A VERY FRIENDLY FIASCO

A FRIENDS-TO-LOVERS ROMANTIC COMEDY

CIDER COVE SWEET SOUTHERN ROMCOMS
BOOK 5

ELANA JOHNSON

ISBN-13: 978-1638764465

CHAPTER ONE

LIZZIE

I sink into the salon chair and meet Morgan's eyes. "I think a little darker."

She runs her fingers through my hair, eyeing it in that way she has. "Darker? Are you sure?" She looks up, and I see the lightning-idea in her eyes.

"What are *you* thinking?"

She flops my hair over the back of the chair, sweeping the sides off my face. "I think you'd be an amazing redhead. And we've got your blonde to the point where we can do it." Joy rides her face, and there's nothing Morgan likes more than reaching for new hair colors.

"A redhead?" I finger the ends of my hair. "Not orange, though, right?"

"Nowhere near orange," Morgan says. "Let's do it." She claps her hands together. "Please?"

I grin at her, and since I need a fresh start in so many ways, I might as well start with my hair. "Let's do it."

Morgan squeals, bounces on the balls of her feet, and says, "I'll go mix up your color. Need a water? Diet Coke?"

"Water's fine," I say, though I'll get a giant soda pop on the way to work this afternoon. I'll need it to go over the forms I need to turn in by Friday. My job is a blight on my existence, and I'm considering a big change in the New Year.

Or I was, until I got promoted a few months ago. Now, I'm still settling into a leadership role. I'm still learning the ropes in the Department Head Row, especially with Matthew Giles just down the hall.

Fine, he's right next door, and the man dominates my thoughts even when I'm not at work. Like right now.

His cologne sits in my nose, though ChemTech is about as far from the salon as I can get and still be in a suburb of Charleston.

A knotted ball of unhappiness sits in my gut, though I laugh and smile with Morgan, tell her all about Claudia's wedding, which has happened since I came in last time. She and Beckett have been married for about three months now, and autumn has started to fall here in South Carolina.

What hasn't happened is anything between me and Matt, though he said if there was any woman he'd go through a packet of red-tape paperwork to date, it was me.

I'm so sick of men saying one thing and doing another.

A couple of hours later, Morgan has me sitting with my back to the mirror, and she's called over four of her co-workers at the salon. They all have their phones out, and Morgan grins at me. "Are you ready for the reveal?"

"So ready," I say in a deadpan.

She ignores my sarcasm, because she's so used to it. It does take a moment—or a day or a week—to get used to my style of humor. Morgan turns me around and her assistant fluffs out my hair, letting it fall over my shoulders.

There's nothing sarcastic about the gasp that cuts through my throat. "Morgan," I breathe. I reach up and touch my hair, just to make sure it's attached to my head. It is, and it's glorious.

"You're a queen," Morgan says. "With a crown of hair on fire."

My hair is red, but not the orangey-red I was worried about. This is a soft brownish-red with plenty of shine and ruby-ness to it. "I love this," I say. Who knew I was a redhead?

Morgan giggles and unsnaps the drape around my neck. "I'm so glad."

I stand and hug her, and she says, "Mm, I love you."

She beams at me when she steps back. "Thanks for trusting me with your hair."

"It's amazing," I say. "You're amazing."

I check out, make my next appointment, as keeping up this new hair color will require regular visits, and head out to my car. Things had lightened there for a couple of hours, but now I have to go to work.

I drive through a sandwich shop and get lunch—and my giant Diet Coke with cherry and vanilla—and head west toward ChemTech.

"Do you really think you can quit?" I ask myself as I leave the city behind. I like talking things out, and sometimes I just need to hear myself say something before it makes sense. I look left as a car passes me. "Why not?" I ask. "We have a ton of savings, so we wouldn't have to work for a few months, at least."

And then what? I ask myself as I glance right.

"Then, we find something that makes us happy, the way Em quit her job and bought the flower shop. She pursued something she's passionate about, and we could too."

And what are you passionate about, Elizabeth? That question flows through my mind in my daddy's voice. He always calls me Elizabeth or some form of a nickname, and I pick up my phone and tap the microphone icon. "Call your daddy tonight and see if you can go to dinner this weekend."

My daddy is my hero, and because he lives an hour away, I don't see him as often as I'd like. Or as often as I should. My momma died over a decade ago, and Daddy's found a way to live alone, something I still haven't mastered.

I reset my phone in my cupholder and get back to thinking about what I'm passionate about. I love fashion, but I don't want to design or sew my own clothes. I love the modeling I do, and perhaps I could do that on a more full-time basis if I wasn't at ChemTech.

I love animals, and one of my favorite things about going home to see my daddy is that I get to walk through his five acres with his dogs, cats, goats, chickens, and donkeys. Maybe I should buy some land out in the middle of nowhere and try my hand at homesteading.

But that would require me to be alone...and I'm not super good at that.

My thinking always circles like this, because the real problem is, I don't know what I'm passionate about and want to spend my whole life—years and years—doing. I was good at math and chemistry in high school, and it felt natural to continue on that path in college and life.

I'm the Regulatory Affairs Department Chair at a chemical company that does everything from research, to development, to sales, to manufacturing. I have a lot of responsibilities, but today, I need to get the paperwork done for a state-required regulation of toxic materials.

Sounds exciting, right?

Trust me, the only bright spot in my day is knowing that Matt is working on something equally as boring next door. And the lunches we share on a near-daily basis.

Today, though, I eat as I drive, and then I pull in the employee parking lot and move to the closest row, where I now have a dedicated parking space. I sigh as I park and reach for my bag. I refuse to carry a brown or black briefcase bag, but I do have a bright teal bag for my folders and documents to travel back and forth in. It doesn't always match my outfit, but it's the cutest bag I've found that still looks professional.

I get out with my bag and find my balance before I duck back down inside to get my soda cup. From there, I click in my heels down the sidewalk to the entrance of ChemTech. I press my badge to the elevator scanner, and I ride up to the fifth floor, where all the Department Head offices are.

It's past lunch, and I work with all men. Routined men, so they'll be out of the lounge and onto their afternoon meetings and tasks. Thankfully. Because I can guarantee that the first man I see will ask me where I was this morning. Then he'll look at me like he knows there's something different about me, but he can't figure out what.

I brush my amazing hair over my shoulder as I step onto the fifth floor and turn toward my office. As predicted, things are calm and quiet, with literally a printer hum hanging in the air. So normal. Mundane. Sleep-inducing.

Someone's on the phone in one office, with another Department Head clacking away on his keyboard in another. I steadfastly refuse to take a peek in Matt's office as I mince my way by, and I turn into my space right next door.

Blast Matt to the moon, because his cologne is stuck in the air in here, and I frown up at the ceiling for its lack of a fan.

"There you are."

I yelp and do the only thing that makes sense in that moment—I throw my forty-four-ounce soda pop in the direction of the voice.

Unfortunately, I do this before I realize Matt has parked himself in front of my desk. "Toledo," I say as the cup hits his calf and explodes all over the floor. At least it didn't do that at a higher elevation and get all over my desk and laptop.

"What was that?" Matt looks down at his pant leg, which is drenched in Diet Coke. He looks at me with plenty of teasing in his eyes, and oh, how I wish he wouldn't. He bursts out laughing in the next moment, and through his gasping wheezes, he says, "You threw... your Coke...at me."

At least he's laughing and not marching down to HR for a complaint form.

I enter my office fully, my pulse settling back to its normal beat. "Why are you loitering in my office?"

He sobers quickly as I put my teal bag on my swooping, curly, two-sided desk. "Loitering?" He presses one palm to his heart like he's going to start reciting the Pledge of Allegiance. "A man of my stature does not *loiter*, Lizzie."

I sit down, my chair squeaking in a way that says it doth protest to my size-sixteen flop into it. I ignore it and meet his gaze. *Mistake*, screeches through my soul, and I look away. "Well, you're here when you surely have something to do in your own office."

Matt clears his throat and says, "Your hair looks amazing."

That draws my eyes back to his. "Thank you," ghosts out of my mouth. *Biloxi*—a US city swear—streams through my mind. Matt has the most beautiful eyes in the world. They're hazel, so this unique color of brown mixed with green, and I swear every fleck is different than another.

"I'm calling the janitor." He gets up, picks up my phone, and punches in a code. A moment later, he says, "Yes, hey, Nate, it's Matthew Giles up on the fifth floor. I have a bit of a non-chemical spill...yeah? Perfect."

He grins widely and meets my eyes. "It's actually next door in Miss Trenton's office. Yep. Thank you."

He hangs up, then stands and closes my door, which

makes my pulse start to pound like a big, bass drum. I played the flute in the marching band growing up, and I dated a drummer. I know beats and rhythms, and this one currently throbbing through my chest is *no bueno— no-no-bue-no.*

Matt turns to face me, pressing his hands behind his back as he leans into the solid door. I want to ask him what he's doing, but my voice has gone on vacation.

"I wanted to talk to you about something," he says. He doesn't seem to have a problem getting his vocal cords to work, but he sure doesn't come over and re-take his seat in front of me.

Okay, I say, but only in my mind. I manage to nod curtly one time, and Matt stands up fully and tucks his hands in his pockets.

"They're doing concerts in the park until Thanksgiving," he says. "I went to one last weekend by myself, and I can't do that again."

"Okay," comes out of my mouth, because I don't know where this is going.

"I was thinking of taking a friend." His eyebrows go up.

Every cell in my body rebels at his words. He knows I want to go out with him. I said it right out loud at Claudia's wedding. The man standing ten feet from me held my hand, and my fingers vibrate with the memory—and the desperation to do it again.

"Are you asking me out?"

Matt grins and shakes his head. "No, because if I ask you out, I have to go get another packet from HR and fill it out."

"*Another* packet?"

"That's what you heard?"

"What happened to the first packet?"

Matt shrugs and advances toward me. He bends and picks up my leaky soda cup and drops it into the trashcan. "I threw it out." He sits back down and smile-stares at me. "I was thinking we could go as friends."

I want to throw something else at him, and I look around my desk for the right object as he adds, "At least for all outward appearances."

My chin lifts instantly. "Outward appearances? What does that mean?"

"I'd love to go to dinner first," he says almost nonchalantly. "Those concerts last a couple of hours, and they only have popcorn and candy and soda there."

Dinner and a concert in the park. A couple of hours each. On a weekend.

"That sounds like a date."

"Only if that's the label we give it." His eyes turn a tiny bit hard. "I'm asking you to go with me as a fake-friend, so we can circumvent the fraternizing rules here at work."

"A fake-friend?" I'm going to start swearing with that

instead of US cities. "That sounds…" I don't know how to finish the sentence.

Dangerous to my health, I think.

A fiasco runs through my mind too.

"Like a way to get past HR and still go out together," Matt supplies. "Is what it sounds like to me. So what do you think?"

CHAPTER TWO

MATT

Lizzie's teal bag perches on the corner of her desk like it might come to life and attack me. Honestly, that would be better than the suffocating silence that's followed my offer for a weekend non-date. Her new hair —the soft, rich auburn—catches the fluorescent light, and I can't stop staring. I've never seen her look more radiant, more beautiful, or more intimidating.

I'm trying to play it cool, but every second she doesn't respond feels like I've asked her to move to Mars with me instead of to dinner and a concert. My heart is doing this ridiculous staccato rhythm, and I swear, if I lean forward just a little, it'll spill out of my chest.

Lizzie leans back in her chair and crosses her arms. I can't tell if she's amused, suspicious, or plotting my demise. Probably a mix of all three—the way my cats do. "So, let me get this straight," she starts, her voice carrying that razor-sharp edge of skepticism I both fear and admire. "You want me to go to dinner and a concert with you. As your *fake friend.*"

"That's right." I nod, trying to keep my tone light. Casual. Like this isn't the most important negotiation of my life. "Just two friends enjoying a nice evening out. Totally platonic. No HR forms required."

Her eyebrow arches. "Totally platonic, huh?"

"Completely," I say, my voice cracking just a little on the word. I clear my throat and press on. "It's the perfect solution. We get to spend time together without breaking any rules, and no one at ChemTech has to know."

She tilts her head, studying me like I'm some kind of complex equation she's trying to solve. "Don't you have *real friends* for this?"

"Byron doesn't like Indie music," I say coolly. My throat is full of sawdust, but I refuse to clear it again.

"Why me?"

Because I've been hopelessly in love with you for months and I'm too much of a coward to just say it out loud. The thought barrels through my mind, but I shove it into the deepest corner of my brain and lock it up tight. No way I'm admitting that. Not yet.

"Do I really have to spell it out for you?" I lean forward like we're sharing some big secret. "Last weekend, I went by myself, and it was depressing. I ate an entire bag of kettle corn just to keep from looking like a total loser."

"Kettle corn is a solid choice," she says, her lips twitching into the faintest hint of a smile. "But I'm not sure how that translates into me accompanying you."

I shrug, forcing a grin. "You're fun. You make everything better. And, honestly, I can't think of anyone I'd rather spend a Saturday night with."

Her arms drop, and for a second, I think I've won. But then she narrows her eyes, and I realize I've underestimated her. Again.

"Would you come pick me up?" she asks, her voice as smooth and lethal as a freshly sharpened blade.

"Sure. Friends pick friends up for events they're attending."

Her lips press together, and I can't tell if she's holding back a laugh or if she's about to muscle me out of her office. Either way, I'm sweating bullets.

Finally, after what feels like an eternity, she sighs. "Fine. Dinner and a concert. As friends."

Relief crashes over me like a wave. "Yeah," I say, grinning like an idiot. "It's going to be so much fun, I promise."

"We'll see," she mutters, but there's a glimmer of something in her eyes—something that looks an awful lot like hope mingling with desire.

I stand, ready to make my escape before I can say or do

anything else to jeopardize this fragile agreement. "I'll pick you up at six. Wear something comfortable. It's an outdoor concert, so there'll be grass and twigs and bugs and things."

"You're not selling this," she says with a half-smile. "Now get out of my office, so I can get this paperwork filed."

I don't need to be told twice. I head for the door, my heart still racing, and throw her a quick wave over my shoulder. "See you later, Lizzie."

As I step into the hallway, I can't help but grin. I did it. I got her to say yes. Sure, it's as a *fake friend*, but it's a start. And maybe, just maybe, my plans to take our friendship into a secret relationship won't end in a complete disaster.

———

BY THE TIME I pull into my driveway, the adrenaline from my "fake friend" win has worn off, leaving me with nothing but nerves and a mild case of buyer's remorse. What if this backfires? What if Lizzie sees right through me? What if I accidentally call it a date and that somehow gets back to Jessie in HR? You should see this woman; she has the perma-frown of a bald eagle and the sharp eyes and beak to match.

"Stop overthinking," I mutter as I pull into my garage and get out of my car. "It's just a friendly dinner and a concert. No big deal."

The moment I step inside, I'm greeted by the unmistakable sound of claws skittering across hardwood floors. A split second later, a blur of gray fur launches itself at my legs, with a slightly darker charcoal only a moment behind.

"Hey, fellas." I crouch down to scratch my felines, Purricell and Purroxide. They're brothers and Maine Coon cats with big personalities and even bigger appetites. Purricell is the most vocal of the pair, and he meows loudly, his tail swishing like he's scolding me for being late.

"I know, I know," I say, heading for the kitchen to fill the food bowls. "I had a long day too, buddy. And I may or may not have just made a complete fool of myself in front of the woman I'm trying to impress."

He meows again, hopping up onto the counter to watch me with those judgmental green eyes. "You remember Lizzie, right? She was wearing the sexiest dress on the planet today, and she took the morning off to get her hair done, and she's a redhead now, guys."

I open the can of food and mix it in with their dry kibble. Purricell yowls and glares, as if he doesn't care about Lizzie, which simply can't be true. Purroxide rubs against my calf, and I think of the Diet Coke Lizzie threw at me when I surprised her.

I grin like a fool, because her defense tactic wouldn't scare away a spider.

Purricell paws at my hand, and I startle back to the

present. "Don't look at me like that," I say, setting the chem-cat's bowls down on the floor. "It's not like you've ever had to navigate ChemTech's dating policy. Or ask the prettiest woman in the state to dinner without actually calling it a date."

The cats ignore me and dive into their food like they haven't eaten in weeks. I lean against the counter, watching them for a moment as fondness tugs through me.

And how pathetic is that?

The nerdy chemical engineer smiling sweetly at his cats, because they're so cute and amazing? "This is why you need a girlfriend," I tell myself as I open the fridge and pull out a can of lime sparkling water. The house is quiet, as I live alone, and all that punctures the humming of the refrigerator is Purroxide's enthusiastic crunching of kibble. It's peaceful, but also a little lonely.

Fine, a lot lonely. I'm lonely, and I can admit it to myself.

I make a drink with an orange-mango packet and the sparkling water and wander into the living room before collapsing onto the couch. My laptop sits on the coffee table, and I open it up, pulling up the ChemTech employee handbook for the second time this week. The dating policy stares back at me, mocking me with its endless rules and regulations.

"Why does everything have to be so complicated?" I ask Purroxide as he joins me, his dinner scarfed down.

He stretches out beside me, his tail flicking against my leg.

The truth is, it's not just the dating policy that's holding me back. It's me. My inability to just say what I'm feeling without turning it into a joke or a half-baked "fake friend" scheme.

I close the laptop, setting it aside, and run a hand through my hair. "You've got two days to figure this out, Matty," I tell myself, hearing it in my mother's voice. "And you can do anything in two days." She always told me that, and I wish she wasn't out in the middle of the Atlantic Ocean and so unavailable all the time.

Because if there's one thing I know for sure, it's that Lizzie Trenton is worth every ounce of effort. Every awkward conversation. Every nerve-wracking moment. She's the smartest, funniest, most incredible woman I've ever met. And I'd walk through fire—or a mountain of HR paperwork if it comes to that—just to see her smile.

Purricell meows, curling up against my side, and I can't help but smile. "You're right," I say, scratching behind his ears. "One step at a time."

I reach for my phone and call my sister. Chanel is my favorite person, and thankfully, she knows to answer when I call, or I'll just pester her until she does.

"Matty," she says, calling me that childhood nickname I grew up with.

I smile as I lean back into the couch and stroke

Purroxide as he snuggles into my other side. "Guess what I did at work today?"

"Solved the energy crisis," Chanel says without missing a beat.

I laugh and shake my head. "No, silly. I'm a chemical engineer," I tell her for at least the fiftieth time. "I don't even work in energy."

"You ate a peanut butter and peach jam sandwich."

"Guilty, but I wouldn't call you about that."

"You finalized the chemical formula for a pill that will cure cancer."

"Now whatever I say will be super-lame."

"You told me to guess." Chanel carries a smile in her voice, and I'm not really upset.

"I talked to Lizzie."

"You talk to Lizzie every day."

"I asked her to go to the concert with me this weekend."

Chanel doesn't immediately fire back at me, and that's how I know what I've done is huge. "So you're going to fill out the paperwork?" she asks. On her end of the line, a baby cries, and it gets louder as she presumably goes to get her three-month-old daughter.

"No," I say, a keen sense of supreme satisfaction pulling through me. "We're going as friends."

"Friends." Chanel says the word like she doesn't know what it means. "But Matty, you don't want to be friends with Lizzie."

"But friends don't have to fill out sixteen sheafs of paperwork to go to a concert in the park."

"Oh, I see what's happening here. You're going to pretend to just be her friend in public while you secretly kiss her in private."

"We have a winner, Purricell." I laugh, and Chanel adds a giggle or two to my voice, but it doesn't last long.

"I worry this is going to turn into a friendly fiasco," she says.

"That's because you worry about everything."

"And you worry about nothing," she fires back. "Matty, you've liked this woman for months. What if this backfires on you?"

Part of me wants to laugh it off the way I do most things. I'd rather just look at life from a glass-half-full perspective than anything else, but what Chanel doesn't get is that a pit of anxiety lives in the bottom of my stomach at all times.

"I've thought through this for months," I say. "ChemTech makes one or both parties turn in a detailed write-up of *every* date. Every single one, Chanel. They have a word count requirement."

"You work for a weird company."

"Scientists are kind of weird," I say, because everyone teases us about that anyway. I might as well admit it.

"So tell me your plan, Doctor Weird," she says.

I do have a Ph.D, and Chanel likes to poke fun at me

about it. "Well, obviously," I say. "I'm going to do a few friendly things with a good friend of mine from work, and I'm going to pour some gasoline onto the sparks between us, and hope that something hot happens."

"Oh, yeah," Chanel teases. "This is going to be a *very* friendly fiasco."

We laugh together, but I'm hoping for exactly that, because my life is as dull as watching paint dry, and I can definitely use something, or rather, some*one*, to liven it up.

And I'm okay if there are elements of it that aren't exactly perfect, as long as there's a lot of me getting to kiss Lizzie.

My phone beeps at me, and I pull it away from my ear. "Oh," I say, surprise and fear rushing through my bloodstream and spiking my adrenaline. "Lizzie's calling, Chanel. I have to go."

"Yep, go," my sister says. "Tell her—"

But I swipe to connect Lizzie's call, because she's never called me after work before, and I'm suddenly dying to know what she has to say.

CHAPTER THREE

LIZZIE

MY FINGER HOVERS OVER THE END CALL BUTTON while the line rings.

Hackensack.

What am I thinking? I can't call him after work. That's not something work friends do. That's what people who are dating do.

And we're not dating.

We're fake friends. I'm honestly not sure which is worse.

Des Moines.

Why haven't I hung up yet?

"Hello?" His voice comes through the phone, warm and curious. "Lizzie? Are you there?"

I blink, realizing I've been sitting here in silence like a complete weirdo. "Hi," I say, my mind blank. "Uh... Matt."

"Do you even know who you called?" It's so unfair that his voice is laced with so much...flirtatiousness.

"Of course I know who I called," I bite back at him. I hope he can't hear how I'm having a mental breakdown in my car in the parking lot at ChemTech. "Sorry to bother you after work."

"You're not bothering me. I was just talking to my sister about you, actually."

Kalamazoo.

"Oh?" I manage, my voice climbing an octave higher than normal. "What about me?"

"About our not-date this weekend."

Not-date. The term makes my stomach do an awful little flip. "Right. That's actually why I was calling."

It's his turn to go, "Oh?" in a vulnerable voice that doesn't sound nearly as flirty now.

My heart squeezes, and I just want an extremely handsome man to ask me out and take me to my favorite restaurant for dinner. I have the perfect first-date outfit too, but I don't want to wear the stunning pink-champagne jumpsuit with a cinched waist and wide legs, my metallic wedges, or my bright red lipstick on a not-date.

Especially now with my red hair. I'm so going to have to rethink my lipstick color for this perfect first-date outfit, but I have a pink I think would work—and it would match my bubblegum-colored cross-body bag.

As I sit there, my outfit morphs, and my desperation to wear it for the not-date doubles. Then triples.

"Lizzie?"

"Yes," I blurt out. "I'm here."

"You called me," Matt says, the amusement back in his voice.

"Yes, I did." My mind races for a plausible reason to call him that isn't *I wanted to hear your voice*, or *I'm overthinking everything you said earlier*.

"I was just wondering what kind of music they're playing at the concert." I practically sigh in relief. "So I can, you know, prepare."

"Prepare?" He laughs, and the sound sends a delicious shiver down my spine. "It's an indie folk band. Nothing you need to study for."

"I like to be informed," I say primly, as if this is a perfectly normal reason to call someone. "I'm the Regulatory Affairs Department Chair. Being prepared is my whole thing."

"Well, Ms. Department Chair, they're called The Hollow Pines. Very chill, acoustic guitar, female vocalist. I think you'll like them."

I nod, then realize he can't see me. "Sounds nice."

There's a beat of silence, and I can almost hear him smiling through the phone. "Is that really why you called?"

"Yes," I lie. "Absolutely. Just wanted the band name. For research purposes."

"Uh-huh." He doesn't sound convinced. "Well, while I have you on the phone, what's your favorite restaurant? For our friendly dinner before the concert."

My favorite restaurant. Such a simple question, but it feels loaded with meaning—and so something my Dream Man would *prepare* for our first date. "I like that little Italian place on Magnolia Street. Bella Notte?"

"Yes, they have great focaccia."

"Have you taken other non-friends there for not-dates?" I ask, something bristling inside me. "Because if so, I—"

"No," Matt says over me. "I've never been on a non-friend not-date before, if you must know."

"I don't even know what we're talking about," I mutter.

"What was that?"

"Great," I practically yell into the phone. "Perfect. Focaccia. I like focaccia."

And I've lost my sanity.

"I'll make a reservation for five-thirty, because the concert starts at seven."

"Sounds good." Another awkward pause. "Well, I should go. I'm still in the ChemTech parking lot, and I need to head home."

"Drive safe, Lizzie."

"You too. I mean—not that you're driving right now. Just, in general. Drive safe in general. When you do drive." I close my eyes, mortified. I hang up as he starts to laugh, mega-mortified that I didn't even say good-bye.

I let my head fall forward onto the steering wheel with a thud. "Tallahassee thunderbolts," I whisper-swear. "What is wrong with me?"

My phone buzzes with a text, and I peek at it cautiously.

Matt: *The Hollow Pines. Look them up. Their song "Whispers in the Dark" is my favorite. Just in case you wanted to do some "research."* 😉

I can't help but smile. Even when I'm freaking out—and he has to know—he's sweet. I start my car and head home, trying not to read too much into a simple text message with a winking emoji.

But seriously, what does that winking face mean, and why does it annoy me so much?

I bet it wouldn't if the not-date on Saturday was a real date.

———

"YOU'RE OVERTHINKING THIS," Emma says, leaning against the kitchen counter at the Big House. Her blonde hair is pulled back in a messy bun, and she's still wearing her apron from the flower shop. "It's just dinner and a concert."

"With a man she's been pining over for months." Tahlia stirs something that smells divine on the stove. "A man who explicitly said they're going as 'fake friends' to get around HR policies."

"I haven't been pining," I say, though we all know that's a lie. "And I'm not overthinking anything."

Emma and Tahlia exchange knowing looks, and then Emma says, "You've been standing in front of the open refrigerator for a while now. The milk is probably warm."

I slam the fridge closed. "I was...looking for the jarlic."

"I put the garlic in twenty minutes ago," Tahlia says, her left eyebrow going up. "I'm feeling like this is a Diet-Coke-secret-spill night."

"No," I say quickly. "There's no secrets to spill." I sink onto the barstool while Emma puts the stack of paper plates on the countertop. "Do you think the not-date is really a real-date?"

"Yes," Emma says without hesitation.

"Of course it is," Tahlia says. Their confidence seeps into me, and I nod.

"But he's never going to use those words," I muse out loud. "Because someone might overhear, and..." I sigh. "ChemTech."

I really need a new job.

"I can't believe you have to document every date like you're writing a lab report," Emma says.

I look over to my bright teal bag. "Yes, well, I looked up the packet online, and we do."

The number of US cities I'd recited then...

I exhale. "So, this is just going to be two coworkers

hanging out on a Saturday night, listening to some indie band in the park." I try on a smile, but it doesn't quite fit the way I'd like.

"While secretly hoping it turns into something more," Emma says as she sets down a few forks, and then a hot pad.

Tahlia follows with the pan of spaghetti and meatballs. Despite the blessed presence of pasta in my life, I groan. "Am I that transparent?"

"I thought you told him how you feel," Emma says while Tahlia says, "Only to us."

They exchange another glance.

"We've lived with you for years." Tahlia pulls out a barstool and sits next to me. "We just know all your tells."

"Like how you keep touching your new hair when you're nervous." Emma takes the last seat on the end of the bar, and I can't believe it's just the three of us here now. And soon enough, Emma and Aaron will be married, and she'll leave the Big House.

I glance at Tahlia, like she might be thinking the same thing as me, but she nods to where I'm absently twirling a lock of my freshly dyed red hair.

I jerk my hand away like I've been hit by lightning. "I'm just not used to the color yet."

"It looks amazing, by the way." Tahlia takes a piece of bread and picks up the plate to offer it to me. "Very *I'm ready for a change.*"

"That's exactly what I was going for," I say. "I'm just not sure if the change I need is in my hair color or my entire life."

"So what are you going to wear on your date?" Emma asks, and just like that, a whole new wave of panic washes over me.

"I don't know."

"What?" Tahlia stops eating and looks at me. "You have the perfect first-date outfit for every situation. How can you not know what to wear?"

"Because I've never imagined a *not-date* with an *actual friend* who I want to be my *very-real-boyfriend.*" My lungs feel so tight, and I suck in a big breath and keep on going. "Because what does one wear for a not-date that might secretly be a date? And why did he say *fake* friends? We're real friends! Why can't we be *real* friends going to a concert?"

My roommates stare at me like I've lost my mind, and to be honest, they're not far off. I slide off the barstool. "I lied. I need a Diet Coke, because I threw my other one at Matt."

"You did what?" Tahlia asks.

Instead of answering, I pull open the fridge and reach for my emergency stash of diet cola. Emma bursts out laughing. "And he still asked you out? Girl, he must really like you."

I don't dare hope, and yet, it's all I feel. Hope, and hope, and more hopety-hope-hope.

I snap the top of the can, and all it does is hiss, *hoooope*, with a big pop on the P at the end.

"So back to the important question," Emma says as I return to the bar. "What are you going to wear?"

I sigh and twirl up a forkful of spaghetti, noting Tahlia served me while I was taking my Diet Coke moment. "I have a few ideas."

"Of course you do," Tahlia says. "Dress? Skinny jeans? One-shouldered sweater?"

I grin at her. "I do love a good one-shouldered sweater."

"Matt'll lose his mind." Emma leans forward and grins at me. "You can do a fashion show for us. Aaron will be here in a few minutes."

My smile fades. "I'm not parading my first-not-date choices in front of Aaron."

"Why not?" Emma asks. "He likes it."

Tahlia starts to giggle, and I shake my head as my grin returns.

"He does," Emma insists.

"He'll do anything for you," Tahlia says between her laughter. "But trust me, Em, he doesn't care about what Lizzie wears on her very-real-date on Saturday night."

I nod enthusiastically, my mouth full of spaghetti with delicious Southern-stewed sauce.

"Hey-hey," Aaron calls from the front of the house. Emma squeals and abandons her food in favor of going to greet him, leaving me and Tahlia alone at the bar.

She sighs, and it contains everything I'm thinking and feeling too. Soon enough, we'll be here alone, and I nudge her gently.

"What are you going to do about the extra rooms?"

Tahlia shakes her head. "I don't know. I haven't decided."

She's told us loads of times in the past that she needs to rent the rooms to pay the mortgage on the house, but I'm not sure about that. Her aunt left it to her years ago, and I don't actually think Tahlia has a mortgage.

I wouldn't want to live in a six-bedroom, four-bathroom, three-story house by myself, I know that. With Hillary, Claudia, and Ryanne gone, the Big House feels so, so...big.

"And for the record," Tahlia says. "You're gorgeous, smart, funny, and Matt would be the *luckiest* man on earth to have you as his real girlfriend, not just his fake friend."

Tears prick at the corners of my eyes, and I lay my head against her shoulder. "Thanks, Tahlia."

"Something smells amazing in here." Aaron Stansfield enters the kitchen with Emma's lip gloss on his mouth, his eyes bright and kind. "Hey, guys."

Tahlia stands and tongs a huge helping of spaghetti onto another paper plate, glowing under his food compliment. "Hey, Aaron. What are you guys watching tonight?"

"Emma has never seen *The Happiest Millionaire*," he says. "Can you believe that?"

"I can't believe there's a movie called that," I say, grinning at him. He really is perfect for Emma, and my happiness for her overshadows the jealousy that attempts to choke me. I even manage to get another bite of pasta past it while Aaron starts to argue his case for a movie made in 1967.

Sixty. Seven.

I so don't watch movies made before I was born, but Emma seems thrilled to have this one on their watch-list.

Aaron, Tahlia, and Emma take their dinners into the living room to start the movie, but my phone has buzzed and lit up with a text from Matt.

"You coming?" Tahlia asks.

"Yes." But I don't look up from my phone. Matt has never texted me after work before, just like I've never lost my mind and called him from the ChemTech parking lot.

"Holy Helena," I curse as I finally comprehend his message. I send my fork flying—spaghetti sauce splattering everywhere—in my haste to pick up my phone and answer him.

My address? I send to him. *I can give it to you at work tomorrow.*

I actually need a favor tonight, he says. *I'm in the car already, and I think I remember you saying you lived over past the high school. Near the orchards? I'm almost there.*

I can't get a full breath. He's coming here now.

Why?

"A favor," I say, my eyes landing on those words. I tap to call him, and thankfully, I don't have time to second-guess myself for calling him twice in one night before he answers.

But it's not him.

"Arooooo-woo-woo!" comes through the line, a very canine sound. Or maybe a ghost getting pulled back into the nether against its will.

"Hello?" I ask.

"Arwoooo-hooo-hooo!"

"Lizzie!" Matt yells over the last of the warbling howl, but I have a feeling the dog he's with—I didn't even know he owned a dog—is filling its lungs for another giant howl.

"Just text me the address, okay? The sooner the better, baby doll."

Before "okay," can fall from my lips, the dog starts another pathetic howl and the call ends.

I stare at the phone, Matt's voice saying *baby doll* ringing through my ears. It echoes on and on and on, even as I quickly type out the address of the Big House and jam my thumb against the *send* button.

CHAPTER FOUR

MATT

Hig lets out another ear-splitting howl as I pull onto Lizzie's street, following the GPS directions to the address she just sent. The Maine Coon in my passenger seat—Purricell, who insisted on coming along—flattens his ears and gives me a look that clearly says, *I blame you for this.*

"You could've stayed home, you know." I reach over to scratch his head. "Hig doesn't like being alone, but he's a dog." And the cats never seem to mind turning their backs on him and marching away.

Truth be told, I wanted to get out of the house too. So when Hig trotted up on my back porch and started howling, I figured I could go for a drive. I severely underestimated the strength of Hig's voice inside a confined space, and I'll take the blame for that.

In the backseat, the massive black and tan German

Shepherd mix continues his mournful serenade. I've been driving him around for twenty minutes, and he hasn't stopped once. My neighbor Mrs. Delaney is a night-shift nurse, and Hig has separation anxiety that could power a small city if only we could harness it.

I turn into a stout driveway that stretches in front of an enormous house and let out a low whistle. The "Big House" really is big—three stories of Southern charm with a wraparound porch and more windows than I can count.

"This is where Lizzie lives?"

With roommates, she'd mentioned, but still.

"Fancy digs," I tell Purricell, who's now pressed against the front windshield, equally impressed. Or maybe he's just trying to get away from Hig's howling.

As I flip the SUV into park, the front door opens, and there she is—Lizzie, her new auburn hair catching the porch light, making it look like she's crowned in fire. She's changed out of her work clothes into a pair of soft-looking leggings and an oversized sweater that slips off one shoulder. My mouth goes dry.

"Aroooooo!" Hig reminds me why we're here.

I hop out of the car and wave sheepishly before turning to the back door. "Sorry about the noise pollution."

Lizzie descends the porch steps, her arms crossed but a smile playing at her lips. "When you said you needed a favor, I didn't realize it involved a canine opera singer."

"He's got range, doesn't he?" I open the back door, and Hig bounds out, immediately heading for Lizzie. "He's nice," I blurt out, because not everyone wants a seventy-pound dog charging them. In fact, I'm pretty sure no one wants that.

Lizzie grins at the dog while I go around the back of the vehicle to get Purricell out. He comes with a leash, because while Hig has weight, he's obedient, and Purricell has attitude that must be contained.

Lizzie's giggles make me light up from within, and I'm drawn to her like a moth to a flame. I'm so getting burned, but I don't care.

"This is Hig," I say. "He belongs to my neighbor, but when she works late, he gets a little...lonely."

"A little?" Lizzie asks, but she's already crouched down and letting Hig sniff and lick wherever he wants. Lucky dog.

The howling traitor wags his tail so hard his entire back end wiggles, and I can't help smiling too. "Of course he behaves for you," I say. "He's been auditioning for a death metal band for a half-hour."

"He just needs some space to run," Lizzie says, scratching behind Hig's ears. "We've got plenty of yard."

"That's actually why I came. I remembered you mentioning living in a big house with a yard." I shift awkwardly. "I hope that's okay?"

"It's fine." She glances up to me, her eyes then trailing down the length of the feline leash. "Is that a cat...on a leash?"

I glance down at my stuffy Maine Coon. "Yep, this is Purricell. He insisted on coming." Purricell gives me a look of utter disdain before slowly, regally stepping forward as if Lizzie will kiss the jewels in his paws. "He's very social for a cat."

"Purricell?" Her lips twitch as she straightens; Hig gives a mournful quarter-yowl, and her hand migrates back to his head. "Like the battery?"

"Chemical engineer humor," I say with a shrug. "His brother at home is Purroxide."

She laughs then, a full, genuine laugh that makes my chest tighten with pure want. "That's both terrible and adorable."

"That's what I was going for." I grin, relieved she gets it. "So...can Hig run around a bit? I promise he won't yowl now that he's properly chastised me for not coming over to get him."

She gives me a coy, flirty, knowing look and turns to gesture to the expansive lawn that stretches along the side of the house. "Sure. It's not fenced, though."

I move to her side, every cell in my body pulling toward hers. "It's okay," I say. "There's a reason he's not on a leash."

"And the cat is." She glances down at Purricell again.

"He doesn't listen," I say by way of explanation. "Go on, Hig. Go run."

The dog gives a joyful bark-yelp and bounds out into the grass while Lizzie and I step out of the gravel parking area and start toward the side of the Big House. Hig fills the world with happiness as he chases shadows only he can see, and I don't have to pull on Purricell to get him to follow—albeit at a dignified distance, of course.

The yard extending from the house toward the one in the distance next door is even more impressive than the front—acres of green space bordered by what looks like an orchard in the back corner

"This place is amazing," I say, slowing my step. "How many people live here?"

"It used to be six of us," Lizzie says, leading me to a set of steps at the back porch. "But three got married recently, so now it's just me, Emma, and Tahlia, who owns the house."

"Wow." I sit down next to her on the steps, close enough that our shoulders almost touch. "Must be a big adjustment."

"It is." She watches Hig race around, a smile playing on her lips. "The house feels too big now, too quiet."

"I can lend you Hig anytime you need some noise."

She laughs again, and I decide right then that making Lizzie laugh is my new favorite hobby.

"So," I say, leaning back on my elbows as Purricell curls up in a Coon-cat-ball and squints his eyes closed, this conversation so lame for a feline. "This is where Elizabeth Trenton lives when she's not terrorizing chemical companies with her regulatory prowess."

"I do not terrorize," she says, but her eyes sparkle in a way that makes me think of kissing her. "I ensure compliance."

"Tomato, tomahto." I wave a hand, part of me full of jitters and the other part completely at-ease here with Lizzie. We watch Hig for a few seconds, as he seems to have found a glow of fireflies and is trying to snap them into his mouth. Every move he makes has some sort of noise attached to it, but thankfully, not his full-on howls.

"You know, it's nice seeing you outside of work." I look over to her, wondering if I can casually take her hand in mine. I'm sitting close enough, and the need to do it gnaws at me.

"Is it?" She turns slightly toward me, and in the soft glow of the porch light, her eyes look almost luminous.

"Yeah," I say. "It's like a different layer of Lizzie." I sit up, because I can't hold her hand while I'm laying back on my forearms. Sudden nerves shower through me. "Like, there's work-Lizzie and home-Lizzie. A different layer."

She's quiet for a moment, watching Hig chase a leaf across the yard as he's given up on the fireflies. "You seem the same to me," she says.

"Yeah, because I'm an open book. What you see is what you get."

She turns toward me, that skeptical look etching across her eyebrows. Oh, I've seen this look before, and I want to erase it from her expression. Worse is the vulnerability she showed me at the wedding.

The wedding where I told her, *If there's anyone I would go through the red tape of paperwork for, it would be you, Elizabeth.*

Then I didn't ask her out. I didn't fill out the packet. Instead, I made up a just-friends not-date, and extreme foolishness fills me from head to toe.

"I don't believe you," she says, and I blink as I try to catch up to the present.

"I'm not that deep," I say.

"No one is the same in every situation." She turns fully toward me now, tucking one leg underneath her. "You have layers too, Matt."

The way she says my name sends a pleasant shiver down my spine. "Maybe a few," I say, the shape of her fingers between mine like phantoms. The wedding was a couple of months ago, but I can still feel where she touched me.

"Like what?"

I consider what to tell her, and Purricell awakens, stretches, and ventures out into the grass, stalking majestically even as he keeps a safe distance from Hig's exuberance. "Well, for one thing, I'm actually terrible at chemistry."

Her eyes widen. "What?"

"Kidding!" I laugh at her expression. "I'm great at chemistry. I just wanted to see your face."

She swats my arm, totally not mad. "You...for Fargo's sake."

My whole soul lights up, because I'd forgotten about her city-swears. "Did you just curse at me in city?" I scoot closer to her and nudge her with my shoulder. "Tell me why you do that again?"

She looks embarrassed for a second, then shrugs. "My daddy doesn't like swearing, so I started using city names instead." A grin spreads across her face, though she refuses to look at me. "Some are stronger than others, just like real swears."

"Very creative, and now I want to know what city names you reserve for...special occasions."

"Wouldn't you like to know?" She faces me with a smirk, but it falls from her face quickly.

I have no idea what I wear on my face, but I shift even closer to her. "I would, actually. I'd like to know a lot of things about you, Lizzie."

Her breath catches, and her throat moves as she swallows. "Like what?"

"Like..." I reach out slowly, giving her time to pull away—which she so doesn't—and tuck a strand of her newly auburn hair behind her ear. "Why you decided to change your hair color."

"Um." She touches her hair self-consciously and lets

her hand drop back to her lap. "I needed a change. I do it every so often, and it's easiest to change my hair."

"It's beautiful," I say honestly, wondering how far I'll go tonight. Just being here is breaking so many rules, and I can't even imagine typing up a record of this conversation. "Makes your eyes look even more blue."

"My eyes are technically green," she whispers.

"I think blue-green," I say, my gaze dropping to her hand in her lap too. "Like the ocean on a clear day."

She rolls her eyes, but her cheeks flush. "That was cheesy."

"Maybe." I grin at her—or rather, the side of her face, since she won't look at me. "Doesn't make it less true."

She looks up; our eyes lock; I forget about Hig and Purricell and the fact that we're sitting on her back porch where her roommates can see us. I just see her—Lizzie, with her blue-green eyes and fiery hair and the way she curses in city names.

My hand finds hers on the step between us, our fingers brushing. It's the lightest touch, but electricity shoots up my arm. Slowly, deliberately, I slide my fingers between hers.

She doesn't pull away. Instead, her eyes search mine, and my heart turns stupid.

"You're trouble, Catalyst." I have no idea where the words come from, only that they're one-hundred percent true.

Lizzie tilts her head, a mischievous spark firing in her eyes. "Catalyst?"

I clear my throat. "Scientific term. Totally objective. Very professional." I curl my fingers around the back of her hand, tightening my grip in that "very professional" way.

"I know what a catalyst is," she says, breaking eye contact and returning her attention to Hig.

"So do I." I follow her gaze and find Hig has finally worn himself out. He's flopped in the long grass at the base of a big tree, Purricell curled up against his chest. I do know that a catalyst is an agent that speeds a chemical reaction, and holding hands with Lizzie has definitely ignited something inside me I've only let simmer in the past.

"Listen," I say. "About Saturday—"

The back door swings open, and we both jump, our hands separating like we've been caught doing something illicit. Which, I suppose, by ChemTech standards, we have.

"Lizzie? Are you—oh." A pretty blonde woman—Emma—stands in the doorway, her eyes widening as she takes me in. "I didn't realize you had company." She cocks one hip like I've crashed a Very Important Party.

Mm, I think Lizzie's been talking about me. With that in mind, I get to my feet as Aaron Stansfield joins us on the back porch. "I told you she wasn't in the house."

He looks between Emma, me, and Lizzie. "I saw her go out front a while ago."

"And yet," Emma says, her gaze locked on Lizzie, who glides to her feet like a Disney princess. "She's out back."

"You remember Matt," Lizzie says, brushing her hands down her leggings. "He had a howler that needed a bit of grass to run around in."

Emma peers through the darkening night toward Hig and Purricell. "You have a dog that big and no yard for him?" When she looks at me again, it's with full accusation.

"He's not my dog," I say as Tahlia comes outside too.

"Oh, here's the party," she says pleasantly.

"No party," Lizzie says. "Matt just needed a place to run Hig for a minute. He was just leaving."

"Yeah, that's what it looked like to me," Emma says.

I've totally failed, I know that. There's no way I can go to a concert in the park with Lizzie. Everyone around us will know we're together—and not as friends. It's like a chemical reaction happening, and those things boil and bubble and don't care who sees them.

"This is Aaron," Lizzie says. "He and Emma were..." She glances at Emma. "He didn't sit with us at the wedding."

"Yeah, but he owns the hardware store," I say, reaching to shake his hand. "I know who he is."

"Nice to meet you, man." Aaron has a good air about

him, and he smiles as he shakes my hand. "I have seen you around the store."

"Yeah." I shoot a look over to Lizzie, who wears a smile that says she knows why. But she doesn't sell me out about my lack of handyman skills in front of her friends.

Hig chooses that moment to add his boisterous bark to the conversation, and he comes bounding over to meet everyone too. "Oh, he's the sweetest," Emma says, going down the steps to meet him.

"Don't let him fool you," I say. "He was performing a full canine aria in my car earlier."

"That's what that was?" Aaron says. "We thought someone was being murdered out here."

"Just my eardrums," I say.

Emma kneels down in front of Hig and lets him lick her face. Gross. "If he's not yours, why do you have him?" she asks.

Lizzie moves to stand beside me, close enough that our arms brush. "Matt was just giving Hig a chance to burn off some energy before taking him home."

"We're going to get ice cream," Emma says. "You guys want to come?"

"No," I say quickly. "I have to get home." I look at Lizzie, who clearly wants to go.

"Give me two minutes to walk him back around the house," she says.

"We'll come pick you up," Tahlia says, and the three

of them head for another parking area behind the house. Lizzie watches them, but I watch her.

"Lizzie," I say, stepping closer because I can. I even let my fingers toy with hers again—out of sight, of course. And I find I like playing with fire. "Have you been talking about me?"

"A little," she says.

"Riveting details, I'm sure," I say.

"Yes, because your mismatched socks keep us all entertained for hours in the evenings." She rolls her eyes, pulls her hand away, and steps over to the railing to pick up Purricell's leash. "Come on, guys. We can go through the house."

It feels like she's kicking me out, but I smile as I whistle for Hig to follow me. It doesn't take long to get the canine and the feline in the car, and then I'm left facing Lizzie.

"Thanks again." I feel fifteen again and not quite sure what to do with my hands or what to say.

"It was the friendly thing to do." Lizzie folds her arms, and I don't think I'm imagining that her tone has gone a bit cold.

I nod and go ahead and get in the car. Hig, bless his heart, makes not a peep on the drive back to my town-home closer to the center of Cider Cove. I successfully return him to his own house, and Purricell and I enter the house to the welcoming yowl of Purroxide.

"Yeah," I say with a sigh. "We're back."

Purroxide rubs against Purricell as if they've been separated since birth, and I pull my phone out of my pocket at the same time it chimes.

My breath freezes in my lungs when I see Lizzie's name on the screen. *Look what I got us for lunch tomorrow!*

A picture appears, and it's my glorious, red-headed catalyst—the woman who spurs me to do things differently somehow—grinning as she holds up a white pastry bag with the circular logo of the Snickerdoodle Porch.

Fifty percent off after eight, she sends next.

What did you get? I ask.

It's a surprise, she says, and though I'm not with her, it feels like flirting. And the inventory at a bakery might be limited this late at night, but I'm certain Lizzie will have gotten a peach cobbler bar if they had any.

I won't make you ruin the surprise, then, I say. *But in case I haven't told you lately, I love the boiled peanut bread pudding from the Snickerdoodle Porch.*

Who could forget that? she asks, and I imagine her smile as she types it.

Can't wait, I say, and no truer text has ever been sent. Now, I just have to figure out how to keep my chemical attraction to Lizzie a secret from everyone we work with.

CHAPTER FIVE

LIZZIE

I stare at my reflection in the bathroom mirror, smoothing my hands over my black pencil skirt for the fifteenth time. My hair is pulled back in a sleek, professional bun, and I've gone with minimal makeup today—just enough to look polished without appearing like I'm trying too hard.

Which I absolutely am.

"It's just lunch," I tell my reflection. "With a colleague. A friend. A fake friend." I grip the edge of the sink. "A very handsome fake friend who held your hand last night and called you a catalyst and made your insides feel like a science experiment gone wonderfully wrong."

Tucson.

I straighten my emerald green blouse—one that brings out the green in my blue-green eyes, as Matt would say—and take a deep breath. I've been at work for three hours already, and I've managed to avoid running into him. But lunch is in fifteen minutes, and I've got a bag of pastries from the Snickerdoodle Porch burning a hole in my desk drawer.

Including one boiled peanut bread pudding that I had to sweet-talk Mabel into dropping by the Big House after she closed.

"You can do this," I say firmly. "You are a professional woman who runs an entire department. You can have lunch with Matt without making a fool of yourself."

The bathroom door swings open, and I nearly jump out of my skin.

A dark-haired woman enters—the worst person possible. Jessie—not Jessica—Humphries, the Human Resources dictator.

My stomach feels like someone has taken a drill to it.

"Talking to yourself again?" Jessie asks, her perfectly threaded eyebrow rising as she nears.

"Just practicing for a presentation." I move away from the sink to let her wash her hands.

Miss Humphries is five-foot-two-inches of pure corporate enforcement—and I thought I was about sticking to the regulations. I'm not even close to Jessie.

Her sleek bob never has a hair out of place, and I've long suspected it's a wig. Even now, standing as close to her as I am, I can't tell, and I jerk my eyes away when she looks at me in the mirror.

Today's navy pantsuit is pressed to perfection, as usual. She's naturally flawless, of course, with smooth skin and dark eyes that seem to take in absolutely everything. In fact, I'm pretty sure she knows Matt held my hand last night just by looking at me.

Oh, and did I mention Jessie is the gatekeeper of the no-fraternization policy that's currently ruining my life?

Why do chemists have to be the stuffiest people on the planet? And why do I have to have feelings for one who has a propensity for breaking the rules? Honestly, I should be talking to a therapist about using words like *propensity* at all.

"I hope your presentation goes better than Ken's paperwork," Jessie says with a sniff. "Some people just can't follow simple instructions."

Everything leaks out of that drilled hole in my stomach. "Oh?" As chemists, we're masters of paperwork, especially us Department Heads.

"He turned in his relationship disclosure forms a day late." She shakes her head like this is equivalent to committing a felony and rips off a paper towel. "And the documentation was incomplete. I mean, how hard is it to record the start and end time of a dinner date?"

"Maybe he was having too much fun to check his watch," I say, immediately regretting the words when Jessie's eyes narrow.

"That's exactly the problem, Elizabeth." She only ever uses my full name, which makes me feel like I'm being scolded by a very tiny principal. "When emotions get involved, professionalism suffers, and we handle very delicate things here at ChemTech."

"Yes, of course," I say. "I turned in all my paperwork on time." Why I'm telling her this, I have no idea. I just need to get out of here.

She lifts her chin and studies her reflection. "It's not like I'm the one who makes the rules, though I'm in complete agreement with them. We have huge government and international contracts. We deal in public safety, with the medicines people rely on. There can be no hint of impropriety."

"Of course not," I say automatically.

"Can you imagine Shawn in Legal having to deal with an international lawsuit because a couple of people first get along too well, and then don't?" She shakes her head, but all I can think is—*is this how people talk about me? You know, Lizzie in Regulatory Affairs will have a heyday with this.*

And there I go again with the uncool word usage.

"That's why we have these policies." Jessie turns toward me, apparently satisfied with her pre-lunch cleanliness routine.

I nod, eager to escape. "Well, good luck with Ken's paperwork."

"I don't *need* luck. I *need* compliance." She smiles thinly. "Have a good day, Elizabeth."

I hurry out of the bathroom, my heart racing. If

Jessie is on the warpath about late paperwork, Matt and I need to be extra careful. Extra, extra, extra careful.

Maybe we shouldn't even have lunch together today. The thought makes my heart turn into a stone, and I hurry down the sterile hallway back to my office.

Once there, I close the door behind me, leaning against it with a sigh of relief. My desk is piled with regulatory forms that need reviewing, but I can't focus on anything except the pastry bag in my drawer and the lunch date—no, friends-only lunch—that's rapidly approaching.

A knock on my door nearly sends me into cardiac arrest. I leap away from the door, and it's a good thing I'm sensible and wear nothing more than a one-inch heel at work. I could've done some real ligament damage with that jump.

"Come in," I call once I'm behind my desk, hoping my voice sounds normal and not like I'm plotting to circumvent company policy.

Matt pokes his head in, and my heartbeat does a great big cartwheel, the stupid thing. Doesn't it know we'll be fired if Jessie even detects one little thump out of place?

Matt doesn't seem to care about any of it. His brown hair is slightly tousled, like he's been running his hands through it, and his hazel eyes light up when they land on me.

"Ready for lunch, my catalyst?" he asks with a grin.

"Don't call me that at work," I hiss, glancing nervously over his shoulder. "And just come in and close the door."

He steps fully into my office and closes the door. "No one's around," he says, but he lowers his voice anyway. "I just ran into Jessie in the hallway. She was on her way to terrorize Ken about his dating forms."

"I know. I had a bathroom encounter with her." I smooth my hands down my midsection and take a big breath. For some reason, I can't look directly at Matt. Instead, I open the drawer and pull out the Snicker-doodle Porch bag. "She's in rare form today."

"All the more reason to stay here for lunch today." Matt's eyes drop to the bag in my hands. "We've done it before."

True, we have. Today, though, it feels like poking an angry bear that woke up too soon from hibernation and can't find food.

"What did you get?" He comes closer, his golden retriever energy off the charts.

I can't help but smile at his excitement. "It's..." I slowly uncurl the top of the bag, watching him.

"You're killing me, Lizzie." He steps closer, and for a heart-stopping moment, I think he might kiss me right here in my office. Something snaps and pops between us, and it sounds like whips cracking and fireworks filling the sky.

I can't look away from him now, and my heartbeat

sounds like the hooves of a thousand horses pounding over dry ground.

Then Matt reaches for the bag, and my reflexes kick in. I swiftly pull it back. "Patience is a virtue, Matthew."

"Not one of mine." His eyes twinkle with mischief. "Do you really want to be caught in here? Eating together, with the *door closed?*" He hisses the last two words like closing a door is akin to a hit-and-run.

He snatches the bag from me, creating a violent sound of crumpled paper. "Come on. Grab your big Diet Coke, and let's go get the good seats away from the fridge." He turns to leave, and since he has my peach cobbler bar, I grab my Diet Coke from my desk and follow him out the door.

As we walk down the hallway toward the Department Head lounge, I'm hyperaware of the space between us. Not too close to raise suspicions, but close enough that I can smell his cologne—that same scent that lingers permanently in my nose

"So," Matt says conversationally as we walk, like we might really be just-friends. "How's your morning been?"

"Uneventful. Yours?"

"I had to review three chemical formulations that all failed safety tests." He sighs dramatically. "Some days I wonder why I went into this field."

"For the glamour and excitement, obviously."

He laughs, and the sound warms me from the inside out. "Obviously."

We reach the Department Head lounge—a comfortable space with plenty of seating, large windows, and a kitchenette that's leagues better than the regular break room. It's one of the perks of our positions, along with the private offices and dedicated parking spaces.

The lounge is already half-full with other department heads taking their lunch breaks. I spot Ken at a table near the window, looking like he hasn't slept in days. Poor guy. Jessie must have really put him through the wringer.

Matt and I settle at a small table in the corner, one we've eaten at before, actually. Before, when I'd watch him while he checked something on his phone, then glance away if he even twitched a muscle.

Before, when I'd ask him platonic questions about his sister and her new baby.

Before, when I'd fantasize about what it would be like to go out with him, laugh with him without anyone watching, kiss him...

He tosses down the pastry bag in a way that makes me hiss, and I glare at him as I turn to go get my lunch from the fridge. Yes, I brown-bag it for lunch, as most do here at ChemTech. While I'd like a hot lunch, I'd rather not ever use the microwave here, so I grab my lunch tote from the fridge, then pull out Matt's brown bag.

Yes, a legit brown paper bag that he's written his name on in black Sharpie. I smile at it, realizing a moment too late how fondly I feel. I straighten my lips and clear my throat as I turn to head back to the table. It's far enough from the others to have some privacy but not so isolated that it looks suspicious, and no one looks at me as I go back.

I hand him his lunch and take my seat, my back to most of the room, thankfully. I unzip my tote and pull out my ham and cheese sandwich.

"Aren't you going to share what's in the mystery bag?" Matt asks, unwrapping his own lunch—a pita pocket stuffed with turkey and cheese.

I smile coyly. "After we eat our real food."

"You're a cruel woman." He smiles back, and he has to take that thing down a notch—and not just to save my thrashing pulse.

"I prefer *strategic*."

"Sometimes it's strategic to eat dessert first." Matt takes a bite of his sandwich, his eyes never leaving mine. He swallows and pulls out a single-serving pineapple cup, a snack-sized bag of chocolate-covered almonds, and another stuffed with Oreo thins.

"You brought dessert?" I ask.

He glances at the bags and quickly puts them back in the lunch sack. "I need them for this afternoon."

I reach for the pastry bag and open it. "You've got barbecue chips in there too, right?"

"No," he says quickly. "I'm out. I had to bring the Funyuns today."

I light up even as I pull out his bread pudding. "I love Funyuns."

More bag crinkling, and then he tosses them to me. "Great. They're yours."

I also happen to adore chocolate-covered almonds, and if I need a three p.m. pick-me-up, I know where I'll be.

I grin at him and lean forward to put the boiled peanut bread pudding down. "It comes with a peanut caramel sauce too," I say. "I can go warm it up."

His eyes widen. "And use the microwave?" He shakes his head somberly. "I would never ask you to do that." He grabs the little cup of sauce and jumps to his feet. I watch him go for a moment, once again forgetting myself. I quickly refocus on my own lunch, hoping no one saw anything they shouldn't.

I've only taken one bite of my cobbler bar before he returns. "So, did your roommates have any questions about me last night?"

I blink at him. "No. Why would they? You've met them before."

"I swear, all my sister does is ask about you," he says.

More blinking. "What would I say anyway?" I lean forward, feeling frothy and dangerous. "This is Matt, guys, and yeah, we work together, but we're trying to date-without-dating because HR will make us fill out humiliating paperwork if we do?" I raise my eyebrows, almost daring him to tell me he doesn't want to go out with me on a real date.

My ribs shake my heart beats so hard. We've been dancing around each other for a long time now, and I've just come out and said we want to be together. But does he?

He grins as if I've said there's a rainbow outside. "That actually sounds nice."

I roll my eyes and rip open his Funyuns. "You're... Biloxi-level ridiculous."

He doesn't miss a beat as he says, "I have an aunt in Mississippi."

I scoff, though it's an action I employ when I'm trying not to melt into a puddle. Matt's phone chimes, and down his attention goes.

He keeps eating while he taps, frowns, and taps some more. I find myself studying him like usual. The way his jaw works as he chews, the little crinkles at the corners of his eyes when he smiles, the way his fingers curl around his can of lime sparkling water.

Those same fingers that were intertwined with mine last night.

"You're staring," Matt says without looking up from his phone.

Heat floods my cheeks, and I flinch. "I am not."

"You absolutely are." Now he does look up, a smug

smile playing on his lips. "It's okay. I'm very stare-worthy."

"And so humble."

"Humility is overrated." He leans forward, lowering his voice, those eyes flashing dangerously now. "Besides, I like it when you look at me."

My heart stutters. "Matt—" I don't know how to continue, and my attention moves to someone entering the lounge.

Jessie.

I immediately lean as far back as I can, noting that Matt does the same.

"Kenneth," Jessie says sharply, making her way to his table. "I need a word."

Every head in the lounge turns to watch the spectacle. Ken looks like he wants the floor to open up and swallow him whole.

He stands, as Ken is no weakling, even up against Jessie. "I've already submitted the revised forms."

Jessie folds her arms, turns on her heel, and heads back toward the door. "I need clarification on a few things."

Matt and I exchange alarmed glances. This is exactly the kind of public humiliation we're trying to avoid.

"First," Jessie continues, her voice carrying clearly across the now-silent lounge. "You failed to document the conversation topics during the appetizer course. The form clearly states that all conversation must be recorded *with timestamps.*"

"We were just talking about the weather, for crying out loud," Ken says as Jessie reaches the door.

"For forty-five minutes?" Jessie's incredulous voice can be heard even as she leaves the lounge.

"We both follow storm chasers, so yeah. For forty-five minutes."

Matt chokes on his sparkling water, and I have to bite the inside of my cheek to keep from laughing. The situation isn't funny—it's horrifying—but Ken's response is almost comical. It's almost like he's *trying* to make Jessie see redder than she already does.

"All conversation topics," I say, smiling at Matt.

"I wonder where he took Julia that has an appetizer course."

"*That's* what you got from that?"

"Well, it was that or the fact that there's more than one person who follows storm chasers in the building." Matt calmly polishes off his turkey pita. "Mm, I put green apples in that today, and it was *phenomenal.*" He grins at me like nothing just happened to our co-worker. "Want me to make you a sandwich with fruit on it?"

I wrinkle my nose and deliberately pull out the biggest Funyun in the bag. "No, thank you, Mister Giles."

He chuckles and zeroes in on his bread pudding.

"This looks amazing." He pours the sauce all over it and digs in.

I watch him enjoy the bread pudding, warmth spreading through my chest. It's such a small thing, but the joy on his face makes it feel significant.

"What?" Matt asks, catching me watching him again.

"Nothing." I smile and take a bite of my peach cobbler bar. "Just enjoying the show."

He laughs and offers me a bite of his bread pudding. "Want to try?"

The gesture feels intimate somehow, and I hesitate before leaning forward and taking a small bite from his fork. The sweet, nutty flavor explodes on my tongue.

"That is good," I admit.

"Told you." His eyes linger on my lips for a moment before he clears his throat and returns to his dessert.

He's just finished it when a series of chimes come through his phone. "Shoot. I have a meeting I forgot about." He looks up, his eyes wide as he takes in the mess on the table between us. "I—"

"Go," I say. "I'll clean up."

That delectable grin crowds onto his face. "I can't wait for tomorrow night, my pretty catalyst."

Before I can respond, he's up and walking away, leaving me sitting at the table alone with my heart racing and a smile I can't quite suppress.

Tomorrow night can't come fast enough.

CHAPTER SIX

MATT

I adjust my collar for the fifteenth time, scrutinizing my reflection in the bathroom mirror. The navy button-down looks good—not too formal, not too casual—but something feels off.

"What do you think?" I ask, turning to Purricell, who's sprawled across the bathroom counter watching me with half-closed eyes. "Too try-hard?"

He yawns widely, showing all his teeth.

"Thanks for the vote of confidence." I unbutton the second button, then re-button it, then unbutton it again. "This isn't even a real date, and I'm losing my mind."

Purroxide meows from the doorway, his tail swishing impatiently.

"I know, I know. I've been in here forever." I run a hand through my hair, making it just messy enough to look intentional. "But this is important. Even if it's just a not-date."

I move to my bedroom, where I've laid out three different jackets on the bed. The weather forecast says it'll be in the mid-sixties tonight—perfect concert-in-the-park weather, but cool enough that Lizzie might need something warm.

That's when I remember the scarf I bought. After our lunch, I'd ducked out during my afternoon break and found this perfect emerald green scarf that would match her eyes.

I dig through the shopping bag on my dresser and pull it out—soft, cashmere-blend fabric with the tiniest hint of shimmer woven through it. Nothing flashy, just elegant. Like Lizzie.

"What do you think?" I hold it up for the cats to see. "Too much for a not-date?"

Purroxide, who has followed me into the bedroom, immediately perks up. His pupils dilate as he fixates on the dangling scarf.

"No." I back away. "This is not a toy. This is for *Lizzie.*"

Too late. He launches himself from the floor with surprising agility for a cat his size, snagging the scarf with his claws. I yank it back, but he's already got a grip, and we engage in the world's most pathetic tug-of-war.

"Let go, you furry little traitor." I pull harder, and

Purroxide responds by growling low in his throat, his back paws kicking frantically at the fabric.

A soft ripping sound makes my stomach drop.

"No, no, no." I finally wrestle the scarf free, but the damage is done. Three small tears and a pulled thread have transformed my perfect gift into something that looks like it's been through a paper shredder.

I collapse onto my bed, holding the mangled scarf. "You're lucky you're cute," I tell Purroxide, who's now washing his paw like nothing happened. "Because you're a menace."

My phone rings, and I grab it from the nightstand. Chanel's name flashes on the screen.

"Hey," I answer, still glaring at my infuriating cat.

"Are you freaking out yet?" my sister asks without preamble.

"And why would I be freaking out?"

"Because you're picking up Lizzie in thirty minutes for your not-a-date, and you've probably changed your shirt four times already."

I glance down at my navy button-down. "Only twice."

Chanel laughs. "You're so predictable."

"I bought her a scarf," I say. "But Purroxide just turned it into confetti."

"Oh, Matty." She sighs, and I practically hear her shaking her head. "You don't need to bring a gift. This isn't prom."

"I know that." I toss the ruined scarf onto my dresser. "I just wanted to do something nice."

"Just be yourself," Chanel says. "That's all she wants."

"That's terrible advice. Myself is a disaster."

"Speaking of disasters, what's your plan if someone from work sees you two together?"

I freeze. I hadn't thought about that. "We're just friends hanging out."

"At a *romantic* concert in the park? After dinner at an *intimate* Italian restaurant?"

"It's not intimate," I say. "It's...family-style spaghetti. That's like, as un-intimate as you can get."

And also why I chose a dark blue shirt. "And the concert in the park is for families, not dates. It's not *romantic*."

"Uh-huh." She doesn't sound convinced, but Chanel never does with me. "Just be careful, okay? I don't want you getting in trouble at work."

I pause. "Shad still hasn't found a job," I say, though I know her husband hasn't found a job. If he had, Chanel would've called screaming with happiness.

"Not yet, and Mom—well, you know Mom's lectures as well as I do."

"I can transfer some money," I say, because boy, do I know my mother's lectures forward and backward. I sink onto my bed. "I can do it from my phone."

"No, you need to go," she says.

"Chanel." I'm already tapping and pressing my finger to the screen for my biometrics to unlock the bank app. "I just forgot it was close to mid-month."

She gives half a sniffle, and I hate it. I hate it with everything I have, and I know she does too. "He had another interview with Prescott today."

"That's great," I say as brightly as I can. "When did you talk to Mom?" Our mother works for the US Navy, and she likes being out on the ships far more than she ever liked being a mother. Dad got us to age eighteen—well, me—and then flew the coop. I finished up with Chanel the best I could, then poured myself into college and my Ph.D.

Honestly, I'm still trying to find my way, as unanchored as I feel.

"This morning," Chanel says airily. "She's still alive, so there's that."

"There is that," I say, my words whisper as I tap to send some money to my sister. "Done, Channy."

"I'm so sorry, Matty."

I shake my head, like this is nothing. "It's fine," I say. "If we can't take care of each other, what do we have?"

And for me, that's a very real question. Without Chanel, Shad, and their little girl, Nora, I'd be a total island.

A stream of loneliness gushes through me, and I get to my feet as I notice the time on my phone. "I should go. I don't want to be late."

"Good luck," Chanel says. "And remember—"

"Be myself. Got it." I hang up and take one last look in the mirror. The navy shirt brings out the hazel in my eyes, and my hair looks decent. Not perfect, but decent.

"It'll have to do," I say to the cats, and then I grab my keys and head out.

BY THE TIME I pull into the gravel lot in front of the Big House, my palms are sweaty on the steering wheel, and I've got a knot in my stomach that could qualify as a new chemical compound.

"It's just Lizzie," I tell myself as I look up to the imposing house, the front door like a yawning, all-consuming mouth. "You've had lunch with her a hundred times. You've talked to her every day for months. This is no different."

Except it is totally different. Because tonight, there's no pretending we're just colleagues. Tonight, we're stepping into something new, even if we're calling it "friendship" for the outside world to see.

I know what it really is—and so does Lizzie. She said it right out loud at lunch today.

I take a deep breath. The evening sun catches on the windows, making the whole place glow golden. It's intimidating in the daylight, but even more so now.

"Just go to the door," I mutter as I get out of the car.

"Knock on the door. Say hello. Tell her she looks nice. Don't stare. Don't say anything weird."

I straighten my collar one last time and head up the walkway. The porch steps creak under my feet, and I reach for the doorbell, only to hesitate.

What if she's changed her mind? What if this whole fake-friends thing is a terrible idea? What if—?

The door swings open before I can press the bell, and I find myself face-to-face with not Lizzie, but Emma.

"Well, well, well," she says, crossing her arms and leaning against the doorframe. "Look who's here."

"Hi, Emma." I try for a casual smile. "How are you this fine evening?"

Emma studies me for a long moment, her eyes narrowing slightly. "Fine."

I'm not sure what I'm supposed to do. Lizzie didn't warn me that there would be a gatekeeper. As a brunette joins her—Claudia, whose wedding I attended with Lizzie a few months ago—I realize I'm in big trouble.

I swallow, everything I can think of to say stupid and obvious. They already know I'm here for Lizzie, so I just look at them. "Hey, Claudia. How are you?"

She smiles, and she seems like my way in. "Is Lizzie...? Should I come in?"

"Maybe," Emma says. "Maybe not. Depends on your intentions."

"My intentions?"

"With our Lizzie." She steps back, opening the door wider as another blonde pokes her head into the foyer.

"Why do you guys always do this?" Tahlia sighs like she's dealing with children. "Come in, Matt. Lizzie's almost ready."

"Yes," Emma says smoothly. "Come in. We need to talk."

"We do this to everyone," Claudia says with a smile. "We've had a lot of practice in the past couple of years too. When Beckett first came, we were still new."

"And you almost clawed out our eyes," Emma says with a grin.

"It was...an interesting start for me and Becks." She leads me into the living room off the foyer, and the Big House expands before me. Everything is even more impressive than I imagined—high ceilings, gleaming hardwood floors, and a grand staircase that leads up to the second floor.

"You've met all of us," Hillary says as she gets to her feet. She's smiling and she steps right into me and hugs me. "Don't let Emma fool you. She's actually the nicest of us all."

"Somehow, I'm not super comforted by that." I smile at her as she steps back. "She looks like she might eat me for dinner."

Emma has adopted a power pose beside a dining room chair.

"Ladies," I say, trying to sound confident as I look

from Emma-the-Warden, to Claudia, to Tahlia, to Hillary, and then finally to Ryanne. She hasn't said anything yet, but she watches me with the eyes of one of my cats—like she knows something I don't, and she might claw off my nose if I make one wrong move.

I clear my throat. "Nice to see you all again. It's been a while since the wedding."

"Yes, it has," Ryanne says. "And why is that?"

"Why is...what?"

Claudia leads me to the chair, and dumbly, I sit in it. *Bad idea*, screams through my head, but the deed is done.

"So, Matt." Claudia sits in a far more comfortable-looking armchair. "You work with Lizzie?"

"Yes, I'm the Chemical Engineering Department Head. She's Regulatory Affairs."

"And now you're taking her on a not-date," Ryanne says, making air quotes around "not-date."

"I mean—yes?"

"Why is that a question?" Emma asks.

"It's complicated," I say. "Our company has some strict policies about coworkers dating."

"So you're circumventing them," Tahlia says, not a question.

"No, we're just..." I search for the right words that won't have these five women skewering me and grilling me for dinner. "Exploring our options."

Hillary snorts. "What does that even mean?"

It means I have my bills to pay and my sister's. I glance toward the stairs, because Lizzie told me she has a room on the second floor. She has to know everyone but her is down here, right?

"Look," I say. "I...like Lizzie, and I want to see if we have somewhere to go, because if we do, I think it could be something really good." I can't even feel my own face right now, and I'm so glad lungs breathe on their own.

There's a moment of silent communication, and then, surprisingly, they all smile.

"He'll do," Claudia says.

"For now." Ryanne lifts her eyebrows at me.

"But if you hurt her—" Hillary points one finger in my direction, and I swear it jabs right into my chest.

"We know where you work," Tahlia says smoothly.

"And where you live," Emma adds with a sweet smile that somehow makes it more threatening.

I swallow hard. "Noted."

"What's noted?" comes Lizzie's voice, and I turn to see—oh.

Oh, wow.

The entire structure of my life tilts on its axis.

My brain shorts out like a dropped beaker. The air leaves my lungs with a violent shove. Somewhere in the back of my mind, my survival instincts scream: *Say something. Smile. Breathe.*

But all I can do is stare.

Lizzie's hair catches the evening light coming in

from the front windows—red and gold and fire and something dangerously close to divine. That pink-champagne jumpsuit curves over her body like it was sewn onto her in secret, with reverence and adoration and possibly black magic. Her smile is small, unsure, but the moment she tosses that bubblegum-pink purse over her shoulder, she looks like she could set the whole block on fire and not even apologize.

My heart? Yeah, it forgets how to beat properly.

"Toledo," I whisper under my breath, because no regular swear word will do. I get to my feet and approach her, everything else in the world fading to nothing.

There is only her.

"You are stunning," I say, my hand sliding along her waist effortlessly. I haven't dated in a while, but apparently, I do know where to put my hands in a situation like this.

I take a deep breath of her as I lean in. "This is the best first not-date outfit I've ever seen."

Someone clears their throat, and I startle away from Lizzie, suddenly realizing I'm surrounded by her friends.

A blush creeps up Lizzie's neck, and she tucks a strand of hair behind her ear. "Thank you, Matt. You look nice too."

I glance down at my navy shirt and dark jeans, feeling woefully underdressed next to her. "I should have worn a tie or something."

"No, you're perfect," she says, then immediately

looks embarrassed. "I mean, you look fine. Great. Very... friendly. For a concert in the park. With a friend."

The interrogation chair scrapes behind me, and I turn to see Emma moving it. "We should go," I say, desperate to escape before I do something stupid—like lean in and kiss her in front of everyone. "Our reservation is at five-thirty."

"What's with the chair, Em?" Lizzie asks.

"Nothing," Emma says as she steps in front of it and sits down. "Just needed an extra seat."

I scan the several empty places on the two oversized sofas in the room, keep my hand on the small of Lizzie's back, and guide her toward the archway that leads back into the foyer.

"So good to see you all again," I say, immediately cursing myself for speaking. I'm not a blasted politician. My feet feel like bricks, but I manage to keep taking one step after another until we blissfully arrive on the porch.

The front door closes behind us, and Lizzie lets out a long sigh. "I'm so sorry about them. They ambushed you, didn't they?"

"A little bit." I grin at her as we walk toward my car. "But I survived." I take her hand in mine. "And you are really—wow. I'd go through them any day of the week just to see you."

She ducks her head and squeezes my hand, and I wonder if we have to go to the concert at all. Friends hang out at each other's houses, don't they? Maybe I can just take her home with me.

My thoughts are too dangerous, even for me, so I cage them while I open the passenger door for her. She slides in, that jumpsuit making a soft swishing sound against the seat, and looks up to me. "Thank you."

I smile and walk around to the driver's side, using the moment to collect myself. When I get in, the car feels smaller somehow, filled with her presence and the subtle scent of her perfume.

The tension in my shoulders eases a bit. Maybe this can work—this in-between space where we're not quite dating but definitely more than colleagues. Maybe we can figure things out as we go.

"So," Lizzie says, breaking the comfortable silence that's settled between us. "Purricell and Purroxide didn't want to join us tonight?"

I laugh, remembering the scarf incident. "Purricell tried to come along, in a way. He destroyed a gift I got for you."

Her eyebrows shoot up. "You bought me a gift? Is that something you do for all the women you're not dating?"

I grin at her. "Yes, I buy gifts for all the women I'm not dating."

As she laughs, I add, "Next time, I'll keep whatever I get in a cat-proof container."

"Next time?" She gives me a teasing smile. "Pretty

confident for a guy who hasn't even made it through the first not-date."

"What can I say? I'm an optimist." I park the car and turn to face her fully. "Ready for some amazing focaccia?"

"Born ready." She reaches for her door handle, but I stop her.

"Wait, let me." I hop out and circle around to open her door, offering my hand to help her out.

She takes it, her fingers warm against mine, and stands. I pull her into my chest, and now she's so close—too close to be only friendly, not close enough for what I really want.

"Lizzie," I whisper, but my voice sounds like I've snacked on rusty nails on the way here.

A couple walks past us toward the restaurant, the man practically yelling into his phone, and reality crashes back in. We're in public. Someone from work could see us.

I reluctantly release her and step back. "Shall we?"

She nods, and we walk toward the entrance of Bella Notte, a respectable distance between us now. As I open the restaurant door for her, the scent of garlic and tomato sauce wafts out, along with the soft sounds of Italian music.

"Reservation for Giles," I tell the hostess, who smiles and grabs two menus.

"Right this way." She leads us to a small booth in the

far corner, with a view out the window that overlooks the downtown park.

I wait for Lizzie to sit, and she gives me a look that's half amusement, half appreciation.

"Very gentlemanly," she comments as she slides in.

"My mother raised me right." I take my own seat across from her. "Though she'd be horrified if she knew I was on a not-date."

"Is she against not-dating?"

"She's against anything that isn't straightforward." I unfold my napkin and place it in my lap. "She'd tell me to just fill out the paperwork and stop being ridiculous."

Lizzie laughs, the sound warming me from the inside out. "I think I'd like your mother."

"She'd like you too." I pick up the menu, though I already know what I want. "She appreciates people who don't put up with nonsense."

"Is that what I do? Not put up with nonsense?"

I peek over the top of my menu. "You threw a Diet Coke at me."

"You startled me." She tries to look indignant, but a smile keeps breaking through. "That wasn't me doing anything but defending myself."

"You curse in city names."

"A lady doesn't swear."

"You color-code your regulatory binders."

She narrows her eyes. "How do you know that?"

"I've seen inside your office cabinet." I grin at her.

"The red ones are for toxic materials, blue for pharmaceuticals, green for agricultural chemicals."

"I'm impressed you noticed."

"I notice a lot about you, Lizzie." The words come out more serious than I intended, and a flush creeps up my neck. I bury myself in the menu, and our server thankfully arrives, saving me from myself.

"Can I start you two with some drinks? Perhaps a bottle of wine?"

I look to Lizzie, letting her take the lead.

"Just water for me," she says, throwing it back to me.

I peer at the menu like I don't know what to order. "Do you have sparkling water?"

"We have spiked seltzer," the waitress says.

I frown and shake my head. "Seltzer is not sparkling water."

She blinks; Lizzie snickers; I say, "I'll take water too, please. And we'll start with the focaccia."

"Excellent choice." She disappears, clearly still not sure what the difference between seltzer and sparkling water is.

"Seltzer is *so* sparkling water," Lizzie says.

I watch her for a moment, taking in the way the candlelight plays across her features. "It's carbonated differently. It totally tastes different."

"Sure, I bet it does." She holds a Ph.D in Flirting, and I am here for it. The air between us crackles with possibility, and I'm suddenly very aware of how close our hands are on the table.

"You know what I was thinking?" I ask, casually sliding my hand closer to hers and then brushing her fingers with mine.

"What?" she asks.

"My sister's birthday is coming up." I keep my focus on her skin, the way it feels along my fingertip, the way someone has just poured a whole bottle of shooting stars into my bloodstream. "And I need to get her something." I raise only my eyes to look at her.

"Okay," she says, blinking.

"I totally need a friend to go with me," I say. "A *female* friend. To help me get the right thing. You know, from a *female* perspective."

Lizzie's blank-eyed blink turns into a glare. "Yeah, that does sound like a roaring good time for a not-date." She has the sarcastic deadpan down pat.

I grin at her. "Yeah, and there's a craft fair and boutique this weekend, with a big food truck rally in the parking lot." I cover our joined hands with my other one. "Would you be free tomorrow to go with me?"

I suddenly have to see her tomorrow too, and I don't know what I'll do if she says no. Probably go Hulk, flip the table, and punch a hole through the roof of this restaurant as I leave.

Lizzie looks up as the waitress returns with our water. That gives us a couple of seconds, and she pulls her hand away to unwrap her straw. I don't like how long it's taking her to answer, nor the semi-calculating look on her face. But I suppose she wouldn't be a chemist if she didn't weigh a lot of factors, lay them all out, and make a decision based on the data.

Right now, I don't care about data. I only care about spending more time with Lizzie.

She takes a delicate sip of water while my heart gets ripped out of my chest. Then she says, "I think I have the perfect outfit for a boutique-slash-food-truck-rally not-date."

CHAPTER SEVEN

LIZZIE

THE PARK BUSTLES WITH PEOPLE AS MATT AND I weave through the growing crowd, searching for the perfect spot to watch the concert. Families spread blankets across the grass while couples claim spaces on the gentle slope facing the stage. Children play tag, and some people have brought their dogs.

No cats on leashes, though, and the thought makes me smile.

"What about over there?" Matt uses the blanket he carries to point to a spot under a sprawling oak tree, not too close to the stage but with a clear view.

"Perfect," I say, surprised at how much thought he's putting into this. I expected to stand awkwardly at the back of the crowd, not have a whole setup. But Matt leads the way, carrying what appears to be his entire living room—a rolled-up blanket tucked under one arm, two folding stadium chairs looped over the other forearm, and a small cooler in one hand.

He must know about my drink anxiety. I just like knowing where my next sip of cold, icy liquid refreshment is going to come from.

I stand back and watch as he unfolds a blanket made of denim squares on one side and spreads it across the grass with practiced efficiency. Next, he sets up the two stadium chairs—navy blue with cup holders and padded seats.

"You came prepared," I say, genuinely impressed.

"I've been to these concerts before." He straightens and gestures to the chairs with a flourish. "Your throne awaits, my catalyst."

"Thank you, Doctor." I sink into the chair, relieved I won't have to sit directly on the ground in my jumpsuit. "You're officially my favorite person right now."

His eyes light up. "Because I brought chairs?"

"The bar is low," I deadpan, but I can't keep a straight face when he clutches his chest in mock offense.

"Here I thought my chemically named cats and insistence that you bring me an obscure bread pudding had raised such a bar."

His charm, wit, and good looks don't hurt either, but I simply take the cooler from him so he can sit down. He does, sitting close enough that our elbows brush on the armrest. The contact sends fiery sparks up my arm, and this feels so much like real dating—comfortable silences, thoughtful gestures, and this constant awareness of each other.

The opening act takes the stage—a young woman with an acoustic guitar and a voice like honey. Her melodies drift through the evening air as the sky turns from gold to pink to purple.

"Want something to drink?" Matt asks, opening the cooler. "I've got several of my sparkling waters and a couple of Diet Cokes." He pulls out a slim silver can of his carbonated water, his eyebrows sky-high. "You know you want to try it."

"Do I, though?"

He shakes his head and pulls out a dripping Diet Coke—with cherry and vanilla. My absolute favorite soda pop, and it's not that easy to find. I take the bottle from him, enjoying the chill.

"This is the real gift," I say. "Forget a scarf."

"Cherry vanilla Diet Coke?"

I twist the lid, the hissing pop of the released fizz oh-so-satisfying. "Oh, yeah." I tip my head back and take a couple of gulps of cola. I sigh happily. "That is so delicious."

I look over to him, expecting to find him watching me and smiling. He's doing one of those, and my own grin falls off my face. "What?"

Matt takes my hand, his Serious Chemist Face stuck in place as he looks up to the stage. "Careful, my catalyst. You're causing a reaction I can't walk back."

My mind short-circuits at his touch combined with his words, making it impossible to reason through what he means.

Sac-Ra-Ment-O.

How am I supposed to maintain this "just friends" charade at work when he says things like that when we're not at work? When he looks at me like I'm the only person in this entire park?

We sit in comfortable silence for a while, listening to the music. As the opening act finishes and the crew begins setting up for the main band, Matt stands and stretches.

"I'm going to grab some popcorn or something. Want anything?"

"I'll come with you," I say, standing too quickly and kicking my bottle of Diet Coke in the process. "Oops."

I watch the bottle fly through the air, landing and bouncing over beside another couple. Then it rolls right next to the woman's bag. I freeze and stare, my mouth hanging open, expecting cherry vanilla Diet Coke to explode everywhere at any moment.

"Come on," Matt hisses, grabbing my arm and towing me away from the scene of the crime.

"I—Matt."

"I have another bottle," he says. "We don't want to be here when that thing goes volcano."

"It's going to be fine," I say, though I don't know that. "I always tighten the lid really good."

He cuts me a look out of the corner of his eye. "What is with you and sending Diet Coke flying?"

"That was an accident," I say, pulling my arm away from his grip. I wish he'd hold my hand again, but I also find myself darting looks left and right, right and left, as we walk over to the concession stand.

The night air has cooled, and I'm grateful for the warmth of my jumpsuit, though I wish I'd brought a light jacket. As if reading my mind, Matt shrugs out of his navy button-down, revealing a pale blue tee underneath, and drapes the shirt over my shoulders.

Unconsciously, I take a deep breath of it, because it holds the very essence of Matt. Then I look at him, and so many unspoken things are said between us.

"You looked cold," he says simply.

I slide my arms into the sleeves, immediately enveloped in his scent. "Thanks."

The line for popcorn moves slowly, giving us time to people-watch and chat. Matt tells me about the first concert he ever attended—a classical performance his mother dragged him to when he was ten—and I share stories about my failed attempt at learning the flute in middle school.

"I was so bad they asked me to just hold up the instrument during the spring concert," I say, laughing about it now. "My mom has a video of it, and I don't know how she never realized I never blew into the thing."

Matt laughs, the sound rich and genuine. "Tell me you still have that video."

Giggles spill from me too, even as I shake my head. "Even if I did, I wouldn't show you."

"I'll ask your dad when I meet him."

That sobers me right up, and Matt steps forward as if he's commented something simple like the sky is blue. "I'll take a large kettle corn, please," he says. "The caramel churro, and—" He looks at me. "You want anything besides that?"

"Red Vines."

"And some Red Vines." Matt pulls out his wallet to pay, and we move down a few feet to pick up our order. I claim my licorice and leave the rest for Matt. Turning back to the crowd, a beautiful sense of peace and happiness moves through me.

There are more people here than I thought would attend a concert in the park, and the atmosphere is bubbling, bright, and vibrant.

Then I see someone I know.

And not just someone I know—Jeff Thornton from Legal and Compliance at ChemTech.

"Boise, Idaho," I blurt out.

Matt follows my gaze. "What is it?"

"Jeff from Legal," I whisper, ducking slightly behind Matt and already looking for an escape route. "He can't see us together."

"Oh, my Miami," Matt says, and I walk away before

we can make a plan. I just need—I don't know what I need. Where is Jeff sitting? He was holding a little girl—his daughter, I'm assuming—and chitchatting with a few other people.

"Lizzie," Matt says from behind me.

"Lizzie," a man calls in front of me. The sky opens and pure light from heaven shines down on Claudia's brother, Luke. He raises his hand in a friendly wave, and I lift my box of candy to acknowledge him too.

He's lounging on the bare grass with a couple of people I recognize from a Halloween party we had a Liam's house last year.

Without thinking, I spin back to Matt. "I see some friends. I'm going to go say hi." I look at him meaningfully. "Alone. You go back to our spot, and I'll text you when it's clear."

Understanding dawns on his face. "Got it." He looks to Luke behind me. "Yep, I'm totally okay leaving you with a bunch of men I don't know." He doesn't move, and his eyes don't come back to mine.

I look over his shoulder, and for the love of all the Diet Coke in the world, Jeff is walking directly toward us.

"It's Claudia's brother," I say. "Jeff is headed this way. We need to know where he's sitting."

"Special Agent Giles is on it." With that, Matt ducks away from me, moving surprisingly well for a man holding an overflowing container of kettle corn and a churro dripping with caramel sauce.

And not a single kernel hits the ground. He really is a superhero, albeit a superhero who could cost me my job. Or at the very least, a great deal of dignity.

I spin away from the still-approaching Jeff and practically run over to Luke. "Hey," I say a bit out of breath.

"Howdy." Luke leans in for a light hug. "What are you doing out?"

I don't appreciate the question, but now is not the time to point that out. "Just enjoying the concert," I say, glancing over my shoulder to see Jeff looking in my direction. "With, um, friends."

Luke narrows his eyes at me.

"Listen," I say, taking his forearm in my free hand. "There's a guy over there that I work with, and I need to stay here with you guys until he's gone. Okay?"

Luke immediately looks up and past me. So do all three of his friends.

"Don't. Look," I hiss. "You guys are the worst." Men certainly don't know how to help out someone in need the way a woman does, that's for dang sure.

"I'm Lizzie," I say. "I can't remember your name."

"Stockton," he says. "This is Marl, and that's Boston."

They all head-bob at me, as if that's how you say hello to someone. "Great," I say. "So great to meet you." I grin like Marl's just made the funniest joke ever.

"Are you okay?" Luke asks in a quiet voice. "That guy, he's not—"

"Lizzie?"

I turn at the sound of Jeff's voice. I force a smile and look from him to his wife, who also has a little girl in her arms. "Hey, Jeff."

"What a surprise seeing you here."

Why is everyone so surprised to see me at a concert in the park? My holy Waco waffle iron, I leave the house sometimes. Maybe I'm an indoor cat, but come on. Me being out on a Saturday night isn't *that* surprising.

"How are you?" I ask. "I'm sorry, I don't remember your wife's name."

"Oh." Jeff looks over to the petite woman at his side, and she smiles warmly. "This is Denise."

"Of course. Nice to see you again." I turn to Luke and his friends. "These are my friends—Luke, Stockton, Marl, and..."

Why does my brain misfire now? *Why?*

"Boston," the last man supplies, extending his hand to Jeff.

As they exchange pleasantries, I stand there with a ticking time bomb in my chest for a heartbeat. This is torture. Absolute torture.

To my everlasting relief, The Hollow Pines come out, which causes the crowd to begin to cheer and roar.

"We need to go sit down," Denise says. She gives me a polite smile, which I return.

"Have fun," I chirp, and Jeff manages a half a smile. Typical chemist, to be honest. I stand there with Luke and his friends while Jeff leaves, and it's not until the crowd swallows him that I take a full breath.

"What is going on?" Luke asks. "Are you here alone?"

"She was with someone," Stockton says. "She's wearing his shirt, dude."

With horror, I look down at Matt's navy blue button-up. It's so not part of my fabulous jumpsuit first date outfit—and Jeff *has* to have seen it. He's not a stupid guy, by any means. I comb my memory, trying to find the moment when he looked at Matt's shirt around my shoulders.

He *had* to have seen it, right?

"Lizzie," Luke says loudly. "What is wrong with you?"

"Nothing," I say automatically. "Thanks for letting me pretend to be here with you guys." I give the same man-nod to each of them that they gave to me. "If you see him again, just say I had to go to the bathroom, okay?"

"I want this story," Luke says, amusement dancing in his eyes.

"Don't you dare text Claudia."

Luke laughs and shakes his head. "Go find the owner of that shirt, and text me if you need help with Jeff again."

Gratitude floods me, and I quickly step into Luke and give him a light hug. "Thank you, Luke."

I turn to leave, scanning, scanning, scanning for where Jeff and Denise have gone. I can't see them, and that only makes things worse. I move through the patchwork of people, finally arriving back at the blanket and chairs where Matt is.

He perks up when he sees me, plenty of questions in his eyes. "Okay?" he asks.

I sink into my chair, suddenly exhausted from the adrenaline—and maybe the quick-step walking I did to get here. "That was close."

"Too close." Matt's expression turns serious. "Is this worth it, Lizzie? All this sneaking around?"

The question catches me off guard. "What do you mean?" I take the kettle corn from him, noting he's only eaten off the top layer.

"I mean..." He runs a hand through his hair, making it stick up in that adorable way that makes my stomach flutter. "Is this not-date charade worth the stress? Maybe we should just—"

The crowd erupts in cheers as The Hollow Pines starts another song, cutting off whatever Matt was about to say. The lead singer steps up to the microphone, her voice carrying across the park as she greets the audience.

Matt and I sit there, the energy and light and life flowing around us, bouncing off an invisible barrier we've somehow erected. Then he smiles softly, takes my hand, and looks to the stage.

As the band plays a haunting melody about finding someone who sees the real you, Matt's thumb traces small circles on the back of my hand. Each gentle movement sends shivers up my arm, and I find myself leaning closer to him, drawn by some invisible force I can't resist.

The music fills me, creating a bubble where nothing exists except this moment—his hand in mine, our shoulders touching, the shared popcorn between us. And despite Jeff being here somewhere, I can't remember the last time I felt this content, this present.

When they play *Whispers in the Dark*, the song Matt told me was his favorite, he leans close, his breath warm against my ear as he says, "This is the one I wanted you to hear."

I close my eyes and let the words sink in—a story about two people finding each other in unexpected places, about taking chances and being brave enough to follow their hearts. By the time the song ends, there's a lump in my throat and a warmth in my chest that has nothing to do with the extra protection of Matt's shirt.

"It's beautiful," I whisper.

Matt's eyes meet mine, and they're filled with something that makes my breath catch. "Yeah, it is."

The rest of the concert passes in a blur of music and shared glances. When the final notes fade and the crowd begins to disperse, I find myself reluctant to leave this perfect bubble we've created.

"Ready to go?" Matt asks, standing and offering his hand.

I nod, taking his hand and letting him pull me to my feet. We pack up in comfortable silence, folding the chairs and blanket and carrying everything back to his car.

The drive to the Big House is quiet, both of us lost in our own thoughts. When Matt pulls into the driveway, the house is mostly dark except for the porch light and a soft glow from the kitchen window.

We walk side-by-side up the path to the front porch, our hands brushing with each step. When we reach the door, I turn to face him, suddenly nervous.

"I had a really good time tonight," I say, my voice softer than I intended.

"Me too." Matt steps closer, his eyes dropping to my lips. "Despite the close call with Jeff."

I laugh softly. "It added some excitement."

"As if being with you isn't exciting enough."

The moonlight catches in his hair, turning the brown strands silver at the edges. He's so close now that I can count the flecks of green in his hazel eyes, can feel the warmth radiating from his body.

"Lizzie," he whispers, and the way he says my name makes everything go weak.

He leans in, one hand coming up to curl around the

back of my neck, and I close my eyes, heart pounding in my chest.

This is it. This is when all my dreams come true.

A high-pitched bark shatters the silence, followed by the sound of something crashing. My eyes fly open just as a small, furry missile launches itself at Matt's legs.

"Oof." Matt stumbles backward as a puppy—a muddy, overexcited golden retriever puppy—jumps up, leaving dirty paw prints all over his jeans.

"Crouton, come back!" Emma's voice carries from around the side of the house. She appears a moment later, looking frazzled, a leash dangling uselessly from her hand. "I can't believe I lost a puppy I don't own."

The puppy—Crouton, apparently—continues his assault on Matt, who's now laughing despite being covered in mud.

"Where did you come from?" I ask, kneeling to grab the puppy's collar, but he's not wearing one.

"Oh, you have him." Emma rushes toward us, the light back in her face. "I didn't see you guys there, and I can't keep this blasted collar on his neck." She shakes the collar, which is still attached to the leash.

"Why do we have a puppy at the Big House?" I ask. Crouton barks at Matt and dances away from him again.

"Tahlia rented him for the weekend." Emma launches herself at the canine, managing to grab him by one paw. "You—collar—come on."

Matt kneels down and wraps the puppy in a big

bear-hug, and Emma manages to get the collar and leash back in place.

She huffs as she stands, then pushes her messy hair off her face. "She's thinking about getting a dog, so she's doing a trial run."

"And how's that going?" Matt stands and wipes his hands down the front of his jeans.

Emma grimaces. "Not great. He chewed one of her shoes, so we brought him outside, but he likes to dig too." She sighs. "And Tahlia had just finished the weeding in the garden, so it's a mess."

"I'm a mess all by myself," Matt says. "So this is my cue to leave." He grins at me, those gorgeous eyes blazing. "I'll see you tomorrow, Lizzie."

"Text me what time I need to be ready," I say, and he nods before he leaves.

"What's tomorrow?" Emma asks.

I ignore her and open the front door. "I'm not answering questions."

"Lizzie."

I sigh as she brings the mud ball inside with her. "I'll send a text, okay? I just...need time to think it through."

Emma's blue eyes watch me, wide and concerned. "Okay," she finally says. "You do like to think through things before you say anything."

It's the scientist in me, so I nod and start for the second floor. As I climb the stairs to my room, still wearing Matt's shirt over my jumpsuit, a sense of loss fills me.

I missed my kiss.

The moment my foot hits the second floor landing, I know one thing: That moment on the front porch won't be my only chance to kiss Matt Giles. After all, I'm seeing the man again tomorrow, and with that amazing thought, I smile my way into my room to relive and analyze every piece of tonight's spectacular not-date.

CHAPTER EIGHT

MATT

A LOUD CRASH FROM THE KITCHEN YANKS ME OUT of the daydream where Lizzie and I slow dance under the stars. I bolt upright, my heartbeat hammering against my ribs.

"What the—?" I spin from the mirror in the master bathroom and race toward the noise, nearly tripping over Purroxide, who's casually washing his paw in the hallway just outside my bedroom like nothing happened.

The kitchen looks like a crime scene. My coffee mug lies shattered on the tile floor, dark liquid spreading across the white surface. My phone—which I'd stupidly left on the counter—sits in the middle of the puddle, screen flickering with the death throes of modern technology.

"No." I lunge for the phone, snatching it from the coffee bath. Purricell sits on the counter, looking supremely unconcerned as he knocks my sugar container onto its side.

"You monsters," I yell, frantically wiping the phone with a dish towel. "I was waiting for a text from Lizzie."

Purricell meows innocently, as if to say, "I didn't mean to," but we both know he didn't mean *not* to.

I can't believe I just thought that. It's something my mom used to say to me all the time when I did something without thinking. *Well, you didn't mean not to, Matty.*

Ignoring the errant thought about my mother, I press the power button desperately, but the screen offers a few pathetic flickers, then returns to black. I close my eyes and breathe in through my nose.

"It's fine," I say. "Everything's fine."

Except it's not fine. I'm supposed to pick Lizzie up in—I glance at the microwave clock—two hours, and now I have no way to confirm our plans.

We'd been chatting about it, and she'd gotten interrupted by her roommates. She'd said she'd let me know if eleven worked, and now I'm not sure what time I'm even supposed to get her.

Purricell rubs against my leg, purring loudly, and Purroxide stalks into the kitchen. He heads straight for the coffee and starts licking it up. Seeing that, I'm not convinced he didn't have Purricell knock over the coffee for him, though how they'd coordinate that, I don't know.

"Don't think you're forgiven," I tell him, but I

scratch behind his ears anyway. "You've created a crisis of epic proportions."

I clean up the mess, salvaging what I can of my dignity, if not my phone. After trying rice, a hair dryer on low heat, and every other internet remedy I can think of, I accept defeat. The phone is dead, and with it, all my recent text conversations with Lizzie.

"I need a new phone," I tell the cats. "Right now."

They stare back at me, unimpressed. They hate my phone, and they're certainly not going to help me get another one.

I point the defunct cellphone at them. "And when I get back, we're going to have a serious talk about boundaries."

———

THE BIG HOUSE looks even more impressive in the daylight—a grand Southern dame watching over her domain. I park in the gravel driveway and take a deep breath, checking my reflection in the rearview mirror. My hair is sticking out in weird ways, not sexy ones, but I have a new phone to go with my casual polo the color of Georgia peaches and khakis.

I grab the small gift bag from the passenger seat—a peace offering for cutting off all contact for the past couple of hours—and head up the walkway. Before I can ring the bell, the door swings open, and there she is.

Lizzie stands framed in the doorway, a vision in a version of a little black dress that is better than anything I've ever seen. The fabric looks soft, but I don't dare touch it, and it flows over only one shoulder, past her curves, and down toward the ground. She's wearing a pair of gold sandals, telling me she's a total queen.

As if I don't already know that.

Her auburn hair falls in soft waves around her shoulders—that bare one making my mouth drier by the moment—and she's wearing just enough makeup to enhance her natural beauty without masking it.

"Hi," falls out of my mouth on accident.

"Hi yourself," she says, smiling. "I was about to call the animal shelter and have them do a well-check on your cats."

I snap back to reality, a chuckle coming out. "A well-check on the cats? Not me?" I step closer, wanting to get a hint of her perfume. I'm rewarded with that tiny touch of citrus, and it only makes me smile more.

"I figured out of the three of you in that house, if something happened, the cats would have something to do with it."

"As it happens," I say. "Purricell drowned my phone in coffee." I hold up the gift bag. "I had to go get another one, and of course, now I don't have your number. I brought you something to make up for the cat-chaos."

Her eyes light up as she takes the bag. "I'll have to thank Purricell."

"Yeah, because he needs more praise." I roll my eyes. It's not like my Maine Coon spent a few extra minutes in the mall to get this gift for her.

She peeks inside and then laughs, pulling out a travel mug emblazoned with "In Case of Emergency, Throw at Matt."

"I figured it was safer than a soda cup."

"It's perfect." She clutches it to her chest, and wow, I've never been more jealous of an inanimate object. "Let me just grab my purse and we can go."

As she disappears inside, I turn around and exhale. "It's fine. See? She's not mad."

Lizzie is awesome, but she totally does have a bit of a grumpy streak. She's very polished, and I roll my neck and ask, "What is she doing with me?"

A beep fills the air, and a woman says, "We have cameras on the front porch, Matt."

I jump about a foot and look around—yep, right there. A camera. I wave to it as pure humiliation fills me. "Hey, there."

"All right." Lizzie returns a moment later, a small crossbody bag in a shimmering, nearly bedazzled black slung over her shoulder. "Ready?"

I give the camera one more glare. "Absolutely." I link my arm through hers, my mind whirring with worry now. I mean, there's no way I can bring her back here tonight and kiss her.

We walk to my car, and I open the passenger door

for her—a gesture that earns me another smile. As I circle around to the driver's side, I catch her checking me out, and warmth spreads through my chest.

"So," I say as I start the engine. "How was the rest of your night with Crouton the Destroyer?"

She laughs, the sound like music that tickles all my desires. "Tahlia decided around midnight that dog ownership might not be for her after all. She's more of a cat person."

"Yeah, cat people are cat people until they're not."

She grins. "Are you going to adopt out Purricell and Purroxide?"

"I'm thinking about it—mostly just Purricell." I back out of the shallow lot, glad there's only one more house on this street past the Big House. "I left my coffee and my phone on the counter, because I'd just spilled on my shirt, and the next thing I know, there's a big crash in the kitchen, and my phone is bathing in coffee."

I glance at her. "I was worried you'd think I was standing you up."

"Never crossed my mind," she says, but there's a slight hesitation that tells me it absolutely did.

"Well, I'm here now," I say. "And I'm all yours for the day."

The words hang in the air between us, heavy with promise. Lizzie's cheeks flush slightly, and she looks out the window.

"So, tell me about your sister," she says after a moment. "What kind of things does she like?"

I smile, grateful for the change of subject. "Chanel's amazing. She's two years younger than me, but sometimes I think she's the more mature one. She just had a baby girl three months ago—Nora."

"That's a beautiful name."

"Yeah, it was our grandmother's." I tap my fingers on the steering wheel, because conversation about my family isn't my favorite. "Chanel's always been into art and fashion—hence the name our mother gave her—but since having Nora, she hasn't had much time for herself."

"So some pampering might be nice."

"Exactly." I signal for a turn, heading toward the Sugar Creek rec center where the craft fair is being held. "Her husband, Shad, is between jobs right now, so I know they won't do anything extravagant for her birthday."

Lizzie nods thoughtfully. "And you want to give her something special."

"Yeah." I don't mention that I've been helping them financially. That's not first—or second—not-date conversation material. "Something that makes her feel like herself again, not just 'Mom.'"

"I get that," Lizzie says. "My mom used to say the hardest part of motherhood was remembering who she was underneath it all."

The mention of her mother catches me off guard. Lizzie rarely talks about her, and I know from bits and pieces that she passed away years ago.

"Your mom sounds great," I say.

Lizzie smiles, a touch of sadness in her eyes. She reaches over and takes my hand, and I dang near drive us off the road.

I've always initiated the contact between us, and this—this—this feels amazing.

"She was," she says. "She would have liked you, I think."

The simple statement hits me right in the chest. "I would have liked to meet her."

We drive in comfortable silence for a few minutes, the air between us charged with something I can't quite name. As we approach Sugar Creek, the traffic thickens, and I spot the colorful flags on the rec center ahead—and plenty of traffic.

"Looks like we're not the only ones with this idea," I say.

"Good thing we have a mission," Lizzie says. "Operation: Perfect Gift for Chanel."

"There you go again, always being the catalyst."

She rolls her eyes at the nickname, but I catch the small smile that plays at her lips.

I finally find parking at the far end of the lot, and we make our way toward the rec center hand-in-hand.

The boutique has spilled out of the rec center and into part of the parking lot, which is why the traffic was so bad. It's a riot of color and sound—vendors selling everything from handmade jewelry to artisanal soaps to custom lawn ornaments. Food trucks line the north side of the lot, something roasted and delicious making my stomach growl.

"Hungry?" I ask.

"Starving," Lizzie says. "But let's look around first. I'm in the zone."

Her determination is adorable, and she tugs me over to the first booth. I watch her way more than I look at anything in any booth as she leads me through the crowd. She approaches shopping with the same focus she brings to regulatory compliance—methodical, thorough, and with an eye for detail.

"What about this?" She holds up a delicate silver bracelet with tiny charms.

"Pretty," I say. "But Chanel's more bold with her accessories."

Lizzie nods and moves on to the next booth, bringing me along with her. Her hand feels perfect in mine, warm and soft and right.

We stop at a booth selling hand-painted silk scarves, and Lizzie gasps. "Matt, look at these."

The scarves are stunning—vibrant colors swirled together in abstract patterns that somehow manage to look both chaotic and perfectly balanced.

"These are gorgeous," she says, running her fingers over one in shades of deep purple and blue.

"Each one is unique," the woman behind the table explains. "I use a water marbling technique."

Lizzie picks up a scarf in rich jewel tones—emerald green, sapphire blue, and deep ruby red. "This is incredible. The colors remind me of stained glass."

I study the scarf, then look at Lizzie. "It's perfect. Bold, unique, beautiful."

Just like Lizzie.

"And practical," Lizzie says. "She can wear it a dozen different ways—as a headband when she's with the baby, or dressed up for when she goes out."

"We'll take it," I tell the vendor, reaching for my wallet.

As the vendor wraps the scarf, I lean close to Lizzie. "Thank you," I whisper, letting my lips brush against the side of her face. Wow, I'm more bold with her than I thought I could be. "I never would have found this on my own."

"I'm sure that's not true," she says, but her eyes soften with pleasure.

I squeeze her hand. "I needed you." The words come out more earnest than I intended, and Lizzie's eyes widen slightly. Before she can respond, my stomach growls loudly.

She laughs, breaking the tension. "I think someone needs lunch."

"Food trucks?" I suggest, tucking Chanel's gift into my messenger bag.

"Lead the way."

We make our way to the food truck area, still hand-in-hand. Who knew there were this many food trucks in the area? "Gourmet grilled cheese," I say.

"Korean fusion," Lizzie says. "That's a no from me."

"Ice cream—maybe for dessert." I turn toward her. "What are you in the mood for?"

Lizzie's eyes scan the trucks as we keep walking, lighting up when she spots one. She crowds in close to me. "Southern comfort food, Matty. I *need* mac and cheese in my life right now."

My feet freeze, and Lizzie almost stumbles as she comes to a stop too. "Matty?"

"Oh." Her cheeks pink up. "I'm sorry. I don't—it just came out."

"My mom and sister call me that."

Her eyes search mine. "And...it's a bad thing? I'm sorry. I won't—"

I place one finger against her lips, rendering her mute. Sparks burn in my fingertip, and I drop my hand. "Sorry."

Lizzie and I stand there in the flow of traffic, people parting left and right around us. "It's fine if you call me Matty."

"Are you sure?" Her mouth barely moves.

"Yeah," I say. "It's...it just caught me off-guard."

Lizzie's mouth lifts into a smile. "I'm going to call that a win." She steps over to the line in front of the bright blue truck with a huge cartoon chicken on it.

"A win?"

"Nothing ever catches you off-guard," she says.

"Are you kidding?" I scoff and pull her closer as another couple tries to squeeze by us. "You threw a full forty-four ounces of Diet Coke at me just three days ago. That *totally* caught me off-guard."

She just shakes her head, and I wonder what she really sees when she looks at me. Is it anything like what I see when I look at myself in the mirror?

"So," I say as we shuffle forward in line. "Tell me something I don't know about you."

She tilts her head, considering. "We've been friends for a while. Why don't you tell me something you *do* know about me?"

I watch her for a minute. "I feel like I'm being set up."

She grins. "You don't think you can pass this simple quiz?"

"So you're admitting it's a quiz." I take another step forward, my mind buzzing now. I really can't fail this quiz, or I'm never getting another date with Lizzie.

"I'll go first to give you time to think." She bumps me with her hip as we step forward again. Lizzie should get an award for flirting, because she's so good at it. "I know that you love chocolate chip cookies, but only with milk chocolate chips. Not semi-sweet. And definitely not dark."

"Dark chocolate is over-rated," I say. "I will die on this hill."

"Your turn," Lizzie says, almost in a sing-song voice.

"You think I don't know anything about you."

"I'm still waiting for you to say something."

"I had cherry vanilla Diet Coke—for you—at the park last night."

She opens her mouth, then nods and we inch forward again.

"And besides, I also know you took dancing lessons a few years ago, and that you really liked them."

Her face lights up. "I did like them." She links her arm through mine while she studies the menu. "Do you dance, Matty? Maybe we can go dancing to, like, plan a company party or something."

She grins at me, and I feel the sunshine behind it.

"I'm not sure I can keep up with you on the dance floor," I say.

"I doubt that." She looks me up and down, and I feel every inch of myself. "You move too well to be completely hopeless."

Heat creeps up my neck at her assessment. "Maybe you'll have to teach me sometime."

"Maybe I will." Her voice is soft, almost a challenge.

We reach the front of the line and I lean into the tiny food truck window. "I'll have the pulled pork sandwich,"

I say. "And we need the mac and cheese in a bread bowl, as well as an order of sweet potato fries with that maple drizzle."

The man in the truck gives me a total that is probably double what I'd pay for these things in a real restaurant, and now I'm paying a ton for truck food. That done, I move out of the way. I step over to her and slide my hand along her waist.

"Is this one of your modeling outfits?"

She leans into me. "Maybe."

"See, I know you're a model." I grin at her.

"It's not a real job," she says, and I detect a hint of wishfulness in her voice.

"Why not?" I ask. "Is there not enough work?"

"I could work more," she says. "Especially with the amount of online shops there are now."

The thought of her confidently showcasing her curves makes me both proud and, if I'm honest, a little hot under the collar. "Then why don't you?"

"It's just a hobby," she says, but I can tell it means more to her than she's letting on.

"Do you have photos? Of your shoots?"

She pulls back, and I drop my hand. "A few," she says vaguely.

I can tell she doesn't want to show them to me, and while I'd normally push her, today, I don't.

"You know, I have been thinking about getting a different job," she says.

Everything inside me perks up at this news. "You have?"

This is huge news. All this not-dating wouldn't have to be a thing if we didn't have to adhere to insane relationship restrictions.

"I'm just not sure what I want to do." She pulls her phone from her crossbody bag and makes a few swipes and taps. Lizzie looks up through her eyelashes, which makes everything male inside me roar.

Then she steps back and hands me her phone.

"What's—?" I look down at the phone, which mutes my voice.

Because it's a professional picture of Lizzie wearing a flowing sundress. She wears a fierce look on her face and bright coral lipstick that makes me focus on her mouth.

Her hair is a dirty blonde in this picture, and I'd forgotten she's a natural blonde. I swipe and another photo comes up. This picture is Lizzie in a sparkly deep forest green cocktail dress that hugs every curve.

She's confident, radiant, absolutely stunning.

This picture burns into my eyes, my brain, and I've never been happier that I'm going to be able to see this for the rest of my life.

"You're incredible," I say, my voice rougher than I intended.

She takes the phone back and tucks it away almost before I even know I'm not looking at her in that cocktail dress anymore. "It's just nice to feel pretty sometimes."

"Lizzie."

She looks everywhere but at me, so I just go on. "You're beautiful all the time. In your work clothes, in your jumpsuit last night, in this dress today. I bet your pajamas would make my mouth dry. It's not about the clothes anyway. It's about you."

I take a big breath as her eyes snap to mine. They're so wide, like she can't believe the things I've said. I can barely believe it.

"You take my breath away." I lean closer, my mind racing with what I might do next. I'm completely out of control, and all I can think about is that camera on the front porch of Lizzie's house.

But how can I kiss her at a very busy food truck rally?

I can't.

"It's not about the clothes, Lizzie. It's you. You're a beautiful person." I press my cheek to hers, the smoothness of her skin against mine pure bliss.

For a moment, I think I've gone too far. Then she pulls back, smiles in a soft and genuine way, and ducks her head. "Thank you, Matty."

Something starts to glow inside me, because Lizzie is an incredible person, and being with her makes me feel incredible too.

———

HOURS LATER, I pull into the driveway at the Big House and turn off the engine but make no move to get out. Neither does Lizzie.

"I had a really good time today," I say, turning to face her.

"Me too." She smiles, and my heart does a somersault in my chest.

"We should do this again sometime." I lean closer, drawn to her like a magnet.

"Definitely." Her eyes drop to my mouth, and I know she's thinking about the same thing I am—our almost-kiss from last night.

I reach up to tuck a strand of hair behind her ear, letting my fingers linger against her cheek. "Lizzie," I whisper.

She leans in, and I can feel her breath on my lips. This is it. This is finally happening.

Her phone rings, shattering the moment.

Lizzie jumps, looking both disappointed and flustered as she fumbles for her phone. "It's my dad," she says, her voice made mostly of air.

"Go ahead," I say, trying not to show my frustration.

She answers with, "Hey, Daddy," and I watch as her expression shifts from annoyance to interest.

"This weekend?" she asks. "Yeah, sure, Daddy, I can help...no, that's not a problem..." She looks over to me, then cuts her eyes away, almost like she'd rather have this conversation alone.

Trust me, I'd like to be alone with her too.

"Actually, Daddy, I might bring someone with me."

My ears perk up at that.

She turns toward me fully now. "Yes, a friend from work." She grins as wide as the sky now. "He's really good with animals; cats, especially."

I scoff, though I can't help smiling.

"Okay, I'll let you know," she says. "Love you too. Bye." She hangs up and turns to me.

"How's your dad?" I ask.

"Great," she says. "Listen, he volunteers at an animal shelter, and they're having an adoption event next weekend. I usually help him out."

"Sounds fun," I say, genuinely meaning it.

"Would you..." She hesitates, then pushes through whatever mental block she has. "Would you want to come with me? It's a lot of work, but the animals are amazing, and my dad makes the best barbecue you've ever tasted, and he said he'd feed us lunch after."

My heart leaps at the invitation—not just to spend more time with Lizzie, but to meet her father, to be included in this important part of her life.

"I'll check the cats' schedule," I say, though I'll clear anything from my calendar to be there with her.

She beams at me, then her expression drops into

uncertainty. "What if someone from work sees us there? It's not exactly team bonding."

I take her hand, running my thumb over her knuckles. "Lizzie, look at me."

She does, her blue-green eyes wide and questioning.

"I don't care who sees us," I say firmly. "I want to go with you. I want to meet your dad. I want—"

The words "to be with you" hover on my lips, unspoken but hanging in the air between us.

Lizzie's phone chimes with a text message, and she glances down at it. Her expression changes, a mix of surprise and something else I can't quite identify.

"What is it?" I ask.

She gasps, then tosses her phone onto the dashboard like it's caught fire.

"What's going on?"

I reach for the phone, but I can't quite reach it. Lizzie stares at the phone, and I see her slipping away from me.

"Lizzie."

"It was from Jessie," she says. "And it was a picture of us." She turns her head toward me, almost robotically. "Standing at the food truck."

CHAPTER NINE

LIZZIE

The ChemTech lobby feels like a prison. The sleek, modern design with its gleaming floors and minimalist furniture usually brings a sense of pride—I work at a place that looks this impressive—but today, it feels cold. Sterile. Like I'm walking into my own execution.

I check the array of clocks on the wall—as if we need to know what time it is in London, Paris, Tokyo, and Honolulu. The one on the far left is local time—7:45 a.m. Fifteen minutes until my meeting with Jessie. Fifteen minutes to decide if my career is worth sacrificing for...whatever Matt and I have going on.

I wish I had a label for it, but it's been two dates and a drop-by with a howler. Is that dating? Is he my boyfriend?

"Absolutely not," I mutter, earning a curious glance from the security guard as I swipe my badge. The elevator doors slide open with a cheerful ding that mocks my mood.

I spent all night alternating between panic and defiance. Matt and I texted from the moment I hit my bedroom until almost midnight, strategizing about what to say, what not to say, whether to deny everything, or come clean. We settled on a vague middle ground—acknowledge we were at the craft fair together, but insist we're just friends exploring common interests outside of work.

I mean, friends can go shopping together. Chem-Tech can't dictate that.

The elevator deposits me on the fifth floor, and I stride toward my office, chin up, shoulders back, the perfect picture of professional composure. Once inside, I collapse into my chair and drop my head into my hands.

My phone buzzes with a text, and it almost takes more energy than what I have to reach for it.

Good luck with the dragon lady, Matt says. *Remember, we're just friends who happened to be at the same place.*

I frown at the phone. Matt does not look at me like he wants to be my friend. He doesn't act like any guy I've ever been friends with. The way he wants to perpetuate this is...well, frankly, I'm confused by it.

And irritated.

Sure, I think. *Friends who hold hands, almost kiss—*

twice—and look at each other like he's starving and I'm a chocolate fountain.

Without ChemTech, I'm sure he'd make his real feelings known. "As if he hasn't already."

I've been out with men before; I know when one is interested in me, and Matt is All Kinds of Interested.

"Maybe just not enough to fill out the packet," I say. "Or not enough to want to truly jeopardize anything."

Those words sting, and I sigh and spin in my chair to look out the windows. With the sun coming up over the building, this western view seems hazy, almost surreal.

I worked hard for my promotion at ChemTech, and I was thrilled to get it. This is my career. My stability. My carefully constructed life where everything makes sense and follows rules and—

And is completely, utterly *boring* me to death.

My phone buzzes again, and this time, when I look at it, my dad has sent me a picture. *Saw these elephants and thought of you.*

The picture of a mama elephant with a baby right at her side reminds me that not everything is as serious as regulatory chemical filing with a government agency.

You used to love elephants as a little girl. I guess I'm not sure if you still do, but whatever. I thought of you, and I hope you have a good week at work.

Dad includes a heart emoji, and suddenly my heart feels too full. Stupid tears even prick my eyes, and this is so not the Battle Mode I need to be in before I walk into Jessie's office.

I still love elephants, I tell him. *Remember how Momma had that crystal pair of them? She loved elephants too.*

She sure did.

I never confirmed that I'd bring Matt with me to the animal shelter adoption event, because the text from Jessie had distracted me. Sitting there in my office, after a night of little sleep, I can't even remember if he said he'd come.

I remember being paranoid that someone from work would see us—which is stupid; my dad lives over an hour away from Cherry Creek and ChemTech. Someone would have to be seriously looking for a specific type of pet to be at the adoption event in Summerville.

What are you doing today? Dad asks, almost like he knows he's let an arrow fly and it's hit me right in the chest.

Maybe getting fired, I think as I look at the text again.

I think I need a new job, I text. *ChemTech is*

I don't know how to finish the sentence. I felt like it was a prison as I walked in this morning, and that about sums it up. *Suffocating*, I finish, and I send that message too.

You're more than ChemTech, Lizzie, Daddy says. *If you don't like it there, get a different job.*

"Doing what?" bursts out of my mouth.

I don't know, but something.

The words flow through my mind in a voice I can't quite place. Not really my dad's, but not mine either. I feel like they sum up everything in my life right now.

What's going on between me and Matt?

I don't know, but something.

What can I do for work if I leave ChemTech?

I don't know, but something.

What's going to happen now that all my best friends have gotten married—or will be married soon enough?

I don't know, but something.

Something always happens, and it's with yet another sigh that I stand, smooth my already-ridiculously-pressed pencil skirt, and leave my office. My heels click-clack against the floor, marking time like a metronome counting down to doom.

In the HR department on the third floor, Jessie's office door is open, but I knock anyway. She looks up from her computer, her dark bob swinging with the movement. For a moment, it looks a little sideways, and I am so right. She wears a wig.

"Elizabeth. Right on time." She gestures to the chair across from her desk and tucks her hair behind her right ear—does she pull it a little bit? I can't quite tell, because my heartbeat is booming as I step into the office, and somehow that makes my vision shake a little. "Close the door, please."

I do as instructed, my stomach knotting as I sit down.

The chair is uncomfortable—deliberately so, I suspect. After all, we wouldn't want anyone to feel at-ease here at ChemTech.

Jessie taps at her keyboard, then swivels her monitor so I can see the screen. There we are—Matt and I at the craft fair, practically standing in each other's arms in front of the food truck. His back is to me, but it's clear his hand rests on my waist, and I'm looking up at him with an expression that can only be described as adoring.

"Care to explain this?" Jessie asks, her voice neutral but her eyes sharp.

"That's me," I say, going with the shortest answer possible. Matt and I discussed this as a tactic, and I told him I'd cave within seconds. Jessie is *scary*, and I'm conflict avoidant.

"And who is with you?"

I feign confusion. "I'm sorry?"

"The man in the photograph, Elizabeth." Jessie might as well have rolled her eyes to go with that snippy tone. "Is that Matthew Giles from Process Engineering?"

I take a deep breath. "It appears to be, yes."

"Appears to be?" She raises one perfectly threaded eyebrow. "You don't know who you were with?"

"Of course I know who I was with," I say, my irritation flaring enough to infect my voice. "Matt and I are friends. We ran into each other at the craft fair in Sugar Creek yesterday."

"Friends," Jessie repeats, looking back at the photo. "And does he always hold his friends like that?"

My cheeks burn, but I hold my head high. "I don't monitor how Matt interacts with all his friends."

"Elizabeth." Jessie removes her glasses and pinches the bridge of her nose. "Let me be clear. A concerned employee sent me this photo because they were worried about potential violations of our fraternization policy."

"A concerned employee?" Anger bubbles up inside me. "What does that mean?"

"They were attending the same public event and noticed what appeared to be inappropriate contact between coworkers." She slides a folder across the desk. "You know our policy."

I take the folder without opening it. "Yes, I'm familiar with the policy."

I would have to be *dead* not to be familiar with the policy. As it happens, I'm very much alive—and I've filled out a packet like this before. Well, not one exactly like this. The last time I got involved with someone at work, the strict dating policy didn't exist. Sure, there was some paperwork, but nothing like it is now.

Yeah, and the guy you went out with is the reason why things are so ridiculous now.

I never want to think about Justin again, so I look up from the folder. The worst part is, Justin quit when the whole scandal went down, and he's never had to live with the aftermath of the revamped fraternization policy.

See, I wasn't the only coworker he went out with. Thankfully, we'd broken up before the true sulfur hit the fan. I wasn't directly involved, but as I sit in Jessie's office, I almost wish I had been.

I wouldn't have been promoted to Regulatory Affairs, and I wouldn't have to work next door to Matt, and maybe I'd be dating a nice man who works as a podiatrist about now.

"Elizabeth," Jessie barks, and I get the hint that it's not the first time she's said my name.

I blink. "Yes, I'm here."

She looks doubtful. "Are you and Matthew in a relationship?"

The question hangs in the air, almost unanswerable.

"He goes by Matt," I say. "Just like I go by Lizzie."

Jessie looks like she's just stepped in a slurry of chemicals that will eat her leg off in the next five seconds. "Elizabeth."

Oh, so she has the *I'm-so-disappointed-in-you* tone down pat too. Her range is incredible, I'll give her that.

"We're exploring the possibility," I clip out. "But nothing's happened yet. We're not in noncompliance."

"Well, that's not really up to you to decide."

"Actually, I think it is."

Jessie's eyebrows shoot up. Surely she's had someone disagree with her. I can't be the first, can I?

"I want the packet filled out anyway," Jessie says, nodding to the nondescript folder in my hands. "Then, if something changes suddenly, you're good."

Filling out this packet is about as far from "good" as I can get, but I simply nod.

"It's fairly self-explanatory."

"I'm sure it is." I've filled out far more complicated forms than whatever is in this folder, I know that.

"With the things we do here, transparency is essential."

Yes, I'm aware of what we do at ChemTech, but I say nothing.

"I'll need that back before anything else happens— even if you just run into each other at the gas station."

I nod, though I want to tell her I drive an electric car. I don't, but I'd love to see her face if I did. "Yes, of course." I rise, refusing to look away from her, and exit before I say something I'll regret later.

Back in my office, I slam the folder onto my desk and collapse into my chair. For five full minutes, I just sit there, staring at the offensive packet. Finally, I pull out my phone and open my job search app. I've had it for months but never actually used it. Now I scroll through listings, looking for anything that might fit my skills outside of chemical regulation.

Nothing jumps out, but one listing catches my eye— a cosmetics company looking for a technical consultant with knowledge of FDA regulations. It's not perfect, but it's something. I save it and keep scrolling.

My phone rings, the name *Heather* popping up. Relief fills me, and I swipe on the call from my modeling agent. "Hey."

"Oh," she says. "I didn't think I'd actually get you."

"You got me," I say.

"I have a couple of opportunities I wanted to run by you." Her voice comes across bright and bubbly as always.

"Excellent," I say. "What do you have?"

"You might not be available...these are day shoots."

"I have vacation days," I say casually. My modeling has always been a side hustle, something I do for the free clothes or to treat myself and my friends with a nice dinner every once in a while.

I've never truly considered actually hustling to do it. If I did, could I have a shoot every single day? Could I make enough money to support myself?

Could I stay in Charleston and do that?

I'm so tired of questions and the unknown answers that don't come with them.

"Okay," Heather says enthusiastically. "Well, let me tell you everything I've got then. There's been a boom in requests lately, and I'm sure you know Karly moved to Newark."

I had no idea about that, but I just say, "Okay."

"So, there's a bridal boutique looking for plus-size

models for their summer collection. Two days of shoot-ing, decent pay."

"Yes, I'd love to do that," I say, surprising myself with how quickly I respond.

"Great! And there's also a department store ladies online catalog—they specifically asked for you after seeing your portfolio. It would be a week-long commit-ment, though. Can you swing that?"

A week away from ChemTech. A week of doing something I actually enjoy. "When?"

"Three weeks from now. I know it's short notice—"

"Book it," I say firmly. "I'll make it work."

We chat for a few more minutes about details, which she promises to email me too, and then I say, "I'm thinking of transitioning to modeling full-time. Don't hold back on any jobs that come up, okay?"

"Wow," Heather says. "Okay. I do usually call you a bit down the list, because I know you can't handle every request."

"Please call me first," I say.

"Making a note...now." Heather laughs and says good-bye. After I hang up, I feel lighter than I have in months. Like I've just made a decision I didn't even know I was considering.

My phone buzzes, and I seriously want to punch a hole in the window and throw it outside. Instead, I look at it.

Emma: *How did it go with HR? I'm dying! You can't still be in there!*

Claudia: *I was just wondering too.*

Ryanne: *Maybe "first thing" at ChemTech isn't really first thing.*

Emma: *She HAS to know by now.*

Tahlia and Hillary don't chime in, because Tahlia teaches middle school and doesn't have her phone glued to her hand the way some of us do. Hillary is on-set today, so she'll be device-free for a while too.

I got the relationship disclosure packet. I have to document EVERYTHING if Matt and I want to date.

Emma: *Are you going to do it?*

That's the million-dollar question, isn't it? Am I going to jump through these hoops for a relationship that's barely started? That Matt keeps referring to as friendship? Or am I going to take this as a sign to make bigger changes?

Before I can answer, another text pops up—this one from Matt: *How bad was it?*

I hesitate before tapping over to his thread. I look at the folder sitting innocently on my desk, and pure fire ignites inside me.

One thing I know: I'm not filling out anything if he's not going to agree he wants to be more than friends. This ruse has to end, or my pen will stay capped.

Meet me for lunch in my office, I send him. *We need to talk.*

CHAPTER TEN

MATT

My heart pounds against my ribs as I approach
Lizzie's office, my lunch bag clutched in my sweaty palm
and her lunch tote slung over my shoulder. The hallway
stretches like a gauntlet, each step bringing me closer to
whatever "we need to talk" means—four words that have
never preceded good news in the history of human
communication.

I've spent the morning in a fog, unable to focus on
anything except Lizzie's meeting with Jessie and what it
might mean for us. For me. For my job.

The job I need to keep if I'm going to continue
helping Chanel and her family, keep my mom's house in
Savannah, and be able to feed my cats their luxury cat
food. I can't even *imagine* what Purroxide will do if I
have to move to generic kitty chow.

I pause outside Lizzie's door and take a deep breath.

I'm not going to lose my job. We're going to fill out the paperwork, and everything will be fine.

The real problem is, no one can ever predict what will happen with absolute certainty, and that's always bothered me. It's why I went into chemistry—I can absolutely predict what will happen, based on the known characteristics and properties of the elements involved.

But me and Lizzie?

Anything could happen—and some of those things could be bad.

The vein in my throat throbs as I knock softly on Lizzie's door. I only make it to three before she says, "Come in."

I ease open the door, praying with everything I have that another Diet Coke—or a knife—won't slice right past my head.

Lizzie sits behind her desk, perfect posture, that auburn hair pulled back in a sleek bun. Her blue-green eyes meet mine, unreadable, and a manila folder sits ominously on her desk. It looks like the rest of the office has been scrubbed completely, packed up like today's her last day.

My heart clenches, squeezing into a tight, cold, hard ball. I stop, every defense in my body flying into place. "Did you quit?"

"What? No."

I relax a little bit. "I got your lunch."

"Close the door," she says.

I turn to do that, and I must've had some extra protein in my shake this morning, because the door gets away from me and slams closed with a horrifying *slap!*

I groan and press my eyes closed. When she doesn't reprimand me or even sigh, I turn to face her. I pass her the lunch tote and take the chair across from her desk. I've sat here a bunch in the past few months since she got made the Department Head of Regulatory Affairs, and I honestly don't know what I'll do if she quits.

"I need this job," I say out of nowhere. So many words tumble around in my head, and I can't make sense of them to order them to march out of my mouth. "I'm sorry about all of this. It's stupid. I know that. I *know* it's stupid, and I've known it since I came up with the idea."

I run out of air, which thankfully makes me stop talking. Lizzie's dropped her attention to her tote, which she unzips and pulls out a chocolate and vanilla pudding cup. The way she stays silent tells me I have a lot more talking to do.

To give myself a minute, I unpack my lunch—turkey sandwich, apple, those chocolate-covered almonds she likes—and push the treat bag toward her as a peace offering. "I'm sorry you had to deal with Jessie alone. I would've gone in with you."

"She didn't know for sure it was you," she says.

"You told her?"

"I had to. She asked me a direct question." She holds

the pudding cup in her hand, and I've never thought of such a thing as a weapon. Right now, it so is.

She hasn't even looked at the almonds. So not good.

"How long are we going to keep this 'just friends' charade going?"

"I thought that's what we agreed on." I set my sandwich down, zero bites taken. "To avoid exactly this situation."

"The situation has arrived anyway." She taps the folder with one perfectly manicured nail. "So what now, Matt?"

I so don't like how she says my name. "We fill out the forms, I guess."

"Do we?" Lizzie leans forward, those eyes now blazing with something that makes me want to slide under the desk. "Because that would mean admitting we're more than friends."

I blink, because this woman can see right through me. Of course she can. I haven't exactly been discreet about how I feel about her—at least when we're on our not-dates.

My heart warms up, and now it's suddenly too big for my chest—and it's bleeding everywhere. "I didn't—I mean—I don't know—I..."

"Minneapolis, Matt," she hisses, and I know I'm in deep trouble when she breaks out the city-swears. "You hold my hand left and right. You almost kissed me. *Twice.* But you can't say what we actually are?"

She gets to her feet, rips her gaze from me, and paces to the window.

I have no idea what to do, but she's not wrong about her assessment. She's also operating with limited information, and words teem in the back of my throat. "I'm trying to protect us," I say, standing too. "Both of us."

"From what?" She turns and fixes me with a stare that pins me to the spot.

"From this." I gesture between us, to our uneaten lunches, at the folder. "From HR breathing down our necks, from having to document every moment we spend together like we're specimens in a lab experiment, from losing our jobs."

"That's not the real reason," she says, and the quietness of her tone is more deadly than her irritation. "What are you *really* afraid of, Matt?"

The question hits me like a chemical burn, unexpected and searing. I look away, my eyes finding the window, the parking lot below, anything but her penetrating gaze.

"My parents," I finally say, the words feeling foreign on my tongue. "They were...not great at being married. My dad left when I was eighteen, right after my high school graduation. Just...gone. My mom buried herself in work, took assignments that kept her away for months, and wasn't in town when my dad left. I put off college to help Chanel get to graduation, and she's about all I've got."

Lizzie's expression softens, but she doesn't throw another question at me.

"Remember how I said Chanel's husband doesn't have a job?" My eyebrows go up too high, and I can't make them go back down. "I pay their bills right now. I bought my parents' house in Savannah for some stupid reason I can't name, only that I couldn't bear to let it go when everything fell apart."

I take a breath, so much out between us now. "I need this job." I turn away from her, feeling like a complete failure. "So that, combined with the fact that I've never really seen a healthy relationship—at least up close—I don't know—I don't know how to do this, Lizzie. I don't know how to be someone's boyfriend or partner or whatever without screwing it up."

I turn back to her, more helplessness pulling through me than ever before.

"So your solution was to pretend we're just friends?" Her voice is gentler now.

"It felt safer." I run a hand through my hair. "If we're just friends, I can't disappoint you. I can't hurt you. There's no paperwork, and there's no risk to either of our jobs."

"But you *are* hurting me," she says simply. "By not being honest about what you want."

I look at her then, really look at her—the woman who's become the center of my universe without me even realizing it. The woman who I think about first thing when I wake up, and smile about when I think of her colored sticky tabs, and who I bring chocolate-covered almonds for, even if she doesn't eat them.

"What I want," I say slowly, giving the words time to line up properly. They arrive, and they pound beneath my tongue. I have to say them. Out loud. Right now.

"What I want…is you, Lizzie. Not as a friend. Not as a colleague. As…everything." I swallow, because I didn't even know I was going to say that.

She doesn't move, doesn't speak, just watches me with those eyes that see right through to my core.

"But I'm terrified," I say. "Because if I mess this up, I lose you completely. Or I lose my job. Or worse, both, and because I have responsibilities—Chanel and Nora and Shad—that complicates everything."

She nods, a small smile playing at her lips.

"What?" I ask. "Why are you smiling like that?"

She rounds the desk, coming to stand in front of me. "If you're really being honest, then—"

"I am."

"Then we should be working together," she says. "Not suffering separately."

I reach for her hand, our fingers intertwining naturally, like they've been doing this for years. "So what are you saying? We fill out the forms?"

"I'm saying I need you to decide what you want more—this safe distance or something real between us." Her thumb traces circles on the back of my hand, sending electricity up my arm. "Because I can't keep doing this halfway thing. It's too confusing, and it hurts too much."

"I don't want to hurt you." I bend my head toward hers and take a breath of her glorious skin. "That's the last thing I want."

"Then stop pretending we're just friends when we both know we're not." Her eyes search mine. "And I know it's new, so if there ever comes a time where you don't want me to be your everything, okay. But right now, I can't keep doing this."

Something shifts inside me, a chemical reaction reaching its tipping point. All the fear, all the hesitation that's been holding me back suddenly seems insignificant compared to the possibility of losing her before I've even had her.

"You're right," I say. "I've been a coward."

"I wouldn't go that far," she says. "You're just scared of this thing. There's a difference."

"Well, I'm done with that." I take a step closer to her, her in that pencil skirt about the sexiest thing ever. "I want to try this—us—whatever that means, whatever forms we have to fill out."

Hope blooms in her eyes. "I'd like to try us too."

I squeeze her hand. "You're worth every page of that ridiculous packet."

She laughs, the sound breaking the tension between

us. "That might be the most romantic thing anyone's ever said to me."

"Are you kidding me right now?" I sweep her into my arms fully and chuckle. "I just said all kinds of things far more romantic than that you're worth some paperwork."

"Oh, you think you did?" She slides her hands up my chest, which shoots a thrill through me.

"I one-hundo did."

She giggles and ducks her head against my chest. "Maybe I need to hear them again. I was a little wound up when you got here."

"Mm." I lean my head down so my mouth lines up with her ear. "I'm pretty sure I said I want you to be my everything."

"I do seem to remember that."

I smile and breathe her into my lungs, my heart, my soul. "Of course you do."

She giggles again, and the sound is magical in the stillness of her office. My free hand comes up to cradle her face, and she leans away from me, her eyes meeting mine. I trace my thumb along her jaw, and up to the curve of her lower lip.

"Matt," she says, speaking my name as a question *and* an invitation.

"I'm done pretending," I whisper, and then I lean down and kiss her, right there in her office, with sixteen pages of HR paperwork still empty on her desk.

Her lips are soft and warm against mine, and she makes a small sound in the back of her throat that sends fire racing through my veins. Her hands come up to grip my shoulders, pulling me closer as the kiss deepens.

I've imagined this moment a hundred different ways, but reality is infinitely better than any fantasy—the taste of her, the feel of her body pressed against mine, the way she kisses me back like she's been waiting for this as long as I have.

CHAPTER ELEVEN

LIZZIE

MATT'S TRUCK RUMBLES ALONG THE COUNTRY ROAD, taking us closer to Summerville and away from Charleston, ChemTech, and all the drama of the past week. I glance at him as he drives, his profile strong against the passing landscape, and a warm fluttery feeling spreads through my chest.

"What?" he asks, catching me staring.

"Nothing," I say, smiling. "Just thinking about how we're on our first official date."

He grins, reaching across the console to take my hand. "Is that what we're calling today? Our first date?"

"Yes," I say. "That's what I'm labeling today."

"So I kissed you a week before our first date? How do we explain that?"

"Who says we have to explain it to anyone?"

He glances over to me and adjusts his fingers in

mine. His touch sends electricity up my arm—a sensation I'm still not used to, even after our stolen kiss in my office five days ago.

Five days of finishing paperwork. Five days of separation at work. Five days of stolen text messages that have made me laugh in my office, grin stupidly at the wall separating me from Matt, and sighing as I lay in bed as he sends me pictures of his cats.

"I still can't believe we filled out sixteen pages of paperwork just to do *this*." I lift our joined hands slightly.

"Seventeen," Matt corrects. "There was that addendum about 'special circumstances' since we work in adjacent departments."

"Chattanooga," I mutter. "I'd forgotten about that one."

He bursts out laughing. "I like that one—Chattanooga. It's got a nice ring to it."

"It's a medium-strength city-swear."

"I'm learning the hierarchy." He sobers and reaches to turn down the radio a little. "So, tell me more about your dad. I want to make a good impression."

My stomach does a slow roll over, which is somehow worse than a sudden drop. Meeting my father on my first real date with Matt wasn't exactly what I'd planned, but now that the paperwork is done and turned in, it was either spend the day with him doing the adoption event, or come alone.

And I didn't want to come alone.

"He's pretty easygoing," I say, though my voice comes out higher than intended. "Just be yourself."

"Which self? My professional chemical engineer self? My cat-dad self? My charming first-date self?" He sighs and looks out his side window. "There's too many selves inside a person. Do you ever feel like that?"

He looks over to me, pure vulnerability in his expression. "Like, there's just so many different situations, and I—well, I haven't met anyone's father in a while."

"Yes, let's talk about who you've dated before."

"Nope." He shakes his head. "This is not first-date conversation."

"It's not?"

"Absolutely not," he says, his eyebrows going up. "Unless you're going to go first? I seem to remember you dating someone at ChemTech a few years ago..."

My throat tightens. "You're right. I don't want to talk about this today."

"Mm hm. That's what I thought."

I look out my side window too. "You're such a people person. You'll be fine."

"I'm a people person?"

I scoff-laugh. "Uh, yes. You're like a golden retriever, Matty. Everyone loves you, and you love everyone."

"A golden retriever?" He sounds so surprised that I face him, grinning.

"You don't like being a golden retriever?"

"I'm—a—cat—person," he says, enunciating each word with strength.

I grin at him. "Well, there are no cats that enter every room with a smile on their face, rushing toward everyone there like they showed up just to see them." I peer closer at him. "Are there?"

We turn onto a gravel road, and a large wooden sign comes into view: Summerville Animal Rescue & Adoption Center. Cars line the entrance, a good sign for the adoption event.

"Probably not," he says.

I settle back into the seat, though we're almost there. "Just be the guy who showed up at my house with a howling dog. Daddy will love that version of you."

"Be the version of myself who makes terrible decisions about pet transportation," he grumbles. "That's ridiculous."

"Then be the guy who sends me pictures of his cats in sweaters."

"It got cold this week," he says with far more power in his voice than he needs to have.

I laugh and shake my head. "I'm going to stop talking, because it's not helping."

"It's helping me," he says, glancing over as he brings the car to a stop.

"I like the cat texts, Matty."

His shoulders go down, and I hadn't realized how tense and boxed up they'd been. "Yeah?"

"Yeah."

He follows the directions of the parking attendant, and I let him come around and open my door for me. Since we're volunteering with animals today, and then eating lunch at my dad's hobby farm, I've worn skinny jeans and a sweatshirt the color of deep ripe purple plums.

I push my door closed and take Matt's hand. As we walk toward the entrance, I spot my father immediately. "There he is," I say.

He's tall like me, with salt-and-pepper hair and the same blue-green eyes I sport. He's wearing his usual uniform of worn jeans and a plaid button-down, sleeves rolled up to his elbows.

"The man with the brown and white plaid shirt."

"Uh huh, I see him," Matt says.

"He's going to love you."

"Lizzie-girl!" he calls, and I put a big smile on my face.

"Hey, Daddy." I quicken my pace, leaving Matt a few steps behind as I hug my father. He smells like aftershave and the outdoors—a combination that instantly transports me back to my childhood.

"You look beautiful, sweetheart," he says, holding me at arm's length as he scans me. "That hair color suits you."

I grin and grin at him. "Thanks, Daddy."

His eyes shift over my shoulder to where Matt

stands. "And this must be the friend from work you mentioned."

I step back, gesturing Matt forward, another realization settling over me. I never told my father that I was bringing a boyfriend, not a coworker. "Daddy, this is Matt Giles. Matt, this is my father, James Trenton."

Matt steps forward with a confident smile, extending his hand. "It's a pleasure to meet you, sir. Lizzie speaks very highly of you."

My father's handshake is firm—I can tell by the way Matt's knuckles whiten slightly—but his smile is genuine. "Good to meet you too, son. Lizzie hasn't brought anyone around in quite some time."

"Yeah, and I forgot to tell you that he's not just a friend." I reach for Matt, glad he easily slides his hand into mine. "We're pretty new."

"Yeah, I figured when I saw you holding his hand on the way over." Daddy gives me a look that says he'll talk to me more about this later. That look morphs into nothing but friendliness as he focuses on Matt.

"Come on, I'll show you guys around. We've got a busy day ahead."

As we follow my father into the shelter, Matt leans close to my ear. "I like him."

"Wait until he starts telling embarrassing stories about me," I mutter.

"Now I'm really excited."

The shelter is a whirlwind of activity. Volunteers

hustle about, moving outside to set up pens for the dogs and arranging cat carriers in the shade. The event will take place behind the building, and the potential adopters are being kept out front for now.

"Matt, what'll it be? Cats or dogs?" He pauses in front of the Cat Castle. "Lizzie, Jenn is waiting for you with the difficult dogs."

"The difficult dogs?" Matt raises an eyebrow at me.

I give him a grin. "I have a way with the troublemakers."

"Is that what I am? A troublemaker?"

"Well, you are a cat person." I give him a quick nudge with my elbow and head for the side of the building that's dedicated to dogs.

"You're a cat person?" my dad asks, and I nearly burst out laughing again. I can't remember the last time I felt this happy, and I pause to look behind me before I enter the canine division.

Matt has crouched down to eye level with a gray tabby, his hand outstretched as he waits for the feline to accept him. He really is amazing, and I duck through the door with every cell in my body buzzing.

"Hey, Jenn."

The brunette standing there with a man and a clipboard looks up. "Praise the stars," she says. "You're here."

"I'm here." I look around, and I don't see anyone else. "Is this it?"

"This is it." Jenn hands me a clipboard. "We have

seven dogs between us, and I want you to be with Lennin and Marcy."

I glance at the clipboard and find that Lennin is a handsome black and brown boxer, and Marcy is a pudgy pit bull mix who has a lot of bulldog in her.

I let Jenn tell me what to do, and together, the three of us get the seven big dogs outside to their special pen. A couple of them have a little bit too much energy, a couple are really shy and would rather not be adopted than have to meet people, and they're all really big animals. A lot of people would rather have a small dog for various reasons, but I kind of like the big boys.

"All right, everyone!" someone says into a microphone, and the noise level goes down as people stop talking. But the vibrancy in the air stays. "We're going to let people back now. Let's have a good event!"

I join my applause with everyone else, smiling as I look for Matt. He's sitting cross-legged on the ground just outside the cat area, surrounded by three kittens who climb over his lap while he grins and grins at them.

He is so a golden retriever, and whoever is in charge of the cats saw it immediately. He's practically a piece of man-candy sitting there, and it's not surprising at all that the first six patrons who come down the path veer toward him and the cats.

"So not fair," I whisper to myself. Anyone would gravitate toward the drop-dead gorgeous man with kittens on his lap.

As I watch, he gently lifts a tiny black kitten and places it in the hands of a wide-eyed little girl whose face lights up with pure joy. Something warm and tender unfurls in my chest at the sight.

"He's a natural," my father says, somehow appearing beside me without me seeing him.

I jump slightly, as if I've been caught watching something I shouldn't be. "Oh! Uh, yeah, he really is a cat person."

"Yeah, I think he's a Lizzie person." Daddy's eyes twinkle with amusement, and I don't contradict him. "He's good with animals, I'll give him that."

"Yeah," I say. "He is."

"How new is new?"

"Today's our first date." I glance over to my dad as the first couple approaches the big dog paddock. "So it would be great if you just took the dadding down a notch when we come for lunch."

Daddy chuckles, and I know I'll get no such favor. "I don't know how to turn down the dadding," he says. "I'll talk to these two. Paddy sent me to get someone to come help with Gizmo. I guess he decided to bring him out just to see if someone will take him."

Gizmo is a hundred-pound mastiff mix with a heart of gold but anxiety issues that make him a handful. He's been at the shelter for months, and they kept him inside during the last open adoption event.

"Sure," I say. "I'll go get him."

Gizmo's whole body wags when he sees me, and I kneel down in front of him and let him sniff me and say hi. "You've got to be a little calmer, bud," I tell him. I get him to sit patiently for a moment, then feed him a bit of dried beef liver.

"Lay down."

Gizmo does, and he gets another tasty treat. I hook his leash to his collar and get to my feet. He stays right at my side as we go down the hall, but he comes to a hundred-pound stop once we step outside.

There is a lot going on, and I stand in front of him and shield him from it. "Come on, buddy. You're with me, and it's fine." After two more bites of beef liver, he comes with me, and I take him toward the smaller dog pen but stay on the other side of the sidewalk.

I sit down in the grass and tell Gizmo, "Sit." He does, which makes a twinge of pride move through me.

A few people say hello to me and Gizmo, but no one really stops to learn more about him.

"Come on, baby-sweets," Daddy says. "It's time for lunch."

The crowd has definitely dwindled, both in terms of people coming to adopt animals and the number of pets in pens and carriers.

I hand him Gizmo's leash and take his hand to get to my feet. I brush off my backside and re-take the leash. "Can we take him home to run on the farm for the afternoon?"

Daddy looks at Gizmo, who sits and looks up at my father with a very doggy smile on his face. "Oh, all right, but I can't keep you forever, Giz."

"Yay, Gizmo!" I crouch down and scrub his yowls. "The goats will love to see you again."

"Goats?" Matt asks as he joins us.

"We're going to the farm." I link my arm through Matt's and bounce on my toes—just once. "Are you excited?"

He grins at me. "Sure, I love farms."

"Have you ever been to a farm?" Daddy asks.

Matt throws me a panicked look that he smooths over when he looks back at my father. "I mean, on a field trip in fifth grade, I think."

To my surprise, Daddy throws his head back and laughs. "Seems like you're qualified then."

My father's hobby farm sits on five acres just outside of town—a modest farmhouse surrounded by a few animal enclosures. Chickens scatter as we pull up the driveway, and two border collies race to greet us, barking excitedly.

"This place is incredible," Matt says, taking in the sprawling yard, the barn in the distance, and the small vegetable garden to the side of the house.

"It's home," Daddy says simply as his dogs fall in beside him. "Come on in. Food's waiting."

The kitchen smells of slow-cooked meat and tangy sauce—my father's famous barbecue recipe that he refuses to share with anyone, even me. We settle around the worn wooden table, and Matt makes appreciative noises at his first bite.

"This might be the best barbecue I've ever had," he says sincerely.

My father beams. "Thank you. It's a family recipe."

"That he won't share," I say as I fork up another bite of macaroni salad.

"It's in my will," he says without any emotion at all. "So you two work together?" He takes a bite of his sandwich.

"Yes, sir," Matt says, his head bobbing. "We're right next door to each other."

"Hmm." Daddy takes a long sip of his iced tea. "And you've got cats, I hear?"

"Two Maine Coons," Matt confirms. "Purricell and Purroxide."

Daddy chuckles. "Chemistry cats. I like that."

The conversation flows easily as we eat, my father asking questions about Matt's background, his family, his interests outside of work. I watch as Matt handles each question thoughtfully, revealing pieces of himself that make me like him even more.

"Lizzie used to be obsessed with animals as a kid," Daddy says, launching into story mode. "When she was seven, she tried to start her own animal rescue in our backyard. Brought home three stray cats, a turtle with a cracked shell, and a baby bird that fell from its nest."

"Guess who I learned it from?" I cock my eyebrow at him, but Daddy only smiles.

"Her mother was allergic to cats," he says. "But Lizzie had already named them and made little collars out of yarn. She cried for days when we had to find them other homes."

The mention of my mother brings a familiar pang, but it's softened by the warm memories and the way Matt listens so intently, like he's collecting every detail about my life.

In fact, his eyes soften as he looks at me. "That sounds exactly like something you'd do."

I nudge him with my shoulder. "See? I have a heart."

"I never said you didn't," he says.

"I'm very regulated," I say with a sigh. "I sometimes feel like a robot."

"How's the job hunt coming?" Daddy asks, and I freeze.

Beside me, Matt does too. And of course, the man can't just let a moment go by where he doesn't say something. It's a tactic I've used on him plenty of times—silence. The man can't stand silence, and if I give him enough of it, he'll fill it with his true thoughts.

"You're looking for another job?" he asks.

"I mean, a little," I say, shooting my daddy a look.

"I didn't know it wasn't common knowledge," he says.

"It's our first date," I reiterate, then I wave him away.

"It's fine." Because it is. I technically told Matt I was *thinking* about getting another job when we went shopping for his sister. I have been thinking about it—a lot.

"The job thing is going okay. There's a cosmetics company looking for someone, and I'm working on my application. I have some modeling gigs lined up too— one's a full week of shooting."

I smile over to him and then Matt. "And they requested me."

"That's amazing," Matt says, and he recovers so well from surprising things.

"That's great, Elizabeth." Daddy finishes eating and starts to clean up. Things between me and Matt still feel a bit tense, but we finish up and take our dishes back into the house.

"You want to see who's new?" Daddy asks.

"That's why we came." I lean in and hug him. "Thank you for lunch, Daddy."

He hugs me back, and I take a moment to just be held by him. Then I step back and smile at him, noticing how much more gray he has in his hair and beard. He still has the lightning in his eyes that he's always had, and he gazes at me with the pure love of a parent.

"Come on," I say, and I lead everyone outside. We walk through the yard, past the chicken coop where hens peck contentedly, and toward a fenced area where several goats bleat in greeting.

"These are the troublemakers," Daddy says fondly.

"That one there is Trouble." He points to a small black goat with a white spot on its forehead. "Lives up to his name."

Matt leans against the fence, watching the goats as one jumps up with his front hooves on the top rung of the fence. "I've never been this close to goats before. They're smaller than I expected."

"These are Nigerian Dwarfs," I say. "Daddy likes the little guys."

Daddy's phone rings, and he says, "I've got to take this," and heads back to the house.

"Never been this close to goats, huh?" I lean into Matt, enjoying that I can press into him without fear or worry about who'll see us.

"They have funny eyes." He straightens, and we move away from the goat pen. Trouble bleats behind us, and then a terrible crash sounds.

I gasp and spin back, only to find dwarf goats spilling out of the broken fence rungs that Trouble has just head-butted.

"Trouble, you menace." The goat doesn't care at all, and just trots past me.

Matt yelps as the goats swarm him, and he backs up with both hands up. "No, goats," he says. "Goats... everywhere."

Trouble bleats again, and apparently that's his goaty battle cry, because he rushes at Matt in the next moment. The other goats even clear the path for him.

Matt, ever the agile chemist I didn't know he was, jumps up onto the fence, avoiding Trouble.

But he's also subject to the laws of gravity, and he topples over the top to the other side. The distinct splat of a body in mud meets my ears, though I can't see Matt as he disappears behind the goat army now bleating at him from the wrong side of the fence.

"Matt," I call, and I opt to go through the broken fence to get to him.

He's sitting on the ground with his back resting against the fence post. "I got the wind knocked out of me," he says.

"And you have a goat eating your sleeve." I swat at the black and white goat nibbling on the fabric, but he comes right back.

The sight is so absurd that laughter bubbles up from my chest before I can stop it. Matt looks up at me, mud splattered across his cheek, and he starts laughing too.

He reaches for my hand and pulls me down beside him. It's my turn to yelp, but I manage to avoid the mud puddle he landed in.

"Sorry," he says, not looking sorry at all as he settles his arm around me. "Chemical reaction. Couldn't help it."

I should be annoyed—these are my cutest skinny jeans—but all I can focus on is the way his eyes crinkle at the corners when he smiles at me, the flecks of gold in his irises, the warmth of his breath against my face.

The goats bleating.

He brushes a strand of hair from my face, leaving a smudge of cold mud on my cheek. Time slows, the world narrowing to just us, mud, goats, and all. When he leans in, I meet him halfway.

His lips are soft against mine, the kiss gentle at first, then deepening as his hand slides to the back of my neck. I melt into him, forgetting about the mud, the goats desperate to get through the fence, and my father probably watching from a distance.

This kiss is different from our first, secret one in my office. That was a beginning, a promise. This is a confirmation, and it makes the earth tilt a little more than it should.

Kissing Matt is my new favorite thing to do, and I can't imagine ever feeling like this with someone else.

He breaks the kiss in the softest way possible, and I open my eyes to find him watching me with such tenderness that my heart stutters.

"Worth the paperwork?" he whispers.

"Worth every page."

The moment is perfect—until a strange expression crosses Matt's face, his eyes focusing on something over my shoulder.

"Um, Lizzie?" he says, voice suddenly tight. "Is that goat supposed to be eating your hair?"

CHAPTER TWELVE

MATT

"So," Chanel says, eyeing me as she passes me a can of my favorite sparkling water. "You've been suspiciously happy all week." She looks at me out of the corner of her eye, and leans down to kiss the top of her little girl's head.

I bounce Nora gently in my lap, buying myself a few more seconds to find my thoughts. "Can't a guy just be in a good mood?"

"A guy, sure. You?" She returns to the kitchen and starts plating up lunch. It's a simple pot of spaghetti and meatballs, but it's something I didn't have to make, so I'm thrilled. "You're always happy, but it's been over the top this week."

"I'm always happy?"

"This is about Lizzie." She doesn't even phrase it like a question as she puts the steaming plate of pasta in front of me. She sighs as she sits down. "I've only seen you like this with one other girl, and that was Katie." Chanel starts to twirl her noodles while I try to breathe.

"I was in love with Katie in high school," I say.

"Exactly."

"I'm not in love with Lizzie."

"It only *seems* like it." Chanel gives me a smile. "I get it. New relationships are super exciting and fun."

"Are they, though?" I tilt my head at her and pick up my fork. I'm not the best at eating with a baby on my lap, but I don't want to give up Nora.

"This one is," Chanel says. "Not everyone is like Rickola."

I groan and twirl up a bite. "Don't say her name."

"You haven't had a girlfriend you've been this happy about in a while," Chanel says. "That's all I'm saying."

I think of Lizzie, and I can't help the smile that spreads across my face. "Okay, I'll give you that."

Chanel leans over her plate to take another bite, looking up at me from beneath her lashes. "Did you fill out the paperwork?"

"Seventeen pages of it." I snap open my sparkling water. "But it was worth every excruciating detail."

"Seventeen pages of what?" Shad joins us from the garage, wiping his hands on a automotive towel.

"Details of his dates with his new girlfriend," Chanel says as I take another big bite of noodles and sauce.

"Oh, you got a girlfriend?" Shad grins, then turns

and steps over to the kitchen sink to wash his hands. "That's great, Matt."

Nora starts to fuss, and Chanel gets up and takes her from me. She puts the baby in her high chair and reaches for a toy in the middle of the table. After setting it on the tray in front of the baby who can't even sit up by herself, my sister sits back down.

Shad joins us with his own plate of spaghetti, and he brings a tray of garlic bread with him. "We're eating this too, right?"

Surprise crosses Chanel's face. "I forgot about that. Thanks, baby." She smiles up at him, and Shad sits down and passes me the bread. The domesticity of the scene makes something twist in my chest—a longing I haven't felt until recently.

"So, is this serious?" Chanel asks. "Or are you still in the 'let's see where this goes' phase?"

I pass her the tray of bread. "The paperwork took us out of 'let's see'," I say. "We're dating, but it's been a week—and we didn't even go out this week."

And let me tell you, I've been inventing my own city-swears about that. Instead, Lizzie and I each filled out a packet for HR, texting madly back and forth about certain answers.

And tonight, she's hanging out with her roommates as they plan their annual Halloween party. The holiday isn't for another six weeks, but apparently, it's a big deal.

"But we got the packet turned in today, and we're

going to brunch tomorrow." I take a crunchy bite of my bread while Chanel watches me.

She always seems to know when I need to say more, and a hint of irritation fires through me. If I wanted to say something, I would.

Unfortunately, Chanel and Shad don't start up a conversation, and it feels like a layer of air presses down on us.

I sigh and roll my neck to stretch the back of it. "You badger me to death."

"I haven't said a word."

"The *silence* is *awful*." I give her a glare, and then look over to Shad. "Does she do this to you too?"

He grins at me. "You're the one who can't handle the silence." He takes a bite of bread. "I'm fine in the quiet."

I sigh like they're both insufferable. "She's talking about leaving ChemTech."

Chanel's eyebrows shoot up. "Lizzie is? Really? Why?"

Three questions in a row. Hey, at least it gives me something to talk about. "She's been thinking about it for a while. She's got some modeling gigs lined up, and she applied for a position with a cosmetics company."

I leave out the part that the cosmetic job is in Columbia, and that it's still in compliance department. She wouldn't be in a leadership role, but with Lizzie, it's just a matter of time.

"She's an incredible model, Chanel. You should see her portfolio."

"I'd love to." Chanel stands and takes her empty plate into the kitchen. "So if she leaves ChemTech, what happens to all that paperwork you filled out?"

"It becomes irrelevant," I say. "No more documenting every elbow brush at the coffee maker in the lounge, or detailing what we talked about in my office when we ate lunch."

But really, for me, there will be no more worrying about who sees us together. I'll be able to parade around Cider Cove, Sugar Creek, and any other suburb of Charleston I want, with the gorgeous Lizzie Trenton.

Everyone will see us and know she's with me. That she *chose* me.

"Wow, she's willing to leave her job?" Shad asks.

My attention zooms to him. "That would be convenient," he says now, something false in his tone.

"What's that supposed to mean?" I ask.

He shrugs. "Nothing. Just...convenient timing. Didn't she just get a promotion?"

"Shad," Chanel warns.

"No, it's fine," I say, though irritation prickles under my skin. My good mood fizzles just as fast as this conversation changed. "She—" I don't have to tell them what Lizzie shared with me, at least not all of it. "This isn't about us."

"Of course not," Chanel says.

"I'm just saying, be careful," Shad says. "I've never seen you celebrate the way you did when you got your Department Head job."

He makes it seem like I'd be unhappy if I lost my job —and I can acknowledge that I would be. I do love my job. But the truth is, there's more than my own happiness at stake.

My sister's eyes flick nervously between us, and I force myself to relax. "That's why we filled out the paperwork," I say, ready to talk about something else. "Hey, how did your interview go today?"

Shad's expression brightens. "Really well, actually. They said they'd pass me to the VP, and to watch my email on Monday for a scheduling link for the final round."

A smile bursts onto my face, and I think of what Lizzie would say. *You're such a golden retriever.*

"That's great," I say, genuinely happy for him. "This is Prescott Electronics, right?"

Shad nods. "Yeah, and I really want it."

The fact that he can show this vulnerability to me makes me so glad that I can help them. Because both of my parents couldn't wait to get away from me and Chanel, I've always felt a bit like an island.

But me and Chanel, we're tight, and I love Shad like he's my own blood.

"I should get going," I say a while later, checking my phone for the first time all evening. No texts from Lizzie, which is unusual. We've been in constant communication since our farm date.

"I'll walk you out," Chanel says, and she passes a fussy Nora to Shad. The baby settles instantly against her daddy's chest, and for the first time in my life, I think I might want a child.

So many things are changing in my life right now, and I suddenly feel completely overwhelmed.

"Matty?"

"Yeah," I say, tearing my eyes from Shad and Nora. "I'm coming."

Chanel doesn't always walk me out—in fact, she hardly ever does—so I know something is up. "Just say it," I say as I join her on the front porch.

To her credit, she doesn't try to feign confusion. "I'm just hoping you're thinking things through with Lizzie." She holds up a hand as I open my mouth to argue. "I know you like her; I mean, you haven't stopped talking about her for months. I know that."

She comes to a stop where the sidewalk meets the driveway, sighs, and faces me. "I'm just worried about you, Matty."

"I am thinking through everything," I assure her. "I'm just also feeling. A lot." I meet her eye, hoping I won't have to say out loud that I spent a lot of years buried in university classes that couldn't lie to me, couldn't abandon me, wouldn't neglect me. I disappeared during all eight years I went to school, and I feel like I'm just barely coming back to life.

Yes, Lizzie is a big part of that, because yes, she makes me feel things I haven't felt in almost fifteen years.

Chanel grabs onto me and holds me tight. "I'm so happy for you."

I cling to her too. "It's like... I don't know, like all the elements were there before, but they never combined in the right way until now."

"Oh no, you're making chemistry metaphors." She groans and steps back, a sisterly smile on her face. "You are *so* far gone."

"Maybe I am." I grin at her. "Is that so bad?"

"No," she says softly. "It's actually kind of wonderful."

We share a smile, and for a moment, I see the same thing I'm feeling reflected in her eyes—hope, a little fear, but mostly joy.

"Just promise me one thing," she says.

"What's that?"

"When you know—really know—that she's the one, don't get in your head and start thinking about Mom and Dad."

I nod, throat suddenly tight. "Is that what you did with Shad?"

"I almost ended things with him." Chanel hugs herself, and I gather her back into my arms. "Because I was so far into my messed up childhood, and I think I've seen you do that, and I don't want you to be in that place."

I can't argue with her, because so much of my past has driven my present and formed my future. I don't know how it can't.

"I love you, sissy," I say.

"I love you too, Matty." She sniffles and steps back. "Go on. Get home before it starts raining again."

I pull my keys out of my pocket and nod at her. The rain has let up a little bit, but the roads are still slick with water. I drive carefully, my thoughts circling back to Lizzie. I should text her when I get home, see if she's decided between Atomic Eggs or Brunched for our date tomorrow morning.

The rain picks up again, hammering against the roof of my SUV, and I slow even further. When I finally turn onto my street and approach my townhouse, I notice a light on inside that I definitely didn't leave on.

My first thought is that I've been robbed, but my security system would have alerted me. My second thought is that one of the cats knocked over a lamp, though that seems unlikely given how lazy they both are.

But that light shining out the front window...I never leave lights on when I leave.

Nothing seems amiss at the house, though. No cars or bikes or anything out front. Not even anything taped to the door the way our HOA sometimes does about community barbecues and when they'll be redoing the asphalt.

I pull into the garage and close the door behind me, heart rate picking up. As I approach the door to the house, I absolutely hear noise inside...like someone talking.

Maybe Purroxide stepped on the remote and turned on the TV. He's done that before, so I carefully turn the knob and push it open with two fingers. I so should keep a baseball bat somewhere.

Sure enough, someone *is* talking in my house, and her voice is tattooed on my brain.

Lizzie.

I step inside and pause as the door swings back toward me. I catch it without making a sound, because Lizzie stands in my kitchen, her auburn hair darkened by rain and curling wildly around her face.

She's wearing an oversized T-shirt that—by the bonds of benzene, that's my tee.

Mine. She's wearing *my* clothes.

I'm suddenly so hot, I might self-combust.

She's holding a piece of cheese, and she picks off a piece of cheese and feeds it to Purricell, who is only one of her captive feline duo.

My cats, I *swear.*

They both sit politely on the counter, their heads cocked as they listen to her say, "We can't tell Matty about the cheese, okay? I know he's got a strict feeding schedule for you, and—"

Not true, but I hold my tongue. *I* don't dictate my cats' feeding schedule. *They* demand things of *me*.

My cats have also never sat so still and so kindly for me.

"—you boys are used to the fancy stuff," she's saying as she turns and reaches for something in a plastic bag. "But my daddy's cats eat this, and they're so happy, so I think you'll like it."

She gives them a brilliant smile, and Purricell meows in response—not a yowl. Not a *hurry-up!* mew. In fact, I've never heard him make such a polite sound.

Kitty Hawk, I think, going right for one of Lizzie's city-swears. I bet it's not very high up on her expletive list, but oh boy, it's at the top of mine.

"Okay," she says as she finishes scooping the wet cat food she brought into two bowls. "You have to eat on the floor. Come on. Jump down."

Purroxide watches her with complete adoration, his usually aloof demeanor nowhere to be seen. Not only that, but he immediately trots to the end of the counter and jumps right down as Lizzie bends over and places the pair of bowls on the floor.

I stand frozen in the doorway, unable to process the scene before me. Lizzie. In my house. Wearing that sexy tee. *Talking to my cats.*

She hasn't noticed me yet, giving me a moment to

absorb the situation. There's something so right about seeing her here, in my space, that it makes my chest ache. Like she belongs here. Like she's *always* belonged here.

"What are you feeding them?" I finally ask, my voice coming out rougher than intended as I step out of the doorway that leads into the garage.

Lizzie startles, spinning around with wide eyes. "Oh my, Tacoma! You scared me!"

"Yes, I can see how *you'd* be scared to find *me* in *my* house." I smile as I approach her. "You look like you got caught outside." I toss my keys onto the countertop and round it to take her—wet clothes and hair and all—into my arms.

She smiles at me, and I'm a little surprised to see and feel how easy she fits in my arms. "Hey," she says.

"What are you doing here? I didn't see your car out front." And I had no idea she knew where I live.

"So don't be mad." She bites her lip, looking suddenly uncertain.

"Oh, I love it when someone leads with that." I grin at her, so she'll know I'm not upset to see her. Quite the opposite, actually. I step back and glance over to where my cats are silently chowing down.

"And I need to know what kind of witchcraft you've worked on my cats. They never sit that nicely for me."

She glances at the cats, who are still watching her expectantly. "We came to an understanding."

"Clearly." I turn back to her, drawn like a magnet to everything about her. "You're soaking wet."

"It's raining," she says, as if that explains everything.

"And you're wearing my shirt."

A blush creeps into her face. "Mine was really wet. I hope that's okay." Her eyes go wide. "I didn't go in your bedroom. I found this in the laundry room, and you know what? I was thrilled to see you don't fold your clean clothes the moment they come out of the dryer."

"Do real people do that?"

She half sighs, half laughs, and that, combined with her wearing my clothes does something primal to my insides. "But you still haven't explained how you got in, or why you're here feeding the chemical cats...what did you bring them?"

"Fish with egg yolk and a little olive oil," she says. "My daddy went fishing today, and he always saves some for the cats." She draws a breath and adds quickly, "It's good for their coats."

"Yes, I'm very concerned about their fur."

Lizzie giggles, and I slide my hand along her waist just because I can. "How'd you get in?"

"You don't lock your front door."

I drop my head and touch my lips to her cheek. "How did you know where I live?"

"Ah, well, I knew it was in this townhome community, and..."

I look up. "And?"

"I called Aaron Stansfield, okay? He looked up your address from an order at the hardware store."

"So your phone works," I say.

A frown of confusion appears between her eyes. "Of course."

"So you could've called for a ride home." I raise my eyebrows. "Instead of for an address of a residence you then broke into."

She says nothing, and I curse the gene inside me that can't stand the silence and is desperate to fill it.

"Where's your car?"

"It just quit on me," she says. "Only a couple of blocks from here, so that's why I called Aaron for the address. You weren't answering."

It's my turn to frown. "I didn't get any calls."

"Maybe the storm affected service."

I take in her appearance again—the damp hair, my oversized shirt, the way she looks simultaneously out of place and perfectly at home in my kitchen. Something shifts inside me, a chemical reaction reaching its critical point.

"Lizzie," I say, my voice barely above a whisper.

Those gorgeous blue-green eyes meet mine. "Yes?"

"Why are you really here?"

Her expression changes, vulnerability replacing her earlier confidence. "I needed to see you," she says simply. "I got some news today, and I—I just needed to see you."

CHAPTER THIRTEEN

LIZZIE

"The cosmetics company in Columbia called," I say, watching Matt's face for a reaction. "They want me to come in for an interview next week."

"That's great," Matt says, but his quick smile doesn't appear. He watches me like he knows I've been stewing about this for hours. "Isn't it?"

I lean against the counter, suddenly overwhelmed. "It should be. It's a good opportunity. Similar to what I do now, just in a different industry."

"But?" Matt turns and opens the fridge. He pulls out a bottle of water and offers it to me.

"It's not sparkling." I stare at it like it might grow fangs and bite me.

"You don't like sparkling."

I take the bottle of water and twist the cap. I take a

quick drink and then run my hand through my still-damp hair as I turn away from him.

It's hard to have real-life conversations when I'm face-to-face with him. I can't believe I'm here, but I found the walls of the Big House suffocating me.

"I've been thinking a lot about what I want, and I'm not sure another regulatory compliance job is it, even if it's with a company that makes products I actually care about."

Matt's eyes feel heavy on the back of my head, but I don't turn toward him. The rain lashes against the back sliding door, and honestly, I feel the storm blowing through me too.

"This feels like a hot chocolate moment," Matt says.

"Hot chocolate?" I can't help but smile, and I turn to look at him over my shoulder.

"Or tea. Or more cheese for the cats, apparently." He nods toward Purricell and Purroxide, who have finished their fish and are now sitting at my feet, looking up expectantly.

"Oh, no, I've corrupted them," I say, grateful for the momentary lightness.

"They were already corrupted. You've just revealed their true nature." Matt moves around the kitchen, pulling out mugs. "So, if not compliance, then what?"

I watch him move with easy confidence through his space. "That's the million-dollar question."

Thunder crashes outside, making me jump. The

lights flicker once, twice, then stabilize. Matt froze when the electricity flickered, but he flies back into motion by putting a kettle over the front burner and lighting the flame.

"Coffee?"

I shake my head. "Hot chocolate is actually perfect."

He gets everything set up, and then reaches for my hand. "Come sit, Lizzie." He leads me into his living room, which is surprisingly cozy for a bachelor pad. A comfortable-looking sectional faces a huge flatscreen TV, and bookshelves line one wall—filled with an eclectic mix of chemistry textbooks, sci-fi novels, and what appears to be a collection of vintage comic books.

"Nice place," I say, taking it all in. "Very you."

"Don't be impressed. I have a cleaning service." He hands me a blanket, and I didn't even know men owned such things. "Do you want marshmallows in your hot chocolate?"

"Is that a real question?"

He smiles at me and goes back into the kitchen. I tuck my feet beneath me and spread the blanket over my lap. I've barely done that when both his cats leap lightly up to the couch and curl into my side.

"Which one is Purricell?" I ask.

Matt looks over from where he's pouring water into mugs. "He's the one with more gray on his face. He's climbing into your lap."

Sure enough, one of the Maine Coons makes himself

nice and comfy right in my lap, and I stroke my hand down Purricell's back. There's something soothing about having another living thing snuggled into me, and my next exhale takes some of my tension with it.

Matt returns to the living room and hands me a mug of hot chocolate, complete with mini marshmallows floating on top. He sits beside me, close enough that I can feel his warmth but not so close that we're touching. "So, tell me about this news that had you breaking and entering."

"Technically, there was no breaking," I say. "Your front door wasn't even locked." I pierce him with a glare and then focus on my mug. It's warm, and that heat sinks into my skin.

I take a deep breath, because I can't stall for much longer, and my hot chocolate will scald my throat if I try to drink it now. "I don't want the job at Marie Bright."

There. I've said it out loud.

I look up and over to Matt, something very raw streaming through me. "I'm sorry. It means I have to fill out paperwork for dropping by tonight."

Matt shakes his head. "I don't care."

"I put in my interest for a couple more modeling jobs," I say. "Fall is fairly busy, as companies are getting their spring lines shot."

"That's amazing, Lizzie." His eyes light up with genuine excitement for me.

"I mean, I don't have more shoots than the two I

booked, but maybe." The real problem, which I don't say out loud, is that I'm not sure I want modeling to be my full-time job. I'm not sure it'll be enough to pay the bills, but as my daddy told me a couple of days ago, I won't know unless I try.

And modeling has always been something on the side of my Very Important Job at ChemTech.

"You don't have to look for something else at all, Lizzie," Matt says.

I look over to him and find him taking a tiny sip of his steaming hot chocolate. "I'm not doing it for us."

Matt's eyebrows shoot up. "No?"

I shake my head. "I just—I haven't been happy at ChemTech in a while. Getting the promotion helped, but really, I think it just delayed me a few months."

"Delayed you from what?"

"From realizing I don't want to stay there for much longer."

I stare down into the creamy depths of my hot chocolate. "I know that sounds stupid—and crazy. I finally made it to Department Head Row, and the lounge is just as good as everyone says."

I sigh, wondering why I can't feel called to do something, the way other people are. "I have a stable job, a good salary, benefits. And I just got promoted. Leaving now would look...." I trail off, unable to find the right word.

"Who cares how it looks?"

I bring my head up at that question, because it's a good one.

Matt sets his mug down on the coffee table and shifts to face me fully. "You should do what makes you happy."

"I have bills to pay."

"Yeah, but you can still do that *and* actually do something that you want to do."

"What I want to do," I repeat softly. The phrase echoes between us, reminding me of our conversation in my office when Matt finally admitted he wanted me—not as a friend, but as everything.

"It's scary," I say. "Stepping away from the safety net."

Another crash of thunder rattles the windows, followed by a flash of lightning that momentarily illuminates the room. The rain sounds like it's coming down in sheets now, and I blink and the power blinks out.

I pull in a breath. "I should call a tow truck," I say, my heart beating as steadily as the rain against the window.

"I don't think anyone's towing anything in this weather," Matt says. He gets up and goes to the front window. "It's not safe out there; the wind is howling."

He turns back to me, and another bolt of lightning highlights his features. "I think you should stay here tonight."

"What?" squeaks out of my mouth. Thankfully, the

lights flicker, shake, and come back on for good. "I can't stay here."

"Sure you can," he says as easily as he does everything else. "I've got two guest bedrooms upstairs."

"Do you?" I ask. "Like...with beds? Do you ever have guests stay with you?"

"One is a library," he says.

"A library?" A smile forms on my face. "How very formal."

He grins too. "The other has a bed. I don't know who'd stay there...someone, maybe."

"Me, I guess." Even thinking about sleeping under the same roof as Matt has my stomach in a tizzy.

Matt sinks back into the couch and reaches for me. That dislodges the cats, and Purroxide gives a simple, "Yow," in protest, but moves.

I lift Purricell as I lay down in Matt's lap, and then settle the cat on my hip. He goes back to purring, and Matt strokes his fingers along my hairline, sending sparks through my ear and down my neck as he brushes his skin against mine.

A beautiful silence falls between us for a couple of minutes. "Are you hungry? Did you get dinner?"

"Yeah," I say. "Tahlia had a whole ton of stuff from school today."

"Yeah, how was the party planning meeting?"

I take a moment to think about it. "You know what?

It was awesome, but all it did was remind me of how much has changed at the Big House."

"Mm, yes, I bet."

"It's stupid, I know." I let my eyes drift closed, images of all of my best friends parading through my mind now. "I mean, did we really think we were all going to live in that house forever?"

"I don't know," Matt says.

I don't either, and I'm irritated at myself that I didn't plan better. Things have been so topsy-turvy for the past couple of years, and while Aaron and Emma aren't quite engaged yet, that'll happen sooner rather than later, and then…

My thoughts always derail here, because I don't know what comes after "and then." I've never been good at open-ended things like that. I want a plan. A schedule. A hypothesis I can test and retest.

"I miss them," I say, hearing the smallness in my own voice. "They come over all the time, and we still have our Big House group chat, but I miss them."

"It's not the same as living with someone," he says.

No, it's not. Hillary's right next door, but Claudia lives about a half-hour away now, as Beckett took a job in Beaufort. They both commute to work now, and they live about halfway between Charleston and Beaufort.

Ryanne and Elliott live in the cutest little house about ten minutes from the Big House, but she's always been the more aloof one—like a Maine Coon cat. I almost always have to reach out to her first, and then she'll get talking.

But yeah. I miss them, and there's no way around that. I just have to go through it.

"For what it's worth, I think you'd be amazing at whatever you choose to do." He traces circles on the back of my hand with his thumb sending a scattering of shivers up my arm.

"Even if it means leaving ChemTech? Leaving you?" The words hang in the air between us, heavier than I intended.

"You wouldn't be leaving me," he says. "Just the building we both happen to work in." He squeezes my hand. "Besides, there are perks to not working together."

"Like what?" I ask, my voice barely above a whisper.

"Like not having to document every moment we spend together for HR." He strokes my hair back. "Like this. I'm going to have to type out that you're lying in my lap and I'm stroking your hair. It's embarrassing."

I sit up, which once again dislodges Purricell. He's had enough, and he gives me a cat side-eye filled with attitude just before he stalks out of the living room. "Sorry," I call after him.

Matt chuckles, and I look at him. "We don't have to give the exact details," I say. "My report is going to say my car died in a rainstorm, and I knew you lived nearby.

So I came here, the storm raged, and I couldn't get home."

He blinks at me. "You're not going to detail every sentence?"

I shake my head, smiling. "I'm not."

"You're going non-compliant." He grins, and oh, there's that happy-go-lucky man who's always made my heart thump a little faster.

"I just think—what can they do? We submit similar enough reports, and that's that." I shrug. "She can call us in and ask questions, but I've been all over the Employee Handbook, and nowhere does it say I have to answer the questions. I have to file the report—and I will."

"I'm just excited to be able to introduce you as my girlfriend without worrying about who might overhear."

My pulse stutters at the word *girlfriend*. We haven't used labels yet, despite the paperwork.

"Is that what I am?" I ask. "Your girlfriend?"

"I filled out seventeen pages of paperwork," he says with a grin. "So yes. That makes it official."

I giggle, feeling lighter than I have all day. Seeing Matt look at me the way he does...he's not even trying to hide anything, and I'm not used to being adored. No one has ever looked at me the way he does, or acted like they couldn't wait to see me, or wanted to cuddle as close as possible on the couch.

It's nice. It makes me feel powerful and feminine.

"It's getting late," Matt says. "I should show you the

guest room." He turns away from me and sets his undrunk hot chocolate on the side table. "Come on, guys. Let's show our catalyst where she can sleep."

Catalyst. He hasn't called me that in a while, and the re-emergence of the nickname warms me from the inside out. I feel like a chemical experiment who's been sitting dormant—until that catalyst is introduced.

In my case, it's Matt, and he makes me foam and bubble and start to question everything in my life.

He takes me upstairs, both cats preceding us. "It's the last one on the right," he says. "The bathroom is right across the hall." He pauses outside the door and reaches into the room to flip on the light. "It's not much, but—"

"I'm sure it's perfect," I say. "Thank you for letting me stay."

I'm going to have to text Tahlia and Emma, at the very least. Who am I kidding? I'll put this on the whole house text, and I'll be lucky if the messages stop before midnight.

The guest room is simple but neat—a queen-sized bed with a crisp white comforter, a nightstand with a lamp, and a small dresser.

I turn in a full circle while he hovers in the doorway. "There are clean towels in the cabinet under the sink. And, um, I can lend you something to sleep in. Unless —" He gestures to the T-shirt I'm still wearing. "—That works for you."

"This is perfect," I say, suddenly feeling shy. "Thank you. For everything."

He nods, his eyes never leaving mine. "Of course. Anytime."

We stand there for a moment, neither of us moving. The air between us feels charged, electric with possibility. I should say goodnight, close the door, text my friends, and get some sleep.

Instead, I step forward, closing the distance between us. My hands find his chest, feeling his heartbeat quicken beneath my palm. "Matt," I whisper, not even sure what I'm asking for.

He understands anyway, leaning down to capture my lips with his. The kiss is gentle at first, then deepens as his arms wrap around me, pulling me closer. I melt into him, all the uncertainty and fear of the day dissolving in the warmth of his embrace.

He always pulls away first, while I'm still floating through the puffy clouds of bliss from kissing him. "Goodnight, Lizzie," he says, his voice rough.

"Goodnight," I whisper back, reluctantly stepping away.

He lingers for a moment longer, then turns and walks down the hall. When he disappears down the stairs, I close the door and lean against it, my heart racing.

Outside, the storm continues to rage, mirroring the tumult in my own heart. I've spent so long playing it safe, following the expected path. Now, with so many new things coming at me from all sides, I wonder if I'm brave enough to weather the storm of change that has arrived in my life.

And if I do choose a new path, will Matt still be there beside me when the skies clear?

CHAPTER FOURTEEN

MATT

I ARRIVE AT ATOMIC EGGS TWENTY MINUTES EARLY, sliding into a booth by the window where I can watch for Lizzie. The hostess gives me a knowing smile as I decline a menu, explaining I'm waiting for someone.

"First date?" she asks.

"No," I say, unable to contain my grin. "But kind of."

"Intriguing." She raises an eyebrow, smiles, and knocks on the table. "Let me know when she's here, and I'll bring menus. Coffee in the meantime?"

"Yes, please." I drum my fingers on the table as the waitress leaves, then check my phone for the time every thirty seconds like this is a blind date. Which is ridiculous, because I spent the entire night under the same roof as Lizzie. And let me tell you, sleep did not come easily knowing she was just down the hall, wearing my tee in bed.

After she called her dad and then a tow truck, I drove her back to the Big House so she could shower and change. She said she'd borrow a car to come to brunch, because she wanted to deal with her car afterward, so she has to stop by the automotive shop.

The memory of her in my T-shirt, chatting it up with my cats, sends a pleasant shiver down my spine. I've never seen Purricell take to anyone like that. Even my sister gets the cold shoulder when she visits.

My phone buzzes with a text from Lizzie: *On my way! Traffic on King Street.*

I send back a thumbs-up emoji, then immediately second-guess myself. Is that too casual? Should I have sent something more romantic? I'm overthinking every interaction, and it's exhausting and exhilarating all at once.

I've already finished my first cup of coffee when I look up and see her walking in. My heart does a double-somersault in my chest. She's wearing a flowing sundress in a floral bright blue that makes her eyes pop and her auburn hair shine. She scans the restaurant, and when her gaze lands on me, her entire face lights up.

I'm on my feet before I realize I've moved, meeting her halfway across the restaurant.

"Hi," she says, a little breathless.

"Hi yourself." I want to kiss her right here, right now, but settle for taking her hand instead. "You look incredible."

"It's just a sundress," she says, but the blush creeping up her neck tells me she appreciates the compliment.

The hostess appears beside us. "Menus?" She holds out a pair of them with a smile for a mile.

"Yeah, thanks." I take the menus and take Lizzie over to the table in the corner. She squeezes my hand as we go, and I can't stop grinning like an idiot.

"What?" she asks as we settle into our booth.

"Nothing," I say, trying to straighten out my golden retriever smile. I totally can't. I open my menu in an attempt to hide behind it, though I already know what I want. "So, did you get any sleep last night?"

"Yeah," she says. "Your guest bed is very comfortable."

"I'm glad to hear it." I pause, deciding to be honest. The menu comes down, as do the corners of my mouth. See? I can stop smiling around Lizzie. "I barely slept at all."

Her eyebrows shoot up. "No? Was it the storm?"

"No," I say, meeting her eyes. "It was knowing you were just down the hall."

The blush deepens, spreading across her cheeks now. "Matty."

"Too much?"

"No," she says quickly. She reaches up and tucks her hair behind her ear. "It's...you know what? I've had this mega-office-crush on you for a while, and I guess it just feels kind of surreal that you...like me."

She holds my gaze for a moment, something blazing in her eyes. Something that tells me that Lizzie doesn't *feel* very likable.

I abandon the menu completely and reach for her hand. "I'm crazy about you," I say honestly. "Tell me why it's hard to believe."

She shrugs one shoulder, her gaze dropping to our entwined fingers. "I just...I've never really had a serious boyfriend." She clears her throat, swallowing immediately after. "I've dated here and there, but..."

"But what?"

"Everyone has been a jerk." She raises her eyes to mine, that blue-green fire shooting at me. "And the last two were chemists. So. Not a great track record."

Before I can answer—or defend male chemists—the waitress comes to take our orders—avocado Benedict with a side of spicy candied bacon for Lizzie, chicken and waffles for me, and more coffee.

"Define what makes a chemist a jerk for me," I say, reaching for my water glass.

Lizzie settles back into the booth. "Well, there was this guy who took me to a fancy restaurant and then forgot his wallet. And his phone. And ran to the restroom while the check came—and then never came back to the table."

My mouth drops open. "How did you get home?"

"I called Claudia," she says. "I texted him a few

times before he said an emergency came up, and he had to run out."

"That can't be true."

"Of course it's not true," Lizzie says with plenty of disdain. "The guy was a jerk."

I slide to the end of the bench and take the two steps to her side. "I'm sitting down," I tell her, because she's just staring at me.

She hurries to slide over, and I crowd onto her side of the booth. I lift my arm around her and pull her closer, and then try to get her closer still. "I can't seem to get close enough to you," I murmur, my lips right against her earlobe. "And I didn't get to kiss you hello."

Lizzie turns toward me, and it doesn't take much movement to match my mouth to hers. "Mm." I don't mean to moan. It just happens, and I take the most amazing kiss for myself and pull back.

She keeps her eyes closed and rests her forehead against mine. "You're not a jerk."

"Thank you, my catalyst."

She lifts her head and looks at me, and she seems like she wants to say something, but she remains silent.

"You're my catalyst, Lizzie. You started all of this. You made me want...more, because of who you are."

Her expression morphs into amusement. "Catalyst is just sort of a long nickname."

"It's not a nickname at all," I say.

"What is it then?"

"It's..." I search for the words. "It's a term of endearment."

"Maybe something like cat then."

"Like a kitty cat?" I run the tip of my nose down the side of her face. "Like, maybe kitten?"

She giggles quietly and pushes one palm against my chest. "Your cats did like me," she says.

"*I* like you...kitten." Yeah, I like the sound of that. A lot. And a lot more than catalyst. It means the same to me, but sounds way more romantic.

"So we've got the avocado Benedict?"

I turn toward the waiter with plates of food in his hands, and quickly slip out of Lizzie's side of the booth. "That's hers."

"And the chicken and waffles must be yours." He sets the plate in front of me as I sit back down in my usual spot.

"Yes, thank you." I beam up at him, and he glances over to Lizzie and back to me before he nods, his smile enormous as he walks away.

Lizzie picks up her fork and spears me with a look as sharp as the tines. "What about you? Any dating disasters?" She cuts into her poached egg while I consider where to start.

"You'll like this. My last girlfriend wanted to do a stay-in cooking date. I was like, okay." I cut off a piece of waffle and start in on the chicken. "I'm not a bad cook or anything, but my idea of dinner was wildly different than hers. She had me using things like tamarind paste and citric acid pearls, and you know what? I accidentally created a small—the *teeniest, tiniest*—chemical reaction."

I spear my chicken and waffle and swipe the whole bite through maple syrup while Lizzie laughs.

"I hope she's been able to get that, ahem, foam out of her carpet by now."

"Carpet?" Lizzie tips her head back and sends laughter toward the sky. "Where did this woman live?"

In her parents' basement, I think, but I simply shake my head at the memory. "She thought I was trying to poison her."

Lizzie glows as she cuts another bite of her brunch.

"It gets worse," I say. "I tried to explain the chemical reaction, thinking she'd find it interesting, but she just got more freaked out." I take a sip of my coffee. "No second date there."

"Her loss," Lizzie says, and warmth blooms in my chest. She looks over to me. "This place is amazing."

"I thought you'd like it." I cut into my waffle, savoring the perfect balance of sweet and savory. "So, I hope this question doesn't end us completely."

"If you think that, maybe you shouldn't ask it." She gives me her Workplace Lizzie look and glances down at her food.

"Oh, it's not that bad."

"Roll the dice then, carpet killer."

I burst out laughing, because I've been called a lot of things, but *carpet killer* has never been one of them.

I grin and grin as I ask, "What is your real hair color? I feel like I've seen you as a blonde, a dirty blonde, a brunette, and a redhead, and as I lay in bed last night." I pause and take a breath to calm my runaway tongue. "I realized I don't even know what color your hair is."

She's just taken a bite, so she doesn't answer right away. I spear another bite and let my mouth keep going. "For what it's worth, I think your hair is perfect exactly as it is. So I don't really care. I just thought it would be nice to know."

She tucks a strand of that fiery hair behind her ear, her head ducking down. "Thank you."

"And I don't just mean the color," I say. "Though the red is stunning. I mean all of it—the way it falls, the way it catches the light, the way it feels between my fingers." I manage to stop myself, and only one more word comes out of my mouth.

"Sorry."

"Don't apologize," she says. "It's nice to be appreciated for who I am, not who someone wants me to be." She nods a couple of times, and adds, "My hair is blonde, Matty. All the way blonde."

I tilt my head at her. "And you dye it because..."

"It actually helps me get more modeling jobs," she says. "But really, the reason I started dying it was to be taken more seriously in a male-dominated field."

I don't know how to respond to that, so I just nod and stuff my mouth with more fried chicken.

After we finish brunch, I suggest a walk along the waterfront. The day is perfect—sunny but not too hot, with a gentle breeze coming off the harbor. Lizzie slips her hand into mine as we stroll along the promenade, and I marvel at how right it feels, how natural.

"I've been thinking about the Halloween party at the Big House," she says. "I'm not sure I ever invited you."

"Am I invited?"

She bumps me with her hip. "Of course you are." She pauses right there on the boardwalk and faces me. "You're my boyfriend, right?

A wave of insanity washes over me, making my vision white for a moment. Then I steamroll into Lizzie, and we stumble back a couple of steps while I right us. "I've wanted to be your boyfriend for ages."

And right there in the middle of the sidewalk, I sober right on up and cradle her face in my hands. "I'm *so* happy to be your boyfriend."

"You better be," she whispers, her lips catching on mine I'm so close to her. I make it a real kiss, every cell in my body in a free-fall.

Wow, I hope I'm not moving too fast. At the same time, all I want to do is go faster.

She has the good sense to break the kiss before we embarrass ourselves in public, and she retakes my hand and continues down the walkway.

"Does your party have a theme?" I ask.

"Yeah." She sighs. "I swear, we make things more complicated than they need to be, but it's famous duos through history." She glances at me sidelong. "Any preferences? I was thinking maybe Marie and Pierre Curie, since we're both science nerds."

"The couple who discovered radium together?" I laugh. "That's perfect. Though I'm not sure how we'd make that into recognizable costumes."

"Lab coats, crazy hair, maybe some glow sticks to represent radiation?" She grins. "We'll figure it out."

"As long as I'm with you, I don't care what we dress as." I bring our joined hands to my lips, pressing a kiss to her knuckles.

Her smile softens. "You're being very sweet today."

"Just today?" I scoff. "I'm always sweet, kitten. Like a chemical sweetener, but without the potential carcinogenic properties."

She laughs and nudges me with her shoulder. "Such a romantic."

"Hey, I already said kitten." I lean over and purr in her ear, which only makes her giggle.

Today is the perfect day, and I have a million things boiling in the back of my throat. Thankfully, my phone rings, cutting off whatever I was about to say. I check the screen and see Chanel's name. "Sorry, it's my sister. Do you mind if I take this?"

"Of course not."

I answer the call. "Hey, Channy, what's up?"

The sound of muffled sobbing comes through the line. "Matty?" Her voice is thick with tears.

Alarm shoots through me. "What's wrong? Is it Nora?"

"Y-yes."

My heart drops to my feet. "Chanel, where are you? Where's Shad?"

"It's not that."

My heart is pounding like a freaking marching band drum line. "Say something," I say. "I'm freaking out."

Lizzie puts her hand on my arm, and I dang near jump out of my skin. She backs up, both hands raised as Chanel says, "She's so sick, Matty. Shad is at the pharmacy getting her meds, and I'm standing outside the ER with a huge bill." Her voice is barely as loud as a breeze by the time she finishes talking.

Chanel sniffles. "It's—I hate calling, but I—"

"It's fine," I say, feeling the life come back into my arms and legs. "It's just money, Chanel."

Only her quiet crying comes through the line.

"Text me the amount, and I'll move the money." I keep my voice as reserved as hers.

"I hate asking you for more," she says. "You already do so much for us."

"You're family," I tell her easily. "This is what family does, Channy. I don't care at all."

"What are you doing for dinner?"

"Well, I'm not coming to your house so I can have Nora get me sick." I manage to chuckle, and Chanel puffs out a half-sob, half-laugh.

"You were here last night," she says.

"Great, so I'm already infected." I smile into the Saturday sunshine, my own worries starting to snake through me. "Hey, I'm with Lizzie, so just text me, okay? I can transfer money in seconds."

"Thank you, Matty."

"Love you, Channy." I sigh as I hang up, and when I look up, Lizzie is watching me with concern.

"Is everything all right?" she asks.

I hesitate, unsure how much to share. This is still so new between us, and my family's financial situation is complicated. I don't want to compromise Chanel's personal problems either. But if we're going to build something real, Lizzie deserves to know the truth.

"Not really." I tuck my phone away. "There's something I need to tell you about my family."

Lizzie's expression grows serious, and she takes my hand again, squeezing it gently. "I'm listening."

I take a deep breath, the weight of my responsibilities suddenly heavy on my shoulders. "I want you to understand something about me and my sister..."

CHAPTER FIFTEEN

LIZZIE

THE BIG HOUSE KITCHEN BUZZES WITH SUNDAY morning energy as I flip another blueberry pancake onto the growing stack. Tahlia sits at the island, scrolling through her phone while Hillary leans against the counter, nursing a cup of coffee.

"I still can't believe you're actually dating Matt Giles," Hillary says, her eyes sparkling over the rim of her mug. "The way you used to talk about him—"

"Oh my *Harrisburg*, please stop." I groan, flipping another pancake with perhaps more force than necessary given the uncooked batter that goes splashing up against the side of the pan. "I was not that bad."

"You were worse," Ryanne says as she comes to a stop beside me. "I gave you so many bags of crispy M&Ms over that man."

I grin at her, noticing Elliott as he settles at the big

dining room table with his guide dog, Luna. "And you made it 'M-and-Matt'." Which is so Ryanne. She knows all my favorite flavors, and she isn't afraid to take a permanent marker and make the candy wrapper into something amazing.

Liam comes in the back door. "Lawn's done," he says.

"Thank you, Liam." Tahlia hops down and gets her not-so-secret stash of cash out of the pantry. She hands him a fifty-dollar bill with a smile, and he settles beside Hillary.

"What did I interrupt?"

"Her obsession with Matt before they started dating," Hillary says.

"Who she's now dating," Tahlia says.

"It wasn't an *obsession*," I say. "It was a...professional curiosity."

The kitchen erupts in laughter, and I can't help but join in. It feels good, all of us together like this. With three of my best friends married now, these moments with my roommates have become rarer and more precious.

Liam's phone rings, and he glances at the screen. "It's Aaron," he says, glancing around at everyone. "Are we ready?"

Hillary bounces on the balls of her feet, and I switch off the stove. "So ready," she says, and I turn and take the plate of pancakes over to the table.

"I'm answering." Liam swipes on the call and comes over to the table too. "Hey, brother. You're on with everyone in the Big House."

"I just saw Emma dash inside her shop," Aaron says. "I feel kind of bad, but I don't know how else to talk to everyone without her."

"She'll be fine," I say.

"Yeah," Ry says dryly. "So you staged a tiny emergency that will end in the perfect proposal. I think she'll be fine."

We all crowd around the phone as Aaron launches into his elaborate proposal plans for Emma. As he describes his vision for transforming the flower shop into a magical wonderland, a pang of something that isn't quite jealousy, but more like wistfulness, pulls through me.

Another friend moving on to the next chapter of her life.

"I think you should maybe consider the clean-up for this," Tahlia says. "Are you going to do it? Because it's Emma's shop..."

"I'll clean it all up," Aaron says. "She just loves that shop so much, and she lets me curate the arrangements for the Boyfriend Corner...I don't think it'll be that hard to get her out there, and she'll know as soon as I get her out of the cooler."

"How are you going to keep her *in* Sir Chills-A-Lot?" Hillary asks.

"A major order," he says. "For my brother's girl-friend's birthday."

Tahlia meets my eyes, and I see that same longing swimming in hers. There, but gone a moment later. I hope I hide my emotions as well, but I know I don't.

"It's not bad," she says, and I nod.

"It's pretty great," I say. "What if she comes out and catches you?"

"I only need a half-hour," Aaron says. "And I'm going to flip her sign to closed for those thirty minutes so the bell doesn't ring when someone comes in."

"Wow, bold," Liam says with a grin. "I think it's going to work great, brother."

"When is this happening?" Ry asks.

"Courtney's birthday is November eighth," Aaron says. "Emma's met Tommy, and she'll do anything to make his girlfriend's birthday awesome—and she'll know he's the type to wait until the last minute."

"Mm, it sounds like you have this planned well," Elliott says.

"I'm going to stage it so I call only a few minutes after Tommy leaves the shop, and I'll volunteer to watch the front of the shop while she disappears into Sir Chills."

"Sounds perfect," Tahlia says.

"Can you send Liam a picture of the ring?" Hillary asks, a bit of a clown smile on her face. She shakes her head as Aaron makes an angry bursting sound.

"No, Hill, I'm not showing you the ring. No one is seeing it before Emma."

"Hey, he knows Emma," I say with a grin. "I wouldn't want any y'all to see my ring before me either."

"I'll be sure to tell Matt," Ry says as she nudges me.

I grin at her and finish up my blueberry pancakes. Nothing will ever be as good as that avocado Benedict from last weekend, but I can't go out to brunch with Matt every day.

"I have to go finish getting ready," I say. "If Matt gets here before I come back down, do *not* sit him in an interrogation chair again." I raise my eyebrows at them and scan the crowd slowly.

"That was all Emma," Tahlia says. "Relax. We won't do that."

"Mm hm." I look at Ry, and something on my face must beg her to help me.

"I've got this," she says. "Nothing will happen to Matt. Go finish getting ready."

I dash upstairs, my excitement for today suddenly bubbling beneath my breastbone. I hear the doorbell ring just as I start brushing my teeth, and let me tell you, I have never brushed so fast.

I hurry down the steps and hear laughter. That can't be bad, right? There can't be an interrogation if there's laughter, but I don't relax until I reach the living room and find Matt standing with Liam, Elliott, and Tahlia.

The three safest people. Hillary and Ry sit on the

couch, seemingly disinterested in my boyfriend. My every cell gets pulled toward him, and I can't help the smile that forms on my face.

I hear clicking as I walk behind the couch, and then whispers. I ignore Hillary and Ryanne, because nothing good can be coming from there, and besides, Matt's here.

He looks unfairly handsome in jeans and a simple gray henley. His face lights up when he sees me, and I swear my heart does a little somersault.

I join the huddle in the doorway leading into the foyer, and Liam makes room for me across from Matt.

"Morning, kitten," he says—and oh, I let my eyes drift closed in a long blink. I employ my inner Purricell and believe that if I can't see them, they can't see me.

Or hear what Matt just called me, though I absolutely *adore* his pet name for me.

But the air inside the Big House has been sucked out. No one seems to be breathing. There's no noise, not even the hum of the furnace or air conditioner, as we're in this weird weather phase where we need both at various times during the day.

Someone moves closer to me, and Matt's familiar scent fills my nose. "I said something wrong," he murmurs. "I swear I'm going to learn how to control my mouth."

I open my eyes and look up to him. He's standing inches from me, and the others have dispersed. "It's fine," I say. "Let's go." I breathe him in, that now-familiar scent of clean laundry and something distinctly Matt.

He links his arm through mine and swings me away from the room, using his body as a buffer between me and everyone else. "See you guys," he says.

"Bye, kitten," Liam teases, and I tense up.

But Matt just says, "Me-Ow," and laughs as he guides me out of the living room. We clear the house, and as we walk toward his car—mine is still in the shop— he says, "It was the kitten. Why did I say that in front of them?" He shakes his head, but a blush seems to fill my whole body.

We reach the car, and he comes around to the passenger side with me. But he doesn't open the door. Instead, he cages me against his SUV and says, "I think we're out of range of your cameras," and kisses me, soft and sweet.

I melt into him, not even caring about the cameras or the kitten endearment. Let my roommates think whatever they want. When we break apart, he keeps one arm around my waist. "Ready for our day of thrilling adventures?"

"If by 'thrilling adventures' you mean going to the bookstore, grocery shopping, and dinner with my dad, then yes, absolutely."

"Hey, don't undersell it." He opens the passenger door for me. "There could be a sale on sparkling water. That's practically a roller coaster of excitement."

I laugh as I slide into the seat. "You have the strangest definition of excitement."

"Says the woman who color-codes her regulatory binders."

"That's different. That's organization."

"Whatever helps you sleep at night, kitten." He closes my door and waves to the front windows as he rounds the front of the car. Holy Helena. The curtains flutter, which means they all saw that kiss, the camera notwithstanding.

I don't care, and as we drive to the bookstore, Matt reaches over and takes my hand, his thumb tracing patterns on my skin. It's such a simple gesture, but it makes my heartbeat flutter.

"So," he says. "I've been thinking about starting a container garden on my patio. Nothing fancy, just some herbs, maybe a tomato plant. A green pepper or something."

"You garden?"

"I'm *going* to garden," he says. "Future tense. Hence the bookstore visit." He glances over to me. "I like to learn one new thing every year, and I've decided that this year, it's gardening."

"It's almost October."

"Which is why I need to get learning."

The local bookshop is quiet for a Sunday morning. We wander through the aisles, Matt's hand comfortably resting at the small of my back as he browses the gardening section.

"What about this one?" I hold up a book with a colorful cover showing various potted plants.

"Perfect." He takes it from me, flipping through the pages. "Look at these little strawberry plants. I could maybe grow those."

I watch him, fascinated by this new side of him. "You're really excited about this."

"I like the idea of growing something," he says, his expression thoughtful. "Creating something living instead of just analyzing things all day."

"Huh," I say, though Tahlia has a garden in the back corner of our yard. I've never spent much time out there, but she seems to love it too.

"I'm going to get this one," he says. "And then we need to pick a menu for tonight. Our next stop is the grocery store."

"I still think we should go with the sweet and sour meatballs," I call after him. He waves at me like I'm crazy. "Nothing to react with!" I sigh when he doesn't even come back at me with something.

Then I follow him up to the check stand. "I just think we need to go simple," I say. "My dad isn't going to care if you can cook or not. It's not like, a test you have to pass so we can keep dating."

"He said he's a meat-and-potatoes man," Matt says as he hands his book to the cashier.

"When did he say that?"

"I don't know. At the animal shelter thing." He smiles at the woman, tucks his card back into his wallet, and takes his now-bagged book.

I can't really argue with him, because he did spend time with my dad without me.

At the grocery store, Matt grabs a cart and immediately heads for the produce section. "Okay, so for dinner I'm thinking a roast chicken with rosemary and lemon, roasted potatoes, and maybe some green beans with almonds. What do you think?"

I blink at him. "Green beans with almonds? What? We just open the can and heat it up in the microwave."

"Sure," Matt says, pausing in front of the non-canned green beans. "But this isn't Tuesday-night dinner. We can take a little more care."

He bags the green beans, the menu apparently set. "Is your dad allergic to almonds? That should've been my question."

"No," I say.

He holds up two lemons, comparing them with intense concentration, though they look the same to me. He deems them good and puts them in the cart. We move through the store together, debating brands of olive oil and whether sweet potatoes are better than regular potatoes—they so are, but Matt disagrees. In the end, he tells me to get what I want, and I put a ten-pound bag of gold potatoes in the cart without a word.

Dad will like those better. It has nothing to do with Matt, I swear.

It feels so domestic, so comfortable, that I almost forget we've only been dating for a couple of weeks.

At the checkout, the cashier—an older woman like my father—smiles at us. "You two are cute together."

"Thanks," Matt says, beaming. "She's pretty great."

"He's okay too," I say, but I can't keep the smile off my face.

Back in the car, Matt loads the groceries while I text my dad to let him know we're on our way. When Matt slides into the driver's seat, he leans over and kisses me again, lingering a little longer this time.

"What was that for?" I ask when he pulls away.

"Just because I can," he says simply.

The drive to my dad's farm passes quickly, filled with easy conversation and comfortable silences. When we pull up to the familiar farmhouse, my dad sits out on the front porch, and he gets to his feet as Matt brings the car to a stop.

"There's my girl," he says as I step out of the car.

"Hey, Daddy." I hurry up the steps to him, where he wraps me in a bear hug before turning to Matt with an outstretched hand. "Good to see you again, son."

"You too, sir," Matt says, shaking his hand firmly.

"James," Dad says. "Sir makes me feel old."

"Yes, sir—I mean, James." Matt grins sheepishly, and my dad claps him on the shoulder.

"Come on in. I've got ice-cold sweet tea waiting."

"We need to get the groceries, Dad."

"I'll get them." Matt trots down the steps and to the car, looping bags over his forearms while I head inside with my father. Thankfully, Matt is fast at everything, and he returns before Dad can start asking questions.

There's nothing he doesn't know anyway.

Inside, Matt immediately heads for the kitchen, unpacking groceries and familiarizing himself with my dad's setup. I watch from the doorway as he rolls up his sleeves and washes his hands.

"Can I help?" I ask.

"Absolutely." He hands me a lemon. "You can zest these while I prep the chicken."

My dad joins us, leaning against the counter. "So, Matt, Lizzie tells me you're quite the chemist."

"I try to be," Matt says. "Though sometimes I think Lizzie knows more about chemical regulations than I do about actual chemistry."

"He's being modest," I say. "He's brilliant."

Matt's ears turn pink at the compliment, and he focuses intently on trussing the chicken. "Different kinds of smart, that's all."

We work together seamlessly—Matt prepping the chicken, me snipping the ends off the green beans, my dad setting the table and telling stories that have Matt laughing until he has to wipe his eyes.

When Matt excuses himself to wash up, my dad

sidles up to me at the kitchen sink. "He's a good one, Lizzie-girl."

"I think so too," I say quietly as I rinse the potato peeler and place it in the dish drainer.

"The way he looks at you..." He shakes his head and rinses out his coffee cup. "Like you hung the moon and stars."

Heat creeps into my cheeks. "Daddy, please."

"I'm just saying, it's nice to see you with someone who appreciates you." He harrumphs. "You haven't had anyone in your life as nice as him in ages."

"Thanks, Dad," I say dryly.

"You deserve the best." Dad nods like his word is law.

Before I can respond, Matt returns, and Dad hands him another glass of sweet tea and nods toward the back porch. After all, a roast chicken doesn't bake in a few minutes.

The sky holds gold in the air, the sunset brilliantly displaying all her glory across the farm. One of the border collies, Pepper, has taken a particular liking to Matt and lies at his feet, nudging his hand for pets.

"Let's go see the goats," Matt says, getting back to his feet and taking Pepper with him.

"I'll be right there," I say as he starts down the steps to the lawn. The thing is, I just want to watch him go visit the goats. I want to see him from afar, and zoom out on my own life with him, and see if I look as happy as I feel.

"You're really falling in love with him, Lizzie-girl."

My heart stutters in my chest at the way my father didn't even try to phrase it as a question. "Daddy, it's way too soon for that."

"Is it?" His eyes search mine, and I don't like what they might find. "I've seen the way you look at him, Elizabeth."

"Don't jinx it," I say, watching Matt lean over the fence to pat one of the goats who's put their front hooves up on the top rung of the fence. "I just...I really like him, okay? Let's leave it at that."

My dad raises his hands in surrender, but his smile irritates me to the point that I just look away.

Matt starts to come back, and he keeps his gaze down on Pepper, clearly talking to him. He is so—perfect. He's perfect, and I find myself wearing a goofy smile that I don't hide before Matt has climbed the steps and is standing in front of me.

"What?" he asks.

Am I falling in love with Matt Giles?

A timer goes off, and Matt lasers in on it. "Chicken is done," he says, and he hurries into the house.

I exhale and lean back in the patio chair.

Wichita—a high-level city-swear.

I am in so much trouble.

CHAPTER SIXTEEN

TAHLIA

I slide my fingertip through a patch of stray glued-down-glitter on my desk, creating a shimmering path across the laminate surface. The classroom is finally quiet after the chaos of twenty-eight seventh graders attempting papier-mâché pumpkins—an ambitious project for the third week of school that I'm already regretting.

"Never again," I vow, surveying the disaster zone. Newspaper strips litter the floor like confetti after a parade, and there's a suspicious glob of paste hardening on the ceiling. How it got there is a middle school mystery I'm too tired to solve.

And when's the last time you tried to find a newspaper? In our digital world, I should've known this project would be my undoing before it even began.

I grab my industrial-sized spray bottle of cleaner and

a rag, attacking the tables with the determination of someone who knows the janitor will give her That Look if she leaves this for him.

"Ms. Tomlinson?"

I turn to find Kiera, my favorite overachiever, hovering in the doorway. She's clutching her perfectly formed pumpkin, which somehow has no newspaper tears or glitter explosions. If I weren't so fond of her, I'd find it annoying.

"Yes, Kiera?"

"I was wondering if I could add more details tomorrow? I want to make the stem look more realistic."

I smile despite my exhaustion. "Absolutely. Just come in during lunch."

Her face lights up like I've offered her a scholarship rather than permission to skip her BFF hangout time for art. "Great, thanks."

As she bounces away, a familiar warmth spreads through me that makes all the budget cuts, supply shortages, and glitter disasters worthwhile. These kids and their unbridled creativity remind me why I became an art teacher in the first place.

I work through the room, this place that is my home-away-from-home, and when I can't stand being in the Big House, I always have a place to come.

I love making my classroom a safe haven, and I love turning off the lights, retreating to my office, locking that door, keeping those lights off, and just being.

At the same time, I love going home to the vibrancy of all my girlfriends, our dinners and parties. But with half of them gone now, going home isn't the same as it once was.

With the room clean, I make it look like I'm no longer in the classroom, and go into my office. My whole body aches, and I sigh as I wake my computer. Emails are constant as a teacher, and I normally hate going through them.

But a necessary evil is still necessary.

I find one from Marianne, the financial secretary here at the middle school. I roll my neck, expecting her to tell me more bad news about the funding for the arts. I've experienced plenty of that, but I'm still here.

"I'm still here," I say to the glowing office and click to open the email.

We got the approval from the Parent-Teacher Organization to repair the kiln! They said we'd have the funds by the end of next month. Can you fill out the attached form and get it back to me by the end of the week?

"Finally." I throw my hands up, because once the kiln is repaired, I won't have to drive my student projects across town to the high school anymore.

Plus, dealing with their Art Department head to get into the kiln is a nightmare. Like, I'm talking *creatures-with-eight-legs* type of nightmare.

I lower my hands and sink into my chair, suddenly aware of the quiet. The school day is over, most teachers already gone. I should be heading home too, but I find myself lingering, answering a few emails and then defaulting to scrolling through photos on my phone instead of heading home to my lonely master suite on the first floor.

There's one from last weekend—Lizzie and Matt making pancakes in the Big House kitchen, looking disgustingly adorable. Another of Emma and Aaron at the hardware store, her helping a customer while he gazes at her like she's the most amazing woman on the planet. A group shot from Claudia and Beckett's house-warming party last month.

My thumb hovers over a picture from two years ago —all six of us squeezed onto the back porch swing, laughing so hard the chains threatened to break. Hillary with her pre-marriage hair, Ryanne grinning at the bag of M&Ms in her lap, Claudia rolling her eyes at something Lizzie said.

The Big House used to burst with energy: midnight ice cream raids, impromptu dance parties, heated debates over which rom-com to watch next. Now the rooms are emptying one by one, leaving echoes where laughter used to be.

Don't get me wrong—I'm thrilled for my friends. They've found their people, their futures taking shape like well-thrown pottery. But where does that leave me? The owner of a beautiful, historic, money-pit of a house with three full floors, six bedrooms and only one occupant in the near future.

I open my Notes app and type: *Roommate search?*

The cursor blinks at me accusingly. I've been avoiding this moment, pretending the Big House won't feel like a mausoleum once everyone moves out. But reality keeps knocking—and my bank account is limping along now that three girls have already moved out.

This must be done—something I tell my students on occasion. How lame would I be if I ignore my own advice?

In the words of my younger brother, "Really lame, Tahlia."

So I leave my email and open a new browser, ready to bring all the strangers right through my front door. That happens with a simple search: *how to find roommates.*

Yes, I have to do this, because I've never had to search for roommates. All of us at the Big House once lived together in college, and finding a complete stranger and inviting them into my house?

Wait, so *this* is actually my worst nightmare.

The results are overwhelming: Craigslist (serial killer central), Facebook (do I really want my third-grade teacher knowing I need roommates?), specialized apps with names like RoomEZ and BunkrBuddy.

Bunker Buddy? What madness have I fallen into? This can't be real.

One click later, and oh-ho-ho, it's real. And not what I want at all in my aunt's house.

I sit back, one question on my mind. *What would Aunt Fern do?*

She left me the house, because I lived with her every summer after the age of twelve. I've loved it since the day my dad dropped me off without even walking me up to the front door.

She was my safe person as a teenager, and her house wraps its arms around me and comforts me every time I walk through the door.

She gave it to me, so it wouldn't go to my dad or his ex-wife. She gave it to me, so someone would keep loving it, caring for it, and experiencing their best life.

At least that's what she said in the letter to me.

A few things she never said? How expensive it is to maintain five acres of landscaped lawn, trees, shrubs, gardens, and more.

How fast the electric bill can add up in the brutal South Carolina summers.

How the timeless beauty and historical significance of the house makes repairs lengthy and costly.

She also never told me that hey, you probably can't do this on an art teacher's salary.

And I haven't had to—until now.

I click on one of the roommate sites and start to create a profile. Name, age, occupation—easy enough. Then I get to the preferences section:

Smoking: No

Pets: Negotiable

Gender preference for roommates: Female

I pause at the last one. I've never lived with a man who wasn't related to me. The thought makes me nervous, though I'm not sure why. It's not like I parade around in my underwear very often. Fine, not at all.

I leave it marked as "female" for now, because this is already a hard first step, and opening the door all the way feels ridiculous.

Then, the big blank description box stares at me, the cursor blinking like a disapproving parent.

Blink, blink, blink.

Say—something—good.

Explain yourself—and the significance—of your house.

Don't—disappoint—us.

I don't really know what to say—again, I've never put up a listing like this, and the horrors of shows like *Worst Roommate Ever* play through my mind as I begin to type.

Historic house in Cider Cove (Charleston suburb). Three floors. Five bedrooms available starting next summer—three on the second floor that share a bathroom and two on the third floor that do too.

Two more full baths on the first level (where I live in the master suite).

Fully stocked popcorn and soda bar most nights.

Dedicated garden space, if interested.

Plenty of parking.

Must love garden gnomes and tolerate early morning baking and lawn-mowing. Owner is 35F art teacher who comes with glitter embedded in her fingerprints. Looking for 30+, responsible, friendly housemates to share this beautiful space.

I add details about rent, utilities, and Wi-Fi. I mention the orchard, the wraparound porch, the new roof, and the history. I don't mention how scared I am of living alone, or how much I miss the sound of multiple coffee mugs clinking in the morning.

My finger hovers over the *POST NOW* button, but I can't quite press it. Instead, I save the draft and whisper to my dark office, save for the blue-white glow of my computer, "Please let the right people see this."

———

THREE DAYS LATER, I'm elbow-deep in yeasty bread dough. The kitchen is quiet except for the hum of the refrigerator and the occasional creak of the old house settling. No Hillary music thumping through the ceiling. No Ryanne binging M&Ms as she tries to placate her mother. No Lizzie muttering chemical formulas while she makes tea in her fabulous clothes.

No Emma crying over a huge order at the flower shop she needs help with, and no Claudia saying we really should repaint the kitchen in Butter Yellow now that we've reached a new decade.

I smile, because I love them all dearly, and I can't imagine better friends and roommates.

Just me, flour up to my wrists, wondering when the Big House started feeling so *big*.

I finish up with the dough and pat olive oil on top of it, then drape a tea towel over the bowl. I leave it on top of the stove, which is off, and move to the sink to wash my doughy hands.

As I wipe my hands on a dish towel, my phone makes a noise I've never heard before. I grab it and settle at the island bartop to find a message from the roommate site—someone responded to my listing, which fine, yes, I finally posted yesterday after a pep talk from Emma.

Sometimes I'm a little slow to accept reality. I can *see* it; I just can't accept it. Two days for me isn't bad, to be honest.

I tap to open the message, curiosity piqued:

Dear Ms. Tomlinson,

I am writing on behalf of a gentleman seeking accommodations in the Charleston area for approximately six to eight months, perhaps longer. Your property seems to meet many of his requirements, particularly regarding privacy and space.

Before proceeding further, I must inquire: Are you open to male tenants? My client is exceptionally quiet, tidy, and rarely home. He would require an entire floor, if possible, for privacy reasons related to his work.

If this arrangement interests you, please respond with your availability for a preliminary discussion.

Respectfully,

D. Hastings

Executive Assistant

I read it twice, eyebrows climbing with each sentence. Executive Assistant? No first name—just a letter? His client?

A *gentleman?*

"How old is this guy?" I ask the Big House.

I didn't put an age *limit* on the listing, but now I'm thinking I should've.

It sounds more like a corporate housing inquiry than someone looking to split the electric bill and argue over whose turn it is to buy toilet paper.

And the tone—formal, almost stilted. Definitely not American. British, maybe? Or just someone who thinks writing like they're in a Jane Austen novel will make them sound trustworthy.

I set down my phone and stare aimlessly out the window, mulling over the message. A male roommate. I've never considered it seriously. The Big House has always been a feminine domain, our own little sorority of adult women figuring out life together post-college.

But the practical side of me—the side that just paid for a new water heater and knows the back rock wall needs serious work—is intrigued. Someone who's rarely home sounds ideal. Someone who can afford an entire floor to himself sounds financially stable.

Someone with an "executive assistant" sounds... important. Or pretentious. Or both.

Eventually, I return to my bread, and as I knead it and shape it and put it in the pan, I find myself wondering about this mysterious potential male housemate. What kind of work requires that much privacy? Writer? Musician? Corporate executive who works from home?

Serial killer who needs space for his collection of victims' teeth?

"Stop it," I say to myself. "This is why you're still single."

I set the loaf to rise one final time, the actions I take done with the precision of someone who stress-bakes often enough to be good at it. The house feels especially empty tonight. Emma's at Aaron's. Lizzie's off modeling and then going out with Matt. It's just me and my thoughts, spiraling in the quiet.

I wash my hands and pick up my phone again, staring at the message.

"A male roommate." The idea sits uncomfortably, especially when spoken out loud.

But then again, so does the idea of being alone in this house.

Instead of replying directly, I forward the email to myself with the note: *Think about this.*

I need to sleep on it, maybe ask the girls what they think. After all, they'd still be visiting often. They should have a say in who moves into their former home.

The kitchen is dusted with flour, a fine white coating on the counters that reminds me of the first snow of winter. It's peaceful, in its way. But too quiet.

I wipe down the counters, thinking about how this house has always been full of life. My aunt filled it with her book club friends, neighborhood children, and an ever-rotating cast of interesting characters she collected like others collect stamps. When I inherited it, my college roommates and I continued the tradition, turning it into our own little haven.

The thought of strangers moving in makes my stomach twist. But the thought of emptiness is worse.

I set the bread to bake and head into my suite to take a bath. They both take about an hour, and bake-bathing is as much a part of my routine as anything else.

"Well, Aunt Fern," I say to the empty foyer as I pass through it. "You always said this house had one more big adventure in it."

I can only hope now that it hasn't already happened with me, Hillary, Claudia, Ryanne, Emma, and Lizzie.

CHAPTER SEVENTEEN

MATT

I step onto the elevator at ChemTech, my brown bag lunch tucked into my briefcase. Just as the doors start to close, a woman's heels come click-running toward me.

It won't be Lizzie, because she's doing her week-long photo shoot this week. It's Wednesday, and I'm facing my third day of eating lunch with Byron and Randy.

I may suffocate before the end of the day, because without Lizzie here, the air doesn't seem to hold enough oxygen.

Jessie steps onto the elevator after catching the doors. "Thanks," she says to the few other people on the car already. She meets my eye and nods.

I give her a big smile and reach to push the five button again to get the doors to close. The sooner I can get to my office, the sooner I can disappear behind a closed door for a little bit.

If this is how ChemTech is going to be without Lizzie, I don't want her to quit.

"You seem happy," Jessie says, like maybe happiness is against company policy.

The truth is simpler and more complicated all at the same time: I'm dating Lizzie Trenton, and it's transforming everything.

"Do I?" I ask. "Must be Hump Day."

She doesn't roll her eyes, but Jessie's existence is like one big eye-roll. She steps off the elevator on the third floor, along with several others, and I continue up to five by myself.

The Department Head hallway has less laughter, fewer impromptu conversations by the coffee machine, and exactly zero surprise sparkling water appearances on my desk.

I miss her. It's only been two days—it's only nine-ten on the third day, for crying out loud—but I miss her like crazy.

I drop into my chair and boot up my computer, my eyes automatically drifting to the wall separating our offices. Tomorrow I'll get to see her at the photoshoot, and the anticipation has me practically vibrating with energy.

My phone buzzes with a text from Lizzie: *Morning!*

Just finished makeup. About to start the winter formal wear section. Still good for tomorrow?

I snap a quick selfie with an exaggerated pout and send it with: *Counting down the hours. The office is boring without you throwing beverages at me.*

I'm sure. I'll reload for Monday when I'm back.

I'm still smiling at my phone when Byron pokes his head in. "Lunch in the lounge again today?"

"Sure," I say, though I'm almost hoping that I choke on my mid-morning snack and have to be airlifted out of here before lunch.

Byron leaves, and I blow out my breath. "Tomorrow," I mutter under my breath. "I won't be here tomorrow, and I'll get to see Lizzie tomorrow."

Tomorrow can't come fast enough.

I pick up a paper clip, unbending it and reforming it like it's personally responsible for batch 214 turning into a gummy brick.

Three failed runs in a row. Same formulation. Same conditions. Same unfortunate resemblance to melted Fruit Roll-Ups.

This isn't a materials issue. It's process. Somewhere between my spec sheet and the floor, something's gone sideways.

I pull up the process flowchart, because this is as exciting as my work life gets. No wonder I want to grow tomatoes on my back patio.

"Heat curve's clean," I say, peering at the screen. "Agitation speed's steady."

Still, something's off.

I pull up my chat with the chemical engineer in the lab on the second floor. Miranda and I chit and chat all day long, throwing questions and answers at each other.

I quickly type out a question and send it. *Did we recalibrate the inline mixer after maintenance?*

Miranda starts typing instantly. *You told me to wait until we ran the new viscosity profile.*

Right. That was before yesterday's batch solidified into what I'm pretty sure could be used to fill potholes.

Okay, do it now. And lock out that line until I sign off. I don't need another five-gallon drum of industrial jelly.

She sends me a laughing emoji and then a thumbs-up.

I sigh and open a new email, ready for some sort of contact with Lizzie that isn't a text about how long her hair and makeup takes each morning for this shoot. I can't wait to actually see it for myself.

Tomorrow.

Subject: *Possibly Reactive Surprises* 😬

Want to grab a soda and talk polymers? I'll bring the goat photos.

I send the email without further explanation, because if I have to troubleshoot this mess again, I'm at least going to do it with the one person in this building who makes volatile compounds easier to survive.

Too bad Lizzie isn't here right now. Normally, I'd just go next door and flop down in the chair across from her, vent out the problem, and she'd brainstorm solutions and ideas with me.

No wonder I'm falling in love with her. She speaks my language.

Lunchtime arrives before anything happens, which is standard for my life at ChemTech. I head into the lounge and find Byron and Randy already set up in front of the windows facing west.

I sigh as I get my lunch out of the fridge, but I have a hard time forcing myself over to the table with my friends. Before Lizzie, these were my regular lunch companions—friendly enough, but our conversations never went deeper than sports, weekend plans, and office gossip.

I finally get myself over there, forcing a smile to my face as I pull out the last chair at the table.

"So," Randy says around bites of his pepperoni pizza pocket. "Are you going to tell us what's got you walking on air lately? Or should I say *who*?"

I take a bite of my potato salad to buy time. "Am I walking on air?"

"Dude." Byron rolls his eyes. "You've been smiling at your phone all week, nearly crashing into walls and stuff." He points his plastic fork at me. "And you're wearing cologne."

I look down at my shirt and tie, as if the fragrance will be visible. "I always wear cologne."

"Not the good stuff."

Randy leans in and stage-whispers, "It's Elizabeth from Regulatory Affairs, isn't it? I know you eat lunch with her instead of us."

Heat creeps up my neck, but I see no point in denying it. "Yeah, we're dating."

Byron falls back in his chair as if I've actually shocked him. "Wow. I wasn't expecting you to admit it."

"We filled out the paperwork," I say. "There's nothing to hide when you have to do that, trust me."

"You two have been dancing around each other for months," Byron says with a good-natured smile. "Good for you, Matty."

"Just don't screw it up," Randy says. "She's way out of your league."

"Thanks for the vote of confidence." I give him a glare and finish my potato salad, already calculating how I can fake a phone call from my sister and go back to my office.

"I'm serious," he says. "She's smart, gorgeous, and terrifying when she wants to be. Remember when she shut down the entire Obelisk proposal with one email about regulatory compliance?"

I do remember, and the memory makes me smile.

Lizzie in Professional Mode is a force of nature—precise, knowledgeable, unstoppable. I can't wait to see her in Modeling Mode tomorrow, because I imagine her to be the same way, just wearing delicious clothes and looking stunningly amazing with professional hair and makeup.

"Earth to Matt," Randy says, waving a hand in front of my face. "You're doing it again."

"Doing what?"

"That dopey smile thing." He shakes his head. "Man, you've got it bad."

"I do not." I shake my head and look over to Byron. "How's the DisneyWorld planning coming?" He has a family vacation coming up, and while I don't care about the planning, it's a conversation topic change I need.

Because florine fumes, Randy is right. I do have it bad for Lizzie.

———

PURRICELL AND PURROXIDE watch me from the bed as I try on my third shirt on Thursday morning. "What do you think? Too casual? Too formal?" I turn in a full circle and strike a pose.

Purricell yawns widely, completely unimpressed with my fashion show.

"You're right. The blue one was better." I change back into the first button-down I tried. "I'm overthinking this."

The cats have been suspiciously well-behaved lately. No knocked-over coffee mugs, no midnight zoomies, no shredded toilet paper. I'm convinced it's Lizzie's influence—they're on their best behavior in case she comes back.

"She's coming over this weekend," I tell them as I adjust my collar. "So keep it together until then, okay?"

Purroxide blinks slowly at me, which I choose to interpret as agreement.

I grab my keys and phone, double-checking that I have the studio address. Lizzie's been sending updates all week about the photoshoot—excited messages about the clothes, the team, how much she's enjoying being in front of the camera full-time.

It's different when it's not just a weekend gig, she texted last night. *I feel like I can really get into the flow of it.*

I want to see that flow for myself. I want to see every version of Lizzie there is.

The photography studio is in a converted warehouse in downtown Charleston. I find parking a block away and walk the rest, my stomach stinging with unexpected nerves. This is Lizzie's world, not mine. What if I don't fit?

The building is nondescript from the outside, but inside it's a hive of activity. I give my name to a harried-looking assistant who checks a list, then waves me through.

"They're in Studio C," she says. "Down the hall, second door on the left."

I follow her directions, passing racks of clothing and people rushing about with equipment. The scent of powder and something more electrical hangs in the air, and it honestly smells a bit like walking into the lab at ChemTech.

The door to Studio C stands open, and I pause in the doorway, taking in the scene.

First, the room is huge, like massively huge. I don't know what I was expecting, but not this.

Second, the wall across from me is made up completely of windows, but all the walls have been painted black. So has the floor. Equipment I'd never be able to identify lines the wall to my right, and racks of clothing fill the back of the room.

Over in the corner, bright lights illuminate a set designed to look like an upscale living room. A photographer adjusts his camera while assistants move reflectors and check lighting. Makeup artists and stylists hover around the edges of the set, ready to swoop in for touch-ups.

And then I see her.

Lizzie stands in the center of it all, wearing a midnight blue evening gown—with, holy Albuquerque, that plunging neckline—that hugs her curves before flowing to the floor in a cascade of shimmering fabric.

There's a slit that starts about mid-thigh, and Lizzie

poses in such a way to really highlight that feature of the dress—one hand on her hip, that knee bent, and the hip cocked.

I can't breathe.

It's over for me.

Somehow, my eyes still send messages to my brain, and I note that her auburn hair is styled in loose waves. She's been painted in dark makeup unlike anything I've seen her wear before, and I'm gone.

Just gone.

Floating somewhere above the world, completely untethered from earth at the sheer beauty of Lizzie Trenton.

She looks like she stepped out of a magazine—which, I suppose, is exactly the point.

The photographer gives her an instruction that makes no sense to me—"Shift your weight, open to the light, and give me negative space on the left."—and Lizzie moves her feet, drops her hand on her hip, and tilts her head.

"Beautiful," the man calls. "More mouth."

Lizzie changes the shape of her mouth, making her lips fuller, more pouty.

Absolutely stunning.

She moves in a way I've never seen before, holding herself with utmost confidence. She possesses grace as the photographer straightens and says, "I need Maria."

Another woman steps over to the camera, and they

start to look through the photos. Lizzie has transformed again. She's sagged, which is incredible, because I sort of thought modeling would be her standing there, looking pretty.

It's so much more than that.

It's power, and grace, and beauty, and knowledge all in one moment.

She's absolutely magnificent.

"Okay," Maria says. "Lizzie, we want to move on to the video." She steps out from behind the camera and over toward Lizzie. They start to confer, and Lizzie nods along as Maria gives her instructions.

Then the photographer steps back into his position, Maria steps out, and he calls, "Chin forward, then down. No, too much. Beautiful. From there."

Lizzie walks forward, those hips going left-right, left-right in a way that has me reaching for the wall to support myself. Except there's no wall there.

I nearly topple over, because watching Lizzie in this element has melted my bones.

"Again," the photographer calls. He consults his viewing screen. "Think about your collarbone, Lizzie, okay? Stretch from it, not your shoulder."

I find myself trying to do what he said, but I actually can't feel my collarbone.

Lizzie takes her place near the back of the set, turns in a perfectly fluid movement, and then walks forward while stretching from her collarbone, because the photographer steps back and claps. "Brilliant," he yells, obviously happy with Lizzie's walk.

I mean, it looked the same to me, but I'm such a ruined puddle of a man, I can't really tell.

He confers with Maria again, and the makeup artist goes in to touch up Lizzie's lipstick. Watching her mouth like that...I have to look away or I might spontaneously combust. But I can't, and somehow, I also don't catch on fire.

"All right, my princess." The photographer leaves his mess of equipment and steps out into the set. He starts talking to Lizzie, who's ultra-focused as she nods along. He puts his hand on her hip in a way I really don't like, but Lizzie doesn't even flinch.

Everyone gets back into position, and he calls, "Mouth breathing secrets. Smile with your eyes, not your lips. Lizzie! Let me see what it looks like when you know you're the sexiest woman in this room—because you are!"

She glides forward, that hand on her hip again, and I completely short out. There is no way she can do that walk better, and I sink into a chair next to a rack of clothes that honestly look like rags compared to Lizzie in that gown.

The photographer shouts something in another language, and the entire crowd in the room breaks out into applause. I join them, because it's for Lizzie, and she deserves the adulation.

"Let's change to the skinny jeans," Maria says, and Lizzie gets bustled away with three people and through a door in the back, assumedly to change.

I can sit there and watch her magnificence all day, so I do. A woman approaches me about the time Lizzie comes out in a pair of skinny jeans the color of the deep blue sea, and the fact that they've been painted on her body isn't lost on me.

I'm pretty sure the woman says something to me, but I can't—my brain—

Then Lizzie looks over to me. I realize in that moment that everyone is looking at me.

"That's just my boyfriend," Lizzie says, her smile growing as she steps away from her entourage.

She says something to the photographer, who nods, and then she's gliding toward me in those spectacular jeans and a tank top the color of lilacs in the spring.

"You came," she says, reaching for my hand.

I manage to stand up, though my legs feel a little numb. "Wild horses couldn't have kept me away." I squeeze her fingers, careful not to mess up her perfect appearance. "You look *incredible*."

"These clothes are amazing," she says.

"Yeah, but so are you."

"I was just asking him if he needed anything to drink," the woman says.

Lizzie and I both look at her, and then Lizzie says, "He'd love some sparkling water."

"Coming up." The woman smiles and takes her clipboard and herself out of Studio C.

"Lizzie," Maria says, and Lizzie turns toward her.

"Go." I let go of her hand. "Just pretend I'm not here."

Lizzie smiles at me and gives my hand one last squeeze. "We're breaking for lunch in about an hour. Can you hang around until then?"

"Absolutely." I can hang around all day long, but I keep that to myself for now.

She returns to the set, and I sit back down to keep observing. The woman with the clipboard returns, two bottles of sparkling water with her.

"I'm Heather," she says. "Lizzie's agent."

"Oh, sure." I shake her hand enthusiastically. "Lizzie loves you."

Heather grins. "She did say you were a charmer."

My chest squeezes at the thought of Lizzie talking about me with her professional friends. I expect it with her roommates, but Heather doesn't live in the Big House. "That's a good thing, I hope."

"Mostly." She smiles kindly, and she has a good air about her. "She seems happy."

"I'm trying my best."

Heather nods toward the set. "She's really good, you know. Has a natural instinct for what works on camera."

I watch as Lizzie transitions seamlessly between

poses, each one looking effortless and elegant. "I can see that."

"I've been trying to get her to do this full-time for years," Heather says. "She's finally considering it."

"Yeah, we've talked about it," I say. "I think she's fantastic."

"Take some pictures if you want to," Heather says. "Behind the scenes stuff. Lizzie sometimes posts those on her social media."

"That's allowed?"

"Marco and Clara Jane won't mind as long as you don't get in the way or post anything before the campaign launches."

I have no idea who Clara Jane is, but I do notice everyone wearing gorgeous clothes. Only Marco, who I'm assuming is the photographer, wears black from head to toe.

Awkwardness descends on me as I pull my phone out. I have no idea how to get the right angle or lighting. Heather wanders away, and I take an occasional photo with my phone. Lizzie in a different shirt, conferring with the stylist. Lizzie getting a makeup touch-up, eyes closed as the artist works.

Lizzie laughing with one of the assistants between setups, this time in a vibrant blue shirt that makes everything about her deeper.

That last one is my favorite—her head thrown back in genuine laughter, eyes crinkled at the corners, completely unposed and natural. Joy radiates from her, and I find myself staring at it long after I've taken the shot.

Too soon, my time at the studio comes to an end. I have dinner plans with Chanel and Shad, and Lizzie has several more hours of shooting ahead.

"I'll see you Saturday?" I ask as we say goodbye near the exit.

"Definitely." She rises on tiptoes to kiss me quickly. "Thanks for coming. It meant a lot to have you here."

"I wouldn't have missed it."

I walk to my car feeling like I've been given a precious gift—a glimpse into a part of Lizzie's life that few people get to see. She trusted me enough to let me in, to show me this other side of herself.

At home, I scroll through the photos I took, lingering on that perfect candid shot. Without overthinking it, I text it to her with the caption: *This is what beauty and joy look like.*

I set my phone down and head to the shower, expecting a quick response. When I check again twenty minutes later, there's nothing. No problem—she's working.

I feed the cats and check again. Still nothing.

By the time I leave for Chanel's, an hour has passed with no response. A knot forms in my stomach as I drive, my mind racing through possibilities.

Is she upset I sent the photo? Did I overstep by

capturing that moment? Was my caption too much, too revealing of how I feel?

Or worse—did something happen? Is she okay?

I check my phone at every stoplight, but the screen remains stubbornly black. By the time I reach Chanel's house, anxiety has twisted my insides into a pretzel.

"You look terrible," Chanel says when she opens the door. "What happened?"

I hold up my phone, showing her the sent message with no response. "I think I messed up."

Chanel peers at the phone, her brow wrinkling. Behind her, Nora fusses, and I go to get her. "By sending her a nice photo? That doesn't make sense."

"Maybe the caption was too much." I pick up my niece and bounce her on my hip, saying, "Sh-sh-sh. How are you, baby?"

"She's doing better." Chanel closes the front door and hands me back my phone. "The caption is fine, Matty. It's not exactly a marriage proposal."

"Then why hasn't she responded?"

"I don't know. Maybe because she's working? Maybe her phone died? Maybe she's thinking about how to respond?"

All reasonable explanations, but they don't ease the tightness in my chest. I try to focus on dinner with my sister and brother-in-law, on snuggling with little Nora, but my eyes keep drifting to my silent phone.

Maybe she's mad I took photos at the photo shoot, I think. *But Heather told me I could.*

Hours later, as I drive home alone, the screen remains dark. No new messages, no explanation, no word at all from Lizzie.

I stare at the photo one more time as I lay in bed—Lizzie's face caught in that perfect moment of uninhibited happiness. Pure beauty, from way down deep inside who she is.

I thought I was capturing something utterly beautiful and happy, but now all I feel is dread.

What if I've somehow gotten her in trouble by taking a forbidden photo?

CHAPTER EIGHTEEN

LIZZIE

I SINK DEEPER INTO THE COUCH CUSHIONS, MY entire body feeling like a wrung-out dishcloth. Five days of photo shoots—five days of not-smiling-but-holding-my-mouth-just-so, posing, changing outfits, and being taped, painted, and curled by makeup artists and stylists —has left me completely drained.

"Here," Tahlia says, handing me an ice-cold can of Diet Coke. "You look like you need this."

"Bless you." I pop the top and take a grateful sip. The Big House living room is filled with my favorite people, all in various states of relaxation. Hillary and Claudia are sprawled together on a bean bag, while Emma and Ryanne occupy the other couch. It's our first full girls' night in months, and something about having everyone here makes my exhaustion more bearable.

"So," Hillary says, rolling onto her stomach and

propping her chin in her hands. "Tell us everything about the shoot. Was it amazing? Did they treat you well? Did you get to keep any clothes?"

I laugh at her rapid-fire questions. "Yes, yes, and of course. I have several amazing things upstairs, and a hefty discount code."

And a great paycheck—about half of what I make at ChemTech in a month, actually.

"And how's Matt?" Claudia asks, her dark eyes latching onto mine.

Heat creeps into my cheeks as I remember the look on Matt's face when he first saw me in those jeans. Like he'd been struck by lightning. "He's fine," I say lightly.

"Fine?" Ryanne says. "That's the best you can do? The man looks at you like you're Marilyn Monroe when you're just wearing jeans and a T-shirt. I can't imagine his face when he saw you all glammed up."

"Speaking of which," Claudia says, looking around. "Has anyone checked social media? Did they post any behind-the-scenes stuff yet?" She meets my eyes again. "Don't you usually do something like that as a sneak peek?"

"I got a few things," I say. "But the shoot just ended an hour ago." I came straight home and changed into my pajamas for our movie night.

With a start, I realize that I haven't looked at my phone since...I can't remember when. Shooting full-time like that is intense, with early call times for hair and makeup, and the shot list always going at least an hour over when I'm told it'll end.

"I haven't posted," I say, reaching for my phone. "The campaign doesn't launch for another month anyway."

"But you always get a photo with Heather," Tahlia says.

"Yeah, I got that," I say. "With Maria and Marco, too. The team who makes me look good." I swipe open my phone. "I've been so tired, I just flop into bed at night."

My phone battery is nearly dead, and my device makes a pathetic sound to warn me of such a thing. I have several notifications, and more exhaustion pulls through me over going through all of them.

I tap on my texts, seeing messages from everyone in the room with me, my dad, Heather, and—"Knoxville."

"What is it?" Tahlia pauses in her return to the kitchen and looks over my shoulder.

"I forgot to check my messages." I open Matt's text and freeze.

One, it's from yesterday. How did I miss this? Have I really not looked at my phone in over twenty-four hours?

The answer is yes. Or rather, no, I haven't.

Two, he's sent me a picture of myself, clearly at the photo shoot yesterday. A candid moment captured between takes. I'm laughing, head thrown back, completely unposed and natural. The caption reads: *This is what beauty and joy look like.*

Something catches in my throat, and I can't breathe properly.

"Let me see," Emma says, scooting closer. I hand her my phone wordlessly, and she gasps. "Oh my gosh, Lizzie. This is gorgeous."

"Let me see." Hillary takes the phone, and she doesn't gasp like Emma. She's more reserved in her reaction—all I get is some raised eyebrows. She shows it to Claudia, who frowns. She also reserves her judgment and comments for a bit, but my phone gets passed to Ry, who smiles.

"He is amazing, Lizzie." She gives the phone to Tahlia, and I don't want her to be left behind here by herself. So much has changed, though, and I can't rewind time by myself.

"He really sees you," Tahlia says as she hands the phone back to me.

I stare at the photo again. It's not the glammed-up, perfectly posed Lizzie from the professional shots. It's just...me. Laughing. Being myself, as I laughed at something Alisha said about Marco.

Matt saw it; he captured the moment; he thought it was beautiful enough to send to me.

"I can't believe I didn't respond," I say. "He probably thinks I hated it."

"Or that you're mad he took photos during a professional shoot," Claudia says.

"Or maybe that your phone died?" Hillary wears wide eyes with pure hope in them.

"I need to respond." I quickly type out a response: *Sorry for the late reply! My phone died yesterday, and today was INSANE, and I just saw this. It's beautiful! Thank you for capturing this moment.* 🖤

I hesitate and look around at everyone, all of them watching me too. "Heart emoji?"

"Yes," a few voices chorus, and I meet Tahlia's eyes.

"I think you're to heart emoji level," she says. "Which means you better start bringing Matt around more." With that, she smiles and goes into the kitchen with, "I'm bringing out the brookies."

Tahlia loves to bake, and she came home from school today and put together one of my favorite things—brookies. Half chocolate chip cookie, half deep chocolate brownie. It's a glorious combination of sweet and salty, and every bite tastes like comfort and love and chocolate rolled into one chewy, delicious square. I swear, if serotonin were a baked good, it would be a brookie.

So, with my comfiest leggings on, and the day over, this text staring me in the face—it's not until I smell the brookies that I have the confidence to send the message.

I drop my thumb on the send button, and my message goes flying through cyberspace to Matt. I look up and find Ry watching me.

"So," she says. "How serious is this getting?"

All eyes turn to me, and my face flushes again. "I don't know. It's only been a few weeks."

"A few weeks of what appears to be the healthiest relationship you've ever had," Emma says.

"Plus all those months of pining," Tahlia says, returning with a plate of brookies.

She hands it to me as I say, "I *wasn't* pining. I'm so sick of everyone saying I was pining."

Tahlia blinks. "I'm sorry, Lizzie. I—"

"Oh, come on." Claudia laughs. "You were *so* pining after him. I don't know for how long, but at least since my wedding." She looks at Hillary and Ryanne, then Emma and Tahlia. "Remember how she ran out, and he followed her?"

I remember that, and I know everyone else does too. Thankfully, no one says anything, but that only leaves the silence to suffocate me.

I pull a Matt and say, "Fine. I was pining a little bit."

"A little?" Hillary grins at me. "You color-coded your sticky notes based on which ones you used for files you shared with Matt versus everyone else."

"That's just good organization," I say.

"It's obsession is what it is," Claudia says with a laugh.

I take a brookie and then a bite of it, letting the sugar soothe my wounded ego. As I pass the plate to Emma, my fears well up, choking me enough to prevent swallowing.

When I finally get the brookie down, I breathe. "I really like him," I say. "Like, a lot. Maybe too much, too fast."

"Why too much?" Emma asks, and she genuinely seems a bit confused.

I struggle to put my feelings into words. "Because I've never felt this way before. It's scary. What if I'm just caught up in the excitement of a new relationship?"

"Or," Tahlia says. "What if you're finally experiencing what being with an amazing man feels like?"

Her words hit me like a freight train. My previous relationships have been disasters—men who took advantage, who disappeared when things got serious, who never really saw me.

Matt sees me. Really *sees* me.

"I think I'm falling in love with him," I whisper, the admission making my heart race.

The room goes quiet for a moment, and then Hillary breaks the silence with, "Well, duh."

We all burst into laughter, the tension dissolving.

"The question is," Ryanne says. "What are you going to do about it?"

I look down at the photo again, a couple of ideas forming in my mind. "I'm going to show him I see him too."

———

ON SUNDAY AFTERNOON, I stand on Matt's front porch, clutching a small gift bag and trying to calm my racing heart. We've texted at a normal rate since Friday night, but this is the first time I'm seeing him since the photo shoot.

I ring the doorbell, shifting my weight from foot to foot. The door swings open, and there he is—hair slightly mussed, wearing a faded MIT T-shirt and jeans, looking so good it makes my chest ache.

"Hey, kitten," he says, relief evident in his voice. "Come in."

I step inside, immediately greeted by Purricell and Purroxide, who weave between my legs like I'm their long-lost owner.

"The chem-cat traitors have missed you," Matt says with a smile.

"I've missed them too." I bend down to scratch behind Purricell's ears, earning a contented purr. "And their dad."

Matt's smile widens, and he pulls me into a hug as I straighten. "I've missed you more than I can say."

When he pulls back, there's a hint of uncertainty in his eyes. "About that photo—I swear to you, Heather told me it was okay to take it. I didn't realize she might be pulling a joke on me."

He takes a breath, but with Matt, that's only more fuel. "I wouldn't have taken it had I known. She just said

I couldn't post them on social media, and I obviously would never do that. So—"

He cuts off when I put my forefinger against his lips. His eyes widen, and I have no idea what I'm doing. But at least he's not talking anymore.

"I'm so sorry I left you hanging," I say. "I haven't done a week-long shoot in a while, and they're exhausting." I offer him a small smile and drop my hand. "The days are long, and I just get food on the way home, eat it in the car, and drop into bed."

He nods, his eyes scanning down to my other hand, which holds the gift bag. I quickly hide it behind my back, making his gaze jump back to mine.

I smile at him. "Thank you for sending me the photo. It's great."

Relief washes over his face. "I was worried I'd overstepped."

"You didn't." I step into him. "I didn't get my hello kiss, because someone has been stewing for three days."

"Someone else has been too busy to see her boyfriend for three days."

"I slept most of yesterday." I hold up the gift bag. "And when I wasn't doing that, I was out getting you this."

He wears surprise in his expression as he takes the bag. "What's this for?"

"Just because."

He drops it to his side and with his free hand, he

hooks me around the waist and brings me flush against him. He looks like he wants to say something, but in the end, he simply leans down and touches his lips to mine.

Kissing Matt is a magical experience every time, and I never tire of it. He smells like his sexy cologne, and he tastes like chocolate and coffee.

"I'm going to open my gift now," he murmurs, and he moves over to the couch and sits. He carefully removes the tissue paper from the bag and pulls out a simple silver frame.

My heart pounds ridiculously hard. "It's not anything special," I say even as his eyes widen.

"You printed it," he says softly.

"I did." I sit beside him, our knees touching. "No one has ever seen me like you do, Matt. That photo...it's how I want to remember this time in my life. Happy. Free. Seen."

He traces the edge of the frame with his finger, his eyes still glued to my picture inside it. "You are all of those things."

"Because of you." I reach into the bag and pull out the second gift—a small keychain with a cat charm dangling from it. Engraved on one side are the words *Best Fake Friend Ever*.

Matt bursts out laughing as he takes the keychain from me. "You didn't."

"I absolutely did." I grin, watching as he examines the keychain with the two tabby cats on the front. "I mean, I know you don't have tabbies, but the mall is limited in their cat breeds." I lean over and press a kiss to his cheek. "Turn it over."

He flips it over to find my phone number engraved on the back.

"Just so you can always call me, even when the cats have gone rogue," I say.

Matt stares at the keychain, then at me, emotion welling in his eyes. Without warning, he sets the gifts aside and pulls me into his arms, his lips finding mine in a kiss that makes my toes curl. It's passionate and tender all at once, and I melt into him, my hands finding their way into his hair.

"Elizabeth Trenton," he whispers, but his mouth is on mine again in the next moment. I kiss him back, hoping he knows we've become more than having to respond to a text within a few minutes.

He pulls away again, his breath coming quicker now. "You are something else entirely."

"Is that a good thing?" I ask, my voice barely audible.

His answer is another kiss, deeper than the first, and I lose myself in the feeling of being completely, utterly wanted. His hands slide down to my waist, pulling me closer, and his heartbeat races against my chest.

The kiss turns urgent, desperate, and I'm drowning in sensation—the softness of his lips, the strength of his arms around me, the heat building between us.

He pulls back suddenly, his eyes dark and intense.

"Lizzie," he says, his voice rough. "I need to tell you something."

My heart stutters. "What is it?"

Matt takes a deep breath, his hands still holding me close, as if he's afraid I might disappear. "I think I'm—"

A crash from the kitchen interrupts him, causing me to yelp and him to jump to his feet. I practically fall forward into the space on the couch he just vacated, my cheek brushing upholstery before I can catch myself.

Pure embarrassment pulls through me as Matt says, "Purroxide, what are you doing?" in a very stern Cat-Dad voice.

The Maine Coon stands triumphantly above a shattered mug, blinking lazily at Matt. Purricell rubs against my ankles, and I absently reach down to stroke him, getting the very real feeling that his cats—*his cats*—were jealous of him kissing me.

"Did you cut your paw?" he asks while Purricell's purring amps up a notch in both volume and intensity.

"Did you guys stage this?" I ask Purricell, but of course, he doesn't answer. Matt cleans up, muttering things about Maine Coons and how much trouble they are, while I wait on the couch, my heart pounding in my chest.

I wonder what he was about to say—and why I'm so terrified to hear it.

CHAPTER NINETEEN

MATT

I can't stop staring at the photo of Lizzie.

For the third night in a row, I find myself sitting on my couch, Maine Coons draped across my lap, just looking at her face in that silver frame. Her head thrown back in laughter, eyes crinkled at the corners, radiating pure joy. It's not the polished, professional model Lizzie that everyone else gets to see. It's *my* Lizzie—unguarded, genuine, and absolutely breathtaking.

Purroxide headbutts my hand, demanding attention. I jerk my hand away and hiss at him, then do what he wants—pet him. "You saved me from making a complete fool of myself, buddy," I scratch along his ears, which he loves. "I almost told her I loved her."

The words hang in the air of my empty townhouse, pure disbelief radiating from them. *I almost told her I loved her.* After just a few weeks of dating. What kind of lunatic does that?

The kind who's actually falling in love, apparently.

"It's too soon," I say to the cats. "Way too soon, so you keep breaking things when you think I'm being an idiot." Because that obviously saved me from myself.

Purricell blinks at me slowly, which I choose to interpret as sage feline wisdom.

"You're right," I say. "I should give it more time. Make sure it's real."

But that's the thing—it already feels more real than anything I've experienced before. When I'm with Lizzie, everything just clicks into place. It's like a perfectly balanced chemical equation, all elements in harmony.

At the same time, I definitely need to slow down and make sure things don't just exist inside the fantasyland of my mind. I've never had anything too serious before, and it's not like my parents showed me what a kind, loving, committed relationship looks like or feels like.

Heck, the closest thing I have is my relationship with my sister, but even I know that sisterly love and romantic love don't feel the same.

Speaking of sisters, I need to head to Chanel's for our mid-week dinner. I carefully place the framed photo back on my end table, giving it one last look before I grab my keys.

"Behave yourselves," I tell Purricell and Purroxide.

"You can only break stuff if there's a reason, and me being gone for the night is *not* a reason."

They stare back with twin expressions of feline innocence that I don't believe for a second. I'm probably going to return to a shredded pillow or something, but I don't let that stop me from leaving.

I think for a minute about calling Lizzie while I drive but quickly veto the idea. She stayed late at work to get caught up on some paperwork, and I've seen her when she's in catch-up mode. Even a simple phone call can get me in the doghouse.

So I make the drive with only the radio for company, wondering how in the world I can still feel so lonely. It makes no sense, and I hate that I can't just be happy when I'm alone with myself.

It's a problem, I know, but one I don't know how to solve.

A couple of hours later, I'm helping my sister with the final dinner prep when she says, "You're a million miles away tonight." She's stirring a pot of homemade marinara sauce, the rich aroma filling her kitchen.

"Sorry," I say, realizing I'm cutting a cucumber and not a tomato. "Just thinking."

"About Lizzie?"

I glance up to find my sister watching me, no smile in sight. "No. What makes you think that?"

Her smile comes now. "Matty, you've been smiling

at that poor cucumber like it just told you a hilarious joke." She nudges me with her elbow. "Spill."

I set down the knife and lean against the counter. "I almost told her I loved her on Sunday."

Chanel's eyes widen. "Matthew. Really?"

"Purroxide knocked over a mug. Saved me from myself."

"And why would you need saving from expressing your feelings?" She turns down the heat under the sauce and gives me her full attention.

"Because it's too soon," I say. "We've only been dating for a few weeks. People don't fall in love that fast."

"Some do," Chanel says with a shrug. "I knew I loved Shad after our second date."

"That's different."

"Why? Because it's you?" She reaches back and removes the elastic from her ponytail. "You've known Lizzie for months, Matty. Working together, talking every day. The dating part might be new, but your friendship isn't."

I pick up the knife and resume chopping, needing something to do with my hands. "I don't want to scare her off."

"Or maybe you're the one who's scared." Chanel's voice softens. "Not everyone leaves, you know."

The knife stills in my hand. "I know that."

"Do you?" She stirs the sauce again. "Because it

seems like you're waiting for something to go wrong. For the other shoe to drop."

I don't respond, because what can I say? She's right. I've spent my entire adult life waiting for the people I care about to disappoint me or leave. It's easier that way—to expect the worst and be pleasantly surprised when it doesn't happen.

"Mom and Dad really did a number on us, didn't they?"

"They sure did." Chanel tastes the sauce and adds a pinch of salt. "But we don't have to let their mess define our lives, Matty."

The front door opens, and Shad calls out, "I'm home." A moment later, he appears in the kitchen doorway with Nora in his arms. My niece squeals when she sees me, reaching out with grabby hands.

"There's my girl," I say, quickly wiping my hands before taking her. She immediately grabs at my hair, a favorite pastime of hers.

"How was your day?" Chanel asks Shad, rising on tiptoes to kiss him.

"Good," he says. "Really good, actually. They want me to come in for another interview next week."

"That's fantastic." Chanel beams at him and wraps her arms around him. "You're going to get this job."

"It's just another interview," Shad says, but I see the hope in his eyes.

"It's progress," I say, bouncing Nora on my hip. "And progress is good."

Dinner is a lively affair, with Nora babbling from her highchair and Shad sharing details about the potential job. I try to stay engaged, but my mind keeps drifting back to Lizzie. To that moment on my couch when everything felt so perfect, so right.

"You should invite Lizzie to the fall picnic," Chanel says.

I nearly drop my fork, and I shoot a look at Shad. He's done eating, so he stares right on back. "What?"

"The family picnic next weekend. You should bring her."

I look around the table. There are four of us here, and Nora is barely four months old. Whatever took her into the hospital last week is gone, cured, and even she watches me with what I interpret to be a semi-accusatory look.

"It's not really a family picnic," I say.

"We pack a picnic basket with food," Shad says.

"And we go to the park as a family." Chanel smiles at me. "Come on, Matty. It's not a big deal."

I think of the Halloween party that Lizzie invited me to. The "family" picnic is equivalent to that, so why can't I invite her? "Okay," I say just as Chanel says, "Stop overthinking everything, Matty. Sometimes good things just happen."

"I'm not overthinking." I frown at my sister, who

doesn't care at all that she's irritating me. Honestly, I get the same treatment from the cats, so why do I have to come here?

"I'll add Diet Coke to the grocery list," Shad says.

I whip my attention to him. "Diet Coke?"

"You said she likes it."

"I did? When?"

Shad chuckles as he gets to his feet. He picks up his empty plate and mine, and claps me on the shoulder as he walks past me. "I've actually heard it a few times. You talk a lot, brother."

"I talk a lot?" My voice pitches up into disbelief range, but Chanel starts laughing.

I'm not really in the mood for this, so I get up too. I sweep a kiss along Nora's forehead and help clear the table—not saying a word, thank you very much—and then say, "I have to head out."

"Matt, don't be mad," Chanel says, following me into the living room, where I grab my jacket off the back of the couch.

"I'm not mad," I say. "I'm annoyed." I shoot her a mini-glare. "You don't have to mother me, Chanel."

Her face turns blank, and then a look of horror crosses her features. "I didn't—I'm sorry. I wasn't trying to."

I sigh, my irritation fading to acceptance. "I know." I take her into a hug. "I don't expect everything to go wrong, but it's not like I have a lot of evidence that it'll go right."

I step back; she nods; I leave through the front door with the promise, "I'll call you later."

"Invite her if you'd like to," Chanel says from the doorway. "I'd love to meet her."

I wave my hand over my head as I walk down the sidewalk, not bothering to look back. If I take Lizzie to the family picnic and introduce her to Shad and Chanel, that's definitely taking things to the next level.

As I pull my seatbelt across me and fasten it, I mutter, "Yeah, just like blurting out that you love her would be."

"THIS LOBSTER MAC and cheese is *divine*," Lizzie says, closing her eyes as she savors another bite. "I can't believe you remembered this was my favorite place."

"I remember everything you tell me," I say, watching her with a smile. The bistro in Sugar Creek is busy for a Saturday night, filled with the hum of conversation and clinking glasses. Lizzie rendered me mute once more at the Big House, this time by coming down the stairs wearing a one-shoulder shirt the color of bright pink bubblegum and a pair of black leggings.

All of her makeup tonight is pink, from her eyeshadow to her blush to her lipstick. She can transform herself with clothes and colors, and I'm still plain old Matt. It doesn't seem quite fair.

"You remember everything?" She raises an eyebrow and scoffs. "Come on. You forgot about the Inter-department Quest just yesterday."

"That's because I don't care about it."

She reaches for her soda and takes a long drink, appraising me the whole time. "Okay. What's my favorite color?"

I point my fork at her. "That's a trick question, kitten. I should dock points."

"Dock points?" She laughs and runs her hand through her hair. "From what?"

"There's something," I say, though I don't know what. I spear another roasted potato but don't quite put it in my mouth yet. "You don't have one favorite color. You like different colors for different things. Green and purple for clothes, blue and gray for home decor, and yellow makes you happy but you'd never wear it, put it in your house or—" I pick up my Mountain Dew. "Drink it."

Her mouth drops open slightly. "Viva Las Vegas," she swears. Then she gives herself a little shake, and a hint of defiance enters those pretty eyes. "And I drink yellow stuff. Lemonade, for example."

"Do you?" I ask. "Last time we talked about lemonade, you said you preferred a flavored one. Strawberry, I believe, was the winner, and that, kitten, is not 'yellow stuff'."

I stick the potato in my mouth and cock my eyebrows at her, daring her to contradict me again. She doesn't, and I grin, a bit of smugness moving through me. "Ask me another one."

"No," she says. "Your head is already too big."

I start to laugh, but I have potato in my mouth, so that doesn't go so well. I end up choking, and Lizzie yelps as she jumps to her feet. "Call for help!" she yells as I wave her off.

"I'm—fine," I say, reaching for my untouched water glass. I take a big drink, getting the potato pulp down and my airway clear.

"Is everything okay?" A man appears at our table, and he's not our waiter.

"Yes," I say, looking up at both of them. "She was just—" I cut off, because I'd love to know what Lizzie was "just" doing.

"Yes, we're fine," she says crisply as she retakes her seat. "Thank you." She spreads her napkin in her lap again as the man walks away, and when our eyes meet, we both dissolve into laughter.

"Call for help," I gasp out between two breaths. "Were you going to give me the Heimlich?"

"I'm a certified first responder," she says, lifting her chin. "Choking is a real hazard that thousands of people die from every year."

"Thousands?"

"Yes," she says with another hair shake. "Mostly children and the elderly, but yes."

I feel sparkly as I lean toward her. "Well, since you have that certification, I'll need you to come to my family picnic next weekend." My heartbeat races along my ribs, but I don't even dare to blink.

Lizzie's doing plenty of that for both of us. "A family picnic?"

"I've met your dad," I say. "This is just my sister and her husband, and my four-month-old niece, Nora."

She scoops up another bite of mac and cheese. "No parents?"

I shake my head, though I haven't exactly told her all the gory details of dear old Mom and Dad.

"No cousins in the area?"

I shake my head again. "Just us."

"What do I wear?"

"It's a picnic in a park, Lizzie." I grin at her. "We sometimes go to this place in Savannah, but I'll find out what Chanel wants to do this year."

"Savannah? That's a bit of a drive."

"It is," I say. "But we could make a weekend of it. Stay overnight. Not—I mean—separate rooms, of course." My face starts to heat up, and I stab an asparagus spear to be safe. "Unless you don't want to. We could drive back the same day. Or you could say no. That's totally fine too."

Stop talking, Matt.

Lizzie reaches over and covers my hand with hers. "I want to come."

The tension drains from my shoulders, and I look up at her. "Yeah?"

"Yeah." She tilts her head, studying me. "I'm assuming this is kind of a big deal? Me meeting your sister officially?"

"Yeah," I say. "I've never brought anyone to a family event before, even a small one like this, and you know, Chanel's excited to meet you. She's heard a lot about you."

Why do I say every blasted thought I have? I press my lips closed and try to find peace in the silence.

Nope. Doesn't work.

"Shad's got another interview next week," I say. "It's been tough for him. The job market in his field is competitive, and with a baby at home..." I trail off and shrug. "They're doing their best."

"I'm sure." Lizzie takes a bite of her mac and cheese, and I want to reach into her throat and pull out some words, a different topic, something.

"I finished raising Chanel after my dad left us," I say, not quite sure this is what I wanted to bring up tonight. Lizzie pauses, her eyes going round again. "My mom was where she always is—off on another assignment, and my dad left the day after I graduated. He didn't come back for Chanel's, and I promised myself I'd always take care of her."

"Matty, I'm so sorry."

I take a deep breath. "It is what it is. By the time I started college, my mother was stationed permanently overseas, and I still don't know where my dad even is."

"And now you look out for Chanel and her family too," Lizzie says. I don't like how she looks like she's putting pieces together, but that's definitely how she looks. It's the eyes—they're so sharp, so calculating, so stunning.

"I can afford it," I say, trying to focus. "And Nora's worth every penny. Besides, it's temporary. Shad will find something soon." I take a big breath so I can keep talking, because I don't need Lizzie's compliments or her sympathy. "Anyway, enough about my family drama. Tell me more about your upcoming modeling gigs."

I expect her to allow me the topic change, but she watches me silently for too long. I stuff my mouth with too much asparagus, and her expression grows thoughtful, almost analytical. "Can I ask you something?"

I nod, all those veggies still stuck in my throat.

"Do you always take care of everyone?"

The question catches me completely off guard, and I inhale sharply. Big mistake when eating asparagus—word to the wise.

I cough again, but Lizzie doesn't jump to her feet this time. I cough and cough and cough, then manage to wash everything down with a half-glass of disgusting, room temperature, *still* water.

Still. Water.

It's so gross.

When I'm not about to choke or pass out or throw up, I open my mouth to respond, but no words come out.

Do I take care of everyone?

I've never thought of helping my sister to graduate, then sticking close to her so neither of us has to be an orphan as "taking care of her."

It's just what I do—what I've always done.

Lizzie watches me, waiting for an answer I don't have.

CHAPTER TWENTY

LIZZIE

THE CHARLESTON WATERFRONT SPARKLES IN THE morning sun as Matt drives us toward the park where we're meeting his family. I fidget with the hem of my sundress—a flowing violet number that I got from my photo shoot—and try to ignore the flutter of nerves in my stomach.

"So Nora is four months old?" I ask, though Matt's already told me this at least twice.

"Yep." Matt glances over, a smile softening his features. "She's getting so big. She was starting to roll over on Wednesday night."

Ah, yes. His standing Wednesday night dinner with Chanel and her family. It doesn't *bother* me. The fact that he's familial is actually a good thing. It just tells me things about him that I've been stewing on for a week now.

He never did answer my question at the bistro. The waiter had come and offered dessert while Matt looked like he was trying to figure out how to speak Swahili. I let the question go and the conversation flow somewhere else, because it was clear Matt doesn't even realize how much he takes care of other people.

But he so does—and not just Chanel.

He's been out to my father's three times in the past three weeks to help with something on the farm. *I* don't even go that often. He refills the toner in the copy machine at work. He fixed the water line to the icemaker in the refrigerator last year, and we all lauded him a hero.

Which he was and is.

But now that I know more about him, it sure feels like Matt wants to be taking care of someone or something...or he's not happy. And maybe my mind rotates in circles it shouldn't, but I can't help wondering if he likes me because he thinks I need his help, or if he likes me because I'm a person he wants to be with.

A person to love, I think. *Not a problem to solve.*

I sigh almost silently as I look out my side window, then I sneak peeks at him as he drives. There's something different about him today—an energy, an eagerness that makes his usual golden retriever personality even more pronounced.

"Chanel's excited to meet you," he finally says into

the silence. "I think she was starting to think I made you up."

"Why would she think that?"

He scoffs and puts on his blinker to turn left. "Because I talk about you all the time." He glances at me. "And apparently, the stories sound—and I quote—made up."

"Made up? Like what?"

"That cake incident when you first came to Department Head Row."

"That was so real," I say. "I had to throw those shoes away. I never could get all the frosting out of the stitching."

He laughs, and something breaks loose inside me too. This is fine. It's a picnic lunch in a park, with the water nearby. What can go wrong?

As we pull into the parking lot near the waterfront park, I spot a woman who's easily his sister. She's petite with the same warm brown hair as Matt, though hers falls in waves past her shoulders. She watches us with a smile and knowing eyes, and I've seen that exact same look on Matt's face before.

"That's Chanel," Matt says unnecessarily.

"I figured," I say, smiling as he parks. "The family resemblance is strong."

"Oh, yeah? I'll have you know I got all the height. I'm six-two, and she's five-two."

"Wow," I say, giggling around the letters. "That is a big difference."

"We tease about it all the time." He looks out the windshield at the water, then his rearview mirror, where he can surely see the park, then me. "You ready for this?"

There's that flicker again—a hint of vulnerability beneath his easy confidence. Maybe everything I've been stewing about this week is completely irrational. I haven't mentioned it to anyone for that exact reason, and I decide to set everything on a shelf for today.

After all, it's a *picnic* in a *park*.

"I'm so ready." I lean over and kiss him quickly. "Let's go meet your sister."

Matt meets me at the back bumper and takes my hand in his. Chanel waits for us on the sidewalk, glowing with the grin of the Cheshire Cat. She wears a long skirt that's colored like denim, but doesn't drape nearly as heavily as that fabric would. Her top is a cute pink and purple striped number—so Cheshire Cat—and she looks put together and kind.

"You must be Lizzie," she says as we approach. She reaches out her hand, and I clasp hers and shake. "Matt talks so much about you."

"And see, Channy? She's real." He rolls his eyes good-naturedly. "Lizzie, my sister, Chanel Hepsworth. Chanel, my very real girlfriend in the flesh, Lizzie Trenton."

"So great to meet you," I say. "Matt talks about you and your family a lot too."

"Not true," he says automatically, peering past his sister. "Where's Shad and Nora?"

"Over by the big oak tree." Chanel links her arm through mine as she turns to face the park. "We found the perfect spot in the shade."

"I forgot our cookies," Matt says, and he doubles back to his SUV to get them. When he catches up to us only a couple of minutes later, he's carrying the plastic container that Tahlia put the cookies in, as well as a large duffel bag.

"What's in the bag?" I ask.

"Just some stuff," he says. "Blankets, sunscreen, a few toys for Nora."

"And probably the kitchen sink," Chanel adds with a laugh. "Matt always over-prepares."

I give her a smile, but nothing is staying shelved where I put it. Is over-preparing the same as playing the hero? And why can't I just enjoy the fact that Matt wants this picnic to go well and be fun for everyone?

We arrive in a shaded area where a tall, broad-shouldered man stands beside a picnic basket and bounces a baby in his arms. He looks up and smiles as we approach.

"Shad, this is Lizzie," Matt says. "Lizzie, my brother-in-law, Shad, and my niece, Nora."

"It's great to meet you," Shad says, shifting the baby

to one arm to shake my hand. "Matt talks about you constantly."

"So I've heard," I say, smiling.

"I'll take her," Matt says, already reaching for the baby.

Shad hands over Nora without hesitation, and the transformation in Matt is instantaneous. His entire body softens as he cradles the infant, cooing nonsense words to her. Nora responds with a delighted gurgle, her tiny hands reaching for his face and then his hair.

"She's beautiful," I say, stepping closer to peek at the baby's round face.

"Want to hold her?" Matt offers.

"Maybe later." I smile, but the truth is, babies make me nervous. I've never been around them much, and I don't want my non-maternal side to show right now.

Matt nods, understanding without me having to explain. He turns his attention back to Nora while Shad and Chanel start unpacking their picnic supplies.

"What can I do?" I ask, moving toward them.

"No, no." Matt quickly passes Nora back to Shad. "I'll get everything set up. You just relax."

Before I can protest, he's directing the entire operation—spreading blankets, arranging the cooler, positioning the picnic basket just so. Shad and Chanel simply follow his lead, as if this is completely normal.

"He's always like this," Chanel says, noticing my

expression. "Come on, let's sit and chat while the men do the heavy lifting."

She guides me to a spot on the blanket Matt has laid out, and we sit together, her with Nora lounging in her lap, watching as Matt organizes everything with military precision.

"So, how long have you known my brother?" Chanel asks.

"Oh, we go way back," I say with a smile. "A few years at ChemTech. Then he got promoted, and he was too good to talk to anyone who didn't work on the fifth floor."

Chanel looks horrified. "Really?"

Okay, so I can't make jokes like that. My smile straightens quickly. "No, I was kidding," I say. "I mean, it is harder to see people you don't work with as often. I'm sure it was just that."

"But you work on the fifth floor now too," Chanel says.

I nod as Matt pulls out various brightly colored pieces and starts to assemble them. Shock flows through me freely, because what is he doing?

"Yes," I say almost absently. "I got promoted to a Department Head position, oh, four or five months ago now." I leave out the part about my insane crush, and how hard I've worked to get Matt to notice me. How tortuous it's been to work right next door to him and have him not even *see* me. How I invited him to my friend's wedding as a last-ditch effort to get his attention.

With a horrible start, I wonder if all of those desperate acts are why Matt has taken me on. Is he just being nice? Does he just want me to feel good about myself?

Am I *project* to him?

"And you've been dating for about five weeks now," Chanel says.

I tear my eyes from the bouncy seat Matt is setting up. "Yes," I say, nodding at her. "That's right."

"And—what do you think of him?" There's something protective in her tone that makes me smile.

"He's..." I pause, searching for the right word. "He's incredibly thoughtful."

"Yeah, he's always been that way," Chanel says, her voice softening. "Even when we were kids."

"What was he like growing up?" I ask, genuinely curious about the boy who became the man I'm falling for.

Chanel glances over at her brother, who's now helping Shad with the portable grill. "He was always the responsible one. Our parents were..." She clears her throat, and I pat her hand.

"He's told me a few things about them," I say. "He mentioned that your dad left after his high school graduation, and you had what? Three years of high school left?"

"Yeah." She nods, her voice a bit of a ghost. "But honestly, Dad was checked out long before that. And Mom was always working, taking assignments overseas." Chanel picks at a loose thread on the blanket. "Matt basically raised me. He made sure I had breakfast every morning, packed my lunches, helped with homework. He was only fourteen, making grocery lists and figuring out how to stretch the cash my dad left for us."

I watch Matt as he laughs at something Shad says, bouncing Nora on his hip again. The image of teenage Matt taking on adult responsibilities settles heavily in my chest.

"He put off college until I graduated," Chanel says. "Made sure I finished high school. Then he went to MIT and *poured* himself into chemistry." She smiles, though there's sadness in it. "I think he needed an escape from his real life, and chemistry gave him that."

My heartstrings pull for him, because he's so handsome, and so smart, and so *good*.

She draws a big breath and exhales. "He's been back for a few years now. Walked me down the aisle. He's the perfect uncle. All of it."

"Yeah," I say. "All of it."

"It's just who he is," Chanel says. "Sometimes I worry about him, though. He's so busy making sure everyone else is okay that he forgets about himself."

Before I can respond, Matt calls over, "Food's ready, ladies!"

We join the men at the portable grill where Matt is serving up hamburgers and hot dogs. As we gather our food and settle back on the blanket, I notice how Matt makes sure everyone has what they need before serving himself.

He's still at the table, fixing his burger up when Shad says, "So Lizzie, Matt tells us you're a model as well as working at ChemTech?"

"It's more of a side gig," I say. "Though I did just finish a week-long shoot for a department store's spring catalog."

"She's amazing," Matt says, his eyes lighting up with pride as he finally makes it to the blanket. "You should see her portfolio."

"I'd love to," Chanel says. "I used to want to be a fashion designer before life had other plans." She glances fondly at Nora, who's now trying to get tiny chunks of cheese into her hand so she can eat them.

"Speaking of plans," Shad says, glancing over to Matt. "I've got that final interview at Prescott on Tuesday. They called last night to set it up."

"Nice, bro." Matt bumps his knuckles, and then adds, "We should prep for it. I can come over Monday night. We'll run through potential questions, make sure your suit is pressed—"

"Matt," Chanel interrupts gently. "Shad's got this. You already do a lot for us."

Matt looks momentarily taken aback, then shrugs. "Okay, yeah, of course."

A slight tension settles over the group, and I find myself reaching for Matt's hand. He squeezes mine gratefully.

"Is it time for dessert?" I ask. "Tahlia made the half chocolate chip, half brownie cookies I told you about, Matty."

He lights up. "The brookie."

"Oh, I have to see these," Chanel says.

I start to get up, but Matt beats me to it, and he retrieves the plastic container of brookies. "Wow-wow-wow," he says as he takes one out. "They're huge."

"I told you they were as big as your face." I hold one up in front of him, the half dark brownie batter cookie and half chocolate chip cookie obscuring his view. "See?"

"This is genius," Shad says as he takes a brookie.

Nora starts to fuss, and Matt turns to get her out of the play seat. "It's tummy time," he tells her, laying her face down on the blanket. He lays beside her, making silly faces that cause her to giggle.

I watch, thinking about all the ways Matt has taken care of me or made me laugh in our short time together. The Diet Coke he keeps stocked in his fridge even though he hates the stuff. The way he always opens doors, carries bags, makes sure I have everything I need.

It's sweet. Thoughtful. Considerate.

So why does it suddenly make me uneasy?

When it's time to leave, we say our goodbyes. Chanel hugs me tightly. "It was so good to meet you, Lizzie. You're exactly as wonderful as Matt described."

"Thank you," I say, genuinely touched. "It was great meeting you and Shad and Nora too." And I mean it. They are amazing people, and I'm so glad Matty has them in his life.

"Take care of my brother," she whispers before pulling away. "He deserves someone who sees him—*all* of him."

I nod, but I don't know what she means. Matt and I drive away, the afternoon sun casting long shadows across the road. Matt seems content, relaxed in a way I haven't seen before.

"Your family is lovely," I say.

"They liked you," he says. "Chanel texted me already."

I smile, but it feels forced. My thoughts are a jumble of everything I've learned today, everything I've observed.

"You're really good with Nora," I say after a moment.

"She makes it easy. She's a great baby."

"You're good with *everyone*. Making sure we all have what we need, taking care of everything."

Matt glances at me, no smile in sight. "Is that a bad thing?"

"No, of course not." I look out the window, gathering my thoughts. "It's just...you do a lot for other people. I wonder if anyone does the same for you."

He's quiet for a moment. "I don't need anything."

"Everyone needs something, Matt."

He reaches for my hand, holding it gently as he drives. "You're the best thing that's ever happened to me, Lizzie."

The words should make my heart soar. Instead, they land like lead in my stomach. Because in that moment, I see it clearly—the pattern, the role I'm filling. Another person for Matt to take care of. Another project. Another responsibility.

I smile weakly and squeeze his hand, but inside, doubt blooms like ink in water. Does Matt like me for who I am, or for how I fit into his need to be needed?

And more importantly, is there room in his life for someone who *doesn't* need to be saved?

CHAPTER TWENTY-ONE

MATT

I stare at my computer screen, the chemical formulation blurring before my eyes. Monday mornings are always rough, but this one feels boronically brutal. To save my sanity, I check my phone for the seventeenth time in an hour.

Nothing from Lizzie.

Something shifted after the picnic on Saturday. I can't pinpoint exactly what changed, but by Sunday morning, she was texting that she needed to "hang with the girls" at the Big House. Which was fine. Totally fine.

Except she canceled a Sunday afternoon movie date with me to do it.

Except she never rescheduled, and I have no idea when I'll see her again.

Except her texts since then have been brief, almost clinical.

Yes, work is fine.

Just busy with some things.

Talk to you tomorrow.

I rub my eyes and try to focus on batch 216, which is showing the same viscosity issues as the previous runs. But my mind keeps circling back to Lizzie's face in the car when she asked if *I* ever had someone take care of me. The way she squeezed my hand but wouldn't quite meet my eyes, I actually thought *she* might want to be the one to be at my side.

But now...something is definitely off.

My phone buzzes, and I snatch it up so fast I knock over my coffee. The dark brown liquid goes everywhere, and I blurt out, "Argon!" as I lift my phone away from the mess.

My folders and notes, however... A stain seeps through them, and I pocket my phone and head for the lounge to get paper towels. Maybe I'll get lucky and run into Lizzie there again, the way I did the day I got cake-i-fied.

She's not there. No one is there, and I grab the paper towels and head back to my office. Paper dries, so I mop everything up by pressing copious amounts of paper into the coffee and then lay the wet notes and folders out to dry.

When I finally get back to my phone, I find a message from Miranda. My eyes scan it, but I won't type out an answer with my thumbs. Sure enough, the same message has popped up in our chat, and I sigh mightily.

I need to turn up my volume, so I can tell the difference between an idiotic work thing and a text originating next door in my girlfriend's office.

Miranda wants to know if I got her email about the mixer calibration. Disappointment crashes through me at the same time irritation spikes. "There better not be anything wrong with that mixer," I gripe as I send her a quick response.

This is my whole morning, and I wish I could say it gets more exciting. About the only thing good that happens is my coffee-stained notes dry out. Now they're crispy as I pile them all up and put them back in the folder.

I glance at Lizzie's door when I exit my office, my stomach growling. We've eaten together since she moved to the fifth floor, and I have no reason to think today will be different.

My phone chimes, and I hurry away from our offices and toward the elevator. I've ordered her favorite pasta from her favorite Italian restaurant, and let me tell you, getting them to deliver it out here wasn't cheap.

Downstairs, I thank the driver, my smile so stupidly big as I head back to the fifth floor. My own brown bag lunch is still in the fridge in the lounge, but I can go get it in a minute. I can't wait to see Lizzie, but her door is closed.

I knock, already hearing her voice on the other side of the door. She laughs, and that only stretches my smile wider. She says something else, and I wonder who she's talking to.

I knock again, and she says something else. A moment later, the door opens a crack. "Oh, hey, Matt," she says.

I blink at her, because this is not how Girlfriend Lizzie has greeted me at work in the past several weeks.

No, this is how Work Lizzie acts. I hold up the plain white plastic sack with no identifying marks at all. "I got the penne with that brown butter walnut sauce you like." I glance past her as the door opens a little more. "Are you in a meeting?"

There's no one else in her office, but she says, "Kind of." She backs up, which I take as an invitation to enter the room. I do, and she adds, "Emma and I are doing a video call."

She slips past me and goes behind her desk, her eyes saying so much to me as she sits down. "Sorry, Em. Give me a minute."

"Yeah, it's fine," Emma says, and she doesn't exactly sound happy.

Lizzie taps a button—hopefully to mute us—and closes her laptop partway. "Matt, I'm sorry, but she needs a good talking to about Aaron."

"Oh? Is there something wrong?"

"Yeah, she wants to get engaged." Lizzie sighs. "And

she's not sure what he's waiting for, so you know. It's like me trying to play chess with someone who speaks a different language."

I smile at her and set the bag with her special-delivery lunch on the desk. I see she's already started to eat her lunch—a Cobb salad drenched in ranch dressing. I blink away from it, something pinching between my ribs.

"Good luck," I say, the way Work Matt would've two months ago. Like he's just talking to his colleague, not the woman he's fantasized about kissing for the past several weeks.

This is far, far worse, because I've actually kissed Lizzie now—it was my reality—but it feels like it happened to someone else.

"I'll see you later, I guess," I say, already turning away.

"Matty," she says.

"If you don't want it right now, just take it home for dinner," I say.

"Thank you," she calls as I reach the door and start to swing it closed behind me.

"Yep." The door closes with a mighty click and a semi-slam that somehow sounds final.

I stand in the hallway like I don't know which way to turn. Left or right? Where does that hallway go? I look back to my office, then step in that direction.

"What is happening?" I ask myself in my closed-door office. I stand at the windows and look out at the world. In my head, I can't see where things went wrong.

We filled out the paperwork. We had amazing dates. She invited me to her photo shoot. I met her friends, her father. She knows my cats; I introduced her to the only family I really care about and talk to.

Someone knocks on my door, and I turn as if on auto-pilot. "Yeah," I say.

Byron opens the door, and he's holding my lunch. "Salazar is cleaning out the fridge, and he was about to throw this away."

I take a few steps toward him to get my lunch. "Thanks."

"You're not eating with Lizzie today?" he asks.

"She's doing a call with one of her roommates." I flash a tight smile and pray he'll leave.

Instead, he sits in the only chair opposite my desk. Byron watches me for a moment. "Are you guys okay?"

"Yes, of course," I say too quickly. Then, "I don't know. Maybe not." I look to the wall we share, wishing for the thousandth time that I could see through it, see what Lizzie is doing over there, hear what she's saying.

He gets up and closes the door before retaking his seat. "Want to talk about it?"

"Not really." I pick up a pen and start clicking it, my lunch still forgotten in its sad brown bag. "It's probably nothing."

"Sure." Byron offers me a kind smile, and he's a great guy. A family man, with a wife and kids, who's always helped me and been nice to me. "That's why you're stress-clicking and look like someone kicked your cat."

I set the pen down very deliberately, trying to decide how much to tell him. I don't want to betray any of Lizzie's confidence. "She's been...a tiny bit distant since the picnic with my family on Saturday. And I don't know why."

"Did something happen there?"

"No, it was great. Chanel and Shad loved her. They've been texting me all weekend about her." I run a hand through my hair. "Everything was fine."

"Maybe that's the problem," Byron says.

"What do you mean?"

"Sometimes people need space, not solutions." He shrugs. "My wife tells me that all the time. Apparently, I try to fix everything instead of just listening."

I stare at him. "Listening," I say. "I listen to her."

"Yeah, my wife says I *think* I listen, but I actually don't." He gives me a smile that feels sad on the edges. "She tells me I have to listen *without* the intent to do anything. The listening *is* the doing."

"I don't even know what that means," I say, completely confused now.

Byron laughs. "I don't either, buddy, but I've managed to stay married for nine years, so I must be getting better at it." His phone chimes, and he heaves a heavy sigh. "Lab four is going to be the death of me." He stands up and heads for the door. "Just try to listen without the intent to do anything."

After he leaves, I pull out my phone with the *intent* to text my sister and ask her what in the aluminum Byron means.

I think something's wrong with me and Lizzie. She's been acting weird since the picnic. I look up. "I knew I shouldn't have invited her to that thing."

Still, I don't know what was so bad about it. Panic races through me, because if the picnic was fine, then the problem lies within...me. I'm the only other reason she'd take five giant steps back the way she has.

Did you ask her what's wrong? Chanel asks.

Not yet. I'm trying to figure out what I did first.

What makes you think you did something wrong?

"Well, what other reason could there be, Chanel?" I mutter the words as I text-stab them into my phone. I hit send and toss my phone onto my desk, suddenly unwilling to have this conversation.

I tear into my lunch and eat it without tasting a bite. I eye my phone with disgust but pick it up as I swallow my last bite of sandwich. Chanel has texted a couple of times.

Matty, you're a great guy. Surely it's nothing you've done. If anything you do TOO much.

You should just talk to her.

I stare at the text, a knot forming in my stomach. It's the second time today someone has implied I'm trying to *do* things.

I do too much? I ask her, thinking about the lunch I ordered and delivered to Lizzie...without even asking her.

Never mind, I type out quickly, because I've already answered my own question. *It's fine. I'll just talk to her.*

I force myself to focus on work for the rest of the afternoon, though my mind keeps spinning to Lizzie. By the time I get home, I'm a bundle of nervous energy with no outlet.

I make the cats a gourmet dinner, all the while wondering if Lizzie is enjoying her pasta feast for dinner. I expect her to text me, then shake my head. She hasn't texted all afternoon. Why would she suddenly tonight?

I think about texting her while Purricell and Purroxide chow down, but I reject the idea instantly.

"What do you think, guys?" I ask Purricell and Purroxide as I pace my living room. "Should I call her?"

Purricell yawns widely, clearly unimpressed with my romantic dilemma.

"You're right. I should give her space." I nod decisively. "But I can still work on our Halloween costumes. That's not pushy, right? That's just being prepared."

The cats watch with judgment as I open my laptop and start searching for lab coat patterns and glow-in-the-dark accessories for our Marie and Pierre Curie costumes. I make a detailed list of everything we'll need, including specific makeup for Lizzie to look appropriately radiated.

"This is going to be perfect," I tell Purroxide, who has settled on the couch beside me. "She's going to love it."

By midnight, I've ordered everything we need, created a timeline for costume assembly, and even practiced my French accent for the party. The cats have long since abandoned me for their beds, but I'm too wired to sleep.

I pick up my phone, finger hovering over Lizzie's contact. It's too late to call, but maybe a text...that's not too much, right? Only a week ago, we stayed up until this time, texting back and forth like mad.

Just wanted to say goodnight. Miss you.

I stare at the screen, waiting for those three dots to appear that tell me she's responding. They don't.

The next morning, I arrive at ChemTech forty-five minutes early, stopping at the Snickerdoodle Porch for Lizzie's favorite cinnamon roll and a Diet Coke with cherry and vanilla. I leave them on her desk with a note:

Got all our costume supplies! Will have everything ready by Saturday. Can't wait for the party. - M

I'm back in my office when I hear her arrive. There's

a pause, then the soft click of her heels as she approaches my door. My heart leaps, but she doesn't knock. Instead, she sends a text.

Thanks for breakfast! You didn't have to do that.

My pleasure, I say. *Want to grab lunch today?*

I can't. She does include a crying emoji, so that's something. *I just found out about a filing I have to have done by five p.m.* Eyeroll emoji.

I stare at my phone, disappointment washing over me despite the two emojis. *I can bring you something.*

I brought a lunch, she says. *I just need to focus and get things done.*

A strange hollowness expands in my chest. This isn't like Lizzie. She's always been direct, forthright. If something was bothering her, she'd tell me.

Unless what's bothering her is me.

The thought hits like a chemical burn, unexpected and searing. What if I'm the problem? What if all my efforts to be helpful, to be thoughtful, are actually pushing her away?

I try to focus on work, but I can't. I need to know what's going on. So I walk next door and knock, maybe a little harder than I mean to. When she calls "Come in," I push open the door to find her surrounded by stacks of papers, her hair pulled back into a crisp ponytail, a Diet Coke can perched precariously on top of a binder.

"Hey," I say, hovering in the doorway.

"Hey." She doesn't look up from her computer.

"Can we talk?"

That gets her attention. She looks up, those blue-green eyes meeting mine for what feels like the first time in days. "Sure." She blinks. "What's going on?"

"Whatever's going on with you." I step into her office and close the door behind me, pressing my back to the wood. "You've been...things have been weird since the picnic. Did I do something wrong?"

"No," she says too quickly. "I've just been busy."

"Lizzie." I move closer to her desk but don't sit down. "I'm not stupid." I've had plenty of women break up with me, and this is so leading to that.

She sighs and leans back in her chair, those eyes flaming at me. "I'm worried about you."

"Worried about me?" The air leaves my lungs, and I sag into the seat in front of her. "Why?"

"The constant helping. The fixing. The taking care of everything." She stands up, moving to the window. "You're always doing things for me, for Chanel, for everyone. Making sure we're all okay."

"Okay," I say, not getting it.

"Do you even know who you are outside of taking care of people?" She turns to face me, her expression a mix of frustration and something that looks dangerously like pity.

I absolutely don't like that. "I know who I am," I say, and my voice sounds like I've swallowed iron.

"Do you know how to just be with someone without trying to solve all their problems?"

"I'm just trying to help," I say, the words coming out defensive.

"That's the problem." She grabs her purse from her desk drawer. "I don't need you to fix everything for me. I need you to see me as an equal, not a project."

My mouth opens, but no words come out. A project? Is that what she thinks?

"I have to go," she says, slipping past me toward the door. "Byron and Randy are waiting for me in the lounge."

Byron and Randy—what?

Before I can speak, she's gone, the door clicking shut behind her, leaving me sitting alone in her office, her words echoing in my head.

That's the problem.

I sink back into the chair, the scent of her perfume surrounding me. My chest tightens, like something is pressing against my ribcage, making it hard to breathe.

My mind blurs through thoughts as I consider how I've been with her—trying to bring her the things she likes, planning to take her to her favorite places, making sure she's comfortable. I thought I was being thoughtful. Considerate. A good boyfriend.

But maybe I've been suffocating her instead.

The realization hits me with the force of a chemical

explosion, shattering everything I thought I knew about myself.

If Lizzie's right—if I don't know who I am outside of taking care of people—then what happens if I stop? Who am I then?

And more terrifyingly: if I can't be the fixer, the helper, the caretaker...will anyone still want me around?

CHAPTER TWENTY-TWO

LIZZIE

THE BACK OF THE BIG HOUSE GLOWS WITH SOFT lights coming from the kitchen windows. Since Tahlia's a teacher, she usually gets home before anyone else. Emma's flower shop is open until six, so she can catch men on their way home from work who need flowers to make it through the front door.

I commute the furthest, but Em and I usually get home about the same time. Except not tonight. Tonight, I waited behind the safety of my office door until almost everyone had left ChemTech. When only the night security remained in the building did I leave, and I drove into the city to get cookies before returning to this quieter, more quaint suburb where the Big House sits on five beautiful acres.

I've always loved living here, loved this house, loved

my roommates. At the same time, I've been dreaming of bigger, better things—namely a husband and family.

I've had no luck in finding such things, but I thought I had a real chance with Matt.

"You still do." I reach for another oatmeal cookie and ignore my phone as it chimes softly from inside my purse. It'll just be Em or Tahlia, asking where I am now. I told them I had some errands to run after work, and I'd be home later. I've been parked in the back lot for about thirty minutes now, because I don't want to go inside and tell them I may have ruined the only good thing I've had in the dating scene in years.

But the lights don't go out, and my stomach complains that I've only fed it cookies for dinner. Sighing, I collect my things and head inside the house. The back door slams in the annoying way it has when I forget to catch it, and the noise draws the attention of both Emma and Tahlia, who stand at the island, a single mixing bowl between them.

"Hey," Emma says, looking over with a smile that quickly fades. "Whoa. What happened to you?" She faces me fully, her blue eyes as wide as the moon.

"Nothing." I drop my purse on the dining room table with more force than necessary and head straight for the fridge. Maybe I can hid my face in there. "Everything's fine."

A beat of silence fills the kitchen, wherein I'm sure Tahlia exchanges a glance with Emma. "Sure," Emma says. "You always look like you want to murder someone when everything's fine."

I pull out a Diet Coke and crack it open, taking a long swig before I trust myself to speak. "It's just been a bad day."

"A bad day?" Tahlia asks. "Or a bad Matt day?"

The sound of his name makes my chest tighten. I knew I couldn't simply sneak in after they'd vacated the kitchen. I'd told them—told everyone, even our friends who don't live here anymore—about my fears concerning Matt.

I close my eyes and lean against the counter, the cold aluminum can pressed against my forehead. "Augusta."

"That bad, huh?" Tahlia abandons whatever they're baking and comes to stand in front of me. "What happened?"

The dam breaks. "I walked out on him at work today." I set the can down with a thud and meet her eyes, suddenly so angry. Not at him. Or her.

But myself.

"He brought me breakfast this morning—which was sweet, I guess—but then I told him I was busy for lunch, and he showed up in my office that afternoon anyway, wanting to talk."

"The nerve," Emma says, and I give her a fierce glare.

"You don't understand." I start pacing the kitchen. "It's not just bringing me breakfast. It's...it's everything.

That food last night. Him ordering the Halloween costumes and planning everything for the party. He's never in a bad mood, and he never takes time for himself. He's constantly doing things for me, for his sister, for everyone. Making sure we're all okay, that we have everything we need."

I only cut off because I run out of air. My chest heaves, and it's so tight I swear someone has mummified me.

"Sounds terrible," Tahlia says. "A thoughtful boyfriend who wants to make you happy by bringing you things you like and who wants to make your life easier by helping with party prep."

"Yeah, I totally want Aaron to be in a terrible mood every time I see him," Emma says. Neither of them wear a smile, but their voices drip with sarcasm. "I can see why you're upset."

I stop pacing and glare at both them. "It's not about him being thoughtful. It's about *why* he's thoughtful." Because otherwise, I'm the Wicked Witch of Both the East and the West.

Emma pulls out a barstool. "Sit. Explain."

"Yeah, because you said you had concerns about Matt on Sunday," Tahlia says. "But this is—him doing nice things for the people in his life doesn't feel like it should be a concern."

I sink onto the stool, suddenly exhausted. "Okay, real truth."

"Real truth," Emma says.

"I've always thought Matt was absolutely wonderful. He's sunny and happy and has a great laugh."

"I'm putting all of that in the Pro-column," Tahlia says as she measures a half-teaspoon of baking powder into the bowl.

"He works hard, and he's smart, and he's handsome, but..."

Tahlia looks at her recipe, and Emma actually turns her back on me to get the bag of semi-sweet chocolate chips out of the pantry.

"I think—" I'm not sure I can say it out loud, but maybe if I do, it'll sound utterly ridiculous. Then I can call Matt and apologize, and everything will be fine.

But what it if rings with truth? Then what am I going to do? I don't want to break-up with Matt, not when we just started this relationship that has been so much fun.

"I think I might just be another project for him," I say. "Another person he needs to take care of. Another way for him to feel good about himself."

"Why would you think that?" Tahlia asks, glancing at me before she fits the bowl into the stand mixer.

"His sister told me how he basically raised her, even while they had parents at home, and especially after their dad left. How he put off college to make sure she graduated high school. How he still helps her and her husband financially."

I drop my eyes, unable to hold their gazes. "And that's all admirable."

"Yeah, I'd put all of that in the Pro-column too," Emma says.

I wipe the condensation off my soda can. "He's a fixer, and he gets his worth and value from being the one to help everyone, make everything right."

I know, because my mother was like that.

"And that's...bad?" Emma looks genuinely confused.

"No, it's not bad. It's who he is." I sigh, trying to find the words to explain the knot of unease that's been growing in my stomach since the picnic. I look up at them, wishing I knew how to explain better.

"But I don't want him to be with me because *I'm* another responsibility. Because he thinks I need him to save me, or help me, or, or, or swoop in and help me find another job, or buoy me up about my modeling, or agree to every little thing I want, because he thinks that's what I need."

I look at them, willing them both to understand. "I want him to be my partner—and I want to be his. Not his project. Not another test in the lab, where if we dial down bringing in breakfast, he can jack up organizing all our family meals and get-togethers."

My chest hurts, and I pull in one breath, and then another.

Emma stands there, silent and still, one hand resting

on the chocolate chips. "Yeah, I wouldn't want that either," she finally says.

"Has he said that's how he sees your relationship?" Tahlia asks.

"He doesn't have to say it. It's in everything he does." I run a hand through my hair. "The constant little gifts. The way he anticipates what I might need before I even know I need it. How he's always checking to make sure I'm okay. If he asks me one more time if I'm okay..." I let the threat hang there, because I don't know what I'll do. Maybe burst into plasma flames and start shooting out oozing balls of fire.

"It *does* sound like he cares about you," Emma says gently.

"Or maybe he just needs to be needed." I meet her eyes. "What if that's all this is? What if he doesn't actually want me for *me*, but for how I fit into his need to take care of people?"

Tahlia sits down across from me. "Lizzie, honey, I think you might be overthinking this."

"Am I, though?" I stand up again, unable to stay still. "His sister even said she worries about him, because he's so busy making sure everyone else is okay that he forgets about himself. What kind of relationship can we have if he doesn't even know who he is outside of taking care of others?"

Emma blinks and blinks. "Have you talked to him about this?"

"I tried today. Sort of." I sink back onto the barstool, remembering the hurt in his eyes when I said I didn't need him to fix everything. "I told him I needed him to see me as an equal, not a project. And then I...left."

"You left?" Tahlia's eyebrows shoot up. "In the middle of the conversation?"

"I panicked. I told him Byron and Randy were waiting for me in the lounge."

"Were they?" Emma asks.

"No." I drop my head into my hands. "Oh, Canary Islands." Not technically a US city, but a great, high-lever swear nonetheless. Tears prick my eyes, and I close them. Doesn't matter. My voice comes out nasally when I ask, "I messed up, didn't I?"

"Oh, Lizzie." Tahlia comes around the counter and wraps her arms around me. "I get that you're worried about his motives, but you have to talk to him."

"I know." My voice comes out small and muffled through my fingers. "I just—I don't know what to do. I really like him. Maybe more than like him. But I can't shake this feeling that I'm just...an ego-boost. Someone else for him to rescue."

"What would he need to rescue you from?" Emma asks.

"My grumpy attitude," I say quickly. "My unhappiness with my job. My indecision about my future." I raise my head and look at her. "I know you don't get it, because you have Aaron, and you're going to marry him and sail off into his new house, and all that. But me and Tahlia are *still here.*"

I gesture to her, cataloging the pinch of hurt in her eyes. "And it sucks. It *sucks* to be left behind while everyone else is so blissfully happy." I lay my head down again, already regretting saying anything.

Emma steps back from the counter and looks over to Tahlia. "I know that," she says. "I'm still here too."

"But you have Aaron," Tahlia says gently. "It's not the same, and don't worry about us, Em." She shakes her head and wipes at the corner of her eye quickly. "Really, don't. But Lizzie's also right, and she's liked Matt for a long time, and—" She cuts off and looks at me with worry in her pretty eyes. "I think it hurts that maybe he doesn't see her as a worthy romantic partner, but a chemistry experiment that needs to be fiddled with and solved."

That's it exactly, and I give her one nod. "Don't tell the others I said anything," I say. "I'm happy for you all, I swear, and I'm sorry, Em. I don't mean to make this about you and Aaron."

She nods, her mouth tight.

"Really, I'm sorry."

Tahlia picks up the bag of chocolate chips. "Maybe Matt isn't playing chemist," she says. "Maybe him taking care of you is just how he shows love."

The word "love" makes my stomach flip. "Maybe. Or maybe he doesn't know how to be in a relationship without taking on the caretaker role." And I don't need another dad.

"I think you need to talk to him," Emma says. "Really talk to him. Tell him how you're feeling."

"And what if I'm right?" I raise my head again, the fear I've been trying to ignore finally bubbling to the surface. "What if he only wants me because he has some Savior complex?"

Tahlia squeezes my shoulder. "Then you'll know. But what if you're wrong?"

The question hangs in the air, unanswered. What if I am?

———

THE NEXT MORNING, I arrive at ChemTech early, determined to have a real conversation with Matt. No running away this time. I've rehearsed what I want to say, trying to be honest about my concerns without hurting him more than I already have.

He texted an apology last night, and I didn't want to talk to him through my fingers. I want to look him in the face and have a real conversation.

I'm at my desk reviewing documents when a soft knock sounds at my door. That's got Matt's *I-don't-want-to-bother-you* vibes written all over it.

I get to my feet and brace myself for battle before I

remind myself—no. This isn't a battle. It's a conversation with a man I do not want to break-up with.

I invited him here by leaving a bag of cookies on his desk and asking him to come see me when he had a minute today.

My heartbeat ricochets through my chest, and yet, I'm somehow able to say, "Come in."

Matt enters, wearing the same sexy-chemist attire he does every day. Dark slacks, that fitted button up—today's is in pale yellow—with a tie knotted just-so at his neck. His hair is slightly disheveled, like he's been running his hands through it, and there are shadows under his eyes that suggest he didn't sleep well either.

"Morning," he says, his voice careful, neutral. "You didn't have to get me cookies."

His statement echoes exactly what I texted him yesterday about bringing me breakfast. My resolve wavers at the sight of him looking so unhappy, so guarded, so...un-Matt.

"Matt," I say. "We need to talk."

"I know." He puts the bag of cookies that he brought with him on my desk and sits down. "I've been thinking about what you said yesterday."

I return to my seat too, because this isn't a stand-off. "Okay."

His eyes flit around my office, finally landing somewhere out the window behind me. "I don't—I think you might be right."

His words crush my lungs. Just flatten them into crepes, with the two pieces mushed together. I don't know how to breathe like this, and it seems wholly unfair that Matt takes a deep breath.

"I—maybe I'm a little over-the-top with Chanel. That relationship—it's always been me watching out for her. I can't even tell you how many times my mom told me to 'watch out for Chanel, Matty. Watch out for Chanel.'"

He speaks with a bitter undertone to his voice, and that's exactly what I don't want. I never, *ever* want him to think of me like that. Like he's just "watching out for me" out of duty. Absolutely not. That is no relationship to covet.

"I'm really sorry," I say. "That wasn't fair of her."

"Even now, on the one or two times every year that I talk to her, she asks me how Chanel is doing." He shakes his head. "That's not why I'm here. I just—I didn't realize I was doing the same thing to you, or how it would make you feel."

I lean forward, willing him to understand. "I appreciate the gestures, I do. But sometimes it feels like...like you're more focused on taking care of me than on just being with me."

"That's not—" He stops, running a hand through his hair. "I do those things because I care about you. Because I want you to be happy."

"But what about you?" I search his face, desperate

for him to hear me. "Do you even know who you are outside of taking care of everyone else? Do you even know what *you* want? What makes *you* happy? Who you think you could spend *your* life with?"

His expression shifts, something vulnerable and simultaneously angry flashing in his eyes. "Not really," he admits, and it makes my heart hurt.

"So your whole identity *is* wrapped up in being needed." The words come out harsher than I intend, and I see him flinch. "I'm sorry. I don't mean to hurt you. I just...I need to know that you want to be with me because of who I am, not because I'm someone else you can get your own importance from."

I stand up, needing to move—and stop looking at him. He's so...downtrodden, and Matthew Giles is never downtrodden. "Maybe we just need to take a break," I say to the windows and the world beyond. "You might not even want to be with me once you figure out—" I wave to the sunshine outside. "If you aren't getting anything from the relationship except validation that you're a good person, maybe we shouldn't be together."

"I think we're great together," he says.

I turn to face him. "But *I* need you to *want* to be with me—and to see me—as an equal partner in the relationship." I press one palm to my heart. "Not because bringing me breakfast and taking me to my favorite restaurant makes you feel good about yourself."

"Can't both be true?" He looks at me with a hint of confusion, plenty of defiance, and a touch of hurt.

"Maybe," I say, feeling braver and braver by the moment. "I don't want to break up, Matty. I just want you to take a break from me to figure out who you are inside a relationship where your partner doesn't *need* your money, doesn't *need* you to plan the perfect date, doesn't *need* you for anything. Where she *wants* you for you, and she wants you whether you forget what her favorite soda is, or are running late, or have rabid, naughty cats who'll break all her fine china and shred all her childhood stuffed animals she hasn't been able to get rid of yet."

I've said too much, and I sink back into my office chair, spent. I want to replace all the she's I just said to I's, but I'm not quite that brave yet.

"And you know what?" I say, somehow finding more words. I must be channeling my inner-Matt. "*You* deserve to be in a relationship with someone you *want* too. Not just someone who *needs* something from you all the time."

He sits tall and straight, and for the first time ever, he has nothing to say.

"It's not a break up," I say again. "Just a tiny break."

Matt nods, runs his hand through his hair, and stands up. Panic streams through me, because I can't fathom him walking out without saying anything.

He moves toward the door, his movements stiff. "I

just want you to be happy, Lizzie. Even if that means..."
He doesn't finish the sentence, and I wonder what he'll
put there.

He knows I'm not happy in this job. He knows I'm
looking for something else. He knows I want to be with
him. He knows I want him to be happy too. Doesn't he?

He meets my gaze for a moment, a sad smile
touching his lips, and then he's gone.

I stare at the closed door for a long moment, then
reach for my phone. I can't stay here today, not with him
right next door. I call my boss, claim I'm in the deathly
throes of a migraine, and head home to the empty Big
House.

In my bedroom and out of my restricting pencil skirt,
I curl up under the covers, finally letting the tears come.
My phone sits on the nightstand, silent and accusing. I
pick it up and scroll through my contacts, pausing when
I reach Matt's name. It's still listed under favorites, with
a little heart emoji next to it.

I should call him. Tell him I was wrong, and everything is fine between us. Being with him, even if it's not
for the right reason, is way better than being without
him.

But I don't.

Instead, I set down the phone and stare at the ceiling, wondering if I've just thrown away something
precious and wonderful because of my own fears.

I close my eyes and let the tears burn, praying that

when Matt figures out who he is and what he wants, that I'll be on the list.

MATT

THE TOWNHOUSE SMELLS A BIT...CATTY WHEN I walk in Wednesday evening. I immediately stop and look around while Purricell and Purroxide swarm around my ankles. I drop my keys on the entryway table with a clatter that seems to echo through the rooms.

"What did you get into today?" I ask them, my voice flat even to my own ears. I don't see anything out of place, nothing broken, no scratches on my sofa, nothing.

So it's just me who's off.

Purricell meows loudly several times, following me into the kitchen. He jumps up onto the counter, Purroxide not far behind him. They stare at me intently while I try to remember where I am and what I'm doing.

I'm aimless without Lizzie to anchor me. "Is that love?" I ask. "Is that me acknowledging what I want? Does this tell me who I am?"

She's asked me such hard questions, and I frown as I finally remember the cats want dinner. I mechanically fill their food bowls and set them on the ground at the end of the island. Purroxide weaves between my legs, more affectionate than he's been in months.

"At least you two still need me," I mutter, watching them eat. The thought brings no comfort, because apparently being needed is not a good thing.

My phone buzzes in my pocket—probably Chanel wondering why I'm not at our standing Wednesday dinner. I can't face her right now.

Do you even know who you are outside of taking care of everyone else? Do you even know what you want? What makes you happy? Who you think you could spend your life with?

No, nope, nopety-nope, and no, I don't.

I know my day has been the worst one of my life. I know Lizzie left her office almost immediately after I did. I know I've hated every minute of today where I didn't think I could text her and get a flirty answer in return.

Lizzie's questions echo in my head as I wander into the living room and collapse onto the couch. I stare at the ceiling, trying to quiet the storm in my mind.

Who am I if I'm not the guy who fixes everything? The guy who takes care of everyone? The guy who anticipates needs before they're even expressed?

I have no idea.

My parents trained me to be that guy, and I have no idea how to *not* do it.

My phone buzzes again. And again. I finally pull it out with a sigh that can only be categorized as the sigh of the century.

My sister is relentless, and every text makes my lungs a little tighter.

Are you coming for dinner tonight? Nora's been asking for Uncle Matty.

She can't talk yet, but I can tell.

Is everything okay?

I hate disappointing my sister, but then I think, *It's just dinner. She's going to eat it with or without me.*

My presence in her house won't matter. She doesn't need me there.

Doesn't. Need. Me. There.

The words are harsh, but they also feel a little... cleansing. Immediate guilt floods me, but I push back against it. "Chanel doesn't need me to watch out for her."

I sit up, energy buzzing through my veins. "Chanel and Shad don't need me to watch out for them," I say. "They're perfectly capable adults, and they do *not* need me."

The words fill the house, both levels, and stream out into the world. "Hear that, Mom?" I mutter. "It's not my job to watch out for Chanel."

I can't believe the level of animosity I have toward

my parents. Maybe it's always been there, but I've stuffed it way down deep and used other means to try to convince myself that I'm a valuable, desirable man.

Purricell jumps onto the couch and comes toward me, settling on my lap, his weight solid and real. He stares at me with those intelligent eyes, and I scratch behind his ears.

"I need to figure things out," I tell him. "I don't know how, but I do."

My laptop sits on the side table, work files waiting for review. I should distract myself. Should do something productive. But the energy required to reach for it seems monumental.

Instead, I lie there, a chemical engineer Department Head who can't figure out the formula for his own life.

———

THE NEXT MORNING, I arrive at ChemTech at 6:30 AM, determined to avoid any chance of running into Lizzie. The fifth floor is eerily quiet, most of the offices dark. I slip into mine, closing the door firmly behind me.

At some point, I feel the humming energy of the fifth floor, but I keep my door closed, something I rarely do. I can communicate with my team via our chats, and it's not technically required for me to leave my office to eat lunch with anyone, or go down to the labs where the processes I oversee take place.

I usually do it, because I hate being cooped up inside the same four walls all day long—even if one of them is made completely of windows.

I seize onto this bit of information about myself, and I pause in a chat to Miranda about the new calibration on the scanner.

"I hate being cooped up inside all day," I say. "I like getting out of the office, because it's something *I* want to do."

As I'm basking in this part of myself that does what he wants, a message pops up on the screen from the Regulatory VP. *Elizabeth is out again today. Can someone get me the Countess file? She says everything is in it, and it's in the second drawer of her filing cabinet. The office is unlocked.*

I lean forward, my hands automatically sliding onto the keyboard to answer. I can totally do that, and maybe Lizzie will see—

"Yeah." I pull back from the computer and keyboard like they're covered in lava and I'm just now noticing. "That's exactly what'll happen. Lizzie will *see* how eager-beaver you are to help her out."

It's not exactly her, I think.

"You're not doing this," I argue back out loud.

Part of me wails, because I want to be seen as a team player. I want others to like me, and think I'm great, and—

I so get my worth from what I do for others. The real problem is, I have no idea how to stop that.

"Just sit here," I say, staring at the message as the seconds tick by. No one else answers it, and I wonder if they think I'll jump in and save the day. After all, I usually do.

"Not usually," I growl to myself. "Always."

Well, not today. I fold my arms and stare at the message, the seconds becoming a minute, and then two.

This message has taught me a lot about myself, as well as the fact that Lizzie isn't here. I won't have to see her. "No," I say. "I won't *get* to see her."

And I *want* to see her.

Another message pops up, and to my great relief, it's Ken saying he knows where Lizzie's files are, and he'll grab the right one and take it upstairs. I sag in my chair, close the message, and go back to where I left off with Miranda.

Something weird and strange fills me. Almost like pride that I didn't jump in and save the day. It's unsettling, really, and I don't quite know what to do with myself.

To keep my mind off my problems, I throw myself into work, reviewing formulations, answering emails, attending meetings where I say as little as possible. I stay until nearly eight, long after most people have left. The building is quiet again as I walk to my car, the emptiness matching the hollow feeling in my chest.

A package waits on my front porch when I get home, and I eye it like it'll have a nest of snakes inside. I pull into the garage and go inside, greet the cats with, "Hey, fellas," and get them fed before I step out the front door to collect the box.

I scan the label, and when I see who it's from, I drop it. Halloween Haven.

These are mine and Lizzie's costumes. The ones I put together, thinking she'd surely fall in love with me then. The ones she never even signed off on.

Pure foolishness fills me as I stare down at the package. Two lab coats—his and hers. Glow-in-the-dark accessories. Special makeup to make us look like we've been exposed to radiation. Everything for our Marie and Pierre Curie costumes.

For a Halloween party I'm probably no longer invited to.

"Fluorine," I mutter, the chemistry swear slipping out as I continue to stare at the box. I drop my head into my hands, fingers digging into my scalp.

This is what Lizzie was talking about. I ordered all this without even asking what she wanted. I just assumed. I planned everything, because that's what I do. I take care of things. I make sure everything's perfect.

I didn't get how much of a problem my obsessive need to please people is until this moment.

"That's not even it," I say. "You don't need to please

people." Though I do. "You need to do things for them, so they'll like you."

So I can be important. So I can have worth.

I sigh and pick up the box. It is supposed to rain overnight, after all, and I can probably return this stuff and get my money back, but not if it gets ruined in the rain.

I set the box on the kitchen counter and stare at it some more. Purroxide jumps onto the counter next to it, sniffing curiously.

"Don't even think about it," I warn, but there's no heat in my voice. I'm too emotionally spent to discipline the felines.

My phone buzzes, and I pull it out of my pocket. I haven't looked at it in hours, because every time I do, and there's nothing from Lizzie, I want to crunch the device into bits with my bare hands.

Now, I see I've received twelve texts from Chanel, and I've missed three calls. She had plenty to say about me missing dinner last night and not even "having the decency" to text her to say I wasn't coming.

You could've been dead in a ditch, she'd said.

I didn't respond to that message either.

But her latest message makes my breath catch:

SHAD GOT THE JOB!!!!! Call me!!!!

Yes, she has a bit of an exclamation point abuse problem. Apparently, everyone in my family needs therapy.

A surge of happiness cuts through my fog. Shad got

the job. My brother-in-law, who's been struggling for months, finally caught a break. They won't need my financial help anymore. They'll be okay.

And I had nothing to do with it.

The realization hits me like a punch to the gut. Shad did this on his own. Without my help. Without my interview coaching or my business connections or anything to do with me at all.

I should be happy about that. I *am* happy about that. But there's also a weird emptiness that comes with it, a strange sense of...loss I don't fully understand.

I don't respond to Chanel's text. Instead, I pick up the costume box and move it to the corner behind the table and go to bed, the cats following close behind.

"You've got to figure out who you are," I tell myself as I change out of my work clothes.

No, you've got to figure out how to be the man Lizzie wants.

Absolutely not, a third argument comes in. *You've got to figure out what you want, because that'll define who you are.*

"But what if Lizzie doesn't like that person?"

Then so be it, both internal voices say.

———

FRIDAY MORNING DAWNS bright and clear, and I wake with a strange sense of determination. I still feel like boron nitride—hard, brittle, and definitely not shiny —but there's something else there too. A tiny spark of something that might be resolve.

Today, I'm going to try to figure out who Matt Giles is when he's not taking care of everyone else.

I get to work at a normal time. When Miranda asks if I can help with a project that's behind schedule, I take a deep breath and say, "I can't today. I have my own deadlines to meet."

The words feel foreign in my mouth, but also...right. I don't offer an alternative solution. Don't volunteer to stay late to help. I just say no.

Miranda is a professional, and she sighs. "Yeah, they've got us all under the knife right now," she says and walks away. The world doesn't end. ChemTech doesn't collapse. Life goes on.

No one *needs* me.

I still feel like someone has removed a vital organ, but I'm learning that maybe it's like my appendix. It only hurts when it's not functioning properly, and then once it's taken out, everything is right as rain again.

Please, let this be like appendicitis—and I bet no one has ever thought that before.

Another request to get something from Lizzie's office comes in. I once again ignore it, and Byron says he'll get the file.

I focus on myself and what I want, and that's to leave early on this fine fluorescent Friday. I even smile at my own lame joke, one that no one would get but me.

I eat lunch at my desk—alone, and I didn't pack any chocolate-covered almonds—scrolling mindless social media on my phone. When I tire of that, I decide it's time to text my sister.

That's amazing news! Congrats to Shad. He deserves it.

I've barely looked away from my phone after hitting send when she says, *Where have you been?? Are you okay?? I called the hospital, and they didn't have any Matthew Giles.*

You did not call the hospital. I scoff out loud.

Fine, I didn't, but I thought about it. Then I remembered I could see your pin, and you were just at home. She leaves that sitting there, but I'm not going to take the bait. I don't owe her an explanation or a play-by-play of my Thursday evening.

I can see you're at ChemTech, so you must not be sick.

I'm fine, I say.

Then come over tonight to celebrate!!

My instinct is to say yes. To rush over with champagne and presents for Nora and offers to help them with whatever they need during this transition. But I pause, finger hovering over the keyboard.

Is that what I *want* to do? Or is that what I think I *should* do?

I'm still figuring that out when my phone rings—Chanel calling. I answer hesitantly with, "I'm at work, Channy."

"Oh, so you can speak out loud. I was wondering if you were even alive."

"Last I checked, I was."

"Don't be a sassy with me. I've been worried sick. You didn't come Wednesday, you haven't answered texts for days—what's going on?"

I sigh, leaning back in my chair. "I need to figure out who I am."

"I—what? What does that mean?"

I struggle to find the words that I want to say. Chanel doesn't need to know everything, and that thought alone frees me. I don't *owe* her anything. I don't *have* to make her happy.

"Because if I don't know who I am, then I can't know who I want to spend the rest of my life with."

My sister stays quiet for a moment. "This is a Lizzie-thing."

"What gives you that idea?" I ask innocently.

Chanel scoffs. Then says, "Come over tonight," in a quiet, non-pushy tone. "Shad and I want to talk to you face-to-face."

"Channy, I don't—"

"Seven o'clock," she yells over me, something Chanel has literally never done.

"Don't be late." She hangs up before I can argue, so I guess we're both doing things out of the norm for us.

Honestly, it's probably about time.

I stare at my phone as it darkens, torn between irritation and relief. Part of me wants to ignore her, to prove I can say no, even to my sister. But another part—a bigger part—wants to see her, to celebrate with her and Shad, to be part of their happiness.

Is that taking care of them? Or is that just being a good brother who values family?

I don't know the difference anymore.

———

I ARRIVE at Chanel and Shad's house at 7:03 PM just because she told me not to be late, a bottle of champagne in hand. Not because I think they *need* me to bring it, but because I *want* to celebrate with them. The distinction feels important.

Shad opens the door, his face lighting up when he sees me. "Hey, brother." He pulls me into a quick hug. "Thanks for coming."

"Congratulations," I say, and I mean it. "That's fantastic news about the job."

"Thanks." He can't stop smiling as I walk past him. "It's a huge relief."

We move into the living room, where Chanel is

bouncing Nora on her hip. She gives me a critical once-over. "You look terrible."

"Thanks, sis." I hold out my arms for Nora, who squeals and reaches for me. The weight of her in my arms feels like an anchor, grounding me.

Shad pops the champagne, and we toast his new job. It's a good position at Prescott Electronics, with benefits and a salary that will more than cover their expenses. As he describes the role, a genuine happiness that has nothing to do with me expands through me.

When Chanel takes Nora for her bath, Shad and I are left alone in the living room. He leans forward, elbows on his knees.

"I want to thank you," he says. "For everything you've done for us these past few months."

"You don't have to say anything."

"No, I do." His eyes hook into mine, seriously and intensely, and I realize *he* needs to say this. It's nothing to do with me. It's about him, and I wave for him to go on.

"You kept us afloat when things were rough. I'll never forget that." He takes a breath. "But I'm also really excited to stand on our own now. To be the provider for Chanel. I *can* take care of her, Matt."

I nod, sudden emotion storming through me. It's not my job to take care of my sister, not anymore. It's Shad's job, and only Shad's job.

"I'm happy for you," I say, and I find I truly am.

There's no sense of loss, no feeling that I'm no longer needed. Just pride in my brother-in-law's accomplishment and gladness that he loves my sister so much.

"If you need something, please let me know," Shad says next, catching me completely off-guard. "Chanel and I love you and want to be there for you when you need us."

"I—thank you," I say, not knowing how to tell him I've made a mess of things with Lizzie because of, well, being me.

"She's ready for you, Daddy," Chanel says, and Shad claps me on the shoulder as he gets up.

My sister sits next to me on the couch, her expression irritating and heartwarming at the same time.

"I don't want to—"

"Oh, you're talking about Lizzie," Chanel says.

Defeated, I stare at my empty champagne flute. "She thinks I only want to be with her because I need to take care of someone. Because it makes *me* feel good about myself."

"Oh."

I stare at her. "That's all you've got? Oh?"

"Well, I thought you were going to say she told you that you weren't good-looking enough to be with a supermodel, so." She shrugs, her smile widening by the moment.

I blink at her as keen shock moves through me. Lizzie *is* a supermodel, but I've never worried about being good enough for her. Or maybe I have. I don't honestly know. Helping people and trying to make them happy has been my default since I was a child. I don't know how to turn it on and off.

"I like doing things for Lizzie," I say. "I like making her happy." I glance behind me to the hall where Shad went. "He does things to make you happy, right?"

"Of course," Chanel says. "I think...it sounds like Lizzie is questioning the motive behind the things."

"Yeah." I sigh. Lizzie consumes me—her intelligence, her wit, her city-swears, the way she lights up when she talks about modeling.

The way she sees right through me.

"I like her, Channy." I look down at my hands, and they suddenly feel too big for my body. "I want to be with her. This two-day break is killing me already."

Chanel nudges me with her shoulder, and I raise my eyes to hers. "You're so dramatic." She smiles at me. "It's actually one of your best qualities."

"Is it?"

"Look, there's nothing wrong with being a caretaker. It's part of who you are. But it can't be *all* of who you are, and it can't be *why* you're in a relationship. I think that's what Lizzie doesn't like."

I nod slowly, knowing my sister is right. "I know." I release all the pent-up air in my lungs and the tension in my shoulders. "I need to show her I want to be with her. Not because she needs me, but because I need her."

"Do you? Need her?"

The question hangs in the air, and for the first time, I really consider it. Not what I can do for Lizzie, but what she brings to my life. How she challenges me. Makes me laugh. Sees the real me behind the helpful façade.

"Yeah," I say. "I think I do."

Back home, I pick up the framed photo Lizzie gave me. I've been so focused on what I can do for her that I never stopped to consider why I'm drawn to her in the first place. What she does for me, just by being herself.

She makes me laugh. Challenges me. Sees me—really sees me—in a way no one else ever has.

And maybe that's what love is supposed to be. Not one person taking care of another, but two people *choosing* each other, flaws and all. Wanting each other, whether I bring her dirty Diet Coke or not.

Being better together than they are apart.

My gaze shifts to the costume box still hiding in the corner. The Halloween party is tomorrow night. A party I probably shouldn't attend, given our "break."

"But what if I did?" I ask the cats.

Not to win her back with grand gestures or gifts or anything else that screams "let me take care of you."

But to show her who I really am. What I really want.

Her. Just her.

I retrieve the box and open it on the dining room table, pulling out the lab coats and glow sticks. Pierre Curie was devoted to Marie—not because she needed him, but because they were intellectual equals. Partners in science and in life.

"I know exactly what I need to do," I say to my empty house, my cats, and myself, a plan forming in my mind.

The cats watch me with curious eyes as I pull out my phone and start typing. For once, I'm not thinking about what Lizzie needs.

I'm thinking about what *I want*—and what I want is her.

CHAPTER TWENTY-FOUR

LIZZIE

"These cobwebs are never going to look right."
I stretch on my tiptoes to reach the corner of the
entryway arch. The fake spider web material clings to
my fingers instead of the wall, and I mutter under my
breath, "Rhode Island."

It's not even a city. I'm so off my game right now—
since Wednesday, in fact. Fine, since last weekend,
when I went to Matt's family picnic. I can't believe it's
only been a week. It feels like ten years without him, and
each day is the first day, the freshest hurt, the worst realization when I wake up and remember I can't text him
the chemistry pun in my head.

"Here, let me," Emma says, taking the tangled mess
from my hands. She's a few inches shorter than me but
somehow manages to get the cobwebs to cooperate

perfectly. "You've been fighting with that same corner for ten minutes."

"Sorry," I say, stepping back to survey our work. The Big House looks appropriately spooky for tonight's Halloween party—orange and purple string lights draped across the porch, jack-o'-lanterns lining the sidewalk and parking area out front, and various creepy decorations scattered throughout the first floor. "I'm just distracted."

"I can't imagine why," Tahlia says innocently as she passes by with a tray of cake pops decorated as eyeballs. She knows exactly what—or rather who—is distracting me.

I ignore her and follow her into the kitchen, where the counters are covered with Halloween-themed food and drinks. "Do we have enough dry ice?" I peer into the cauldron-shaped bowl we use every time we host this shindig. "I can go get more."

"We have tons," Tahlia says, setting down the tray and turning to face me. "Is he coming tonight?"

My throat tightens. "No."

Emma joins us in the kitchen. "Even after he arranged all the costumes?"

I busy myself by rearranging the plastic spiders around the cauldron. "I'm not going as Marie Curie. I'm just wearing my witch costume from two years ago."

Tahlia frowns like my recycled costume will single-handedly ruin the party. "But you were so excited about the scientist costumes."

"That was before I suggested we take a break." I straighten the already-straight row of cups next to the punch, avoiding her eyes. "I can't exactly show up as half of a couple's costume. That's just lame."

And it makes my heart hurt.

Emma and Tahlia exchange a look that makes me want to throw something.

"What?" I ask.

"Nothing," Emma says quickly, actually taking a step backward. "It's just...you don't seem happy about this break."

"I'm not supposed to be happy about it." I grab a ghost-shaped cookie and bite its head off with more force than necessary. "It's not a vacation. It's a chance for Matt to figure out who he is and if he wants to be with me."

The kitchen falls silent except for the humming of the refrigerator. I still have hours to endure before the party starts, and the throbbing behind my eyes isn't getting better.

"I'm sorry," I say, rubbing my temples. "I didn't mean—I don't even want to go to the party." I move over to the slim cabinet beside the stove and open it. I pull out the painkillers and shake three into my palm.

"You have to come to the party," Emma says in a weak voice.

I throw back the pills dry and face her and Tahlia. "I'm going to come and do one circle around the living room. Then I'm going back upstairs."

"You're not going to stay and vote?" Emma asks.

I smile at her, some of my frustration melting away. "I can just pre-vote for you and Aaron as Aragorn and Arwen."

She beams. "My head jewels are pretty fantastic, and my dress is too."

"I'm sure," Tahlia says, and I switch my gaze to her. She doesn't have a second half to dress up with tonight either, and my heart rips a little bit for her.

"We should've been Tweedledee and Tweedledum," I say.

She grins and ducks her head.

"What are you going to dress up as?" I ask.

"I'm not telling," she says yet again. She's told us that for a couple of weeks now, but the party is in only a few hours.

"Well, I'm going to be a witch," I say. "It matches my mood." I glance around the kitchen, where we have nearly everything ready. Tahlia will order pizza later, and we'll have a riotous feast with too much dry ice, tons of desserts, and plenty of creepy-crawly goodness.

"I have a headache, and I have to call my dad," I say. "I'm going to go lie down for a bit."

My roommates let me go, thankfully, and I do climb into bed and close my eyes. Yes, my head throbs, but the truth is, I miss Matt so much it physically hurts. I miss his laugh, his endless enthusiasm, the way he lights up when he talks about his cats or chemistry or anything he's passionate about. I miss the way he looks at me like I'm the most fascinating creature he's ever encountered.

But I can't be with someone who doesn't know who they are. Who doesn't know what they want. Who's just with me because I fit into their pattern of taking care of people.

My phone rings, and for a heart-stopping moment, I think it might be Matt. But it's my dad's name that appears on the screen.

"Hey, Dad," I say. "I was just about to call you."

"Hey, pumpkin."

I smile, because my nickname changes with the seasons.

"Just checking to see if you're still coming over tomorrow." His voice is warm and familiar, an anchor in the storm of my emotions. "It's soup weather, and you can pass out the candy if any trick-or-treaters come."

Which they won't. Dad lives on a farm outside of town. Plus, it's Sunday. "I think they'll all be coming tonight," I say. "Do you need me?" Hope balloons in my chest. If my dad needs me tonight, I can't stay for the party...

"Nah," he says. "I'll just put a bowl on the front porch."

Something dings on his end of the line, and I close my eyes to try to place it. "Where are you?"

"Grocery store," he says. "I'm thinking of making that chicken and corn chowder. Remember your momma always made it for the first soup of the season?"

I smile. "It was the opener for soup season." I was in college before I realized "soup season" was something my mother had made up. None of my roommates had ever heard of it before. "Sounds good," I say.

"Do I need enough for three?" Dad asks.

The question sends a fresh wave of pain through me. "No, he's...busy tomorrow."

"Oh, I'm smellin' a lie," Dad says. The noise on his end of the line dulls. "Lizzie?"

I wish I could just skip this part. I hate having to tell everyone why Matt's not with me. Thankfully, all my roommates—current and former—know, and hopefully I can make it through tonight without too many other questions.

"We're—well, Dad, we're taking a break." I exhale heavily.

"A break?"

I can practically see my dad's face all scrunched up in confusion. "What does that mean?"

"It means we're not really hanging out right now."

"Well, that's a relief," he says, his tone snippy and dry. "Because you're not fifteen years old. Did you break up?"

"No," I say. "Kind of."

"I don't understand," he says, and I believe he doesn't. I barely understand what's going on, and it was my idea. "What happened? You two seemed happy together."

Memories move through my mind. He's not wrong. I was happy with Matt. He's great. He's—I stop the thoughts before they can derail me.

"It's complicated, Daddy."

"Try me," he says, his tone gentle but firm. "I raised a girl and nursed my wife through all kinds of things. I should be able to understand a kind-of break up, but I don't. You have to explain it to me."

I roll onto my side and try to find the words. Dad and I have had a lot of talks that start with, "You have to explain it to me."

After my mom died, he'd say, *I'm not your mother, Lizzie-girl, but I want to understand. Explain it to me.*

Or, *I don't know what you're talking about, though those words are English. You have to explain chemistry to me like I'm four years old.*

I smile at that memory, a trickle of tears entering my eyes.

"Matty is a fixer, Daddy."

And just like that, I've explained everything in just five words. Okay, two more: "Like Mom."

Dad grunts, his way of saying he heard me and he's thinking. Several seconds pass where I wipe my eyes and try not to sniffle too loudly. "You think he's trying to fix you?" he asks gently.

"Kind of," I say. "Not really, though. More like...he finds value in being Mister Fix-It, and I don't want a husband who thinks he needs to step in and solve every little thing that bothers me." I wait for Dad to quip about how Matt will never be able to keep up, but he doesn't. Now's not the time for it anyway, and I've worked very hard to be more low-key, less high-maintenance.

"So I asked him if he was with me, because helping me gave him worth, or if he was with me, because he wanted to be with me."

"And?" Dad asks.

"And he doesn't know," I say, the sharpness of the words like a three-pronged dart in my heart. "So we're on a break while he figures out...whatever he needs to figure out."

"What do you need him to figure out?"

"Dad," I say, my tone weary. "I don't know."

"Humor me."

"I need him to figure out if I'm enough for him," I say. "Me, right now, as I am. Not who he wants to fix me into being. But just me, right now. Who I am, and who he is. Does he want me? Or does he just want to fix me?"

Dad lets my words sink in, which I appreciate. "Your mother didn't think you needed to be fixed, my darling girl."

I try to give him the same pause he gave me. "I know,

Dad, but that's how she made me feel nonetheless. And I don't want to live my whole life with a husband who treats me the same way. I want to be enough for him just how I am, even if I do have a few things that could be better."

My father is quiet for a long moment. "Huh," he finally says. "That's strange. He never looked at you like you weren't enough."

"What do you mean?"

"The way that man looked at you, Elizabeth...it wasn't like he was checking items off a to-do list. It was like you were the sun, and he couldn't believe his luck to be standing in your light."

Tears prick at the corners of my eyes. "Daddy, that's just because you have cataracts." I partly laugh and partly sob while my father chuckles.

"No, that's just a father who can see two people more clearly than they can see themselves." He sighs, and I know this sound. His memories are firing hard too.

"You know, your mother used to worry about something similar," he says, his voice softening. "She was so independent, so capable. She didn't think she needed anyone. But *needing* someone and *wanting* them in your life are two different things, pumpkin."

I wipe at a stray tear. "I know that. That's exactly my point to Matt."

"Okay," he says. "I just don't want you to push away

someone who makes you happy, because you're afraid of letting him care for you."

"It's not that simple."

"You're right. It never is." He sighs. "But love isn't about keeping score. It's about choosing each other, every day, even when it's hard. *Especially* when it's hard."

I sit with his words, letting them sink in. Have I been so focused on not being Matt's project that I've missed what was right in front of me? A man who genuinely cares for me, who sees me—really sees me—in a way no one else has?

"I don't know what to do, Daddy."

"Yes, you do," he says simply. "You're just scared to do it."

I sniffle then, definitely loud enough for him to hear. "I have to go get ready for the party," I say.

"Yeah, go," Dad says. "I'll have the chowder tomorrow—enough for whoever wants to come. Emma. Tahlia. Whoever."

I appreciate that he doesn't specifically name Matt, though we both know who he means. "I love you, Dad."

"Love you too, Lizzie-girl."

After we hang up, I stay in bed, watching the sunshine leak out of the day. The first guests will arrive in less than two hours, and I still need to get ready. But the moment I sit up to do that, my bedroom door creaks open.

Tahlia stands there, and the big energy coming through the doorway says she's not alone. "Can we come in?" she asks.

I nod, and she leads in everyone. I start to cry again at the sight of Hillary and Claudia, Ryanne and Emma.

"Oh, it's not good," Hillary says. She climbs on the end of my bed and crawls right up next to me. "Come here, honey."

I fold myself into her hug and let my other roommates take up supportive positions around me. "Why are you all here?"

"To help with the house," Ryanne says.

"Becks is doing the music," Claudia says. "We should all be praying we don't regret *that* decision."

That gets me to smile, and I hate that it's not as happy as it could be.

"Liam and Elliott are expanding the parking down to our place," Hillary says. "And then we found out that you were up here, and..." She looks around at everyone. "We can't have crying on Halloween."

"Halloween is tomorrow," I say in a pathetic voice, though I love that they're here. My found family, who always rallies when one of us needs something. The thought brings both comfort and a pang of sadness. I love these people, but lately it feels like everyone is moving forward except me. Hillary and Liam are married and living next door. Claudia and Beckett are thriving in their new jobs. Ryanne and Elliott are already trying for a baby. Emma and Aaron will be engaged in the next couple of weeks.

And me? I'm stuck in limbo, too afraid to move forward, too restless to stay still.

"Hill?" Liam calls from somewhere beyond my bedroom. We all turn toward the door, which is open. My heartbeat patters in my throat, because no men ever come up here.

"There's a box here for Lizzie," he calls, and Hillary slides away from me and rolls off the side of the bed. She jogs around the bed and across the room. "A box?" She leaves, her footsteps echoing back to us as she walks down the hall.

She says something else to Liam, who answers, but their voices are rumbles, not words. Hillary returns, her eyes as wide as the great big box she carries. "This came for Lizzie," she says.

"What?" I wipe my face completely free of tears. "Who sent it?"

"Liam said it was in one of those yellow delivery vans," Hillary says. "There's no return address." She tips the box toward those of us still clustered on my bed. "It just has your name on it. Not even an address."

"Let's open it," Ry says, clapping her hands and standing.

"It doesn't weigh very much," Hillary says, moving to the end of the bed and setting it down. She looks at me, part fear and part excitement in her expression. "Should we open it?"

"Let her do it," Claudia says. "This has to be from Matt."

My heart clenches at the thought, and I scoot out of bed. It's a plain box, with my name written in black marker. Yes, the handwriting looks like Matt's, but I take a moment to look at Hillary, then Ry, then Emma, then Tahlia, and finally Claudia.

She radiates a light she'd probably call *Here Comes the Sun*, and nods at me.

The box has been secured with clear packing tape, but it comes off pretty easily. Inside, I can't see anything through mounds and mounds of light blue tissue paper. I start pulling it out by the handful until I get to—I gasp.

Then I lift up the black, vintage-style dress. I blink, trying to open my eyes wider and wider each time, so I can see more and try to understand quicker.

Ry takes the dress from me with a low whistle. "What else is there?"

I pull out a package of glow stick, a small velvet box, and a note.

I look at Ry, who has held up the dress to her body. That's when I see the pinned note that says "Marie Curie" on the collar.

My breath stalls in my throat and my eyes drop to the smaller items in my hands. "He's written me a note," I scratch out.

"Read it," Tahlia says, and I can't even imagine how much this hurts for her.

I meet her eye and nod, then look down at the note in Matt's horribly-chemist handwriting.

There's only one person I want to get radioactive with — you.

P.S. The velvet box isn't what you think. Open it anyway.

"It's got to be jewelry," Hillary says, having read the note over my shoulder. I hand it to Claudia, who scans it quickly and passes it on.

"I think so too," she says.

I set down the glow sticks and open the velvet box. Inside is not a ring, but a delicate silver necklace with a pendant shaped like a chemical element symbol—Lr, for Lawrencium.

Another note is tucked beneath it:

Element 103, named after Ernest Lawrence. One of the rarest elements on earth. Just like you, my catalyst.

Tears blur my vision as I lift the necklace from the box. It's beautiful, thoughtful, and so perfectly Matt.

"Catalyst," I say, lifting my eyes from the most perfect love letter anyone has ever written me. "Cat. Kitten."

"What?" Emma asks. Then she goes, "Cat? Kitten—oh."

Yeah. Oh.

I clutch the necklace to my chest, my heart racing as I look around at everyone. "What do I do now?"

"You put on that dress," Tahlia says firmly, pushing herself off the bed and taking it from Ry.

"And get your hair all chemical," Hillary says.

"And brush on some era-appropriate makeup," Claudia says.

"And you go find your Pierre Curie," Ryanne says.

I stare around at all of them. "Do you think he's here?"

"No," Emma says. "So where would he be, Lizzie?" She unzips the dress Tahlia still holds. "Get in your scientist costume and go where only you know he'll be."

CHAPTER TWENTY-FIVE

MATT

I shift my weight from one foot to the other, my bow tie suddenly feeling like it's strangling me. The sun has already gone down behind the Big House, and it's going to be full-dark soon.

If Lizzie doesn't come out soon...

I shove the thought away. The package was delivered only forty-five minutes ago, and if I know Lizzie—and I do—she'll want to go all-out to become the best Marie Curie she can be.

Or maybe I'm delusional. I should be at home with my chem-cats, eating a whole pizza out of the box while all the spooky shows play on the TV.

I lean against Lizzie's car, trying to look casual while my insides perform the chemical equivalent of a nuclear meltdown. "This was either the best idea you've ever had or the stupidest," I grumble to myself, adjusting the sleeves of my vintage, tweed suit jacket. The Pierre Curie costume is historically accurate down to the period-appropriate shoes, which pinch my toes in ways I hadn't anticipated.

A car pulls into the driveway, and I instinctively duck behind Lizzie's vehicle. A couple dressed as Gomez and Morticia Addams emerges, laughing as they head toward the house.

Not Lizzie.

I check my phone for the thousandth time. No messages. No indication that she received my gift, opened it, hated it, loved it—nothing.

She could have at least texted to say she got the box, I think, then immediately feel guilty. I have no idea what alternate plans Lizzie has made for this party. I can't imagine she'd not attend, and my thoughts circle around the guy from the concert she latched onto.

Lizzie doesn't like to do things alone—would she have arranged another costume, with someone else?

I can't imagine she would do that, but she didn't have our planned costume until very recently.

My thoughts circle again, and I wish I could turn off my mind.

As I wait, my mind drifts back to the past few days—the loneliest of my life. Not because I was physically alone, but because I finally had to face the emptiness inside me. The void I've been filling with other people's needs since I was fourteen years old.

Who am I if I'm not the guy who fixes everything?

I've come up with a few things.

I'm the guy who loves chemistry jokes. Who talks to his cats like they understand English. Who drinks sparkling water instead of seltzer and thinks the difference matters. Who gets excited about new formulations and indie bands and the perfect ratio of chocolate chip cookie to brownie in a brookie.

I'm the guy who loves my sister and her family, and I'm learning to love goats. If I have more time out at Lizzie's dad's farm, I'm sure we'd become best friends.

And I'm the guy who's in love with Elizabeth Trenton.

Not because she needs me. Not because I can fix her problems or make her life easier or find her a new job.

But because she makes me laugh. Because she challenges me. Because she sees the real me behind the helpful façade I've been hiding behind for years.

Because she's the only person who's ever asked me what I want.

And what I want is her.

Another car arrives, this one carrying what appears to be the entire cast of Scooby-Doo. They park directly behind me, blocking me in. Great. Now I'm committed to this plan, for better or worse.

"Hydrogen peroxide," I mutter, straightening my bow tie again.

The front door of the Big House opens, spilling

warm light onto the porch. My heart leaps into my throat, but it's just Tahlia dressed as—holy helium, that's the best Cinderella costume I've ever seen—as she greets the new arrivals.

I check my phone. This party doesn't officially start for another four minutes. What if Lizzie didn't get the costume? What if she got it but decided not to wear it? What if she's upstairs right now, laughing at my pathetic attempt to win her back?

No. I refuse to spiral into worst-case scenarios. I'm done with that kind of thinking.

Another group approaches the house—a zombie horde complete with realistic makeup and tattered clothes. They stumble past me, groaning convincingly. The party is picking up steam, and I'm still hiding behind a car like a stalker.

"This is ridiculous," I say, pushing off from the vehicle. "I should just go up there and—"

The front door swings open again, and my words die in my throat.

Lizzie has always taken my breath away, and tonight is no different.

She stands framed in the doorway, that little black dress I bought for her gleaming under the porch lights. Even with the ruffles and the high collar, she steals my breath and renders me mute.

Her auburn hair falls in soft waves around her shoulders, and around her neck—my breath catches—the Lawrencium necklace glints in the light.

She's looking for something. For someone.

She's looking for me.

She takes a hesitant step onto the porch, and I step out from behind the car just as another pair of party-goers—Mister Incredible and Elastigirl—approaches the house.

Our eyes lock across the yard, and the world narrows to just her. The noise of the party spilling out of the house fades. Everyone else blurs into nothingness. There's only Lizzie, looking at me with an expression I can't quite read.

I take a step forward. Then another. My heart pounds so hard I'm surprised it doesn't burst through my Pierre Curie costume.

"Hi," I say when I reach the bottom of the steps, acutely aware of the costumed guests streaming past us.

"Hi," she says, her voice soft but steady. "You're here."

"I'm here." I climb the first step, then the second, bringing us to eye level. "I got you something."

"I noticed." She touches the necklace at her throat. "It's beautiful."

"Like you." The words come out before I can stop them, but I don't regret them. I'm done hiding how I feel. "Lizzie—"

"Matty," she says at the same time.

We both laugh nervously, and she gestures for me to go first.

I take a deep breath. This is it. The moment I've been rehearsing for days.

"I've been doing a lot of thinking," I say. "About what you said. About who I am outside of taking care of those I love." I step forward, up onto the porch with her, close enough to catch the scent of her perfume—jasmine and clarity and home.

"You were right. I've been defining myself by what I do for others. By how needed I am. But that's not why I want to be with you, Lizzie."

I glance past her, catching a few familiar faces in the gathering crowd—Hillary, Claudia—but they fade into the background. This moment is only ours.

"I don't want to fix your life. I want to live it with you. As your equal. Your partner. Your...Pierre." I gesture to my goofy costume with a smile that finally feels real.

Her lips twitch, eyes softening. That's encouragement enough, and I have so much more to say.

"I love bringing you breakfast and surprising you with your favorite things. Not because it makes me feel important. But because *you* make *me* feel like I matter. Like I'm seen. I help you not to prove my worth, but because you inspire me to be worthy."

I reach for her hand. When she lets me hold it, relief

floods through me. "I don't need you to need me, Lizzie. I just want you to *want* me. The real me. The one who talks too much, obsesses over chemical formulas, and owns naughty cats with idiotic names."

She smiles. "I do like your cats."

"They like you too. Honestly, I think Purroxide was planning a coup if you didn't forgive me."

She laughs, the sound like a sudden shift in pressure—everything light and right.

I reach into my pocket. "I have one more thing."

Her breath catches. My heart skips. "It's not a ring," I say quickly, opening the small box to reveal a silver charm bracelet with a single, tiny beaker etched with the word *US*.

"I thought we could add charms together," I say, clasping it around her wrist. "Not because we're trying to fix each other, but because we're building something. A reaction. An equation neither of us could balance alone."

I meet her eyes, the tears brimming in them giving me strength.

"I've said it before," I say. "And I will say it again and forever: You're my catalyst, Lizzie. You don't just make me react—you *change* me. You make me want to be better, not so you'll stay, but because you're the only person I've ever met who made me believe I didn't have to *earn* love to deserve it."

I take a breath. Then I say the line I've rehearsed more than any other: "I love you. Fully. Bravely. Chemically."

A beat. Then softly, as I lower my forehead to touch hers. "I'm Doctor Matthew Giles, and I want Elizabeth Trenton. I want her to choose me. I want *us* to build a whole amazing life together."

"Shreveport," she says, and I know from her tone it's one of her highest-level city-swears. "You can't just say all that like it's not going to wreck me."

I grin at her. "I know someone who can fix whatever gets wrecked, kitten." I press my lips to her temple. "But he's kind of busy right now, so he probably can't do it. He's still working on who he is, but I'm going to figure that out completely, okay? But I want to do it *with* you, not while we're on a break."

She looks up at me with stars in her eyes. "No more breaks." She grabs the lapels of my Pierre Curie jacket and pulls me toward her, her lips meeting mine in a kiss that melts every synapse in my brain.

I wrap my arms around her waist, pulling her closer, pouring everything I feel into the kiss. Behind us, cheers fill the air, but I barely hear them. There's only Lizzie—her warmth, her softness, the taste of her lips, the pure combustion between us.

She pulls away as quickly as she kissed me, and she stands in my arms as she grins over to the crowd of roommates and party guests. They continue to applaud, and let me tell you, seeing Beauty and the Beast whooping for you is a wild ride.

Emma jumps up and down—and an elven princess doing that is no small feat—and Hillary-as-Dolly-Parton has her phone out, no doubt capturing the moment for everyone to watch later.

"Wow," Lizzie says, her cheeks flushed as she faces me again. "That was…"

"A successful experiment?" I grin down at her.

She laughs that gorgeous laugh that makes my cells sing. "Definitely. Though we might need to repeat it a few times to verify the results."

"I love the scientific method," I say, grinning like an idiot.

She smiles, that radiant smile that first captured my heart. "So, Pierre, are you ready to show these people what happens when two elements with a strong attraction come together?"

"Absolutely, Marie." I offer her my arm. As we turn toward the party and everyone else flows back inside, she tugs on my arm and causes me to pause. It's just the two of us on the porch, and she looks up at me with that chemist intensity she has.

"Before we go in, Matty…"

I wait, because when she gives me silence, I fill it. Of course, that's never worked with her, but tonight, she looks to the gaping front door of the Big House and back to me.

"I love you, too," she says, and I could die the happiest man on earth in this moment—all because Elizabeth Trenton loves me.

CHAPTER TWENTY-SIX

EMMA

THE BELL OVER THE DOOR JINGLES AS I LOOK UP from the arrangement I'm working on. Thomas, Aaron's younger brother, rushes in with that frantic energy only last-minute shoppers possess.

Fernunculus. This isn't going to be good. I glance down at the seven orders I still need to finish before I close, and then up at Tommy as he arrives at my counter. I am never doing early morning pick-ups again. It makes my night-before too hectic.

"Emma, uh, hi."

"Thomas."

"Thank goodness you're still open." He runs a hand through his dark hair, which is shorter than Aaron's but just as thick. "I, maybe—fine, completely forgot today is Courtney's birthday, and I need something amazing. Like, now."

I stab my flower pen into the pot and cock my hip. "Hollyhocks, Tommy." I sigh and look away, because we both know I'm going to help him out. He's been dating Courtney for months, and they're so stinking cute together.

He grins at me. "Hollyhocks. Is that a good plant-swear or a bad one?"

"Depends on how much you're willing to spend on your girlfriend." I wipe my hands on my apron and move around the counter. "What does she like? What are you hoping for?"

He shrugs helplessly and looks around my flower shop like he's never been inside one before. "Something that says 'I'm not a terrible boyfriend even though I waited until the last minute to get you a gift'?"

"So something expensive, then." I grin at him and lead him toward the premium arrangements. I glance over to my Boyfriend Corner, and it's looking pretty sparse. I need Aaron to come refresh it, so I have something for the ladies to buy on their way home from work.

"How long have you two been together now?" I glance over my shoulder at Thomas.

"Uh." He looks at me blankly. "I think it's six months and four days today."

"Wow, that's exact." I give him a smile, because yes, Tommy likes being exact. I point to a lush arrangement of stargazer lilies and white roses. "This one says 'I'm thoughtful and romantic' rather than 'I panicked and grabbed the first thing I saw.'"

Tommy's eyes widen. "Perfect. Can you add something extra? Maybe some of those purple things she likes?"

"Purple things?" I practically spit the words out. Surely Thomas did not just call my gorgeous flowers "purple things."

He pulls out his phone and looks up at me with panic in his eyes. "I'm—I don't know what they're called. Can we check in the fridge?"

I pick up the arrangement, sigh, and start toward the back of the store. "Fine, but Tommy, I have a ton to do. How long can you wait for these?"

"Maybe like a half-hour?" he guesses as he follows. "Can you do it, Em? I'll pay double."

Oh, he'll be paying double all right. Not only that, but he's dreaming if he thinks he can come inside Sir Chills-A-Lot with me.

"Give me a few minutes," I say. "You'll have to wait out here." I point to my consultation room. "But you can sit here if you want."

"I'm going to go out front and call Court." He exhales heavily. "Thank you, Em." He grabs onto me from behind, nearly knocking me forward and spilling the arrangement from my hands.

I grunt and brace myself as he gives me the most awkward hug of my life. "It's fine, Tommy," I say.

He releases me, and his footsteps hurry toward the front door. Relief rushes through me, because while I love Tommy like my little brother, he's still a bit odd. And now I have even more to do.

I pull open the door to Sir Chills, and the blast of cold air hits me as I step into my beloved cooler, my sanctuary of perfect temperature and humidity. Aaron teases me about his name, but Sir Chills has earned his place in the flower shop.

I set down the arrangement I brought from the front and turn to find some "purple things" to add to it. "Lilac, lavender, lisianthus."

That last one is real—and it's perfect for this arrangement. As I work, I hum along to the soft music playing through the shop's speakers, completely in my element. Time doesn't really exist inside Sir Chills, but my fingers keep track of the minutes by starting to sting when I've been inside for too long.

I do have gloves I wear when I have to be in here for a while, but this job is going to be fast. I've started three of the other arrangements, and if I'm lucky, I'll be out of here by seven.

It'll be dark by then, and I hate driving home in the dark. But we're moving into winter now, and it's going to be my reality.

I'm just finishing the arrangement when my phone buzzes in my apron pocket. A text from Aaron.

Busy day?

I smile, though a slip of irritation runs through me. We've been dating for over six months too, and while I know lots and lots of couples go out for longer than that, I'm ready to be engaged.

Aaron and I have talked about marriage a ton. I know I want to do it in the spring or summer, and I want to do it in his backyard. I'll do the flowers, of course, and Aaron will build our altar.

My eyes move to my very naked left hand. If only he'd put a ring on it.

Tommy just came in, I tell him. *He needs a last-minute birthday gift for Courtney.*

Typical Tommy. Need any help?

I'm good. See you for dinner?

Can't wait. Love you.

I tuck my phone away, a warm feeling spreading through my chest. He loves me, I know. But I might need to have another conversation with him about moving forward. I remind myself that Aaron is very busy all the time, not just around major holidays and during wedding season.

He runs the hardware store next door, and literally everyone in town needs something from him on a daily basis.

Tommy's arrangement looks wonky. "Probably because you tried to take something that was already done and add to it." I step back, knowing this never goes well for me.

I fiddle with this bloom and then that one, finally telling myself that it's not my arrangement, and Tommy isn't going to care. I don't normally send vases full of flowers out the front door without being completely happy with them, but I have so many other things to do.

Finally, I stop pushing this petal that way, and then that one the other way, and sigh. "Good enough." I pick up the new arrangement and turn toward the door.

I make it out into the hall, where I pause outside the consultation room. Tommy's not there, and I don't see him standing at the register either.

"Tommy," I call, and I've just set the arrangement on the counter when I realize my shop...is no longer my shop.

I suck in a breath at the hundreds of tiny fairy lights twinkling from the ceiling. I step out from behind the counter to find a path of rose petals across the floor, leading toward the front of the store.

I walk alongside them, not wanting to crush them beneath my feet. My heart pounds and pounds as I take in the flickering candles on all the tables, the bookcases, the pretty displays I spend hours creating.

"Hello?" I ask, but no one answers me.

I round a particularly tall cabinet and peer over to my premium display cabinet. There's no one there. I look left to my Boyfriend Corner—and gasp.

My boyfriend stands there, and Aaron looks nervous and wonderful in a suit I've never seen before.

"Wisteria," I whisper.

"Surprise," he says softly.

My brain struggles to catch up. "Where's Tommy?" falls out of my mouth.

Aaron takes a step toward me, his smile both shy and certain. "He'll be back in a bit to get the arrangement, but he's not picking up Courtney until seven-thirty."

Realization flows over me. "You sent him over here." My heart pounds against my ribs like it's trying to escape.

"Emma." Aaron takes another step closer, reaching for my hands. They're still a bit cold from Sir Chills, but he doesn't seem to mind. "From the moment you opened this shop next to mine, you've brought color into my life. Before you, I was all nuts and bolts—practical, predictable. You taught me to see beauty in unexpected places."

Tears blur my vision as I glance around at the Boyfriend Corner, which is now laden with gorgeous red rose bouquets. There must be a hundred roses here, and I pull my eyes back to his.

Aaron drops to one knee, and I can't breathe. "I love you endlessly. Everything in my life means nothing without you. I would get caught in any rainstorm to be with you, and I can't wait to build everything and anything with you."

He holds up a ring with a round diamond surrounded by tiny sapphires the exact color of my eyes.

I press both hands to my pulse, willing it to calm so I can hear everything he says.

"Emma Newberry, will you marry me?" He looks at me with such hope and love, the whole world opening up before me.

"Yes," I whisper, my throat so tight and dry. "Yes." My voice comes out louder now. "Yes, I'll marry you."

His face breaks into the most beautiful smile I've ever seen as he slides the ring onto my finger. He stands and pulls me into his arms, lifting me off my feet in a spin that sends a squeal out of my mouth.

When he sets me down, his lips find mine in a kiss that feels like coming home. He's definitely not the Doberman now, and when he pulls away, he says, "I ordered all of these from you."

"What?" I ask as he sways with me.

"The roses," he says. "I didn't order them from someone else."

I pull in a breath, the warmth of Aaron's arms around me as I look at the gorgeous roses again. "I made these," I say. "For the Harmon's anniversary."

I search his face as he grins. "Yeah, that was Fonda's sister. I've been holding them all in my office for the past twenty-four hours."

"No wonder you wouldn't let me come over for lunch today." I gaze around at everything, noticing photographs of our park plot, and us when we'd won the Cider Cove grant.

"How did you do all this?" I ask, amazed. "I was only in the cooler for a few minutes."

"Thirty-seven minutes," he says. "I thought you'd never come out." He brushes a strand of hair from my face and gazes at me with such love. "I love you, honeybee."

And it's the easiest thing in the world to say, "I love you too, baby."

CHAPTER TWENTY-SEVEN

TAHLIA

"All right," I say as I pull out my aunt's cookbook. Not that I really need it. I've made her pie crust—the flakiest—dozens of times. The trick is in the ice-cold water, I'm telling you.

And on this Saturday in November, the Big House is empty. So I'm prepping pie crusts for the Friendsgiving I'm hosting for two teacher friends next week.

I pause, fingers coated in flour, and listen to the house breathe. The Big House has always had its own rhythm—creaks and sighs that Aunt Fern taught me to interpret like a language. Right now, it's saying something that sounds suspiciously like *lone-ly*.

"I know," I whisper back, patting the dough into a disk. "I miss them too."

Three years ago, this kitchen would have been chaos on any given Saturday. Hillary sleeping late and then rushing to eat breakfast before heading out for some class she'd signed up for. Claudia arguing with Ryanne about politics. Emma arranging flowers on every available surface. Lizzie walking in so often, always wearing a different outfit for us to see.

Now the kitchen is pristine. Too clean. Too quiet. Too empty.

I reach for my phone and turn up the volume on my playlist, but it's like trying to fill the Grand Canyon with a water gun. The space is too vast, the silence too deep.

Come next summer, I'll be completely alone. Lizzie's already talking about a summer wedding, though Matt hasn't officially proposed yet. Emma and Aaron will be married in May. Everyone's moving forward, and I'm still in the same place. Still baking. Still alone in the Big House.

"We might have to dust off that roommate listing," I tell the dough as I fold it into triangles and slide it into the fridge. I'd gotten a few more inquiries—that all sounded like regular people in their thirties—but for some reason, I don't want new roommates while I still have my old ones.

So I'd pulled the listing and told everyone who'd asked about it that the rooms had been rented.

Donald Hastings wasn't one of them, because we'd only messaged back and forth a few times—enough for me to get the name Donald for the D—and then he'd gone silent. I'm sure he has wildly important things to do, and I tell myself I do too.

After all, I'm making a chocolate pecan pie this year, and everything has to be perfect. Claire and Julie don't have plans with their loved ones for the holiday, and the moment I'd heard that, I'd offered to do a Friendsgiving at the Big House.

See, everyone will be off doing something except me. Hillary and Liam are going to her parents' in Columbia. Claude and Beckett will be at his aunt's. Ry and Elliott are celebrating with his brother and mother. Emma and Aaron will feast on turkey at his parents' in downtown Cider Cove. Lizzie and Matt have accepted an invite to his sister's house.

For about two seconds, I thought about calling Jason, just to see what my brother's plans are for the holiday. But I don't really want to fly to Seattle, and I don't want to answer his questions, and I don't want to defend myself or the decisions I've made.

Thanksgiving should be relaxing, and getting together with him is the opposite of that. I'll just text, the way I always do.

And that meant I needed something for myself to do on Thanksgiving. Aunt Fern used to say the Good Lord would provide, and the very next day, I'd overheard Claire and Julie talking about their non-plans for the holidays.

I'd seized the opportunity to have them here, though

they both teach math and I'm in the arts. I've known them both for a few years, and they seemed genuinely happy to be coming.

While the pie crusts chill, I pour myself a glass of sweet tea and take it to the swing on the back porch. "Ahh," I sigh as I sit and toe myself back and forth. The arrival of November means things have finally cooled, and the evenings are utterly gorgeous.

The Big House faces east, so we get morning sunshine on the front and glorious sunsets in the back. I take a sip of sweet tea, enjoying the easiness of the night.

Aunt Fern used to say the Big House was at its most honest in November—no leaves to hide behind, no flowers to distract, just the bones of the place standing strong against the wind.

I turn to my phone, as usual, but I'm sick of social media. I play a few games, and tap on my email out of habit more than anything else. I take a big drink of sweet tea as I scan, but when my eyes land on an email from D. Hastings, I suck in a breath.

Not ideal with all that sweet tea in my mouth.

I choke. Then cough, liquid dribbling out of my mouth though I try to keep it in. My chest hurts.

I sputter, and as a last resort, spit out the sweet tea I haven't managed to swallow.

My eyes burn, and too many holes in my face are dripping with who-knows-what.

And I'm like that as I read an email from a man I haven't heard from in weeks.

Dear Ms. Tomlinson,

After further consultation with my client, I am pleased to inform you that he would like to expand his initial inquiry. Rather than a single floor, he is interested in renting the entirety of both the second and third floors of your residence in Cider Cove, South Carolina.

The second floor would be for his personal use, while the third would accommodate support personnel (myself included). This arrangement would ensure the privacy and space that is essential to his work.

Could you please provide a quote for this expanded rental, along with floor plans detailing bathroom access, entrances, and general acoustics of the property?

Respectfully,

Donald

I stare at the message, unsure whether to laugh, cry, or scream. Donald had cut off our communication quite suddenly, and now this?

But this could solve some of your problems, I think.

Then I snort, and oh, that's not a good idea. Sweet tea goes up my nose and sends me into another round of coughing. I hurry inside for a towel, and I get de-tea'ed before returning to my phone on the porch swing.

Words like *support personnel* and *bathroom access* and *general acoustics* meet my eyes. In theory, I know what these words mean. In the order Donald has arranged them, I do not.

I have a lot of questions, but the loudest one is—*when would they move in?*

I may have gotten myself into a pickle, because though I know Lizzie and Matt are getting married now, I can't rent the upper two floors in the Big House until they do.

And they aren't engaged and haven't set a date.

So how in the world can I answer Donald?

Once I allow that second question to come forward, the dam breaks.

"A man, Tahlia?" I ask myself. "Two men—at least. Who knows what other 'personnel' this guy has."

And what does he do where he needs so much privacy?

Why doesn't he just rent one of the mansions in Charleston?

What would Aunt Fern think of me renting out most of the house to strangers? Would she understand that I'm trying to preserve her legacy the only way I know how?

"Stop it," I tell myself, because I can bury anyone in questions, myself included. "Answer him."

I check the timestamp on the email, and it came in only a few minutes ago. I still think Donald and his mystery client are overseas, so if he's emailing me at six p.m. in South Carolina, it's got to be midnight or later wherever they are.

I've been charging my roommates seven-fifty for their rooms, plus another seventy-five for utilities. See why I can't live here myself? There's no way I can pay almost five hundred dollars per month just for utilities.

But perhaps Donald and his client can.

"And then some," I whisper. I don't need to gouge them, but I can certainly quote them a higher price and give myself some negotiating room.

Mr. Hastings,

It's so great to hear from you again! I had assumed you were no longer interested in the Big House. For the entirety of the second and third floors—which is five bedrooms and two baths total—plus utilities, the rent would be $5500.

I look up, my thumbs already tired of tapping out this email. I hate doing things like this on my phone, but I just need this done. Fifty-five hundred is about fourteen hundred over what my roommates pay now.

Or paid, when all five of them were living here.

Common areas such as the kitchen, laundry room, one bathroom, and main living spaces on the first floor would be shared, though I am the only current resident and teach middle school Monday through Friday.

Also, I'm not sure when you might be interested in moving in, but I still have two of the rooms rented at this point. The third floor is empty, however, and available for immediate occupancy. The second floor wouldn't be available until summer at the earliest.

My heart sinks, bumping against each of my ribs as it does. They're not going to want to wait seven more months to move in. There are plenty of places to live and rent in the greater Charleston area.

But let's keep chatting! Let me know your thoughts.

Best regards,

Tahlia

I hit send and immediately stand from the swing. It pitches back and then forward, clipping the backs of my legs and nearly sending me to the ground.

I grunt and move out of the way, casting a glare to the swing for...swinging. Literally what it's supposed to do.

This is going to require so much more than a few pie crusts. I return to the kitchen and get them ready to bake —anything to distract myself from the pit in my stomach. I slide them into the oven and eye my phone.

In the end, I am not a strong person, and I tap to open my email to see if Donald has responded in the past fifteen minutes.

Sweet buttered biscuits, he has.

Hello Tahlia,

The terms are acceptable. My client appreciates your prompt response and is pleased with the arrangement.

I can confirm that I will be the only staff member residing on the third floor. Both my client and I are extremely respectful of domestic boundaries and prefer quiet, structured environments.

A few additional questions, if I may:

- Are the rooms on each floor connected, or entirely separate?

- Would it be possible to use one bedroom as a sitting room?

- Is there one bathroom per bedroom, or are they shared across floors?

- Would it be permissible to install a small refrigerator upstairs?

Thank you for your response to these inquiries.

Respectfully,

Donald

The questions are thoughtful, thorough—and oddly charming. It's clear this is not just some random tenant. Whoever this is, they're used to having things done their way. And if Donald is answering so quickly, this mystery client has to be sitting next to him. Why can't he just email me himself?

I leave my phone on the counter and hurry across the house to my master suite to retrieve my laptop. Pie crusts don't take long to bake, and they can go from not-quite-done to burnt in literally seconds.

So I can't leave them alone while I try to craft the perfect response to this new email.

I set up at the bar and copy Donald's questions into the reply box. Then I can see them as I answer them.

Donald,

I'm happy to answer any questions you may have.

Each bedroom is a separate room. None of them are connected, except by hallways. You can absolutely use the rooms for anything—sitting room, an office, etc.

There are three bedrooms and one full bath on the second floor, as well as a small storage room/closet.

On the third floor, there are two bedrooms, with a full bath between them, with an entrance to the bathroom directly from each bedroom. In the United States, we call these a Jack-and-Jill bathroom. There is a small storage closet on the third floor as well.

There is a full living room, kitchen, laundry room, and one-and-a-half baths on the main level. You can absolutely put a small refrigerator in any of the rooms—there are plenty of outlets in each room.

I'm happy to send photos or a video walk-through if you're interested.

Let me know!

Tahlia

It feels odd to use an exclamation point with the formal Donald, but I send the email anyway. I don't have to alter how I write to match his style.

With the message whizzing across the ocean, I can't sit still. I slide from the barstool and pace the length of the island. Thankfully, the timer on my pie crusts goes off, and I distract myself by pulling them out and setting them on a baking rack to cool.

That done, I can easily go right back to obsessing over Donald and his emails.

I tip my head back and look up to the ceiling. I imagine I can see through the plaster and paint to the floor above, and then the one above that. "I don't know what else to do," I whisper to the Big House. "I can't keep this place going on my own."

It's not just the money, though that's a real concern. It's the emptiness. The Big House was never meant to be inhabited by just one person. It needs voices and laughter and the chaos of lives being lived within its walls.

I exhale and roll my neck, stretching out the stress there. I have nothing else to steal my attention, so I dive back into my email.

"He's fast, this Donald," I say when I see I have another email from him. Perhaps I'm wrong about who Donald is—I've been imagining him as a white-haired, close-to-sixty-year-old man who types everything with only his pointer fingers.

Tahlia,

Thank you for the detailed information. My client is very pleased with the layout and amenities as you've described them.

This arrangement could work beautifully. My client has authorized me to inform you that we would like to proceed. Formal arrangements will be made in the new year, after the holiday season.

In the meantime, we are prepared to pay a substantial deposit of $11,000 USD to secure the entirety of the second and third floors until you're able to rent them both to us. It is essentially a first and last months' worth of rent—my client doesn't want this house to go to other renters.

Would this be acceptable to you?

Respectfully,

Donald

I read the message three times, my heart fluttering in my chest. "Eleven thousand dollars." I laugh but can't quite extinguish the spark of hope that ignites in my chest.

And these guys are so from overseas.

My imagination starts to wander as I picture who they could be, and why they want to come to America. Not only that, but why South Carolina? Why Cider Cove?

I want to tell everyone on the Big House group text, but I refrain. I don't want Emma and Lizzie to feel like I'm rushing them out of their rooms, and besides, nothing is finalized yet.

But maybe with one more email, it will be.

Donald! This sounds great! I've attached my standard lease agreement with the monthly rent+utilities filled in, and I added the deposit amount for you as well. The dates are left blank for now, and we can keep discussing those in the New Year.

Payment information and the address to the Big

House are included. If your client would please sign the agreement and send the payment, then the top two floors are yours whenever we can make it work for both of us.

Thanks so much!

I send the email, sit still, and try to listen to the Big House. It's still quiet, but something about the silence feels...different now.

Like maybe she's waiting for her next big adventure as we both welcome new people through her doors.

CHAPTER TWENTY-EIGHT

LIZZIE

Sunlight streams through the curtains of my childhood bedroom, painting golden stripes across the quilt my mother made when I was ten. I stretch, feeling the familiar creak of the twin bed beneath me. For a moment, I'm transported back in time—a teenager again, with nothing more complicated to worry about than chemistry homework and whether my crush noticed me in the hallway.

But I'm not that girl anymore.

I reach for my phone on the nightstand, smiling at the text Matt sent me about ten minutes ago.

Merry Christmas Eve, kitten. Can't wait to see you. Leaving in 30 minutes.

Two months after our Halloween reunion, and Matt still gives me butterflies. We've been inseparable since that night on the Big House porch when he showed up in his Pierre Curie costume and laid his heart bare.

I type back: *Drive safe. Dad's making his ooey gooey cinnamon rolls.*

Sans raisins, because Matty doesn't like them.

I swing my legs over the side of the bed and pad to the window, looking out at my father's farm. The morning frost glitters on the pasture, and the goats are already out, their breath forming little clouds in the December air. Trouble, the ringleader, stands on his hind legs against the fence, probably plotting his next escape.

So much has changed since Halloween. I quit ChemTech the Monday after the party—one of the scariest and most liberating decisions of my life. Now I'm modeling part-time and working at Glow Cosmetics, a small manufacturer in Charleston that specializes in natural skincare products. I'm their compliance consultant, where I can use my regulatory experience in a field I actually care about, and it leaves my schedule flexible enough to take on as many modeling jobs as I want.

And Matt has been my constant through all the changes, the clean-out of my office, Emma's engagement and constant wedding talk, everything.

"Sugarplum," Dad calls from downstairs. "I can't remember if it's a yes to raisins or a no!"

"Coming!" I grab my robe and head for the door. Christmas Eve with my dad and Matt—my heart feels full to bursting. And tomorrow, Chanel is hosting all of us at her place for dinner.

Downstairs, the kitchen smells of cinnamon, coffee, and the pine garland Dad always drapes across every available surface in the month of December. He stands at the counter, gray hair tousled, wearing the "World's Best Dad" apron I gave him years ago.

"There you are," he says, adding sugar to his coffee. It's too much, but I figure he has to enjoy life too. "Thought you might sleep all day." He looks at me like I've done something wrong by sleeping past dawn.

"It's only eight-thirty." I join him in the kitchen and make my own cup of coffee—mine with plenty of cream.

"When you were little, you'd be up at five on Christmas Eve." He grins and steps over to the bowl of dough on the countertop. "Couldn't *wait* for Santa and were convinced he might visit you a day early."

I smile though I don't remember that, then grab the bag of raisins and put it back in the pantry. "No raisins, Dad."

He looks scandalized for a moment, and then he nods. "All right. You can get out everything we need for the frosting." He starts to roll out the dough, liberally layering on melted butter and cinnamon sugar while I get out cream cheese and powdered sugar.

"So," Dad says as he starts to roll up the dough. "How's the new job going?"

"It's amazing." I can't help the smile that spreads

across my face. "I'm designing a compliance system for their new skincare line, and they actually care about my input. Plus, I did three shoots last week for their spring campaign."

I shrug. "I mean, it's makeup, but I did one with my red hair, then went to the salon, and did one with my new brunette look." I reach up and push my now-dark brown hair out of my face. "Hair color really does influence the type of makeup people should wear."

"Mm hm." With the dough rolled properly, he picks up his big kitchen knife and starts cutting rounds. I pick up the pan and spray it, then lay the cut rolls inside, swirl-side up.

We work together in the kitchen for a few minutes, until Dad has the rolls all resting for their final rise and he's checking on the ham he's already started.

"When is Matt getting here?"

"Soon," I say, glancing at the clock. "He should've left by now, and he's stopping by his sister's house to get an apple pie for our pie bar later."

"I love me some apple pie," Dad says with a smile. "Maybe we should have it with our breakfast."

"It's your house," I say, because I'm not going to tell my dad he can't have pie for breakfast, just like I don't mother him about the amount of sugar he puts in his coffee.

"Do you think Matt will care?"

I glance over to my father. "I don't think he's going to swat your hand away."

"Never hurts to stay in the good graces of your girl-friend's father." He closes the oven and wipes his hands on a dish towel. "Especially when that father owns a shotgun."

I cock my hip and glare at him. "You promised not to do the overprotective father routine." Besides, it's not like he's never met Matt. We come out to the farm at least twice a month, and sometimes more.

We retreat to the back deck, where it's not exactly warm, but it's not too cold either, at least by Southern standards. I love coming to the farm, because it's so different than the city, even the suburb where I live.

The world feels slower, and I need that in my life right now. After a while, the sound of tires on gravel comes from around the front of the house, and my heart does a little skip. "He's here," I say, getting up and heading for the steps that will take me into the yard and around to the front.

"Hold on there, speedy." Dad catches my arm. "You might want to put on something besides your pajamas first."

I look down at my teeny tiny shorts and tank top, my robe over my shoulders but open in the front. "Lafayette," I mutter. "Be right back."

Ten minutes later, I'm dressed in jeans and a soft cream

sweater, my hair brushed and a touch of makeup applied. Not too much—Matt has seen me in full glam and in no makeup at all, and somehow manages to look at me the same way regardless. I add the final touch—earrings in the shape of a string of Christmas lights—and head downstairs.

Matt is already in the kitchen, helping my father set the table. They talk and laugh like they're best friends, and when he finishes, Matt doesn't immediately ask what else he can do.

He's wearing khakis and a dark green sweater that'll surely highlight the flecks of gold in his hazel eyes, and his hair is slightly windblown, as always. He looks up when I enter, and his whole face lights up.

"Hey, you," he says, setting down the plates in one big stack to come greet me. He wraps his arms around my waist and presses a quick kiss to my lips. "Merry Christmas Eve, kitten."

"Merry Christmas Eve." I lean into him, breathing in his familiar, woodsy scent. "I see you've been put to work already."

"Your dad said I had to earn my keep." He grins over at my father, who pretends to be busy with the coffee pot.

"I brought pie," Matt says. "And presents." He nods toward a laundry basket full of beautifully wrapped packages. "And...cats."

"You brought your cats?"

"I didn't want to leave them all day on Christmas Eve," he says.

I laugh even as I step out of his arms and go to greet Purricell and Purroxide. "You leave them home all day while you go to work at ChemTech."

"It's *Christmas*, Lizzie."

"You didn't have to bring presents," Dad says as he joins us in the living room, but I can tell he's pleased.

"Of course I did." Matt looks at me with wide eyes, then trains his oh-so-innocent expression on my father. "It's *Christmas*, and it's my first time here." He scoffs and sits down on the end of the couch. "Don't need to bring presents."

Dad chuckles and looks at the Maine Coon in my lap. "I take it these felines aren't farm-ready."

Matt laughs and shakes his head. "Not even close, but I brought Purricell's leash, and we can put the litter box on the sunporch." He jumps back to his feet. "I'll do that now."

"Purroxide won't come out," I say.

"He's just mad at me, because I told him it would be a short drive," Matt says. "See if you can work your Lizzie-magic on him."

Something passes between us—a look, a feeling, an understanding. *This is what wholehearted feels like, I think. This is what it feels like to be fully seen and fully loved.*

Dad clears his throat as Matt leaves with the litter box. I just wait for him to say what he wants, and after the door to the sunporch slams, he says, "Your Lizzie-magic?"

"I possess very little," I say. "Mostly only with cats." I grin down at Purricell, who's sitting very still while I scrub his neck. "Fine, just these two cats." I turn toward the carrier and smile at Purroxide as he peeks his nose and ears out.

"Come on, buddy. It's just my dad's house."

Purroxide takes a careful step out, holding his paw up for an extra moment, like he can't trust the couch to hold him up.

"Don't let them near the tree," Matt says as he rejoins us. "Tell them, Lizzie, because they won't listen to me."

"No tree, guys," I say. "You can't go anywhere near the Christmas tree." I peer at Purricell, then Purroxide. "No. Tree."

"Yow," Purroxide says, and he hops to the ground. He takes a few steps toward the Christmas tree, stops, and looks over his shoulder at me.

I tilt my head at him and fix him with a fierce glare. "No."

The cat seems to enjoy the attention, because he holds it for several long moments. Then he sits down and faces the tree with another, "Yow-elll."

"Good boy," I say as I nudge Purricell onto the floor too. "How long until the cinnamon rolls are done?"

The timer on the oven goes off, and Dad gets up. "Right now. We just need to whip up that frosting and give them a minute to cool." He bustles into the kitchen to do that, and Matt slides onto the couch with me, effortlessly putting his arm around me and pulling me close.

"I had to anchor my tree to the wall, and it only has half the balls I originally put on it." He shakes his head. "I *feed* them, for scandium's sake."

I grin at the element-curse and press my lips to his cheek. "You're my favorite person, but you brought a lot of gifts."

"Dude, they are so lame." He sighs as he looks past me to the laundry basket of gifts. "I put a couple of them in a bigger box just so they didn't look so stupid."

I laugh and lean into him, sinking into the warmth of the love between us.

"Let's eat," Dad says, and Matt and I go into the kitchen. "I think Elizabeth's feline-magic comes from that kitten she kept in her closet when she was eight."

Matt stalls in pulling out my chair. "You had a secret cat?"

"I knew my parents wouldn't let me keep it," I say.

"Yeah, leaving it for us to find during her momma's book club meeting seemed like a better idea," Dad says dryly.

"Minneapolis." I throw Dad a look as I finish pulling out my chair and sit down.

Matt grins at my city-swear. "Is that what you said when you were eight?"

"No," I say exactly the way I imagine Purricell or Purroxide would if they were asked.

"Elizabeth started the city-swears in high school," Dad says, and I should be used to him throwing me under the bus at this point. He sets the pan of ooey gooey frosted cinnamon rolls on the table, where he's already put a bowl of fresh fruit, coffee, and orange juice.

Matt never finished putting out the plates, which actually makes me super happy, and I reach out and take one off the stack.

"Did you tell your dad that we were looking at getting a cat together?" Matt reaches for the serving spoon in the fruit and puts some berries on my plate.

"No," I say. "I haven't told him that yet."

Dad's wearing his surprised expression, and I can't quite meet his eyes. I'm not sure why, but it's whatever.

"Well, technically, it would live at my place," Matt says. "But Lizzie would have visitation rights."

"How very generous of you," Dad says. "Getting a pet together sounds like this is a serious thing."

It's not a question, but Matt answers anyway. "Yes, sir. Very serious."

The warmth and strength in his voice makes my heart do a little flip. We haven't talked about marriage explicitly, but it's there in the background of our conversations about the future. A shared understanding that we're building toward something permanent.

"How's your sister doing?" Dad asks, smoothly changing the subject. "First Christmas with the baby, right?"

"Yes," Matt says, his face softening the way it always does when he talks about Nora. "She's almost seven months now. Chanel's gone all out—matching family pajamas, professional photos with Santa, the works."

"You're spending tomorrow with them?" Dad asks.

"You're coming too," I say, shooting Dad a look as he puts a cinnamon roll on my plate. "You already committed, and you're not sick."

"I wasn't going to back out."

"Mm hm."

"They're excited to have you," Matt says, volleying his gaze between me and my dad. "Shad's been practicing his Christmas ham recipe for weeks."

"I'm sure it'll be delicious," Dad says.

I can admit I'm a little nervous about Christmas Day at Chanel's. See, my dad isn't the only one coming from my side of the family. All of my roommates and their significant others are coming too.

That's right. Chanel is hosting the Big House roomies, my dad, and all the husbands and fiancés. Plus me and Matt.

I honestly don't know how we got to that point, and it sounded like a good idea until this moment.

"It's going to be amazing," Matt says as if he can sense my trepidation.

When we finish eating, we move to the living room, where a modest Christmas tree stands in the corner, adorned with the same ornaments Dad's been using since I was a child.

"Present time?" I suggest, and Matt nods as he stands guard in front of the tree, his arms folded as he glares at Purricell.

The cat stalks away, and Matt watches him go. "Yeah, that's what I thought." He sighs as he comes over to his laundry basket of gifts.

He plucks one out and hands it to me. "Ladies first."

I tear into it, gasping when I see what's inside—a delicate silver charm in the shape of a high-heeled shoe. "For your bracelet," Matt says, taking it from me and carefully attaching it next to the beaker charm he gave me at Halloween. "To celebrate your modeling career."

"It's perfect," I whisper, admiring how it catches the light. "Thank you."

"My turn," Dad says, handing Matt a flat, rectangular package. "This one's from me."

Matt unwraps it carefully, revealing a digital photo frame. His expression softens as he studies it, and he grins at my father. "I've always wanted one of these."

"You can send pictures to it from your phone," Dad says. "Or Elizabeth can. She takes a lot of selfies."

"I do not, Dad." I roll my eyes, but secretly, I love a

good selfie, and I'll totally send them to Matt's digital picture frame. "Your turn," I say, handing Matt my gift.

He unwraps it eagerly, his eyes widening when he sees what's inside. "No way," he breathes, lifting out the vintage chemistry set. "Where did you find this?"

"Antique store in Columbia," I say, pleased by his reaction. "The owner said it's from the 1950s. All the chemicals have been removed, of course, but I thought you might like it for your office."

"I love it," he says, examining the detailed illustrations on the box. "This is incredible, Lizzie. Thank you." He leans over to kiss me, and Dad excuses himself to start cleaning up the kitchen.

Though we haven't finished opening the presents, I curl up next to Matt on the sofa, my head resting on his shoulder.

He plays with the charms on my bracelet. "About that cat."

I look up at him. "Did you find one?"

"Kind of." He traces patterns on my palm, his eyes warm and flecked and wonderful. "It's not a Maine Coon, but Purricell and Purroxide need a little sister. We could name her Purrmanganate."

I burst out laughing. "That's terrible."

"It's *brilliant*," he says. "We could call her Maggie for short."

"Like you call any of your cats by a short name." I

grin at him. "So we're going to start calling them Cell and Oxide?"

"We could," he says airily.

Yeah, we could, but I know Matty, and he won't. He *likes* to scold the felines with their full names.

He holds me close, and for a moment, we just breathe together, content in the knowledge that we're exactly where we're meant to be.

"We should probably get going soon," I say reluctantly. "The Big House party starts at seven, and I still need to pack my overnight bag."

"Oh, all right." Matt sighs and shifts to get up.

We find Dad in the kitchen, loading the dishwasher. "Heading out?"

"Yeah," I say. "I need to grab my things upstairs, and then we'll go."

"I'm going to leave the presents for you guys," Matt says.

"Yeah, sure," Dad says as I head for the stairs.

I have my foot on the first step when I hear Matt clear his throat behind me. "Actually, James, if you have a minute, I was hoping to ask you something."

I keep going up a few steps so they can't see me, my heart suddenly pounding. What could Matt possibly need to ask my father? He starts to speak, and I scamper away, not wanting to overhear this. If Matt wanted me to know, he'd have asked in front of me.

One thing I know: I'll find out eventually, because Matt and I don't keep secrets from each other.

CHAPTER TWENTY-NINE

MATT

The cats are staring at me like I've lost my mind.

"Stop looking at me like that," I tell Purricell as I adjust his tiny bow tie for the third time. "It's Christmas. You're *supposed* to look festive."

He gives me a slow blink that clearly communicates his feline disapproval, while Purroxide attempts to back away from his own bow tie. I catch him before he can escape, securing the red velvet around his neck.

"It's just for a few hours," I say. "And it's a special day."

More special than they realize. My hand drifts to my pocket for the hundredth time this morning, feeling the small velvet pouch hidden there. The ring inside represents everything I want—a future with Lizzie.

I glance at the clock. We need to leave for the Big

House soon, and my heart is already doing the chemical equivalent of a potassium-water reaction. Explosive. Unpredictable. Potentially magnificent.

"She's going to say yes," I tell the chem-cats, though I'm not entirely sure which of us I'm trying to convince. "Her dad already gave his blessing."

My mind drifts back to yesterday in James's kitchen, after Lizzie went upstairs.

He'd looked at me with those same blue-green eyes Lizzie has, somehow already knowing what was coming. "I'm listening."

"I love your daughter," I'd said, my voice steadier than I expected. "I want to spend the rest of my life with her." I took a deep breath. "I'd like your blessing to ask her to marry me."

James hadn't hesitated. "You have it," he'd said, clapping me on the shoulder. "But fair warning—she's stubborn as a mule and particular about everything."

"I know," I'd replied with a grin. "That's part of why I love her."

Now, standing in my bedroom with two disgruntled cats in bow ties, I'm ready to take the biggest step of my life.

"Okay, guys," I say, giving them each a scratch behind the ears. "Let's go—and Purroxide, nothing about today is about you. No yowling on the way over."

———

PURROXIDE YOWLS the whole way to the Big House, the menace. He's urged on by Hig, who showed up on the front steps howling while I stuffed the chemistry cats into their carrier for the second time this year—and the second time in two days.

So as if we aren't a giant ball of chaos, the Big House seems to match our energy, with cars filling the front parking area, and people spilling out of them and heading up the front sidewalk. Chanel and Tahlia have been planning this meal for weeks now, and as the guest list grew, my sister didn't think her house would be big enough. Tahlia loves having people at the Big House, so we moved the party here.

The door stands open, and Tahlia and Emma loiter in the doorway, welcoming everyone. Cheery lights hang from the eaves, shining even in the daytime. Christmas music blares from somewhere inside, mingling with laughter and chatter.

An enormous blow-up Santa stands at the corner of the sidewalk and the porch—and that so wasn't there a few days ago.

"Yooowwwww!" Hig yelps, causing Beckett and Claudia to turn toward my SUV.

I roll down the window. "There's nowhere to park up here. Should I go around back?"

"Yeah, it's not too hard," Claudia says, and she gives me quick instructions for how to get to the additional parking behind the house. It's six more minutes in the car with unhappy animals, and by the time I pull up behind the Big House, I'm seriously doubting every choice I've made in my life.

But I soldier on, gathering the cat carrier while Hig bounds across the yard toward the back yard. A moment later, the back door opens, and Lizzie rushes outside wearing a red sweater dress that makes my brain short-circuit.

I freeze next to the back door of my SUV, because she is so gorgeous, and there is no way I can ask her to marry me. I can't even breathe.

"Hig," she says pleasantly, like she knew all along I'd bring an extra dog for Christmas dinner. She moves to the railing on the back porch and waves, and I just love her in her dark hair and the way she comes quickly down the steps to greet me and the chem-cats.

"Merry Christmas," she says, kissing me quickly before reaching into the backseat to get the pan of rolls my neighbor gave me. She has to work today—thus why Hig was found yowling on my front steps. "Everyone's already here."

"Everyone?" I ask, my throat suddenly dry. "I'm last?"

"Yeah, but it's no big deal." She glances at me. "Tahlia and Chanel still have lots to do before we can eat." She glows with holiday cheer. "Wait till you see Nora. She's wearing the *cutest* little Christmas outfit."

We make our way inside, where the scent of roasting

turkey and apple pie spices fill the air. Tahlia, dressed in a green velvet dress with a smudged apron protecting it, directs operations from the countertop, where she's pouring green beans into an enormous baking dish. Aaron and Elliott work to set the extended dining table. Hillary and Liam are entertaining Nora, who's dressed as a tiny elf.

And in the midst of it all is my sister, who catches my eye and gives me a quiet look that makes my face heat up. "Matty." Chanel leaves her post at the stove to come hug me. "Merry Christmas."

"Merry Christmas." I hug her tightly, trying to sound normal and not like a man about to have a coronary.

"Nice bow tie," she whispers in my ear. "Matches the cats."

I look down at my own red bow tie—yes, I'm coordinating with my cats today—and adjust it nervously. "I'm too dressed up, right?"

"It's fine," Chanel says underneath the laughter that erupts near the island. "Leave it." She swats at my hand, and I let it fall back to my side.

A collective "Aw," rises into the air, and I turn to see Lizzie has released the cats from their carrier, and she and all of her roommates crowd around them.

"They're the cutest things ever," Hillary says.

"We need a cat," Claudia says.

"To go with our two dogs?" Becketts asks, shaking his head. "You've lost your mind."

"They're adorable," Tahlia says. "You can dress up your dogs, Claude."

"That's what we need to do," she says.

"Aw, Luna likes them." Ryanne smiles fondly at her husband's guide dog, who sits primly while Purricell inspects her Christmas dress. Panic streams through me, because the chem-cats aren't used to any dogs except Hig. But Luna has a calm presence, and it's Elliott who crouches down to pet them.

"Hey, brother." Shad appears and hands me a bottle of sparkling water.

"Hey." I pull him into a hug, and whisper-ask, "Tahlia is aware of the plan, right?"

"Yep."

We separate, and I nod once before I catch Lizzie watching me. I fix a smile on my face when I really want to throw up. "Nora is an elf," I say when I press into her side.

"I think she's a bit overwhelmed by the crowd."

"Join the club," I say.

Lizzie giggles and links her arm through mine. "You're the social one, Matty. You don't like this?"

"I do," I say. "Where's your dad?"

"Out in the living room," she says. "You could go join him out there if you're overwhelmed in here." She looks at me with her big Lizzie eyes, and I'm not going anywhere.

I take a sip of my sparkling water, my first instinct to

ask what needs to be done. If I'm busy, then I can't stew on the pouch in my pocket. But this isn't my show, and if Tahlia or Chanel need help, they'll ask someone. Doesn't have to be me.

"Look how cute you two are," Hillary says, joining me and Lizzie. "You match."

I look at my bowtie and Lizzie's dress. "Kind of," I say.

"It's Christmassy," she says.

"Yeah, but I didn't coordinate with him," Lizzie says, her gaze moving to Claudia and Beckett.

"Yeah, Claude takes clothing coordination seriously," Hillary says. "I'm lucky if I can get Liam to wear something besides his biking body suits."

"I do not wear those for anything but biking," he says, handing her a cracker with dip on it. "Taste this. It'll blow your mind."

Hillary eyes it warily. "What is it?"

"Buffalo wing dip." Liam grins at her.

"You want a divorce, don't you?"

Liam bursts out laughing, and some of my nerves dissipate in the warmth of their banter. This is what family feels like—teasing and inside jokes and the comfortable chaos of people who love each other.

Tahlia claps her hands for attention. "Dinner in five minutes! Everyone, find your name card at the table, please."

The next few minutes are a flurry of activity as final

dishes are brought to the table, drinks are poured, Lizzie goes to get her dad, and fifteen people try to find their assigned places. Somehow, Tahlia and Chanel have managed to combine three tables to create one long feast-worthy setup that stretches down one wall and L's into a second area.

I find my place between Lizzie and Chanel, with James across from us. The cats have their own little station in the corner, complete with festive bowls for their Christmas dinner.

"This is amazing," I say, looking around at the elaborate spread. "You guys outdid yourselves."

"It was mostly Tahlia," Chanel says. "I just followed orders."

"Not true," Tahlia calls from the head of the table. "Chanel made the most incredible cranberry sauce I've ever tasted."

Once everyone is seated, Tahlia raises her glass. "Before we eat, I just want to say how special it is to have everyone here. Our Big House family has grown and changed, but days like this remind me that we'll always be connected." She smiles, her eyes suspiciously glassy and bright. "To family—both the ones we're born with and the ones we choose."

"To family," everyone echoes, clinking glasses.

This is what I want, I realize with sudden clarity. Not just Lizzie, but this—belonging to something bigger than myself. Being part of a tapestry of relationships that support and challenge and love each other through all of life's changes.

Tahlia catches my eye from across the table and gives me a subtle nod. My heart rate doubles instantly.

It's time.

"Before we start," Tahlia says. "I know it's not Thanksgiving, but I thought we might go around and share something we're grateful for this year. It's been a big one for a lot of us."

Everyone murmurs in agreement, and Emma starts by raising her glass of cranberry cocktail. "I'm super grateful that Aaron and I won the contest in the park, and that we'll be getting married next year."

"And I'm grateful I finally figured out how to get Emma to think of me as boyfriend-material." He chuckles while Emma cuddles into his side.

"I'm glad Becks and I figured out how to work together, live together, and most of all—what color to paint the kitchen."

"Oh, boy," Beckett says with a grin. He puts his arm around Claudia, and they really are the most sophisticated couple here. "I'm grateful Claude still married me, even though I wore shorts to our wedding."

Everyone laughs, with several of them telling him how they liked his short-suit. I have to admit, it wasn't bad. Not what I'd wear, but not bad.

"I'm thrilled I still live right next door," Hillary says. "And that I didn't kill Liam's orchards this summer." She beams at him, and he wears nothing but love in his face for her.

"I'm glad we're back in South Carolina," Liam says. "California ain't for the weak." He laughs, and several people join him.

"I'm glad I have Luna and Ry," Elliott says. "To help me see what's most important." That sobers things a bit, which is actually good for me.

Ryanne weeps as all eyes move to her. She shakes her head into the silence, and then she takes a great big breath. "I've been stocking up on a flavor of M&M I don't normally eat all that much."

Elliott pulls her closer and kisses her cheek. Ry looks at him, and then lifts up a bright yellow package of peanut M&Ms.

Beside me, Lizzie gasps, and at the end of the table, Tahlia sucks in a breath. "Ry," she says.

Ryanne nods. "Elliott and I have a little peanut on the way, and I'm real happy about that."

A roar of congratulations follow, with Emma and Lizzie getting out of their seats to go hug Ry and Elliott. This is joy. This is family. I want to be part of this for a long time, and I suddenly understand why Lizzie has been upset about her roommates and best friends moving out and moving on.

Things settle again, and James clears his throat. "I'm so grateful to be here. It's been a while since I've had so much excitement in my life, and I love it."

Lizzie reaches over and squeezes his hand, and we look at Tahlia.

She wipes her eyes, laugh-cries, and shakes her head. "I'm just so happy we're all here doing this." She looks around at everyone. "Thank you for coming." She nods and looks at me.

Oh, it's my turn.

I stand slowly, humiliation running through me. My mind shouts at me to *sit down*, because no one else stood up.

My legs might give out beneath me. "I, um—" I clear my throat. "I'm grateful for a lot of things this year. For my job, for my sister's family being here." I glance at Chanel, who gives me an encouraging smile.

"But mostly," I say. "I'm really glad Lizzie didn't shove me out of her office when I brought up the idea of us using our friendship as a front for what I really wanted."

I turn to look at her, and the rest of the room seems to fade away. "For the way she sees me—really sees me. For how she challenges me to be better. For her city-swears and her Diet Coke addiction and her uncanny ability to make my cats behave."

A ripple of laughter goes through the room, but I barely hear it. I'm focused entirely on Lizzie, whose eyes crinkle as she smiles, but fill with wariness when she looks at me again.

"When we met, I was a guy who thought his value

came from what he could do for others. But you showed me that I'm enough just as I am." I take a deep breath and reach into my pocket. "You're my catalyst, Lizzie. You change everything for me."

I drop to one knee beside her chair, and she gasps, her hand flying to her mouth. "Holy Butte."

The room goes completely silent.

Butte. That's a new one.

"Elizabeth Trenton," I say, shaking the ring out of the velvet pouch. The solitaire diamond with tiny lab-created rubies on either side, set in platinum, glints like the happiest Christmas engagement ring in the world.

I look from it to her, scared out of my mind. "Will you marry me, kitten?"

Lizzie stares at me, tears filling her eyes, and for one terrifying moment, I think I've miscalculated everything.

Then she launches herself at me, nearly knocking us both to the floor. "Yes!" she cries, wrapping her arms around my neck. "Yes, yes, a thousand times yes!"

The room erupts in cheers and applause. I slip the ring onto her finger with shaking hands, and she stares at it in wonder. "It's perfect," she whispers. "It's absolutely perfect."

She looks up and kisses me, and the celebration turns to cat-calls. Purricell rubs along my side, and right on cue, Hig pitches up into a yowl on the back deck.

Lizzie laughs, and I join her as we find our feet. Someone grabs Lizzie, leaving me to my sister. Chanel hugs me fiercely, whispering, "I'm so proud of you, Matty."

James shakes my hand, then pulls me into a bear hug. "She's lucky to have you, son."

In the midst of the chaos, I find myself at the center of more love and acceptance than I've ever experienced.

Lizzie and I come back together, and she leans her forehead against mine.

"This is the family I've always wanted," I whisper, my voice thick with emotion. "Thank you for introducing me into it." I kiss the top of her head, my heart so full it feels like it might overflow. "Thank you for showing me what I really wanted all along."

"And what's that?" she asks, looking up at me with those beautiful blue-green eyes.

"You," I say simply. "Just you. And all of this." I gesture to the room full of people who have become our extended family. "A place to belong."

She kisses me again, and I know without a doubt that I've found my home. Not in a building or a job or even in what I can do for others.

But in Lizzie.

"I love you," I say.

She beams at me. "I love you too."

———

Oh, boy, I think "being fake friends" is the best thing

that ever happened to Matt and Lizzie! I hope you liked them too!

Read on for a couple of sneak peak chapters at the next book in the Cider Cove series - **A VERY ROYAL ROOMMATE** - and find out exactly WHAT is going on with D. Hastings, and his mysterious client who wants to rent Tahlia's entire house...

Get new free stuff every month, access to live events, special members-only deals, and more when you join the Feel-Good Fiction newsletter. You'll get instant access to the Member's Only area on my new site, where all the goodies are located, so join by scanning the QR code below.

SNEAK PEEK! A VERY ROYAL
ROOMMATE, CHAPTER ONE: TAHLIA

I LOOK IN THE MIRROR IN MY MASTER SUITE, feeling very much like that teenage girl who finds out she's a princess. "This is as good as it gets."

The first weekend of June means freedom for me. Three glorious months of it, though I still feel the bone-weary tiredness of the end of the school year.

My hair is freshly blonde, where I've put in accents just to give my already pale hair more color and texture. Curls bob around my chin, but I won't look elegant the way Lizzie will, or stunning the way Em will.

They're getting married today. Yes, together. A joint ceremony at the Dorothy, one of Charleston's premier hotels. The past few months have been wild with ups and downs and twists and turns and changes.

I suppose that's life, but it's been crazy here at the Big House.

And it's about not to be.

Emma's already moved out, and Lizzie has most of her things packed and boxed and waiting on the back porch. Matt's chemistry buddies, who are also Lizzie's former co-workers, are going to come move them into his townhome while they're on their honeymoon.

I leave my reflection in the mirror and flow out of the master suite in my deep blue gown, exiting to the foyer and pausing as I look through the high arches and into the living room. In in my mind, I see Emma weeping there as she tells us that Aaron's grandfather's backyard —where he lives and has been renovating the house for the past many months—has to be dug up.

"New—pipes," she says with a hiccup. "There's no way we can get married there next month."

Hillary had sat on one side of her with her arm around her, and Lizzie moved from where she'd been standing on the other side of the coffee table. She smashed herself in between Ryanne and Emma—much to Ry's displeasure—and hugged her tightly too.

"What do you need?" she'd asked.

I see myself reach out and pat Emma's leg, my voice almost a ghost as I say, "Whatever we can do, we will."

"We have the orchards," Hillary says.

"*You* got married in those orchards." Emma gives Hillary a grateful look, but shakes her head. "Everything is booked. You have to book the good venues *so* far out."

"What about here at the Big House?" I ask, though

I can't even imagine what that'll take to pull off. I'm not a wedding planner by any stretch of the imagination.

Emma shakes her head. "No, Tahlia. It's too close to finals for you. I can't ask you to do that."

I'd nodded, mostly relieved, then feeling guilty about being relieved.

Now, standing in my foyer, I'm that same yo-yo of emotions I've been since Emma and Aaron got engaged in early November. Happy—desperate—glad for them—worried about my bank account—celebrating as they shop for a dress, taste cake, and book bands.

Then crying in the shower so no one can hear.

And now I stand ready to leave the Big House by myself. I'll meet up with the others at the Dorothy, where Emma will walk down the aisle first, with Lizzie behind her.

"So you'll get married with me." Lizzie had beamed with the words, and her selfless suggestion carries enough energy to propel me out of the house. On the way there, I repeat the same mantra I've said at least five hundred times in the past six months.

"It's going to be fine." Check my mirror. Flip on my blinker. "It's a few hours, and you'll know a lot of people there."

Additional words flow through my mind, but I don't acknowledge them. I don't have to dance, though the ballroom in the Dorothy is made for such things. I don't even need to stay much past the ceremony and the dinner.

At the same time, I don't want to miss a moment of this dual wedding.

So I won't be leaving early, and, "It's going to be fine. It's a few hours, and I *want* to be there. These are my friends, and they're not abandoning me."

They're moving on, and moving on is what humans are meant to do.

Not only that, but Donald has confirmed that he and his still-nameless client will be arriving next weekend.

I'm going to be able to keep up with the maintenance on the Big House, and I've lived with five other women before. I can handle two proper men who each have their own floor.

Before I know it, I'm parking at the Dorothy, and walking in with other fabulously dressed people. Claudia rises from a couch just inside the door and links her arm through mine with the words, "Wow-wee-wow, T. This dress is Bonanza Blue and looks amazing on you."

I relax at her side, because Claudia is glamorous and always knows exactly what to say to put me at ease. I grin at her, and she smiles and leads me through the foyer and down a hall, away from where the other guests are being directed.

"They're down here." Claudia brushes her own curled hair out of her face. "We've been waiting for you."

"I'm not late, am I?"

"No," Claudia says with a wave of her hand. "Not really. Becks and I were just early, because I was worried about traffic. Hill just got here, and we haven't seen Ry yet."

"I bet she's freaking out about her dress." I give Claudia a raised eyebrow, and she doesn't argue.

"She's seven months pregnant," Claudia says instead. "And no dress is going to conceal that."

"I don't know why she even wants to. They've been so ridiculously excited about the pregnancy."

"And it's been so easy," Claudia says. Her phone chimes, and I have no idea where she's stashed that thing. She wears a deeper, darker shade of blue for her bridesmaid's gown, and hers has sequins—of course—and looks like it's been sewn onto her skin.

She turns down another short hallway and then pushes through ultra-tall double-wide doors. "Here we are," she says, stepping back to let me enter first.

The bridal suite is blindingly white everywhere. The summer sunshine streams in through walls and walls of windows, and I pause on the threshold of the room to take it all in.

"I want to get married here," I say.

Lizzie turns to look at me, and her face lights up. "Tahlia's here."

Emma comes around a dressing screen, fiddling with the glittery belt around her waist. "Tahlia's—oh, Tahlia's here." She rushes toward me, and because she's not wearing her shoes yet, she can move quite fast.

"You look beautiful," I say as we embrace. She's opted for a ballgown with layers of uneven tulle that falls in carefully designed layers from her waist to the ground.

"This dress is the real showstopper," Em says as she steps back. "I mean, holy hydrangeas, Tahlia. You look *amazing*."

I smile at her and cock a hip in my own gown. It's not as fabulous as Emma's ballgown, nor Lizzie's mermaid gown, but it fits me well, and it's well-suited to my personality.

Hillary steps into my arms and says, "She's right. You look fabulous."

"No one is fixing me up with anyone," I say. "I don't need you to fill my dance card or anything."

Hillary pulls back, her auburn hair shining in all the bright light. She too wears blue, and she's done her makeup to match, of course. Subtle hints of eyeshadow and liner, with a pale pink lip that only draws my eyes back to hers.

Her dress is lighter than mine, but not quite sky-blue, and it seems to be made of wispy, cottony clouds that have been dipped in the ocean, caught the deep blue sea, and been hung to dry.

It's a fit and flare—like mine—but mine is satin and lace while Hillary's is feathers and gauze.

I love that we have a range of blues, and that Lizzie

and Emma both love the color enough to use it in their weddings.

"All right," Ryanne says in her grumpy-cat voice. "I'm here, and I didn't fall down. Go find Liam and Beckett."

I turn toward the still-open doors to see Elliott kissing his wife, and then Ryanne faces us in her version of the perfect blue bridesmaid dress while he waves to us all and then turns his guide dog around to go back the way he came.

"They're in the groom's room," Hillary calls after him. She moves to the doorway and adds, "To your left, El. The next hallway on your right. It's the only door there."

"Thank you," he calls, and then Hillary brings both doors closed. She leans against them and smiles around at all of us.

"I swear, he thinks I can't go anywhere by myself," Ryanne says.

"I think it's adorable," Hillary says. "He takes good care of you, Ry."

I nod even as I hug her. "He is amazing," I say. "And so are you. Your dress is stunning." Her baby bump keeps us apart, and as she steps back, I rest my palm against it. "How's the baby?"

"He's grumpy today."

"So like his momma, then," Claudia says as she eases into a Ry-hug too.

"I'm not grumpy," Ry says. "It's just so hot outside." She falls back and then sucks in the biggest breath ever. She makes a big fuss over Lizzie's dress, and then Emma's, though we've all seen them both. But if you want a big reaction, Ry's your girl, and I do love that about her.

Two of my best friends marrying their perfect matches in one gorgeous ceremony. It should be the stuff of fairy tales—and it is, for them. For me, it's a bittersweet reminder that after tonight, I'll officially be the only one left in the Big House.

Just for a week, I remind myself, the *It's fine*, immediately following.

With all of us there, we help Lizzie put on her veil, as it's a Whole Thing that pulls behind her for fifteen feet. She'll go second down the aisle to the altar, and when she's ready, she stays by the door, her bouquet clutched in her hands.

I turn my attention to Emma, who's had Hillary braid her hair into a crown. Now, we all place tiny, delicate flowers into the plaits until she's a queen and completely ready for her groom.

I meet her eyes, my smile big and bright as I nod. "You're ready."

"I'm ready?" Emma's voice cracks, and Claudia swoops in.

"No crying," she says. "Em, you promised me."
Emma shakes her head. "No crying."

The problem is, Em cries about everything. Happy things. Sad things. Frustrating things. Amazing things. All things.

"Come on, ladies," Hillary says. "It's our time to shine." She stands in front of Lizzie, who hasn't moved a muscle. Her father should be waiting in the hall, and since Emma doesn't have her father in her life, she's opted for her grandmother to walk her down the aisle.

I love my friends and the way we've all managed to find each other, find the people who care about us, and not worry about what anyone else thinks.

"I want to be on the end," Ry says, and I step to her right side. Claudia joins me, with Hillary on the other end. The four of us will walk down the aisle first, the entire wedding party for the brides. Aaron said his brother doesn't care to walk down the aisle, and Matt's sister is already married and doesn't need to be in the spotlight all the time.

That leaves it for the four of us and the brides, and my heart bobs around in my chest as we walk down the hall. Thankfully, Claudia seems to have gotten all the memos, and she knows to take us to Door B—"B for bride," she says—where we wait for the wedding planner to open it.

It only takes a few minutes, and then the doors open, seemingly on their own. Golden light fills this room, with its marble floors and pillars with the inlaid metallics that surely influence the sunlight coming into the ballroom.

The space is one enormous round, with a huge domed top that steals my breath. I manage to take a step when my girlfriends do, and the crowd rises to their feet when we start down the aisle.

Aaron stands there, looking stunning and dapper in his jet-black tuxedo—with a black leather tool belt under his jacket and around his waist.

"What he got in that thing?" Claudia murmurs, but I don't answer. I have no idea what Aaron has equipped his tool belt with, because it looks empty to me.

Matt steps forward, and I grin at him too. He's also wearing an all-black suit, with a shockingly white jacket with huge lapels and a very chemist-lab-coat pocket on the right side.

"Mm, I approve," Claudia says.

"They both look great," Ry says.

We reach the end of the aisle, where I hug Matt first, and then Aaron, and I follow my friends to the first row, where Chanel has saved a seat for me with her husband and daughter.

I give her a side-squeeze and a smile, glad I have a place here.

The string quartet transitions to Pachelbel's Canon, and everyone ooh's as Emma appears at the entrance, her grandmother beaming beside her. Grams wears a perfectly Southern hat in pale blue on her head, perched just like a bird's nest. It seems like Emma walks her down the aisle more than the other way around, but they both shine with pure radiance.

Emma reaches Aaron, who says right out loud, "You're gorgeous," and kisses her cheek. They link arms, and Claudia guides Grams over to her side of the first row.

The music shifts again, and Lizzie appears. Her blonde hair cascades in soft waves over her shoulders, and her dress—a stunning off-the-shoulder mermaid that showcases her curves perfectly—makes several guests audibly gasp. Matt stands at the altar, looking at her like she's the only person in the room.

I blink back tears. These are happy tears, and I don't need a mantra to feel it and know it. My friends found their people. That's worth celebrating.

The ceremony blurs by in a haze of vows and rings and perfect kisses. I cheer with everyone as Aaron dips Emma low to seal their I-do with a kiss, and then wipe my eyes when Lizzie and Matt kiss in a more subtle way.

The crowd moves on to dinner, where I'm seated with Claudia and Beckett, Hillary and Liam, Ryanne and Elliott, and Grams. I chit and chat, keeping my smile fixed on my face, but there's an empty ache in my chest that won't go away. I love these women fiercely— my college roommates, my found family, my support system through every up and down of the past decade. And now they're all paired off, moving forward with their lives, while I'm still...me.

Tahlia Tomlinson, middle school art teacher, owner of a too-big house, perpetually covered in some form of glitter and paint, or flour and chocolate.

There's dancing. A cake cutting. Bouquet tossing—which I'm conveniently in the restroom for. Through it all, I maintain my smile, even as the evening wears on and my face begins to ache from the effort.

Finally, I hold a two-foot sparkler in each hand and stand with dozens and dozens of other guests as the newlyweds, now changed into less formal clothes, come out of the Dorothy. I yell and scream, congratulating my friends as they get into a limousine and drive away.

Others turn toward each other, hugging and smiling, the energy falling fast now that the subjects of our celebration are gone. I don't have anyone, and I stand there in the darkness, wondering if anyone would notice if I simply...melted into it.

———

THE DRIVE back to Cider Cove is quiet, just me and my thoughts and the occasional flash of headlights from passing cars. The June night is thick with humidity, pressing against my skin even through the car's air conditioning.

I turn down the familiar lane to the Big House, the lane as familiar to me as breathing. The moon is high and full, casting silver light across the front lawn and making the white columns of the porch glow like ghostly sentinels.

Still in the road, I slow to a stop, squinting at the house, knowing immediately that something isn't right. There's a light on in one of the second-floor windows—a window that should be dark because Emma moved out last week.

My heart rate kicks up a notch. Did I leave a light on? No, I'm obsessive about turning everything off before I leave—and I haven't been up to the second floor since I went through it after the cleaning service came five days ago.

I blink, my eyes moving to the front of the house, where I was going to park. Nothing looks amiss there, so I park and sit for a moment, debating my options. Call the police? Go in and confront whoever it is? Drive back to the Dorothy and pay an astronomical amount for a room?

"Get it together, Tahlia," I whisper, reaching into my purse for the pepper spray I keep on my keychain. "This is your house."

I slip off my heels, grab my phone, and quietly make my way up the front porch steps. The key turns silently in the lock, and I step into the foyer, listening intently.

There's movement upstairs. Footsteps. And...is that humming?

What kind of burglar hums while robbing a place?

I tighten my grip on the pepper spray and creep toward the staircase, wincing as a floorboard in the living room creaks beneath my bare feet. The humming stops abruptly.

"Hello?" a male voice calls down. "Is someone there?"

The voice is smooth, cultured, with just a hint of an accent I can't quite place. European, maybe? Definitely not local.

Before I can respond, footsteps approach the top of the stairs, and a figure appears.

In the dim light of the bedroom light he's turned on upstairs, I make out broad shoulders, tousled dark hair, and a strong jaw. He's wearing what looks like expensive loungewear—dark pants and a fitted T-shirt that hints at a well-maintained physique.

For a split second, I'm too stunned by his appearance to remember I'm supposed to be terrified.

Then reality crashes back, and I raise my pepper spray, finger on the trigger.

"Don't move!" I shout, my voice embarrassingly shaky. "I've already called the police, and they're on their way."

The man freezes, save for his hands lifting in surrender. "Easy, there." He for-sure has an accent, but I still can't identify where it's from. He takes a step down the staircase. "I'm not—"

I mirror his forward movement by going backward, out of his sight. My hand shakes, and I've never sprayed pepper spray before. I don't even know if it'll work. He probably thought this house was abandoned, though that makes no sense.

He keeps coming, and I'm over by the arched entry when he reaches the bottom of the steps. "Don't come closer to me," I say.

A flicker of amusement crosses his face, quickly replaced by concern. "Tahlia? It's me, Callan Irwin."

I blink, pepper spray still aimed at his face, though he's too far away for me to incapacitate him now. *Callan Irwin.* That name strikes a gong in my memory, and it's beautiful music in the beginning, and then the sound goes dissonant.

"There was a change of plans," he explains slowly, keeping his hands visible as he does the unspeakable—he comes closer. "Donald sent an email this morning. When we didn't hear back, he called and left a message explaining we'd be arriving tonight instead."

I haven't checked my email or voicemail all day. "How did you get in?"

"The key was under the fake rock in the back parking area, exactly where you told Donald it would be." He actually hooks his thumb over his shoulder, which seems too casual of a movement for someone as sophisticated as him.

My emergency key. Of course. I'd told Donald about it in one of our exchanges, in case there were any issues with the move-in.

"What's your name again?" I ask. "And where's Donald?" Not that I can confirm anything by meeting him. We've never met in person, nor have we exchanges pictures. "You're not supposed to be here for another week."

As the initial surge of adrenaline fades, embarrassment floods in to take its place. I lower the peppery spray as Callan reaches to snap on a lamp.

Light floods the living room, and that alone would stun me for a second. Callan's good looks do it for a lot longer than that. He's clean-shaven and stunning with the light in his eyes now. His hair makes me want to become a stylist, just so I can drag my fingers through it.

The man works out, and all worries about my mystery tenant being a seventy-year-old hermit working on his boring European memoir vanishes.

I can't get a proper breath, especially when Callan smiles. "We did email and call," he says.

"I was at a double wedding all day," I say, surprised my voice works at all.

He runs his hand through that hair in a completely

unfair move. If he knew what that did to females, he wouldn't do it.

There's something familiar about that smile, about the way his eyes crinkle at the corners, about his nervous hair-pushing gesture. Something that tugs at a distant memory I can't quite grasp.

"Have we...?" I start, then shake my head. "Never mind. I should probably put this away before I accidentally blind you." I tuck the pepper spray back into my purse.

"Probably wise." Callan moves closer, showing off his striking blue-gray eyes. "It's nice to finally be here, Tahlia. I've been waiting a long time."

I frown. "Donald said—"

Callan reaches the end of the couch, and he's only two paces from me when I gasp. I know this man. I know those eyes. I know this name.

He emerges from the depths of my memory like a ghost rising from another world, another life.

"Cal?" I whisper, the nickname falling from my lips before I can stop it.

His smile falters for just a moment, then returns brighter than before. In the next moment, it also falls into something far more sad, more anxious.

Yeah, he should be worried.

He has some nerve showing up here. How did he even find me?

He ducks his head, and I tell myself it's *not* the most

adorable thing in the world. Maybe twenty years ago, it was. *Maybe.*

Then he lifts his eyes to mine, where they hook and don't let go. In fact, Callan Irwin has never really let me go. Especially when he says, "Hello, Tally," in that super-smooth, ultra-sexy, perfectly recognizable voice. "It's been a long time."

I can't believe I'm standing here, in South Carolina, with the gorgeous Tahlia Tomlinson in front of me.

Finally, I think, so many stars filling my bloodstream. They fizz and sparkle and foam, making my whole body tingly.

Unfortunately, Tahlia wears a look of complete distaste, colored by pure shock. My carefully laid plans of the past nine months crumble before me. Faced with her, I have no idea what to say though I've practiced and practiced for this moment.

I've planned what I'd wear, and where I'd stand in her house—the Big House, she calls it. I've studied the land, the house, where the parking is. Google Maps is an amazing thing, after all.

I can't even tell you how many hours of sleep I've

lost as I've stood at the table in my study, the blueprints of this house spread before me.

Now that I'm here, face-to-face with the stunning woman my teenage best friend has become, my mind blanks.

Gone are the speeches—and I've delivered plenty of stupid speeches.

Gone are the witty barbs I'd rehearsed with Donald.

Gone are all my defenses.

"What are you doing here?" she gasps out, one hand pressed to the middle of her chest. She wears the sexiest dress I've ever seen, and I've been to parties and dinners with princesses and duchesses. They're nothing compared to Tally in that blue gown. I close my eyes to imprint the memory there, almost overjoyed to have this new image of her.

"Things didn't end the way I wanted them to the last time we were together," I say simply.

Tally falls back another step, fire entering her expression. She cocks one curvy hip, which nearly sends me toppling to the ground as she weakens me. I reach out and grip the back of the couch.

"You left in the middle of the night," she says. "The last time we were together." She scoffs, holds my gaze with her fierce glare as she turns on her heel, and marches across the tiled foyer. "It's late, and I'm tired. You're a week early."

"Tally." I take a few steps to fill the doorway as she opens the door to her master suite.

"We'll talk in the morning." She turns back to me in her open doorway, and we face off there, the innocent foyer between us. "Or maybe we won't. Then *you'll* see what it's like to wake up and have the person you're waiting to talk to gone."

She snaps her fingers, and I flinch. "Poof. Disappeared. Vanished."

"Tal—"

She backs up and slams the door, effectively silencing me. I sigh and hang my head again. "Well, that didn't go so well," I mutter to myself.

Honestly, what did I expect? Tahlia Tomlinson to open her arms and welcome me back into her life without a single explanation?

I have explanations, but some of them I can't say. Some of them I don't want to. Nothing was ever good enough for Tahlia, because I'd known I'd hurt her.

I've never forgotten her, and I've always felt terrible about the way our friendship ended. I scoff at myself and head back to the second floor. "Friendship, right," I say as I climb the steps in this gorgeous Southern plantation house.

Both Tally and I know we were *way* more than friends when I "poof. Disappeared. Vanished," on her. That's what happens when you tell someone you love them.

I groan as I roll my neck, going past the first two bedrooms to the last one at the end of the hall. It's bigger by twenty square feet, and it has the most comfortable bed.

I flop down on that bed and stare up to the ceiling. When I first returned to Notovella to take my role as the Special Envoy of the Crown, I never spoke of Tahlia. Not a single person besides the two of us knows what we were to each other—and that poses a huge problem for me.

See, Don goes everywhere with me, and he's not a stupid man. In fact, Donald Hastings is the one and only person my mother trusts to do this "ridiculous experiment" with me, and I'm quite fond of him too. I certainly don't want to lie to him.

He's known since the get-go that I have ulterior motives for this...sabbatical to the United States. He's never asked what they are, but the moment Tally and I get in the same room, Donald will see and feel the fireworks.

Because, oh, the sparks between us...hot. Instant. Powerful.

"She slammed the door in your face," I whisper to myself. After all, I don't know how sound-proof this old house is, and this bedroom sits directly above Tally's master suite. "Perhaps she doesn't feel those sparks the same way you do."

Perhaps, I grant to myself, and the thought makes my

eyes sigh closed in a combination of disappointment and annoyance. I know how to hide these emotions from my parents and my older brother. I have no idea how I'm going to keep them from Don.

There will be so many questions, and now that we're not under the protection of the Vellation palace...he's going to want answers.

Tally wants them too.

I sigh, wondering how in the world I can answer her question. *What are you doing here?*

I can't speak the truth—I've never forgotten her, and we have unfinished business.

But if I don't, I don't think she'll let me stay in her house for longer than this one night.

Perhaps I don't want morning to come after all.

Perhaps, I agree with myself.

———

MORNING ARRIVES, as it always does, and I go through my normal AM routines. Shower, shave, scrub my teeth, dress in slacks and a white shirt. I have no meetings this morning, so I leave the tie hanging in the closet, and then I face the closed door of the bedroom.

"Can't stay here," I tell myself, and it's not the first time I've given myself this pep talk.

I leave the bedroom and take the stairs down to the first floor slowly, one hand skimming the pristine dark wood banister. The Big House is quiet. Not silent, like the palace at night with its marble corridors and servants who speak in "Yes, sir," and "Right this way, sir."

Oh, how I hate the word "sir."

Worse is "your majesty."

And don't get me started on "his highness."

If I hear that one more time... Thankfully, here in Cider Cove, I won't.

The kitchen is quiet, which I should be used to, but this is a different kind of quiet. The kind that hums with memory and stillness and something else I can't quite name.

Maybe it's hope. Maybe it's dread.

My stomach tightens at the emptiness of the room. I'm not sure what I expected—Tahlia in another ball-gown the exact crimson of my country's flag, her hair swept up in a messy bun, flour on her cheek as if she's stepped out of one of my daydreams?

Instead, the kitchen is empty.

Except for the tortoise.

He's a foot across if he's an inch, and I can't move. The tortoise with a faint trail of strawberry across its beak sits in the middle of the kitchen floor like a forgotten sculpture from a modern art exhibit. It doesn't move. Just stares at me with centuries-old judgment and the energy of someone who's witnessed empires fall.

"Good morning," I say, because I was raised properly, and because this reptile might very well be Tally's first line of defense.

It does not respond.

It does not blink.

I think it might be breathing, but how can one truly know through the shell?

I take a slow step around it. The creature's eyes track me like a security camera in a museum. I nod respectfully and skirt the perimeter of the room. If this is some kind of ancient guardian or enchanted roommate, I'd rather not trigger a curse.

I open the fridge, find the orange juice Don put there last night, and pour a glass. The tortoise shifts— barely—and now it's facing me, its beady gaze unrelenting.

"I'll leave the lettuce untouched, Your Majesty."

It exhales through its nostrils like a tired librarian.

Tally appears in the doorway then, and suddenly the air leaves the room. She's wearing leggings and an oversized T-shirt that says *Support A Local Artist* in glittery letters. Her hair is twisted up with a pencil—an actual pencil—and she's barefoot, her toenails painted a soft peach.

She looks exactly like herself, and nothing like the girl I left behind. A woman now. One who could break me with a look—and did last night.

"Morning," I say, too casual, too light.

Her eyes narrow slightly. "You're still here."

"I live here now." I lift my juice in salute. "Or so I was told by your lease agreement, which I read quite thoroughly."

Her lips twitch, but she doesn't smile. She doesn't move either.

The tortoise takes a single step forward. I swear I hear the echo of doom.

Tally follows my gaze. "I see you've met Shellvador Dalí."

"That's...yes. We met."

"He's got a surrealist soul." She crosses to the stove. "Don't get on his bad side. He's chewed through better men."

"I believe you," I say, watching as she opens the oven and the scent of cinnamon and sugar wraps around me like a memory. Sweet, warm, unforgettable.

Like her.

Tally pulls out a tray of golden spirals, her movements efficient, practiced. She sets them on the stovetop and turns toward me, arms crossed now.

"So, Callan," she says, her voice as cool and sharp as the edge of a paper cut. "Are you going to explain why you're really here?"

I lift my juice to my lips, having dodged far harder and harsher questions than this. I've never wanted to tell the truth more earnestly than I do right now. But honestly, my reappearance in America—in Tally's life—has already shocked us both.

"I needed a change of scenery," I say with perfect neutrality. Mother would be so proud. "Somewhere quiet. Peaceful. Where one can walk into a kitchen and find a giant tortoise."

She doesn't laugh, but snorts. "He's not a giant tortoise. He's a regular pet-shop-tortoise."

"Yes, I see that."

She eyes me. "You could've gone anywhere."

"I wanted to come here."

"Why?"

I hesitate, because the truth is far too messy to deliver over cinnamon rolls and citrus.

Because I've never stopped thinking about you.

Because I watched your life unfold from a distance and realized I wanted to be in it again.

Because you're the only person who ever saw me without the title, without the pressure, without the expectations.

But I can't say any of that.

So I go with, "Because I remembered the fountain."

Her brow furrows. "What fountain?"

"In your back garden. You used to pretend it was a wishing well. You said if you made a wish and threw in a gumball, it'd come true."

Her arms drop slightly, and the air whooshes right out of her lungs. She looks at me with pure vulnerability, then seems to realize it and stitches it all back together. "I don't know what you mean."

I keep my distance, but I want to run to her and remind her of everything we shared. "Yes," I insist. "You told me you used to come here in the summers and throw gumballs in your aunt's fountain."

"My aunt's?" She echoes my accent, and a very strong urge to leave the room races through me. So I say *ah-nts* instead of those pesky little creatures who invade picnics.

It's not a crime. It does, however, clue her in to where I've been living.

Perhaps.

"You don't remember?" I ask.

She brushes frosting over her baked goods. "I haven't thought about that fountain in years. Aunt Fern had it removed years ago."

"That's too bad," I say softly. "I wish I could've seen it first. I've been thinking about it a lot."

It. I nearly scoff but manage to keep it in.

I've been thinking about *her*.

The silence that follows is thick, stretched tight between us like an old swing set chain. And then she blinks, shaking herself free.

"Well," she says briskly. "Wishes don't always work out the way we want."

"Perhaps not," I say and finish my juice. My stomach just feels like acid now, and I'm sure it won't be the only thing I regret today. "But sometimes they still bring you where you're meant to be."

She exhales, and for a moment, I think she might soften. But then she motions toward the cinnamon rolls. "Take one and go. I have to deliver the rest."

"To whom?"

She hesitates, eyeing me like I'm still the burglar in her house she wants to get rid of. "There's an old man who lives behind us. Me." She takes a quick breath. "He's eighty-seven and thinks I'm his granddaughter."

I grin. "I can't help but feel like I'm being set up." Is this a test to see if I'll eat an elderly man's breakfast?

"Only if you're allergic to raisins."

I take a cinnamon roll anyway and bite into it. It's warm and gooey and perfect.

"Still the best baker I know," I say, reaching for a paper towel and dabbing at my mouth.

Tally watches me intently, her eyes actually narrowing. I quickly throw the paper towel down.

"Flattery's not going to work," she says. "I never baked for you when we—before." Her face turns a delicious shade of pink I'd like to see over and over again.

"I wasn't trying to flatter you," I say. "I speak the truth."

She opens a Tupperware container and starts transferring the rolls from the pan to it. "You're going to need to tell me the truth eventually."

"I will."

"When?"

I pause. "When I know you won't slam the door in my face."

Her hands still, the cinnamon roll halfway to the container. "Then you might be waiting a while."

I nod, though my heart twinges in my chest. "I've developed quite the sense of patience."

She looks up, and our eyes lock again. That same magnetic pull I felt last night tugs at my spine. She breaks the moment with a sigh and turns away. "Come on," she says, grabbing the container. "If you're going to live here, you might as well meet Mr. Beasley. He hates everyone under forty and thinks Elvis faked his death."

"Perfect," I say and follow her to the back door. "We'll get along splendidly."

She snorts, and it's the closest I've heard her come to laughing. As she opens the door, sunlight spills in—bright, golden, and relentless. I blink against it, stepping out onto the deck beside her.

"Are you going to church?" she asks.

I frown. "No. Why?"

"You're wearing church clothes." She shoots me a look out of the corner of her eye, then moves down the steps. "In the summer heat. You're going to melt."

I've lived the past twenty years being uncomfortable. A little heat isn't going to touch that. "I'm—"

"Good morning, sir," Don says as he rises from the sleek black rental we'll have during our time here in the South.

"Sir?" Tally echoes.

I glare at Don, but it doesn't stop him from straightening his tie and jacket—talk about being overdressed for a quiet Sunday in our new home—and opening the back door of the town car.

A man rises from the back seat—one on each side. Honestly, I'm surprised the second man had the wherewithal to open his own door. But he did, and the pair of personal security men step out, button their jackets, and face me as a single unit.

For the love of the crown.

Tally turns to me, confusion dawning in her eyes. "Don? Is that Donald?"

"Yes," I say tersely as my personal assistant starts toward us, his meticulously shiny shoes crunching over the gravel. The security detail comes with him, and all the oxygen in the air gets sucked right out of the sky.

"Why does your assistant have a security team?" Tally asks.

I open my mouth, but I have no idea what to say. What I know: There's no way I'm keeping my royal status a secret for very long. Heck, she could type in my name to her Google search and know ninety percent of my public life in less than point-two seconds.

And just like that, the very private door I've been hoping, praying, and planning to reopen between us slams shut all over again.

Acting quickly, with three men advancing toward

me, I take a step and move in front of Tally, turning my back on them. Our eyes meet, and I ask, "Could you make me a simple promise?"

She stiffens, her eyes flicking past me—toward the suits—and back again. They're hard, guarded, and I hate the way she looks at me. "What is going on? Are they all going to live here?"

Unfortunately, I think.

"I'll tell you everything," I say. "I swear. But not here, not right this second."

She glares, and I'm certain she'd pop that curvy hip and fold those arms if she wasn't carrying the cinnamon rolls.

The crunching of their footsteps come closer and closer. "Don't take everything you hear at face value," I say quickly, dropping my voice to something just shy of a whisper.

She says nothing, but her eyes don't leave mine.

"And I'd love it if you could promise me—don't look anything up online until I can tell you everything from my own mouth."

She doesn't respond. Her eyes flick to Don, to the guards, then back to me. There's fire behind them. Uncertainty. Hurt.

I take a breath. Step closer. Flutter my fingers against hers. She sucks in a breath, and I lean closer. Don's going to say something at any moment.

Your Highness. Majesty. Sir.

They all echo through my head as I whisper, "Tally, please."

———

Ohhh, there's something going on here that we don't know about - that TAHLIA doesn't know about. Will she make that promise to Callan? And then what?

Find out in A VERY ROYAL ROOMMATE, the last book in the Cider Cove RomCom series, by scanning the QR code below with your phone.

Just His Secretary, Book 1: She's just his secretary...until he needs someone on his arm to convince his mother that he can take over the family business. Then Callie becomes Dawson's girlfriend —but just in his text messages...but maybe she'll start to worm her way into his shriveled heart too.

Just His Boss, Book 2: She's just his boss, especially since Tara just barely hired Alec. But when things heat up in the kitchen, Tara will have to decide where Alec is needed more—on her arm or behind the stove.

Just His Assistant, Book 3: She's just his assistant, which is exactly how this Southern belle wants it. No spotlight. Not anymore. But as she struggles to learn her new role in his office—especially because Lance is the surliest boss imaginable —Jessie might just have to open her heart to show him everyone has a past they're running from.

Just His Partner, Book 4: She's just his partner, because she's seen the number of women he parades through his life. No amount of charm and good looks is worth being played...until Sabra witnesses Jason take the blame for someone else at the law office where they both work.

Just His Barista, Book 5: She's just his barista...until she buys into Legacy Brew as a co-owner. Then she's Coy's business partner *and* the source of his five-year-long crush. But after they share a kiss one night, Macie's seriously considering mixing business and pleasure.

———

Bonus for newsletter subscribers! Just His Neighbor, Prequel: She's just his neighbor...until his dog—oops, his brother's dog—adopts her.

Get this book by joining my newsletter here: https://readerlinks. com/l/3887964 **or scan the QR code on the next page.**

A Very Terrible Text, Book 1: Sometimes the thumbs slip…

She's finally joined the dating app everyone in Cider Cove is raving about…when she accidentally sends a message about wanting to meet up for a first date to her enemy.

A Very Bad Bet, Book 2: *Sometimes a wager only makes things more fun…*

She's got seniority over the obnoxious grump next door, and she's determined to beat him out for the top job in their charming home-town. But a bold bet spins their rivalry into a flirty attraction that could change everything.

———

A Very Merry Mess, Book 3: *Sometimes the holidays are messy...*

Christmas is the season of joy, mistletoe, and, unfortunately for Ryanne, the pressure of bringing home a date. When she vents to Elliott, her best friend and co-manager at the small-town office supply store, he impulsively grabs her phone and texts her mother that they're dating.

Date. Ing.

A Very Disastrous Dare, Book 4: *Sometimes a person speaks before thinking...*

She's just bought the flower shop and he's taken over the hardware store for his dad. Sounds peachy, right? Sure, until they both want an assistance grant from the city...and now Emma and Aaron are rivals *and* neighbors.

A Very Friendly Fiasco, Book 5: *Sometimes the friend zone is breached...*

Sometimes the friend zone is breached...

He's her office crush, and she's the colleague he can't stop thinking about. But with HR's no-fraternization policy breathing down their necks, Lizzie and Matt have to get creative if they want to explore what's brewing between them—starting with a "fake-friend" date to a concert in the park.

A Very Royal Roommate, Book 6: Sometimes a crown changes everything...

When her childhood best friend (and boyfriend...) shows up to rent the second and third floors of the Big House, she has no idea he's actually a prince—or that their former falling out is about to turn into something far more complicated than a simple roommate situation.

Elana Johnson is a USA Today bestselling and Kindle All-Star author of dozens of clean and wholesome contemporary romance novels. She lives in Utah, where she mothers two fur babies, works with her husband full-time, and eats a lot of veggies while writing. Find her on her website at feelgoodfictionbooks.com.